PASSION'S AWAKENING

Virginia was aware that his grip had tightened on her hand, but she didn't care. She was fighting for his daughter's well-being. "Daniel, you have to give Mary more room to grow, to experience new feelings."

"And you are very good at making people experience new feelings, aren't you?" He suddenly pulled her against him, his lips coming down on hers.

Before she could react, she was trapped in a kiss that was so powerful and maddeningly overwhelming. Instinctively she began to struggle, her brown eyes flashing with fury, as she slapped his face. "How dare you!"

Though Daniel's jaw stung from the blow, he pulled her closer and kissed her more forcefully. Virginia fought again to free herself but his hold was too secure and his mouth seemed to follow hers no matter which direction she turned her head. Virginia stopped struggling as an unfamiliar warmth spread slowly through her, taking possession of her senses. His kiss was far different than anything she had ever experienced, the feelings he aroused in her far more powerful than any she had ever felt, and the moment her arms encircled his neck, she knew she was in trouble, but there was nothing she could or wanted to do about it. . . .

ZEBRA HAS THE SUPERSTARS
OF PASSIONATE ROMANCE!

CRIMSON OBSESSION   (2272, $3.95)
by Deana James

Cassandra MacDaermond was determined to make the handsome gambling hall owner Edward Sandron pay for the fortune he had stolen from her father. But she never counted on being struck speechless by his seductive gaze. And soon Cassandra was sneaking into Sandron's room, more intent on sharing his rapture than causing his ruin!

TEXAS CAPTIVE   (2251, $3.95)
by Wanda Owen

Ever since two outlaws had killed her ma, Talleha had been suspicious of all men. But one glimpse of virile Victor Maurier standing by the lake in the Texas Blacklands and the half-Indian princess was helpless before the sensual tide that swept her in its wake!

TEXAS STAR   (2088, $3.95)
by Deana James

Star Garner was a wanted woman—and Chris Gillard was determined to collect the generous bounty being offered for her capture. But when the beautiful outlaw made love to him as if her life depended on it, Gillard's firm resolve melted away, replaced with a raging obsession for his fiery TEXAS STAR.

MOONLIT SPLENDOR   (2008, $3.95)
by Wanda Owen

When the handsome stranger emerged from the shadows and pulled Charmaine Lamoureux into his strong embrace, she sighed with pleasure at his seductive caresses. Tomorrow she would be wed against her will—so tonight she would take whatever exhilarating happiness she could!

Available wherever paperbacks are sold, or order direct from the Publisher. Send cover price plus 50¢ per copy for mailing and handling to Zebra Books, Dept. 2403, 475 Park Avenue South, New York, N.Y. 10016. Residents of New York, New Jersey and Pennsylvania must include sales tax. DO NOT SEND CASH.

Ecstasy's Fire
ROSALYN ALSOBROOK

ZEBRA BOOKS
KENSINGTON PUBLISHING CORP.

ZEBRA BOOKS

are published by

Kensington Publishing Corp.
475 Park Avenue South
New York, NY 10016

First printing: July, 1988

Printed in the United States of America

Chapter One

"Are you absolutely *sure* you want to go through with this, Virginia?" Mark Langford asked. He pulled his workworn wagon to a clattering halt in front of the ornate Victorian house. While he waited for her answer, his gaze was reluctantly drawn to their elegant surroundings. He pressed his lips together tightly while he took in everything from the intricate detailing of the cornice of the elaborate house to the perfectly trimmed ornamental shrubbery that circled the house and separated the well-kept grounds from the pastures and vegetable gardens that lay beyond.

Finally his gaze returned to the beautiful girl who sat primly on the hard wagon seat beside him, her head held high with determination. He smiled despite his misgivings when he realized how carefully she had dressed for the occasion. She wore a very plain-looking brown muslin dress that was both high-necked and long-sleeved. She had pulled her long, luxuriant mane of dark brown hair straight back and had severely fashioned it into a small knot, low at the base of her head—very matronly, indeed.

But his smile faded when he remembered just why she wanted to look so very proper, and the feeling of impending doom closed in on him again. "I really don't think this is a very smart thing to do, Ginny. It's still not too late for you to back out."

"I have no intention of backing out," Virginia Connors stated adamantly. Her hands curled into tight fists on her lap when she turned to face her friend.

From the moment they passed the gatehouse and Virginia caught the first glimpse of the large, stately three-story house so elegantly hidden behind the spreading Spanish oak trees that her own ancestors had planted over fifty years ago, she had been forcefully reminded of the true grandeur of Valley Oaks.

The shadows that had darkened her heart for so many years turned suddenly cold, chilled by the bitter hatred which had become so much a part of her. The lifelong resolve to see justice finally done grew even stronger inside of her, gripping her by her very soul, until she felt true, physical pain. But she tried to hide those embittered emotions when she looked at Mark again. She knew he still had no idea of the real reason she had returned to East Texas, because if he had even started to suspect what was truly in her heart, he never would have volunteered to bring her here.

"Don't feel you *have* to try to get this teaching position. Mother was sincere when she invited you to stay on with us for a while longer, until you can find a teaching job somewhere else. Anywhere else. Maybe there will be an opening at the school in Pine soon. Or maybe over in Pittsburg. I hear they may even start up a college there."

Again he looked at their surroundings, and his

frown deepened with disgust. "I don't see how you could consider coming to teach here anyway. Going to work for a *Pearson*. After all they have done to your family in the past, I'd think you'd rather starve to death than go to work for one of them. I don't understand why you even applied for the position."

"I told you . . . teaching jobs are hard to come by these days, especially around here. And why not work for a Pearson? Why not earn back some of what was stolen from my grandparents so many years ago?"

"Is that why you are doing this?" He was clearly trying to understand.

"Partly. Besides, as you said, all those things happened in the past, before I was even born. I'm tired of looking back. I'm ready to look forward." And if the truth be known, she had been looking forward to a chance like this for as long as she could remember. She smiled at Mark, revealing teeth that were pressed together with pure determination. "Are you going inside with me, or would you rather wait for me out here?"

"I'm going with you," he muttered as he flicked the reins and drove the wagon under the carriage porch. He shook his head to show he still clearly disapproved, but he realized he was not going to change her mind. No one was.

As soon as Mark brought the wagon to a halt closer to the front door, he hopped down from the driver's seat and hurried around behind the wide-planked bed to help Virginia. "But I really do wish you wouldn't go through with this. I think living here will only make you miserable." What he failed to mention was that her living there, under the same roof with a wealthy widower, with only the man's freeservants and his young daughter to serve as chaperones, was going to make *him* extremely miserable as well. He just wished that she somehow understood.

Virginia was too busy trying to control her own anxious heartbeat to argue any further with Mark about her decision to work at Valley Oaks. Too much depended on her getting that job, on her getting into that house. Concentrating on what she might say to the man once she was inside, she pressed her lips firmly together and took a deep breath while she let Mark help her down.

Though she was tired of having to defend her decision constantly, when she was finally on the gravel drive and ready to approach the house, she smiled at her friend to reassure him that she had indeed thought this out. Her smile only seemed to make his frown deepen as he self-consciously adjusted his suspenders.

Poor Mark. He was so set against her applying for this job. She wondered if he would ever come to suspect that she'd never have even known a Pearson had returned to Valley Oaks if it had not been for his letters. After two years of the place being vacant, except for the freeservants who had been kept on as caretakers after Old Caleb's death, she had begun to hope that eventually the house and the land that surrounded it would be put up for sale—though she had no idea how she could have ever come up with the money to purchase any of it.

Until Mark had written her about Daniel Pearson's sudden arrival in Camp County, she would never have known Valley Oaks had once again been made into a working cattle ranch. Nor would she have known that the man who had just moved in was looking for a private tutor for his daughter. Virginia was grateful to Mark for having kept her informed of all the latest occurrences at Valley Oaks. But she dared not let him know how he had been the one to provide her with all the vital information she had needed to at last devise a feasible plan to get Valley Oaks back. If she were to tell him, he'd never forgive himself.

"No, Mark, you're wrong about that. I'm actually looking forward to living here," she told him while she looked again at the beautiful house she had only managed to steal glimpses of during her childhood. Because Old Caleb Pearson had insisted that no one trespass on his land, and knowing the delight he took in bringing pain and heartache to any Elder, she had rarely chanced it. And even when she *had* risked coming onto his land, though it was land that never should have been his in the first place, she had never risked getting close enough to get a good look at the old man himself.

Only once had she ever actually set sight on the man who had brought ruin to her family, and that had been from a distance. It was on a day when he had come into town, while she and her grandmother were standing outside Sutcliffe's Dry Goods Store. Virginia had been only eleven at the time; she could barely remember now what Caleb Pearson had looked like, even at a distance; but she could remember how his appearance had struck her as deceiving. He had been a thin man, dressed in a fashionable frock coat and trousers. He had not looked at all like the horribly evil beast she knew him to be. In fact, he had appeared almost harmless, like any other man. It had been her first lesson about how deceptive first impressions could be.

Virginia had never caught sight of any of Old Caleb's family during her secret visits to his land, though she had known that he had at least one

9

married brother who came to visit occasionally and who had brought his wife on some of those visits. And once, when Virginia had been very, very young, she knew Caleb's brother had also brought an older child with him, a child who sometimes came to visit on his own.

Because everyone in town knew what a cruel and heartless man Caleb Pearson was, they'd all enjoyed keeping up with what went on out at Valley Oaks and eagerly spread gossip about the man, or his brother and his brother's family. If anyone who happened to be headed out to Valley Oaks stopped in town and mentioned his destination, by nightfall the whole community was aware of it.

Caleb himself had never married. Rumor had it that he foolishly hoped that Virginia's grandmother, Essie Elder, would one day decide to leave her husband, Joseph, and come running to him. But there had been little chance of that; Virginia knew her grandmother hated Caleb Pearson with a vengeance until her dying day—hated him for what he had done to Joseph, for the ruin he had brought upon them both.

The hate Essie Elder had felt for Caleb had not gone with her to her grave, for it lived on in the breast of her only grandchild. It was a hatred Virginia had been taught to nurture and carry deep within her heart—a hatred she had known all her life.

"I still wish you would reconsider," Mark muttered when he turned and walked with her up the wide-planked steps and across the open, sparsely furnished veranda that ran along the recessed wall at one side of the house.

"There's nothing to reconsider," she said with a light shrug that was meant to further reassure her friend. She squared her shoulders and reached for the large, ornate doorknocker. The brass ring rapped sharply against the thick double door with nearly the same strong, heavy rhythm as her own heart.

Running her tongue over her lips apprehensively, she stepped back and gazed again at the splendid surroundings. The bitter hatred that now overcame her left her feeling as if someone had spilled acid inside her. For two generations, even before Texas had first seceded from Mexico, Valley Oaks had been the Elder family's home—until Caleb Pearson had somehow cheated her grandfather out of nearly everything he had owned.

Though Virginia had never been told the whole story, she knew enough to realize that Valley Oaks should have been hers—that Caleb's nephew really had no right to live there. Many times her grandmother had started to tell her just how Caleb had taken Valley Oaks from them, but the poor woman had always become too emotional to finish the story, and her grandfather had never wanted to talk about it, obviously ashamed that he had allowed anyone to cheat him and his family so completely.

As Virginia understood it, Caleb had already started to work for her great-grandfather, Matthew Elder, when her grandfather, Joseph Elder, first met her grandmother-to-be, Essie Henderson, at a big picnic which was held there at Valley Oaks once a year. Caleb and Joseph both fell in love with Essie that very day, and both courted her—but in the end, Essie chose Joseph to marry. And Caleb Pearson had immediately set out to destroy their happiness by pretending to be Joseph's closest friend and offering him advice on how to invest his money—advice that eventually sent Joseph into financial ruin.

When Joseph had no other choice but to sell his

11

house and his land, Caleb mysteriously came up with the money he needed and bought Valley Oaks for a paltry sum. With no conscience to guide him, Caleb Pearson then forced Joseph and Essie to leave their beautiful home, though rumor had it that he hoped Essie would one day return alone.

And Caleb had been very careful to see that his takeover of Valley Oaks had been done legally so Joseph would have no lawful means of getting his land back. Even now, Virginia knew the law would be of no help to her in her bitter quest for personal justice; she was completely on her own. And as the very last of the Elders, she was determined to see justice finally done. She would avenge the wrong committed so long ago and set things right again. Valley Oaks would once again belong to an Elder.

To Virginia, it seemed an eternity before they heard any movement from within the house and another eternity before the sound of heavy footsteps reached them. Finally the door swung open and a large Negro woman dressed in a brightly colored print dress and red headscarf appeared before them, greeting them with a curious smile. "May I help you?"

"Yes," Mark answered quickly with a polite nod. "I am Mark Langford, from up the road a ways, and this is Miss Virginia Connors, a guest in our home. She is here to see Daniel Pearson."

"Is he expectin' her?" The woman's wide brow wrinkled and her lips puckered into a peculiar twist while she tried to remember if she had been told anything about either of them.

"In a way," Virginia was quick to answer. "I told Mr. Pearson in my last letter that I would stop by to meet with him a few days after I arrived in Pine, to see if I met with his approval. I arrived only yesterday but am very eager to meet with him, so I came on."

The frown disappeared from the woman's face and was promptly replaced by a look of pure surprise. *"You* are the woman from Pennsylvania who wants to tutor Miss Mary? Master Daniel didn't tell me you was goin' to be so young. Why, you's still a child yourself."

Virginia felt it revolting, the way the woman had referred to Daniel Pearson as her master—the days of masters and slaves were long gone—but she said nothing about it for fear of creating trouble when she needed to make the best first impression she possibly could. "Mr. Pearson was not made aware of my age, merely of my qualifications."

A broad smile stretched across the woman's face. "Come on in, both of you. I'll go tell Master Daniel that you's here." As the woman spoke, she stepped back and opened the door wider to give them room to come inside.

Mark escorted Virginia through the open door into the entrance hall. Virginia noted the highly polished floors with their many thick, luxuriant carpets; the pale-blue wallpaper, with its intricate gold pattern; and the elegant, carved staircase that curved upward. There was a huge crystal chandelier which hung from a thirty-six-foot ceiling in front of that wide, gleaming staircase.

All her life she had heard how very grand the house was, inside as well as out. With a sudden feeling of disgust, she wondered how happy such surroundings could have possible made Caleb in those last lonely years of his life. He'd had so few friends to share it with. What good was all this wealth and elegance?

"Master Daniel will see you now," the black

woman said. Her broad, toothy smile never dulled while she waited for Virginia to join her. She seemed pleased as a peacock about something, and Virginia could not help but wonder what it was.

"I'll go with you," Mark said, and moved forward to walk along at her side.

"No, Mark, please . . . stay here. I'd rather meet this man alone. I really want to do this on my own."

Mark looked displeased by her decision, but did not argue with her again. "If that's the way you want it."

"It is. Please, wait for me here. I shouldn't be very long. I'll hurry."

"I'll be all right. I still don't like the idea of all this, but if it really *is* what you want, take all the time you need. I'll wait in one of those chairs." He gestured to two dark blue medallion-backed chairs against the far wall.

Taking a deep, steadying breath, Virginia joined the woman and followed her until they were both out of Mark's sight. When the hallway turned to the left and ran along the back of the house, Virginia began to realize just how large the house really was. Eventually, she was led into a room with no windows and only one other door. The room was walled ceiling to floor with recessed wooden bookshelves and anchored in the very center with a huge pinewood desk.

A man with thick, dark brown hair sat at the cluttered desk with his head bent low, reading from a ledger that lay open in front of him. Before he looked up to acknowledge their presence, the black woman disappeared from the room.

The man's attention was clearly still on his work. Virginia's gaze was drawn to the many shelves of leather- and clothbound books, then to the sturdy hardwood and leather furniture that surrounded the desk. The room had such a strongly masculine quality that it even smelled masculine. She breathed deeply of the rich mixture of leather, pipe tobacco, and pine oil, and frowned when she found it so pleasing to her senses. So were the soft colors of tan and gold that predominated in the well-chosen carpets and furniture.

When the man finally looked up from his ledger, her attention returned to the desk. The man had rudely ignored her entrance. She was startled when their eyes met, because she had not expected Daniel Pearson to be so handsome. Not when his uncle had reportedly been such an ordinary man, except for his uncanny blue eyes. "The eyes of the devil," her grandmother had called them.

Virginia now understood what her grandmother had meant, because Caleb's nephew possessed the same eyes — eyes so pale that they were almost colorless. Eyes that could look right through a person. She shuddered and tried to swallow, but her throat was too dry.

She had also not expected him to be so young. He looked to be in his late twenties. But she realized that he was probably closer to the age her parents would be if they had lived. She frowned while she took in his appearance. Not only was he younger than she had bargained for and far more handsome, but judging by the width of his shoulders, he was far larger, far more intimidating. When he came forward around the desk, she was further dismayed to discover he was taller than most men and, though quite muscular through the chest and across the shoulders, quite trim: the close cut of his dark blue trousers revealed a very narrow waist and extremely lean hips and thighs.

Quickly returning her gaze to his face, trying to

15

keep her expression noncommittal, Virginia waited for him to finally speak. When he did, she was further disturbed by the deep, commanding quality of his voice.

"*You* are Virginia Connors?" he asked, obviously surprised. He crossed his arms in front of his chest and came to stand before her, and because he had rolled his sleeves up several inches above his elbows, she became immediately aware of how sleek and firm his forearm muscles were. Judging by his casual dress and his strong build, she decided he was not quite so lazy as his uncle had been.

"Yes, sir, I am Virginia Connors." She held out her hand for a formal greeting, but when he did not unfold his arms to accept the gesture, she dropped it awkwardly at her side. His gaze bore through her as if she had done something terribly wrong, as if he condemned her for something.

Though she had a strong urge to look away, her light brown eyes never strayed from his intense, pale blue gaze. Her heart hammered wildly as she wondered if his obvious look of displeasure was because he had somehow discovered exactly who she was. She knew that if he had, he would realize she had ulterior motives and he would never hire her. He might even go as far as to physically remove her from his house. She held a burning breath deep within her while she waited for him to indicate aloud whether or not he had guessed who she was.

"I had no idea you were so young. You didn't mention your age in your letter. I assumed you'd be much older, especially traveling alone the way you were."

"I didn't think age mattered. I felt I needed only to mention my qualifications as a teacher," she responded quickly.

16

"Just how old are you?"

"Nineteen. I'll be twenty next month." She was starting to feel irritated by the way he kept harping on her age, but she tried not to show it.

"Only nineteen?" He frowned and uncrossed his arms.

"I assure you I have completed all the required courses, and with very high marks. Not only do I have my teaching certificate to show you, I have a letter of recommendation from the headmistress," she explained while she pulled open her handbag and reached inside for the papers she had brought with her. Haughtily, she slipped them both out and thrust them into his hands. "I'm sure you'll find I'm quite qualified for the position I seek."

Daniel stared at her a long moment, then at the folded papers in his hands. A glimmer of amusement shone in his eyes as he began to unfold the papers and read their contents. The corners of his mouth twitched as if he had a sudden urge to grin about something, but before he spoke, his facial muscles hardened again and his expression was deadly serious. "It says here that you just recently graduated. You have no experience teaching?"

Virginia bristled at the fact that he had found her situation so amusing, even if only briefly. "Just the experience that came with my training," she admitted truthfully. "But that does not make me any less qualified to teach."

He studied her strong determination. "Doesn't it worry you that some people might not consider it quite proper for an unmarried lady as pretty and young as you to live in the same house with a recently widowed man? And I assure you, you *would* have to live here with me. Besides the bunkhouse out back, and the gatehouse, which are both already

17

occupied, there are no other living quarters on the place."

"I feel your house servants should qualify as proper chaperones, and I would certainly expect a room with a sound lock on the door," she answered quickly. She had anticipated the question because it had also been one of the first things Mark and his mother had thought to ask her the day before, when she had first told them how she had applied for the tutoring job.

The man tilted his head and continued to stare down at her. "But people still might talk."

"Let them. Teaching jobs are hard to come by at the moment. I'm not about to let wayward gossip hinder me when finding work is so very important to me. I really do want to teach, and I'd like a chance to teach your daughter."

"Exactly how did you find out I was looking for a private teacher all the way up in Pennsylvania? The only advertisements I placed were in the local newspapers."

"With teaching jobs so few these days, that sort of news travels quickly." She felt a sudden constriction in her throat. She had not liked the suspicion she had detected in his voice.

"I see. Then you must already realize that you will be responsible for teaching only my daughter, and even though there is just the one child, you will be expected to spend your entire workday with her. You will be expected to teach even in the summer."

There was still a hint of suspicion in his voice; she was determined to dispel it. "I'm not opposed to working year-round. And though it would not bother me to have a classroom of twenty students, I look forward to being able to focus my attention on one child. I believe it will be a rewarding experience

18

for both of us, because I do intend to bring your daughter to her fullest potential."

Continuing to stare curiously at the woman who stood so proudly before him, Daniel stepped back and rested his weight against the edge of his desk. He found he was struck not only by her extreme beauty, but by the fire and determination deep within those shining brown eyes. She truly was dead set on making a good first impression and, as a result, getting that job. Maybe age really did not matter. "Since you have come so far, and I have yet to find anyone else appropriate for the job, I suppose I could at least hire you on a trial basis . . . if you have no objection to that. But of course, that is only *if* my daughter approves of you."

"What sort of trial basis?" Virginia wanted to know.

"I'll guarantee you one month's employment. After that, I'll consider the situation as it is then and decide whether or not to keep you on permanently or find someone else better suited to the position."

"That's fair enough," she said agreeably, knowing she would do everything she could to please him in that month's time. "When do I begin?"

"First, you have to meet with Mary's approval," he reminded her and headed toward the door. "We might as well find out what she thinks right now."

Virginia wondered if she was supposed to follow him or wait there.

"Aren't you coming?" he asked impatiently when he turned to see why she was not right behind him.

"Of course," she muttered, irritated that he had been arrogant enough to assume she would know exactly what he wanted. How very like a Pearson! It took all the effort she had to keep a pleasant smile while she moved across the library to join him.

At first they walked in silence, but when they approached the same staircase near the vestibule Virginia and Mark had first entered, Daniel started to explain a few things he felt she should know. "Mary's rooms are upstairs. Just across the hall from mine."

While they turned to ascend the staircase side by side, Virginia wondered exactly where her room would be. On the third level, where the steep lines of the roof probably only allowed enough space for one or two narrow bedrooms? Or on the same level with Mary's room? That would also put her bedroom very close to his bedroom—possibly close enough to be able to sneak from her room into his without being detected. She wondered what secrets she might discover hidden there.

Neither Virginia nor Daniel glanced back to where Mark sat keenly watching them while they slowly climbed the staircase together. Neither saw the intense frown on the young man's face when Daniel Pearson placed a casual hand at Virginia's elbow just before they reached the top of the stairs.

"She may be sleeping," Daniel went on to warn Virginia as soon as they had stepped away from the stairway, out of Mark's sight, and headed for the only closed door. "She is still recovering from a serious accident."

"An accident? What sort of accident?" Virginia asked with a frown that came as much from the thought of the child having been in an accident as from the strange things that were happening inside of her. She tried her best to ignore the warm, tingling sensations the man's simple touch had triggered, even through the sturdy material of her sleeves—when what she should have felt, if anything, was pure repulsion.

"A very serious carriage accident, I'm afraid. She

almost died as a result of her injuries." His grasp on her elbow tightened and the flutterings that resulted inside of her became too strong to ignore any longer, no matter how much she wanted to ignore them.

"When was this?" She finally had to pull her elbow away from his grasp in order to get control on what was happening inside of her and better concentrate on what was being said. Even after she had effectively freed herself, she could still feel a lingering warmth. It worried her that the man could have such a strong effect on her. It was bad enough that he was so incredibly handsome.

"The accident was eight months ago. Mary suffered a concussion and several broken ribs. That's why she hasn't been able to attend school. She's had recurring headaches and bouts with severe depression; but she's been doing well enough here lately that the doctor feels she should have enough strength and stamina to start catching up on some of her lessons at home. That's the reason I placed that advertisement." His face hardened and his blue eyes narrowed when he went on to explain, "Besides, I don't want her going to the school in Pine. The children in that town are heartless and make fun of her when I'm not around to stop them. Mary doesn't need that."

Virginia wondered if the girl had something else very wrong with her that he had not bothered to mention. Or was the child treated so cruelly in town simply because she had the unmistakable misfortune of having been born a Pearson? She well remembered the attitude the townfolk had always held toward Old Caleb. Everyone despised him—despised him for what he did to Joseph, and rightfully so.

Just before Daniel reached for the doorknob, he paused and turned back to face Virginia. His face grew harder still and his gaze bore down into hers with clear warning when he spoke his next words. "Mary does not like to be reminded of her accident. See that you don't mention it. She's a strangely sensitive child."

"I won't even let on that you've told me," she agreed, raising a curious brow.

"Just see that you don't," he said, his voice still cold. His expression was so grim it sent chills racing down her spine. "It's not something we discuss in this house."

Virginia could not help but wonder why that was.

Chapter Two

Daniel rapped on the doorframe twice, then swung the door open without waiting for any response. Virginia wondered why he had bothered to knock at all and it took a lot of self-restraint not to say something about it. Even a child deserved more consideration than that.

"Mary?" she heard him say after he had entered the room, but there was no response. "Mary, wake up."

It was not until he had flung the door open wider and stepped aside that Virginia actually saw the child seated on a narrow window seat across the room. And though Daniel had warned her his daughter was still recovering from a serious accident, she had not expected to see a child so thin or so pale.

"Mary, I'd like for you to meet Miss Virginia Connors. She has asked to become your new teacher," Daniel said as a way of introduction for the two.

"Hello," Mary said in a voice so tiny that Virginia almost didn't hear her. Virginia supposed that was because the child appeared to have fallen asleep and had been so suddenly wakened.

"Hello, Mary," Virginia said with a warm smile. She approached the child, aware how forlorn the little girl looked seated next to a large multipaned window, staring out into the yard below. "Mind if I sit down beside you?"

Rather than answer, the girl scooted to one side to give her enough room. She continued to stare out the window.

Glancing outside in an effort to see just what held the girl's attention, Virginia found nothing out of the ordinary but went on to remark, "What a lovely view you have."

"I guess," Mary responded. She finally pulled her gaze away from the window and looked down at the small folded hands pressed together in her lap. Tresses of light brown hair fell forward to cover her thin face.

"As beautiful as it is out there, I'd think you'd want to be outside enjoying the sunshine rather than staying cooped up in your room like this," Virginia said in an effort to keep a conversation alive. She had never seen a child so withdrawn. "There are so many beautiful butterflies out today. Do you like to watch the butterflies dance about?"

"Mary prefers to be inside," Daniel quickly supplied and took a step toward them.

Virginia frowned at the way he had intruded in the conversation she was trying to establish with his daughter, but said nothing. Instead, she tried again to draw the girl out with more questions. "Can that really be true? You don't like to go outside?"

Mary's face lifted and her pale blue eyes went tentatively to her father, as if deeply intimidated by his presence, but cut back to stare at her folded hands before she answered Virginia's question. "Not very much."

When Daniel took another step in their direction, Virginia noticed the girl's shoulders tense, as if she expected something terrible to happen to her. It was extremely upsetting to realize the child actually cowered from her own father. What sort of monster was Daniel Pearson? More and more, Virginia realized he was exactly like his uncle. She seethed with repressed anger, more determined than ever to have this job if for no other reason than to protect this poor child from her own father.

"If you don't like to go outside, what *do* you like to do?" Virginia tried again.

"I don't know," came the answer from beneath a still bent head.

"She just sits and looks out that window, mostly." Daniel obviously felt it was his duty to supply a better answer. "But she won't have much time for that once you get her started on her lessons, that is, if Mary likes the idea of getting back to them. What do you think, Mary? Isn't it about time you started again with your schooling?"

Mary looked up at him, as if it was expected of her to look at him whenever she spoke to him. "Yessir."

"Do you like Miss Connors enough to —," Daniel started to ask, but was interrupted by a light knock on the doorframe behind him.

The servant who had greeted Virginia at the front door stood just inside the open doorway and peered into the bedroom cautiously. "Parson me, Master Daniel, but Mister Pete asked me to come up here and tell you that he needs to talk to you for a moment downstairs. It has somethin' to do with that new foal of yours."

Daniel's face tensed with concern. "What's wrong? Did he say?"

"No, just that he needed to talk with you right away."

"Tell him I'm coming," he said, and while the servant hurried back down the hall, he turned to Virginia with a dark frown. "Stay here. I'll be right back."

Virginia was appalled at the way the man seemed to show more concern over a foal than he did over his own daughter, but she tried not to let her feelings show. She smiled sweetly. "Take all the time you need. Mary and I can use this time to get better acquainted, can't we Mary?" She bent her head low in an attempt to get a closer glimpse of the child's face.

"I guess," came the timid response.

Daniel paused only a moment before he spun around and headed out the door. Virginia watched while the girl's tension slowly melted away; her small shoulders relaxed a degree the moment Daniel's footsteps could finally be heard on the hardwood stairs, growing rapidly fainter. Virginia kept her gaze on Mary's bent head, and waited with a warm smile until the girl slowly chanced to look at her.

"What do you think about my coming here to be your private teacher?" Virginia asked. She let her gaze wander through the elegantly furnished sitting room, pretending to be interested in her surroundings. She wanted to give the girl a chance to study her without having to feel awkward about it.

"If you were my teacher, would that mean I'd get to stay here?" she asked.

"Yes, I would move in and teach you here at home," Virginia answered, still not daring a long look at the child.

"Does that mean I would not have to go away to boarding school this fall?"

Virginia clearly detected hope in Mary's voice, and when she finally turned back to really look at the girl, she could see by the relief in her wide, crystal blue eyes just how worried the child had been.

Finally getting a closer look at the girl's face, it occurred to Virginia how very much Mary resembled her father. They had the same unusual eyes and the same strong features, though the girl was decidedly thinner and her skin far more pale. "Boarding school? No. As I understand it, if your father likes my work, I am to remain here as your teacher for quite some time."

"I guess Amanda is not getting her way this time," Mary said, amazed, and for the first time attempted a smile. It was a pretty smile that brought a bright sparkle to her eyes.

"And who is Amanda?" Virginia asked.

"Amanda is one of Father's friends. A very close friend. I'm suppose to call her Auntie Amanda," Mary told her. Her nose wrinkled devilishly to reveal how little she cared for this close friend of her father's, then her expression turned very serious. "I overheard her and Father downstairs talking one night about sending me back east to a good finishing school. It was right after Dr. Harrison told my father I was well enough to start back to school." Suddenly Mary's hand flew up to cover her mouth as if she'd said something she should not have.

Virginia wondered if the child's sudden concern had been over her having admitted to eavesdropping or because she had mentioned the accident. It occurred to Virginia that Mary might not be quite so against discussing the accident as Daniel had led her to believe; but because she had promised, she decided not to pursue the subject. "Well, it looks like your father decided to hire a private tutor for you

27

instead, doesn't it?"

"I wonder if Amanda knows. I'll bet she's mad as a wet rooster," Mary said and clapped her hands gleefully. Dimples formed in her narrow cheeks. "She was so set on sending me back east. I can't believe Father went against her wishes."

Virginia could not imagine anyone wanting to send a child so young away to school and have to give Daniel credit for having made the right choice for the girl, at least in this instance. "You don't like Amanda very much, do you?"

"I hate her." Mary's response had been quick, her tone bitter.

"Hate is such a strong word," Virginia cautioned her. "Maybe you just dislike her."

Mary tilted her head and looked at Virginia a long moment with her face drawn into a thoughtful frown. "No, I hate her, all right. But I think I like you."

Virginia had to smile at such a timid but open declaration of affection. It was so very like a child.

"I like you, too," she responded quickly. It was the truth. Even though she had hoped not to, she found herself being drawn to the little girl. She had not wanted to become emotionally involved with anyone in the household; but with a child like Mary, she could not seem to help but care. She had a deep, inner desire to help this motherless child however she could while she remained her teacher. After all, it was certainly not the little girls' fault she had been born of a Pearson, and as long as she did not actually possess the heart of one, she deserved any help Virginia could give her.

It was a relief to note that Mary clearly did not have the same cold and ruthless inner traits as the rest of the Pearson family. Virginia quickly con-

28

cluded that although the girl had inherited her father's looks, she had to be more like her mother inside. For the first time Virginia wondered what Mary's mother must have been like and felt truly sorry for the girl, who'd lost the only caring element in her life at such a tender age. She wondered how the woman had died and how long ago it had been.

"Can I trust you to keep a secret?" Mary wanted to know, capturing Virginia's full attention again.

"Of course; we are friends now, aren't we? Friends can always trust each other with secrets," Virginia assured her.

Mary looked at the open door and listened, then spoke in a hushed voice so anyone outside the room would have a hard time hearing her. "I do like to chase butterflies. And sometimes I like to go out into a field of wildflowers and lie down in the grass so that they fly right over me. One time I sneaked off and did just that, and a big yellow butterfly landed right on my nose."

"No!" Virginia pretended disbelief while wondering why the child had to sneak off in order to play with butterflies.

"Yes, it did, right on my nose," she said, raising a tiny finger to point out the very spot where it had landed.

"Then you *do* like to go outside," Virginia concluded.

"Yes, but I can't go outside alone. Lizzie don't have enough time to spare, and when Father goes with me, he won't let me do none of the things I really want to do."

"And who is Lizzie?" Virginia asked, realizing there would be plenty of time to work on the child's grammar later on.

"Lizzie is our housekeeper. She's the one who just

came up here to tell Father that Mister Pete wanted to talk to him. Her momma worked for my great-uncle as a house girl. She started out as a slave, I think, but that was a long time ago. Lizzie and her husband, Moses, lives upstairs. She tells great stories and makes the best raisin pie you ever put to your tongue."

"But she doesn't have time to go outside with you?"

"Not very often. She has to see to her housework first. But sometimes, if I help her fold the clothes, she'll go outside with me for a little while."

Virginia considered the situation. The child was clearly starved for fresh air and sunshine. "Well, I certainly am glad to learn that you don't truly hate the idea of going outside as you first led me to believe, because I plan to conduct some of your lessons out in the yard. There's lawn furniture already set up under the shade of the oaks in the side yard, and I thought it'd be a perfect place to study on hot summer afternoons."

"Really?" Mary asked eagerly. "Do you suppose we could take time out to watch the butterflies?"

"We will have to. Can't study insects without giving full attention to the butterflies," Virginia assured her.

"You promise?" the girl asked, as if afraid to believe her good fortune.

"Promise what?" Daniel asked as he entered the room.

Mary's smile disappeared.

"I was telling her a few things I plan for us to study," Virginia quickly put in, having sensed Mary's reluctance to answer. "I want her to learn more than just the basics. Not only will we read, write, and learn arithmetic — I want her to know as much about the world around her as possible. I think she should learn art, history, and science. I also want her to know all about nature. There's a lot to be learned out of doors." She looked at Mary and the two exchanged a knowing glance.

Daniel nodded thoughtfully and though he spoke to Virginia, his gaze remained on his daughter. "Then am I to understand that she approves of the idea of having a tutor?"

"Oh, yes!" Mary responded eagerly, but then, as if she'd shown more emotion than she should have, she added in a much more controlled voice, "I really like Miss Virginia."

"Good . . . I like her too," he admitted to the child, then turned to Virginia, expressionless. "Come downstairs with me."

Virginia's stomach was a knot of apprehension while they descended the stairs together in silence. Mary had said she liked her . . . did that mean she could have the job, at least for a month? She wished he would give her some indication, some sign of what he had decided.

When they came to the bottom of the stairs, Daniel gave Mark a questioning glance but made no effort to speak to him. Instead he gestured for Virginia to step ahead of him, then directed her back to the library.

It was not until they were inside the room that he finally spoke to her again. "So, do you think you can handle a child as peculiar as Mary?"

"I foresee no problems," she replied, wondering how a father could refer to his own child as peculiar. True, Mary had initially seemed very withdrawn, but Virginia had already broken past that. She felt all Mary really needed was someone to show her a little extra attention to help make up for the terrible loss

31

of her mother. And it was something she would gladly do for the girl. "I hope you don't mind my asking, but how long has it been since her mother's death?"

Daniel tensed visibly while he worked the muscles in his jaw. He hesitated as if trying to decide whether or not to answer her. Finally he spoke. "Eight months."

Virginia could sense that Daniel did not plan to offer her any further information concerning his wife's death and realized it was none of her business, so she did not question him further. The woman had died only eight months ago; Mary had obviously not had quite enough time to get over such a traumatic loss. No wonder the girl seemed so forlorn, so lost! Virginia wondered why Daniel did not show as much remorse as his daughter did. He seemed more angry about his wife's death than grief-stricken; but then, Virginia did not really expect a show of true concern from a Pearson.

Daniel was just as cold and distant as she had expected, even toward his own daughter. The man had shown no sign of even having a heart, so far as she could see. He was exactly like his uncle in that respect, caring only about himself. If by some remote chance he did indeed have a heart hidden away somewhere deep inside him, it was clearly in the possession of some evil demon. Although she felt truly sorry for Mary, she was glad Daniel Pearson had proven to be so cold and ruthless. It would make it that much easier for her to do what she had returned to East Texas to do.

"Since Mary says she likes you, I guess it's settled," Daniel said, breaking into her thoughts. "When can you start?"

Relief washed over Virginia like a warm tide. She

had the job, and he did not suspect a thing. Though she felt like jumping for sheer joy, she remained ever so proper in both her manner and her speech. "I'll have my belongings brought over first thing tomorrow, if that is all right with you."

"Where are your things? I'll send Pete and Jack for them," he offered.

"That won't be necessary. I already have someone who has promised to bring them in his own wagon."

"The young man seated in the entry?" he asked.

"Yes—he has promised to help me."

"I see. Well, then, I guess that's all we have to discuss until tomorrow," he said, indicating he was ready for her to leave.

"There is one other thing," she stated hesitantly. "I believe we have not yet discussed my salary." Though she would take the job even if he refused to pay anything for the first month, she thought he would be less inclined to become suspicious of her motives if he thought salary was the main reason she wanted the job.

"Ah, yes, salary. Since I play to supply you with meals and a place to stay, I'd expect you to consider those benefits part of your payment—and you will be allowed to have your Saturday afternoons and Sundays to yourself," he began, as if preparing her for the worst. "But of course I plan to pay you, too. Would twenty dollars each month be satisfactory?"

Satisfactory? She could not believe he was willing to pay so much, especially when he was indeed going to supply her with both room and board. She stared at him dumbfounded, knowing she could buy four good dressed with only one month's salary. Why, if she wanted, she could buy a horse for less than twenty dollars, and a carriage to go with it for forty more!

33

"Twenty dollars would be most satisfactory," she said, wondering whence this sudden burst of generosity had come. Pearson men were not known to have such loose purse strings. Or was it possible he had become so used to having money that he had no real grasp of its value?

"Fine," he said simply, then looked at her expectantly. When she did not say anything more or make a move toward the door, he asked, "Is there something else?"

Realizing he expected her to leave and had no intention of escorting her out, she stammered, "No, there's nothing else. I was just about to leave."

He looked at her curiously, then asked, "You weren't expecting me to show you the way back, were you?" Then his eyebrows arched with realization. "You were, weren't you?"

"No, of course not. After all, I'm no longer a guest; I am now in your employ," she said, trying to sound convincing. Inside she seethed with anger, knowing he had purposely sought to make her feel foolish. "And I am certainly able to find my own way back."

"I can walk you back," he said quickly, taking a step in her direction.

"No, don't bother . . . you're a very busy man, and I've already taken up too much of your time. I'll see you tomorrow and will be ready to start to work the day after." Then, with a terse nod she spun on her heel and left the room quickly, eager to put as much distance as possible between herself and that arrogant beast.

It was not until she and Mark were well away from Valley Oaks that she was able to push aside her anger and humiliation enough to think about how good it would feel to take Valley Oaks away from that awful man, no matter how she had to do it. Even so, it had taken Mark's sharply insistent tone of voice to pull her thoughts back to what was happening around her.

"Virginia, did you get the job?" he asked, carefully pronouncing each word of the question as if it was the second or third time he had been forced to ask it.

"Yes. I move in tomorrow and start teaching the very next day," she told him, feeling a renewed surge of excitement.

Knowing the news was not going to sit well with Mark, she braced herself for another of his attempts to change her mind. She was a little surprised when his only response was to softly mutter, "Oh."

"Have you ever met his daughter?" she went on to ask.

"No, can't say that I have. I hear the man rarely takes her into town, or anywhere else for that matter. Even if he did take her out, unless he was headed to Cason for some reason, he wouldn't have a reason to pass by our house. Why do you ask? Is she a nice child?"

"To my surprise, yes, she is. When we went upstairs, I got to talk with her alone for a moment. It's as if she had no Pearson blood in her at all. I'm going to enjoy being her teacher."

There was a long pause before Mark asked, "And what did you think of Daniel Pearson?"

"Now there's a typical Pearson," she muttered with a rueful smile, and for the first time since they had left Valley Oaks, Mark smiled, too. "But he plans to pay me twenty dollars a month. For twenty dollars I easily can put up with the likes of him."

"Well, if you're happy, then I'm happy." Oddly, he did not sound happy. "Do we take your things over tomorrow morning or wait until the afternoon?"

35

"Morning—I'd like time to unpack the books and the school supplies I'll need and to get my belongings put away before I have to start my teaching the next morning," she explained, then frowned sadly. "But I had hoped to find enough time to go by the cemetery and visit Grandmother's and Grandfather's graves before starting to work. Can we do that now? I realize the cemetery has to be at least an hour's drive from here, but I really would like to see where they were buried."

"Sure, there's plenty of time," Mark told her, "just as long as I get back in time to milk and feed the cows at dusk."

On the way to the cemetery where Essie and Joseph Elder were buried, Virginia fell into a dark, gloomy silence. Several times Mark tried to get Virginia's thoughts off her grandparents' deaths by asking questions that had to be answered by more than a simple yes or no. "Sure is great having you back after so long. How much has the countryside changed since you left?"

"Not much, really," she responded, glancing around at the tall, stately pines that lined and shaded the narrow dirt road, then beyond to the rolling meadows and the distant wooded hills. "But then, I've only been gone five years." She wondered where that word "only" had come from, for they had been five of the longest years of her life.

"Well, *you* certainly have changed in those five years," he commented ruefully.

"For the better?"

"For the most part," he said with a teasing glint in his pale green eyes. "You were a far easier person to understand before your grandmother sent you to Pennsylvania so you could live with that great-aunt of yours and attend that city school."

36

"And what is it you don't understand about me?" she wanted to know.

"For one thing, I still don't fully understand why you would even want to work for a Pearson. I remember how much you hated them when we were kids. It's not too late for you to back out and stay with us until you can find another job."

He looked at her then with so much honest concern it made her reach out and take one of his hands in her own. Quickly she laced her fingers through his. "Mark, we've already been through this three times. I really don't want to discuss it again."

Mark frowned but curled his fingers through hers and wished he could be satisfied with her decision, but he could not. He did not like the idea of Virginia living in the same house with a man like Daniel Pearson, virtually alone except for his house servants and his own little girl. It was not that Mark felt he could not trust Virginia, because he knew he could; but he sure as hell couldn't trust Daniel Pearson. Virginia was simply too naive, too unaware she was about to enter the lion's own den and could very well find herself eaten alive before it was over. He wished he had the courage and financial stability to ask her to forget about working at all and marry him instead. But even if he had the money, it had been five years since she left; he could not be sure how she felt about him now.

"Mark, I want you to know I'm grateful for your concern, but I really have thought this thing through and it is exactly what I want to do," Virginia went on to assure him.

"And I *am* concerned. I want you to know that. But I also want you to know that I'm here for you if you need me. I always have been and I always will be."

"I know — you always have. Remember the time you saved me from that awful snake?"

Mark laughed. "I remember the scream you let out when you first realized it was right beside you. It curls the hair at the back of my neck just to think about it. But now that I reflect on it, I'm not so sure that I saved you from the snake as I am that I saved the snake from you!"

"Too bad we couldn't remain those carefree children forever," Virginia remarked with a nostalgic sigh. "It's a shame we had to grow up and become adults with adult responsibilities and adult problems."

"Oh, but what an adult you've become," Mark was bold enough to remark. "You aren't anything like that skinny little freckle-faced kid I used to catch turtles with. I find it hard to believe you're the same girl. Maybe if you fixed your hair in tousled braids, it would help."

"Or smear a little dirt on my face," she added. "And maybe tear my skirt along the hem."

"That's something I had forgotten about you, Ginny. You always were tearing your blasted skirts on a tree limb or on some briars."

"Except for the time you finally felt sorry for me and loaned me a pair of your old britches," she reminded him.

"Oh, the trouble I got into for that." He shook his head as he remembered how angry his parents and her grandparents had been.

"You? I was the one who had the most trouble sitting down the next day!"

The two of them continued to laugh and recalled their fondest memories of the past they had shared — back when the two of them had been young and oh-so-carefree. They had become such constant companions, especially in the summer, that people in town sometimes mistook them for brother and sister. Because the Langford farm was very close to Virginia's grandparents' small house, they were able to visit often. Their homes were scarcely a mile apart, and they had worn the path between the two houses bare to the ground.

"I'm glad to know that the five years have not changed the closeness we shared," Virginia said and reached over to pat the top of the hand which still held onto hers. "I had worried that it might."

Mark's grip tightened around her hand. "So did I. Five years is a long time. Look what all has happened."

Virginia thought again of her grandparents and immediately fell silent. As soon as the cemetery was within sight, tears began to form in the corners of her eyes and an anger of immense proportions began to stir deep within her breast.

Chapter Three

Mark waited while Virginia knelt just outside the cemetery gate to gather a large handful of the delicate bluebonnets which grew in thick, rounded blue-and-white bouquets near the freshly whitewashed wooden fence. He had seen the tears in her pale brown eyes and realized just how hard the visit would be for her.

Virginia had been very close to her grandparents. The summer Virginia was barely three, her parents had been burned alive in a horrible steamboat accident near Shreveport, and Joseph and Essie Elder had taken their only granddaughter into their home. Despite their difficult financial circumstances, they loved her and willingly provided for their only grandchild as best they could. Later Essie decided Virginia could get a far more valuable education back east and sent her granddaughter to live with her only sister in Pennsylvania.

Both Joseph and Essie had died during the five years Virginia had been away at school, and though she had wanted to return, she had been unable to attend either funeral. Because she had never seen their graves, Mark knew he would have to show her exactly where they'd been buried. How he dreaded the moments ahead.

"I'm ready now," Virginia said quietly.

When she stood, her arms were full of the dark blue wildflowers. She looked at him expectantly and he offered her a sympathetic smile before he bent forward to swing the rickety wooden gate open. The two then walked in silence along one of the well-worn paths until they stood before the jutting gray headstones that marked Virginia's grandparents' final resting place. Appropriate to Virginia's mood, the bright afternoon sun slipped behind a thick white cloud and cast an eerie shadow over them.

"The town took up a collection to get her a gravestone," he explained. He had intentionally avoided referring to her grandmother's death in the letters he had written to her after the horrible tragedy occurred. "They realized you would probably not have the money to buy one."

The constriction in Virginia's throat was too painful to allow her to speak at the moment. She simply nodded her gratitude. Knowing her grandmother's grave was properly marked meant a lot to her, but finding out the townfolk cared enough to see to it meant even more.

"You'll want a moment alone. I'll wait for you by the wagon." He wished there were some way he could make the moments ahead easier for her, but he knew there was little anyone could do to make the pain more bearable. Aching for her, he bent forward and placed a gentle, caring kiss on her cheek, then left her.

A faint breeze wafted through the small country cemetery and tugged gently on the few strands of her hair that had come loose to curl at her hairline. She watched Mark leave. His thoughtfulness and the

41

understanding he had for her need to be alone in her grief made the tears she needed to shed come that much quicker. When she turned back to face the two narrow headstones that sat side by side, her vision was too blurred to allow her to read the inscriptions. Slowly she knelt down between them and placed half the wildflowers she had gathered at the base of each.

"Grandma? Grandfather? I've come back," she said aloud. Her voice was so strained by the painful emotions that clutched at her throat, even she had barely heard it. "And I want you to know that the reason I am here is to set things right again. I am about to move into the house at Valley Oaks." Her lips quivered as she attempted a rueful smile. Glancing heavenward, she wondered if they could somehow see her. "An Elder will once again live there—right there—right where we belong."

The anguish she felt knowing her grandparents would not be there to share in her eventual moment of triumph grew so overwhelming that her shoulders began to quiver and her head dropped forward from the sheer weight of her sorrow. Sadly, she reached out and touched the cold surface of one of the headstones.

"Grandfather, you would be glad to know that I intend to undo all the evil that was done against you thirty years ago. I've come to get Valley Oaks back. It's something I've always intended. My mother's blood and your blood still flow proudly through my veins, and because of that, because I am indeed an Elder by birth, Valley Oaks should and will be mine—*ours*."

Her hand trembled when she brought her fingertips down to lightly touch the deep engravings of the name Elder and the dates each had been born and had died. Her voice grew stronger but was bitter when she vowed aloud, her eyes pressed closed, "I will avenge the pauper's life you both were forced to live, I promise you that. There's a Pearson living there at Valley Oaks again. His name is Daniel. He's Caleb's nephew and every bit as cruel and heartless as Caleb was. But I want you to also know that while I'm there I plan to do whatever it takes to undermine that man and get our land back. *Whatever it takes.*"

Virginia's grief became too much for her. The force of it crushed her until she had to cross her arms in front of her and bend forward to ease the pain. Unable to right herself, she pressed her forehead against the cold stone while her body quaked uncontrollably with the tears she needed to shed.

Morosely, she remembered how she had always hoped to return to the loving arms of her grandmother when she had finally finished school, the teaching certificate the dear woman had thought so very important clutched in her hand. But because of the tornado that had swept through her grandmother's house late one night just over a year ago, while her grandmother slept, Virginia's dreams of a happy reunion with the woman she had loved most in the world could never be fulfilled. She would now have to live her life alone, truly alone.

The thing she regretted most as she finally purged herself of her tears was the fact that her grandmother would not be at her side when she finally reclaimed Valley Oaks in the name of Elder. She now wished the dear woman had not been so adamant about her going back east to get a proper education. Had she stayed home, Virginia might have been able to do something to save her grandmother from such a tragic fate. Her grandmother might still be alive.

Although Virginia had always wanted to be a teacher, she knew even before she left for the east that she had more important things to see to first. And although she would have preferred to achieve her ultimate goals while her grandmother was still alive to enjoy the spoils, she was still as determined as ever to put the ownership of Valley Oaks back in the hands of an Elder, where it rightfully belonged—before she could possibly consider going on to do anything else with her life.

"Grandmother, I wish you could somehow be with me when I finally show the world what disreputable, ruthless people the Pearsons really are and prove once and for all how Old Caleb cheated Grandfather out of everything he owned—all the while pretending to be his best friend."

Her fists curled so tight that her fingernails dug deep into the palms of her hands. "Oh, Grandma, how I wish you could be with me when it happens. How I would love to have seen you once again be the mistress of Valley Oaks, living in the grand style you so deserved."

Virginia glanced heavenward and wiped the tears from her eyes with the back of her hand while she further vowed in a soft, trembling voice, "B-Because I *will* make them pay for what they have done. Valley Oaks *will* be ours!"

When Virginia finally found the strength to stand again, she gazed down at the two stark slabs of stone one last time, then sadly turned and walked away. Mark had remained beside his wagon but went forward to meet her at the gate and put a supportive arm around her shoulders when she came to him. "Do you feel up to stopping by your grandparents' place? I have most of the more important things already at our house, but there are many things still locked up in the smokehouse that I imagine you'll want to go through."

For fear she would start to cry again at the mere thought of having to go through her grandparents' personal belongings, yet knowing it needed to be done, Virginia merely nodded a reply and allowed him to lead her back to the wagon. Though she doubted she would find much of value to anyone else—her grandparents had been forced to live as paupers for much of their lives—she did want to gather the things that would hold a fond nostalgia for her.

By the time Mark had put the wagon into motion again, turning back the way they had come, Virginia was too overcome by hope, hopelessness, and dread to give anything else much thought. Curiously, she wondered just what awaited her discovery in her grandparents' smokehouse and in Mark's attic. She became so absorbed with her sometimes hopeful, sometimes painful speculation that all thoughts of the poor little girl who was soon to be her student and the child's hideously arrogant father were temporarily pushed from her mind.

Though her efforts proved futile at first, she struggled to bring to a stop the hot tears of anguish that continued to stream silently down her cheeks. But the closer she got to where her grandparents' small house had once stood, the harder it was for her to hold back such overpowering emotions; yet with Mark's knack for inane conversation, and the tranquil beauty of the multicolored wildflowers, dark clovers, tall trees, and green grasses which surrounded them on all sides, she managed finally to get her emotions back in control and the tears stopped.

It was not until they had traveled through the thickly wooded area that bordered her grandparent's land to the southwest and finally had the homestead in clear sight that her heart began to break all over again. All that remained of the small four-room house which had at one time been her home was one weatherbeaten chimney and part of a wall. With a fresh flow of tears, she wondered if her grandmother had wakened and realized the immense danger she was in before she died. Virginia closed her eyes and prayed that her grandmother had been spared a final moment of such horror.

"Mark!" she sobbed aloud when she opened her eyes once more and saw the stark pillar of brick and the jagged piece of wall. Heartbroken, she raised her hand to cover her mouth; her forehead creased when she spoke her next words, fingertips gently pressed against her upper lip in a futile effort to stop the trembling. "I had no idea the tornado was so devastating."

"I tried not to make it sound as bad as it really was," Mark admitted. "You still had almost a year of school to get through, and I realized it was going to be hard enough for you to keep your mind on your studies just knowing your grandparents were both dead. You didn't need nightmares added to your grief. I guess I wanted to protect you from the horror of it as long as I could."

Virginia continued to stare at where a house had once stood, then across the yard to where two wooden sheds, one much larger than the other, remained virtually unchanged. Her insides began to shake again uncontrollably. Why couldn't the tornado have taken the sheds instead of the house?

As she silently cursed Fate for having been so unreasonably cruel, her gaze was curiously drawn to the smooth blanket of lush green field grass that now grew where a six-foot-deep basement should have been. She stared at the spot a long moment before finally gathering enough courage to ask, "Did the rest of the house blow completely away?" She wondered how they had ever found her grandmother's body if so much of the house had been destroyed.

"No . . . not completely. But what remained was mostly mangled roof and broken walls too dangerous to leave sagging like they were. Stephen Shattles and Craig Clifton came over with me the next day and helped clear away most of the wreckage. What was salvageable we either loaded into my wagon and took to my house or locked up in the smokehouse there."

Virginia's gaze went from the thick green grass to the jagged edge of the wall that still stood, and then to the tiny weathered building that had been used as both a smokehouse and a woodshed. She wondered why Mark had chosen the smokehouse instead of her grandfather's barn, which was so much larger, but his next words explained it all.

"I'm afraid there was not very much left for us to salvage," Mark waned her while he reached into his trouser pocket. "Come on—I've got the key with me. You can look through what's in there, if you want."

Virginia drew in a deep breath that she hoped would help steady her, but it only made her that much more aware of how violently her insides had started to tremble. She wondered where she would find the courage and inner strength to see her through the ordeal ahead while she followed Mark to the only door of the smaller of the two buildings. She watched while he slipped a key into the padlock and turned it until the lock opened.

The shed had been built with an extra skirting of boards around the base to help keep rodents and snakes out of the food stored there, and Mark and Virginia had to step high to get inside. Virginia's boot heel caught, causing her to stumble, but she managed to keep from falling. It took a moment for her eyes to adjust to the darkness. There were no windows, and the only light other than the small shafts that streamed in from two narrow air vents near the roof came from the open door behind them.

"This is all the furniture we could find that was not destroyed," Mark said apologetically, as if he believed it was somehow his fault that the tornado had done so much damage.

He gestured to some of the things closest to them and began to give her a brief inventory of what was left. "That table, that sewing stand, and those three chairs are about all the wooden furniture that was not either smashed or ruined by the rain itself. That bed grill over there is bent out of shape just a little, but since it was repairable, I kept it for you. And the stove is still in real good shape. I oiled it well so it would not rust. There's a whole pile of pots and pans on the other side of it. Some of the pots have a few dents, but they can still be used for cooking. If you don't need them, maybe you could sell them to someone who does. Someone just starting up house who can't afford to buy new."

Unable to respond, Virginia stepped forward and began to examine some of the smaller items. Her eyes were immediately drawn to the huge wall mirror that had hung by the front door for as long as she could remember. Stepping closer, she ran her hand gently over the dusty wooden frame and felt a great sense of comfort at being able to touch the smooth, solid surface. Realizing there was not a crack or chip to be seen in the mirror itself or in the frame, she looked curiously at Mark.

"Don't ask me. By all rights it should have been smashed to bits, because we found it all the way in the bedroom, lying face down on an overturned dresser. And I really think it's because of that mirror's protection that so many of the things we found inside the dresser were not ruined."

"Where are those things now?" she wanted to know. She remembered that the dresser was where her grandmother had kept the tintypes of her parents.

"Those are some of the things I took over to our house. It's all up in the attic, packed away in boxes. There was also a trunk filled with quilts and bedspreads that were not ruined by rain. I carried it on out of here, too. It's up in the attic with the rest."

Virginia continued to brush the dust from the mirror with her bare hand until it better resembled what she remembered. "Can we take this with us? I want to keep it."

"Sure, that and anything else," he told her. "Whatever you want. The rest you can keep locked up in here, at least until you decide whether you want to sell this place or rebuild. I don't need that lock for anything else."

Virginia thought about that. She still hadn't made up her mind about whether she should sell this small plot of land or not. After all, it had never been her grandparents' real home . . . Valley Oaks had been that. Even though her grandmother had spent more of her years living here than at Valley Oaks, this place had never felt like home to her grandmother. But then again, because it did hold memories of what was to Virginia a fairly happy childhood, and because it was attached to Valley Oaks by a common boundary to the north, Virginia felt it might be worth keeping.

"Hey, remember this?" Mark interrupted her thoughts while he held up her grandfather's leather razor strap and shook the dust from it. "Remember how your granddad used to threaten to use it on both of us whenever we really misbehaved? But then he never actually did. Now that I'm older, I realize he never really would have."

Virginia's laughter helped ease some of the pain she had buried so deep inside. "But I remember how at the time you were not too sure about whether or not he would ever really use it. Remember how you were so worried about it that you actually hid the thing from him that day we accidentally set fire to the backyard?"

"He may not have used the strap on us, but the switch he broke off that old hickory tree outside sure did set fire to me," Mark said and rubbed the area he remembered had hurt the most. He looked back at the six-inch-wide razor strap he still held out well away from him as if he feared it could strike all by itself. He shook his head warily, saying, "Just think of the damage that man could have done if he ever *had* used this thing on us."

"Might have done us some good," Virginia mused while she pulled the heavy mirror away from the rest of the things, then tried to lift it; she realized it would take the both of them to carry it to the wagon.

By the time they loaded the mirror, the sewing stand, and several other items and Virginia locked the shed to protect the rest, the sun hung low in a cloud-dotted, fading blue sky. The shadows cast by the tall trees which had at one time shaded her grandmother's house had grown long and distorted, and though the sun had not yet dipped from sight, the warmth of day had already started to give way to the coolness of the coming night.

Though Mark, his mother, and his little sister,

Jessie, were eager to visit with their guest again that night, as they had until the wee hours the evening before, Virginia chose to retire shortly after supper. Mark and Jessie had already brought down the many boxes of her grandparents' belongings from the attic and had placed them in Virginia's room. After she got ready for bed, Virginia spent the next few hours going through everything, box by box, item by item, heartache by heartache.

Among the more personal belongings Virginia came across was a sealed envelope of her grandmother's. It had been addressed to Virginia in Pennsylvania but had obviously never been posted. Curiously, she ran her fingernail beneath the flap and slipped the letter out. Her heart began to hammer hard beneath her breast as she set the envelope aside and stared at the folded paper. She knew that whatever the message, it would cause her more sorrow, make her that much more aware of all she had lost.

Slowly she unfolded the two pages. But when she first glimpsed her grandmother's handwriting, her anguish became so severe that she almost could not bear the pain. Quickly she folded the paper back and held it closed between her hands. She decided to wait and read whatever was inside later . . . much later, at a time she might be able to better cope with such a strong rush of emotion. Yet her curiosity would not allow her to actually set the pages aside.

She made an effort to swallow back the heartache but found it impossible to do. The pain had become too much a part of her. Carefully she reopened the letter and focused first on the date scrawled at the top. She saw that the letter had been written years ago, only a few months after her grandfather's death. She realized it was going to be a letter from a deeply bereaved woman, a letter that would surely

51

break her heart, a letter her grandmother may have decided was not worth posting, but which had meant enough to her not to actually destroy in the years that followed.

Virginia's hands began to tremble with such force that she could not hold the paper still. She finally had to lay it on the bed beside her in order to read the message.

The first paragraph was devoted mostly to Joseph's funeral. It contained much of the same information she had read before, in a letter that had indeed been mailed to her at about the same time. But the second paragraph contained information so unexpected that she snatched the paper up into her hands again and reread the words carefully.

Ginny,

"I cannot tell you the pain it brought me to learn that Joseph did not own this house and never had. Nor did he own any of the land that surrounds it. To discover he had been renting both the house and the land and no telling what else from Caleb all these years was almost more than I could bear. How very like Joseph to want to hide that final indignity from me. How dearly I wish Caleb Pearson were still alive! Oh, how I would love the chance to march up to that man and rip those savage blue eyes right out of his face with my very own fingernails.

When I think of all the humiliation Joseph was forced to endure because of that horrible man, it breaks my heart. And to think that by letting me believe he salvaged this small patch of land from all he had lost, he was forced to suffer that final humiliation all alone! If only I could have found out . . . I would rather have starved in the streets than live in any house owned by Caleb Pearson. Just as soon as I can find someplace else to live, I intend to move out of here. I have no desire to stay in this house and pay Caleb's heirs rent. No Pearson will ever get such satisfaction from me.

The vengeful letter continued for another page and was so full of bitterness and despair that it filled Virginia with more hateful anger than she thought she could bear. The letter made her realize that in the end, her grandparents had not owned even the small patch of land they had lived on for most of their lives. Caleb had taken *everything* from them. The house was not hers to sell, nor was the land around it. That realization made Virginia more determined than ever to see justice finally served . . . to make Valley Oaks her home, once and for all.

With hands quaking now more from the intensity of her ever-growing anger than from her deep-seated grief, Virginia continued the task of sorting through her grandmother's belongings. Though most of the things she came across touched her memory in some way, like the tintypes of her parents, and her grandmother's Bible, Virginia was surprised to find a black velvet pouch in among the items she had yet to explore. Strangely, the pouch had been sewn shut. Something that felt solid was inside. Quickly breaking the thread with her teeth, she pulled the unfamiliar pouch apart and was further surprised to discover a thin metal case plated in bright gold.

She had never seen the case or the pouch before. Doubting that it truly belonged to her grandmother, Virginia slipped the golden box out onto the bed beside her, unlatched it, and looked inside: a beautiful emerald necklace lay in a pool of black velvet.

She was certain there had been some sort of mistake. Even her mother, who had married a merchant from Longview, had never had anything so grand. But the inscription carved into the underside of the lid let her know she was wrong, for it clearly read, *To my beloved Essie, with all my heart*.

A new rush of tender emotions flooded Virginia when she realized the necklace had to have been a gift from her grandfather, possibly an engagement or wedding present. It had likely been given to her grandmother before Caleb had managed to ruin them.

Staring closely at the intricate necklace and realizing its worth, she wondered why her grandmother had never sold it, for they had so often been in need of money; but then she realized it must have held too much sentimental value for her grandmother to ever consider selling it. And because it had meant so much to her, Virginia knew that she would never be able to sell it, either. No matter how destitute she ever found herself, she would never part with the necklace.

Though she had thought she was all cried out, tears once again forced their way into her eyes as she pressed the metal box to her breast and realized the necklace represented the one thing money could never buy: the necklace was a gift to her grandmother from her devoted grandfather, and therefore it represented love in the purest sense of the word.

Reluctantly she set the golden case on her pillow so she could give it further consideration before going to sleep. She then continued with her search of her grandmother's belongings, wondering what other secrets she might discover.

By the time Virginia finally finished going through the last of it all, she was so emotionally drained that sleep came quickly: a sleep that was so deep, so badly needed, that she had to be startled awake by a sharp knock at her door the following morning.

"Who is it?" she called out as she sat up in bed, trying to focus her sleep-dazed thoughts on her unfamiliar surroundings. The bright morning sunlight that streamed in through the window beside her bed only served to confuse her more.

"It's just me," Wyoma's voice called to her through the door. "You told me you wanted to get an early start today, so I thought I'd better make sure you were awake. May I come in?"

Slowly Virginia's thoughts came together and she remembered where she was. Today she would move into Valley Oaks. Today she would take that first step. "Yes, of course — come in."

Mark's mother entered the room with a bright smile on her face, but it quickly faded when she glanced at Virginia and realized the poor girl had cried so long and hard the night before that her eyes were still a little swollen, even after a good, long sleep. She glanced at Essie's things still scattered about the room and noticed first the tintypes of Virginia's parents, then the golden jewelry case on the pillow next to where the girl sat.

Wyoma's brows rose with curiosity, but she didn't ask about the case nor about any of the other items strewn around the room. Instead she reached for Virginia's wrapper, which was draped over one of the tall, rounded posts at the foot of the bed, and handed the garment to her. "You'd better hurry and get dressed. Breakfast will be ready in about fifteen minutes." Then, turning to raise the window and let the fresh morning breeze into the room, she smiled again and added brightly, "It looks like we're going to have another beautiful day."

"What time is it?"

"Almost eight," Wyoma responded before turning back around.

"That late?" Virginia hurriedly slid out of bed. Rather than bother with her wrapper, she went directly to the washstand to quickly wash herself before putting on the clothes she had so carefully laid out.

"Yes, Mark has already eaten. He's out taking care of his chores so he'll be ready to leave whenever you are. I know you wanted to get an early start . . . but because I heard you still up and moving about until late last night, I decided to let you sleep a little longer. You'll need to be well rested. Moving is very hard work, even when you have a lot of help."

Virginia was afraid Mark's mother was about to start again with all the many reasons she should stay there with them for a while, and she tried to think of a way to gracefully change the subject without seeming too obvious. "Did Mark say what time he would be ready to start loading my things into the wagon?"

"No, but by the time you get all this repacked, he should be finished with his chores. And before you start putting any of this back into those boxes, you need to eat. Breakfast is about ready. Come down as soon as you're dressed."

Wyoma moved to leave the room, but paused with her hand resting on the knob, then turned and looked at Virginia as if she considered saying something more.

"What is it?" Virginia asked, bracing herself for another argument meant to change her mind.

Wyoma stared at her a moment, then shrugged her shoulders. "I just wanted to tell you how sorry I am about your grandmother's death—your grandfather's, too. And I wanted to tell you that if you *ever* need me, just let me know; I'll be there for you. You're like a daughter to me." She smiled sadly before she turned and left the room.

used me just as she showed. I'll be more too that
when their features on me, as she would could
leave me alone and sell the cows.

Chapter Four

By the time Virginia finished breakfast and went back upstairs to pack her things, Mark had returned and was ready to start carrying her belongings downstairs to load onto the wagon. With additional help from his mother and nine-year-old Jessie, Virginia was completely packed by ten o'clock and the workworn wagon was loaded, secured, and ready to leave by eleven.

Before she climbed aboard, Virginia turned to Wyoma and hugged the woman close. "Thank you for making room for me and letting me stay here. I know I didn't give you much notice."

"No, you didn't," Wyoma admonished lovingly as she reached up to tuck a wayward strand of hair back into her otherwise neat chignon. "But then, you know you are *always* welcome here."

"Always," Mark put in with emphasis.

Virginia smiled gratefully at his mother, who looked so much like him. "I realize that. And I want you to know how very much I do appreciate all you've done for me. I'll never forget your kindnesses."

Wyoma searched the younger woman's troubled

expression and frowned deeply, as if she somehow sensed her mission. "Don't go, Virginia. Stay here with us. Now that Jeanne and Catherine are both married and gone, we've got plenty of room."

"Yeah, Ginny, stay here with us!" Jessie piped up. Her wide green eyes glimmered with hope. Though the little girl couldn't have had very many memories of Virginia before her arrival two days ago, she'd quickly become attached to her new friend and was very eager to convince her to stay.

Virginia reached out to smoothe the short wisps of hair which had come loose from the girl's braids and hung limply at her hairline. Although Jessie had Mark's identical eyes, the girl looked more like her father. Virginia smiled as she remembered what a friendly, laughing man Mark's father had been. "I couldn't stay if I wanted to . . . I've made promises I can't break. But I'm not going to be that far away. I'll come to visit you often."

"Promise?" Jessie's pinched expression showed that she did not fully believe her.

"I promise," Virginia said in earnest as she pulled the girl to her and hugged her close.

"And will you bring one of those books back with you so we can read us another story?"

"I promise." As a teacher, Virginia winced at Jessie's poor use of grammar; but as a friend, she decided it was not a good moment to correct the girl. "I'll come visit and I'll bring a book for the two of us to read."

Having accepted Virginia's words as truth at last, Jessie's tentative frown lifted to a bright, beaming smile. "Okay." Then, as if all her problems had been duly solved, she turned and skipped off toward the barn, her braids hopping gaily about her thin shoulders.

"Well, since you still seem dead set on seeing this through, I guess we'd better get going," Mark grumbled and held out his hand to help Virginia into the wagon. Then, with a deep scowl, he climbed up beside her and snatched the reins. With a brisk flick, he sent the horses into a lively canter.

Clearly Mark was still very upset about her decision to work at Valley Oaks, and Virginia knew there was little she could say that would change his attitude. She remained quiet for most of the ride, hoping his mood would lift before they had to say goodbye; she wanted them to part on good terms. Though she was starting to sense that Mark wanted something more than friendship with her, which was not at all what she wanted, at least not yet, she did hope they'd remain the best of friends. They had shared too much of the past not to.

Mark finally broke the thick wall of silence he had thrown up between them about the time they had the elaborate ironwork gate that marked the entrance of Valley Oaks again in sight.

"You know how I feel about this," he began. His mood was still as sour as ever.

"And you know how I feel about it," she countered.

His scowl deepened until a zagged notch formed between his eyebrows. "Well, you'd just better keep that promise you made Jessie and come to visit us often."

Virginia could not help but smile at his boyish pout: it was an expression that brought back a virtual flood of childhood memories. "Have I ever broken a promise that you know of?"

He thought about that. "No, I guess not."

"Then what makes you think I would break that one? Now that the Porterfields have moved away, you're the only truly close friends I still have left around here. Where else would I spend my free time?"

"Daniel Pearson might find a way to prevent you from having any free time to spend *any*where," he muttered. More and more it was becoming evident that Mark was jealous—very jealous.

"He can't do that. He has already promised me my Saturday afternoons and my Sundays," she reassured him. "And with the days getting longer, I might even have a little time during the evenings for a quick visit."

Unable to come up with any fresh arguments and realizing the old ones had gotten him nowhere, Mark finally gave up his efforts to change her mind. "Let's just hope he *keeps* his promises and lets you have that time off."

Mark waited until he had helped her down and taken her arm in his before he spoke again. "Will you be allowed to have visitors here, do you think?"

"Not during my teaching hours," she answered quickly. She could feel her heart jump apprehensively at the mere thought of it. She did not want Mark coming over at all for fear his visit might in some way cause Daniel Pearson to link her to her past, more specifically to her grandparents. "And I prefer you didn't come until I am quite settled in and well on Mr. Pearson's good side. But eventually, I suppose it would be all right for me to have company, as long as it did not interfere with my work. Remind me and I'll ask him before you leave," she said, though she dearly hoped she would not have the chance. She was not yet sure how she'd explain knowing Mark so well, unless she claimed she'd met him when she first arrived in town and acquired his services, and his wagon, to get her things out to

Valley Oaks.

That would ring true enough, since Pearson had seen Mark the day before; still, Virginia did not want to tell such a lie in front of Mark. He would never understand her desire to keep the truth a secret—at least for a while.

As it turned out, Virginia had worried for nothing. As soon as they entered the house, Lizzie informed them that Daniel was not even there. "He had to go to town early this mornin' and said he'd be late in gettin' back, but left me with full 'structions about where Miss Connors here is to stay. Follow me on back and I'll show you which rooms is yours."

Wanting to know as much about Virginia's living arrangements as possible, Mark followed them both and was glad to find that her rooms were going to be at the back of the house on the ground floor, well away from the other bedrooms in the house.

While Virginia stayed behind to explore her spacious new bedroom and the adjoining sitting room, Lizzie and Mark left to find someone to help Mark bring her belongings in from outside. Virginia was pleased to see how much room she would have for her things, especially since she had acquired so much the day before. And if Daniel Pearson did not already have someplace else in mind for her to teach, she could make a nice little classroom out of the sitting room. With its many windows to let in fresh air and with its bright yellow-and-white wallpaper, the room would be perfect.

After Lizzie finally located her husband, Moses, and one of Daniel's stockmen who was not too busy with other work to help, Mark saw to it that all of Virginia's things were unloaded and carefully carried to her new rooms. He stayed to make sure Virginia would not need him for anything else, frowning when he realized how delighted she was with her rooms.

As requested, there were locks or strong bolts on all the windows, on the door to the hallway, and on a second door that Virginia realized must lead into another room. When she unbolted that smaller door and tried to open it, she discovered it was also bolted on the other side. That piqued her curiosity enough to wonder what lay beyond. But it was not until she left the room to walk Mark back to the front door that she realized the mysteriously locked door in her sitting room led directly into Daniel's library—a room where she suspected many secrets might be kept . . . secrets that might help her to accomplish what she had come to do . . . secrets that *must* be hidden away in there, because he had made the effort to close the hall door as well.

The thought of it made her heart race. She hoped to find undeniable proof of exactly what Caleb had done to get Valley Oaks; but she would settle for any shady information concerning the Pearson family. Although not completely fond of the idea, she knew she would resort to blackmail if that was what it took to get Valley Oaks back. After all, Caleb had to have resorted to much worse in order to overtake Valley Oaks in the first place.

It was not until Virginia had told Mark goodbye and had watched him drive away that she thought of Mary and realized she hadn't seen the child yet. She turned to find Lizzie standing in the doorway watching her as if she had nothing better to do with her time than keep an eye on her, and she asked the woman where Mary was.

"She had to go into town, too, to see the doctor and to get a new supply of her medicine. They should be back here before dark. Meanwhile, you can go on and get yourself unpacked and all moved in. I'd help you unpack your things, but the blackberries done been picked and washed. They came early this year, and I got cannin' to do." Then she turned toward the back of the house, her wide, colorful skirts swishing back and forth as she walked, giving Virginia an occasional glimpse of her bright red slippers.

On her way back to her new rooms, Virginia stopped to give the knob on the door to Daniel's personal library a try, but found it was locked, too. But the other doors in the hall had been left wide open, leading her to believe even more that there were indeed important things to be discovered inside that room, things Daniel Pearson wanted kept secret. She made it one of her highest priorities to find a way to get inside that library to see if she could discover exactly what those secrets were.

For the next few hours, Virginia was satisfied simply to unpack her things and put them away in the huge dresser and closet that had been provided, but soon the urge to explore her surroundings while Daniel was gone became too great to ignore. Finally, she put her unpacking aside and left her room. First she glanced into all the main rooms on the lower floor, deliberately avoiding the one leading off the dining room, which she was certain was the kitchen; she did not want Lizzie to realize she had left her rooms and was spying around.

When she next went quietly up the stairs, she was glad to find those rooms had also been left unlocked and the doors were open, which enabled easy inspection of each—including Daniel's own bedroom, which she was unable to resist and entered cautiously.

Much as she'd expected, the room was large enough to be a sitting room on one end and a bedroom on the other. A twelve-foot-high, elaborate plaster ceiling and gleaming oak floors that caught the reflection of the sunshine streaming in through many windows made the room seem even more spacious.

With an added touch of elegance, the wide, hand-carved mantel over the fancy brick fireplace matched the floor exactly, as did the wall trim and most of the furniture in the room.

At the end of the room sat a five-piece Rococo parlor suite. It was upholstered in pale-blue silk brocatelle and included a sofa, a rocker, and three armchairs. On the far end of the room was a bedroom suite made in a matching design with a two-level cheval dresser, a tall washstand, an armoire, and an oversized four-poster bed draped with a pale blue quilted bedcover made of the same material as the sofa and chairs.

Though she had intended not to venture far into the room, the incredible size of the man's bed lured Virginia further. To her amazement, the thing was wider than it was long—large enough to sleep three people in easy comfort. She wondered why anyone would need a bed so large and felt sorry for whoever had the chore of changing its sheets.

Stepping closer to the strange-looking bed, Virginia reached out and pressed down on the plump, rounded surface. As she expected, the mattress was stuffed with either fine cotton or feather down. Tilting her head to one side while she continued to stare at the it, she wondered which side Daniel slept on or if he slept right in the very middle. When she realized what had crossed her mind, she blushed and tried not to wonder what it was he wore to bed, remembering the short nightshirt of her grandfather's that allowed her to see to much of his spindly legs.

Ready to clear her thoughts of such dangerous considerations, she glanced around to see what else she could discover about Daniel Pearson that was not quite so disturbing. She noticed a tall shaving cup and a long razor on the cheval dresser, near the tall, beveled mirror. A porcelain-backed hairbrush and a small hair comb lay on the same dresser, on the higher of the split surfaces. Beside the hairbrush was a brass penny bank that resembled a small dog.

On the elaborate washstand beside a tall water pitcher that matched the wide, inset bowl lay a nailbrush and a small cake of pure white, store-bought soap. A dark blue towel hung perfectly folded across a small porcelain towel rack.

Curiously she moved closer to the dresser and pulled open first one drawer, then another. She found they were filled with perfectly folded clothes; there were apparently no hidden secrets. That's when it occurred to her how exceptionally neat his room was, just like the rest of the house. Nothing in his entire bedroom was out of place. She wondered if that was more because of his own habits or because of Lizzie's conscientious attention to detail. She decided it was probably Lizzie's doing, because she could not quite fathom a Pearson making the effort to be neat, especially when someone else was paid to clean up after him. She wondered how Lizzie accomplished as much as she did.

When Virginia walked back to the door, she paused to give the room one last glance. Again her imagination proved determined to place Daniel in that huge bed. A rapid pulse pounded deep inside her chest at the mere thought of the man lying there before her, beckoning her to come forward with a meaningful smile. She had to press her eyes closed to put the embarrassing image out of her mind. It was then she decided she had better leave before her thoughts got any worse; but when she finally turned to do just that, she bumped shoulder first into Daniel Pearson, who stood purposefully blocking the doorway. Her heart forgot to beat while she stood staring guiltily up into his incredibly blue eyes.

"Looking for something?" he asked with an easy drawl as he stretched an elbow up and leaned casually against the doorframe. His eyes studied her rapidly paling expression.

"I—I was just getting acquainted with the house," she stammered; then, realizing he was not supposed to be home yet, she demanded almost accusingly, "What are you doing here, anyway? Lizzie told me you were supposed to be gone most of the day."

His eyebrows arched with surprise. "I come and go as I please in my own home," he informed her quietly, unwilling to admit that he had hurried with his errands in town because of her. His own tone of voice was deceptively calm, but his expression was grim as he added, "And I might remind you that because this *is* my home, and because *that* is my private bedroom, you should at least have the courtesy to stay out."

Wide-eyed and mouth agape, Virginia continued to stare helplessly into his angry face, knowing full well he had every right to be angry. Having been caught in the very act of spying, she had no choice but to apologize and offer an excuse, no matter how feeble. "I know I should have, and I'm sorry; I didn't intend to go in there. I guess I let my curiosity get the better of my good judgment."

"And was your curiosity satisfied?" he wanted to know. His hard expression slowly relaxed and showed traces of the pure amusement at her situation.

The tiny smile that tugged at the outer corners of his lips drew her full attention for the moment, making it hard for her to concentrate on an answer. When she did not reply to that original question, he ventured to add, "Or would you like for me to give you the grand tour of my own personal bedroom? We could start with the bed . . . ."

Horrified, Virginia did not wait for him to finish his lurid statement. She shuddered just before she pushed past him and fled down the hallway, back the way she'd come. All she could hear as she hurried down the stairs, desperate to get to her own rooms, was the rapid pounding of her heart and the sound of deep, masculine laughter as it echoed through the house.

Only after Virginia had noticed Daniel cross the yard toward the barn late that afternoon did she again venture from her room. Still mortifed by what had happened earlier, as much by the way she'd run from him as by what he'd been about to suggest, she decided the best thing for her was to stay out of his sight and finish unpacking her things. But having seen him finally leave the house, she gathered her courage and, as soon as she had all evidence of her past locked away in a trunk, in case Daniel should decide to pay her room a visit in much the same manner she had his, she went in search of Mary. She wanted to assure the child that they would indeed begin classes the following morning, and if the day was a pretty one, they would devote part of the afternoon to outdoor studies.

Not wanting to bother Lizzie, she went upstairs to look for Mary. As expected, the girl was in her room, perched on the same window seat she'd been sitting on when Virginia was first introduced to her. This time Mary sat leaning back, her knees drawn up to her chin, her eyes closed.

The door had not been closed all the way; Virginia peered inside before bothering to knock, to see what the child might do with her time when she was alone. Virginia had not expected to find her sleeping so late in the day, but then remembered the girl was still recovering from an accident.

Quietly she pushed the door open and stepped inside, not wanting to waken her, but finding she wanted a closer look at the sleeping angel. Today the window beside the girl was open and a gentle spring breeze drifted into the room, bringing with it the sweet scent of freshly mown grass. Clutched tightly in Mary's tiny arms, close to her heart, was a brightly colored cloth doll. It was not until Virginia stepped closer still to get a better look at the doll that she noticed the puffiness around Mary's eyes. Her heart twisted with concern when she realized Mary had cried herself to sleep. She wondered what could possibly have happened to cause such a thing in a child to young.

While Virginia stood pondering the possibilities, Mary's arm slipped from the doll and fell to the cushion; the movement woke her. She blinked with sleepy confusion when she saw Virginia standing only a few feet away.

"What are you doing here?" There was no suspicion in her voice, only a child's true curiosity.

"I came to talk to you, but found you had fallen asleep. I could not decide whether to wake you or not."

Mary frowned. "I guess I was tireder than I thought. We had to get up real early to go into Pittsburg today. Had to go see the doctor again.

Have to go once a month."

Realizing the child was giving her the most obvious reasons for having fallen asleep so she would not guess the truth, Virginia decided not to let on that she had noticed her red and slightly swollen eyelids.

"And did you have a good time?"

Mary's frown deepened and she reached for the hem of her dress and held the ragged edge out for Virginia to see. "No. I fell down in the street and tore my dress. Father became so angry with me that he jerked me up by my shoulder and shouted at me in front of everybody. And then he refused to speak to me again all the way home."

"Did you hurt yourself?" Virginia asked and glanced at the girl's legs for any signs of injury.

"I skinned my knee, but I didn't mean to. It was an accident," she said, her voice pleading with Virginia to believe her. She pulled up her skirt to show the white bandage that covered the injured knee.

"Of course it was an accident, no one falls down on purpose," Virginia said with an understanding nod. "No one could possibly blame you for something like that."

"Father did. He got real angry with me about it." Mary's lower lip quivered and her pale blue eyes glimmered with fresh tears. "He sent me up here for the rest of the day to sit and think about what I did. I've made him so angry this time he'll never forgive me."

Virginia was instantly furious with Daniel Pearson for having shown such cruel judgment. "That's ridiculous. He was probably just upset that you hurt yourself. And I imagine as hot as it was today, he was already feeling irritable before you fell down. As soon as he has had a chance to cool off, I'm sure he'll forget about it."

"Do you think so?" Mary asked. A tiny ray of hope gleamed in her still-worried blue eyes.

"I know so. He was just tired from the trip and irritable from all the heat," she said, though she did not believe a word of it. Simply put, the man had no heart to guide him, even when he dealt with his own daughter. Poor Mary! Then, to help take the girl's thoughts off of her misery, Virginia glanced at the doll still clutched next to her heart and said, "What a lovely doll you have there. What's her name?"

"Shirley Anne," Mary responded quickly and held the doll out for Virginia's inspection.

"Shirley Anne? That's a nice name." She reached for the doll's well-stitched hand and shook it gently. "Glad to meet you, Shirley Anne. I'm Virginia Connors—Mary's new teacher."

Mary giggled at the thought of a grown-up introducing herself to a doll.

"What's goin' on in here?" they heard Lizzie ask from the doorway, and they both turned at the same time.

Virginia noticed Mary did not drop her smile when Lizzie entered the room, as she had for her father the day before. Obviously, Lizzie offered no threat to the child.

"Miss Virginia was shaking hands with Shirley Anne," Mary explained with open delight, then pretended to listen to some response the doll had made. "And Shirley Anne says that she likes Miss Virginia and wants to know if she will be her teacher, too."

"As long as Shirley Anne behaves herself, she is more than welcome to join our class," Virginia assured her.

Mary giggled again. "I'll make sure she behaves herself."

Lizzie chuckled as she wagged a stubby finger at

Mary. "Shirley Anne's not the one I worry about. Just you make sure you behaves yourself, young lady. Miss Virginia's class is for learnin', not playin'. But for now, you and Shirley Anne need to get on downstairs to the dinin' room and eat your supper before it gets cold."

Mary hopped down from the window seat and hurried out of the room to do as she'd been told, leaving Lizzie and Virginia to follow at a more leisurely pace. When Lizzie failed to mention anything about her own meal, Virginia decided to ask about it.

"Where do I eat? Mr. Pearson never said," she asked, though she suspected she would be eating in the kitchen with Lizzie.

"You will be eatin' in the dinin' room with Master Daniel at eight-thirty," Lizzie informed her.

"At eight-thirty? But I thought you just said dinner was ready now."

"Miss Mary's dinner is. She always eats at seven o'clock, then goes straight on upstairs to wash up and get on into bed."

"She eats alone?"

"Yes, ma'am," Lizzie responded. Though Lizzie's expression remained noncommittal, Virginia could sense that the woman was no more pleased with the arrangement than she was. "Master Daniel goes up to see that she's all tucked in a little after eight, then he comes back down to eat his own meal at eight-thirty. He likes to eat his supper late. And he told me this mornin' that you would be eatin' your evenin' meal with him."

"Oh, he did, did he?" Virginia asked, anger immediately evident in her voice. He could at least have consulted her about when she would prefer to eat, and with whom. "Well, we'll just see about that," she countered.

Lizzie paused at the foot of the stair and looked at her with surprise.

"Where can I find Mr. Pearson?" Virginia asked. Her pale brown eyes narrowed with determination. "I think we need to have a little discussion and get a few things straight between us."

"He's probably out in the barn," Lizzie answered hesitantly. "But I wouldn't disturb him none if I was you. He doesn't like womenfolk goin' into the barn. He says they get in the way out there. Besides, he don't take too kindly to people goin' against his wishes. He won't want to hear it if you have it in mind to complain."

Virginia did not stay to argue. With her hands clutched into tight fists at her sides, she marched straight out of the house in search of Daniel Pearson. Since Lizzie had mentioned the barn as a good possibility, that was the first place she went.

Finding the wide center doors open, she ignored Lizzie's warning to stay out, hiked her skirts a few extra inches to avoid the trampled mixture of hay, sawdust, and God knew what else, then went directly inside. To her disappointment, the only person she found in the barn was an older man with thinning brown hair and a slender build—definitely not Daniel. But at least he was able to tell her where Daniel was, how he had ridden off to check on a downed fenceline that appeared to have been cut, and that he'd probably be twenty minutes or more getting back.

Aware that if she waited for his return, she'd miss the opportunity to eat with Mary altogether, she went straight back to the house. Entering through the kitchen door, she marched directly into the dining room, where she found Mary already seated and

Lizzie applying a light sprinkle of table salt to the food on her plate.

"Set another place. I intend to eat with Mary," she said with so much determination that Lizzie decided it best not to argue and quickly did as she'd been told.

By eight-thirty, Virginia had already bid good night to Mary and retired to her own rooms. She was propped against her pillows reviewing the lesson plans she had put together for the following morning, drowsy with fatigue, when a sharp knock at her door startled her. She went to the door and opened it a few inches, just wide enough to be able to peer out into the hallway, to find herself face-to-face with a very angry Daniel Pearson.

"May I help you?" she asked tentatively while her right hand rose to clutch the narrow ruffle that circled the modest neckline of her cotton nightdress. Though she knew he could not actually see her through the wooden door, she suddenly wished she had thought to take the time to slip into her robe and glanced back at where it lay across the foot of her bed, well beyond reach.

"I have something I must ask you," he said just before he abruptly pushed his way into her room, unaffected by the loud gasp she let out as she pulled away from him. "I want to know why you aren't in the dining room as you're supposed to be."

Horrified he had forced his way into her bedroom without having given her any thought whatever, Virginia hurried to get her robe and held it in front of her like a shield, clutching the material so tightly that her knuckles turned white.

But the effort had come too late, for Daniel had already caught a glimpse of her feminine shape through the thin material and had permanently committed it to memory.

It was not until she had put several feet of distance between them that she finally tossed her head back and spoke, "I have already eaten."

"So I heard. And I also heard how you were indeed told ahead of time that I expected you to eat with me at eight-thirty, and how you then took it upon yourself to change my plans without so much as consulting me. I think you need to be reminded just who is the boss around here."

It took all the restraint Virginia had to keep her voice level and not argue with the man. He had made a good point. He was the boss, and if she wanted to continue to work here, she had better do what she could to please him. "I am well aware that you are the boss. I also know you are the man who will be paying my salary, and I did try to find you so that I could tell you how I would prefer to eat earlier than eight-thirty; but you were gone to check on a fenceline."

Rather than create more hostility, which could work against her in the long run, she forced herself to remain calm and tried to sound as agreeable as she could when she continued, "But if it would please you, I will quickly put my hair back into place, dress, and join you in the dining room for supper."

"Yes, it would please me very much," he said, his voice still harsh, though some of the anger had left his stark blue eyes. "But you don't have time to play around with your hair. Supper is going to be cold enough as it is. Just put on a dress and come on into the dining room. And from now on, remember that you are expected to join me for all evening meals, which are promptly served at eight-thirty."

The muscles in her jaw worked furiously as she

continued to struggle with her temper. "Yes, sir. I will try to remember that, *sir*. Eight-thirty."

He stood in the middle of her room, glaring down at her a moment longer, his anger fully returned, then spun and marched out of the room with as much determination as he had shown when he entered. The moment the door slammed behind him, Virginia felt her legs go suddenly weak and she sank quickly to her bed, aware that if she did not sit down immediately, she would surely crumple to the floor in much the same manner her pink silk robe had.

Never had she witnessed such barely controlled anger in a man; never had she felt such intense fear. Suddenly Virginia became deeply worried. She shuddered as if a chilling wind had curled up her spine. Had she somehow gotten herself into a situation she would not be able to handle with quite the same ease as she had first thought?

Chapter Five

When Virginia appeared downstairs moments later, she wore one of her more matronly dresses, bought not only to better suit her rigid teacher's image but to make her look older. The dress was simple in cut, bore no lace or fancy trim, and was made of a plain, dark blue muslin. Though she did not take the time to twist her long hair into a tight bun at the back of her head, in the manner she preferred to wear it, she did tie the long tresses back with a dark blue ribbon to keep it off her shoulders and out of her way.

Daniel did not seem affected by her appearance one way or another when she entered the dining room. He merely assisted her with her chair. His only remark was to say how glad he was she had decided to join him after all . . . as if she had had any choice in the matter.

Though she silently seethed with deeply repressed anger, Virginia forced herself to eat the second meal that was placed before her, while making every effort to seem cordial. She did not want to be tossed out of Valley Oaks before she ever had a chance to look around for something that would help her get the place back. She now felt almost certain that a clue to how she would be able to accomplish her goal lay hidden away somewhere in Daniel's library just waiting for her to discover it.

She was more hopeful than ever that there was still evidence to be found which would work against Caleb Pearson. Why else would the room be kept locked, if not to protect such dark family secrets? And until she could find out more about what it was Caleb had done to her grandfather, she fully intended to do everything she could to get along with the arrogant young nephew who now sat across the table watching her like a hawk.

While she continued to smile ever so politely at the man who stood between her and what she wanted most, Virginia tried to keep in mind how when the end finally came, the painful effort would be worth it. She would have Valley Oaks and would have restored her family's heritage; and all Daniel Pearson would be left with was his overwhelming arrogance and his cold-blooded black heart.

"Are your rooms suitable?" he asked after several minutes of heavy silence.

"Yes, they are quite suitable. The sitting room will make a lovely classroom."

"Classroom? Didn't Lizzie show you the room I've already had made ready for you?" he asked while he studied her questioning expression. "Evidently not. I'll show it to you after we finish eating. My uncle used the room as a study, but I found all the windows too distracting when I'm trying to get any work done and have decided not to use it."

"Your uncle's study?" she asked, as if she was totally confused. Though she had been slipping in and out of her own thoughts throughout the meal, he now had her full attention.

"Yes, this house used to belong to my Uncle Caleb. He left it to my father when he died, and then

78

when my father died a couple of months later, it was left to my mother. But she felt she would never have a need for the place and gave it to me. In the three months I've been here, I've made a few changes. One was to move Caleb's books and mine into a different room than what Caleb used as a library. If I try to work in a room with too many windows, I'm tempted to forget the work and end up back outside. I love the outdoors."

Virginia had already guessed as much by the golden glow of his skin and the gleaming highlights in his dark brown hair. "And you have already made the room into a classroom for Mary?"

"Sure—it seemed perfect. There was already a desk in there and there are plenty of shelves for whatever books you might have and several cabinets for storing whatever school supplies you'll need. I've already bought some supplies that I figured you'd want to have on hand. Whatever else you'll be needing, just let me know and I'll buy it the next time I'm in town."

Caleb's desk? Her heart jumped with sudden hope. She wondered if Daniel had bothered to clean it out, or might some of Caleb's papers still be inside? Suddenly she was eager to go see. "The room sounds perfect. But you don't have to bother showing me where it is . . . I can have Lizzie direct me. Finish your meal."

She pushed her chair back and placed her napkin on the still half-filled plate before her as she prepared to leave the table.

"No bother," he assured her in a firm voice while he too laid his napkin aside. His stern expression warned her that she had better wait until he had stood before rising from her seat. "I want to know your reaction to the room. If it's not what you want,

79

I'll prepare another room that better suits your needs."

Hating herself for being so easily intimidated by the man, Virginia waited until he had stood and indicated that she should stand too. She had never been very good at protocol, and she'd suffered harsh scoldings from her great-aunt because of it. She could almost hear her Aunt Sophie's voice instructing her to show more self-restraint and allow a gentleman to be a gentleman. But then she wondered how any of that could apply to Daniel: he was certainly no gentleman.

"This way," Daniel said, gesturing at a door which led to the main corridor.

When she got up, he placed his hand at her elbow, which to her dismay sent a tingling wave of warm chills up into her arm and through her body. She wondered what magic powers he possessed that caused her to react to his touch so strongly. Why did she suddenly find it so hard to concentrate on anything else?

Determined to ignore the strange sensations while he escorted her across the hall and into the back of the house, she tried to focus her thoughts on her surroundings instead of on the light touch at her elbow. Soon she was led into a room that had possibly been added on as an afterthought. Perhaps it had been specially planned to protrude from the rest of the house so that its oversized oriel windows would jut away on three sides.

Before Daniel moved further into the room to light the lamps, Virginia was able to see the silvery outlines of the moonlit gardens that lay just outside the uncurtained windows. A torchlit yard was easily seen through the windows at the back of the room. But once Daniel had the lamps lit and the room glowed with its own light, the view in the windows became their own mirrored images and Virginia was once again made very aware of the man who stood in the room with her, just a few feet away.

"The room is extraordinary," Virginia said quite frankly when she brought her gaze from his dark image in the glass to the room itself. The floor was of polished oak, as were the baseboards, the recessed bookshelves, and the window sashes. The walls had been papered in pale green with dark green trails of ivy leaves either hand-painted or artfully stenciled near the intricately carved plaster ceiling. Several books bound in leather had been left on the shelves near the desk.

A closer inspection of the books revealed that they were all references of one type or another and would prove useful in her teaching. The rest of the shelves in the room were empty. Curious to see what supplies he had provided for her, she opened one of the oak cabinets that had been built along the inner wall and discovered a large store of paper and pencils, two bottles of ink, several ink wells, and plenty of pens. There was even a small wooden easel with a slate board and enough chalk to last a year.

"It's been a while since I was in school," Daniel said, following her across the room and standing only a few feet behind where she had knelt to feel the paper he had bought. "I got the things I remembered my teacher used, but if there's anything I forgot, I'll go into Pine and get it for you later in the week. If Abernathy's doesn't have it already in stock, they'll order it immediately."

"It may be later on in the week before I realize what I will need," she said as she closed the cabinet and stepped away from him. She hurriedly moved to the large oak desk. She had found his nearness more than a little discomfiting and wanted to keep a good distance between them.

In an attempt to hide her eagerness to explore the desk, Virginia casually pulled one of the three top drawers open and peered inside. She was disappointed to discover it completely empty; there was not even a layer of dust. She then opened another drawer; again, it was empty. Frowning, she pushed the drawers closed, knowing the rest of the drawers would prove the same.

"I had Lizzie go ahead and clear the desk out for you," he said with a pleased smile while he slowly moved toward her until he was again beside her. "The room is ready for whenever you want to move your things in. I figured Lizzie had already told you about the room so that you could start arranging everything the way you wanted it. I told her to bring you back here and let you see the room as soon as you were settled into your rooms." His smile quickly lowered into a thoughtful frown as if he might be trying to decide whether Lizzie had failed him or not.

"It was almost seven before I was finished unpacking," Virginia said by way of explanation. She certainly did not want to get Lizzie into any trouble.

"Oh, yes, you took a little time away from your unpacking to do some exploring, as I recall," he said, and a trace of amusement lifted his frown into another dangerously charming smile. "How is it you missed this room in your explorations?"

"I did notice the door, but I thought it probably led to a closet," she admitted honestly. It was so close to the kitchen she'd decided to leave it alone. She'd been too afraid she would alert Lizzie to the fact that she was no longer in her room unpacking — but she was not about to admit that to him. "And I didn't feel I had a right to go snooping around in your closets."

His eyes sparkled while he considered what she'd just said; his smile widened. "Yet you felt it was perfectly all right to go in and snoop around my bedchamber."

Virginia felt the blood rising to her face, leaving her cheeks hot and flushed. "I explained that—I didn't mean to go in; it's just that the room had been left open and I was curious."

"Curious about what deep, dark secrets might be hidden away in a gentleman's private bedroom?" he taunted her and leaned forward, eager to watch her reaction.

"You certainly are no gentleman," she said defiantly, with far more bravado than she actually felt.

"And did you discover that fact during your search of my room?"

Her heart climbed to her throat as she tried to decide if he was still teasing or if he had started to suspect her real reason for being at Valley Oaks. She felt her flushed cheeks grow suddenly pale as all the blood rushed to her hammering heart. Her legs ached; they seemed almost too weak to support her weight. "I've already apologized for having gone into your room and I can promise you, I'll never go in there again." Having discovered that there was nothing of value to her there, she knew that was a promise she could keep. Her interest was now centered on what might be hidden away inside the library.

"That's not a promise I've asked for," he said with a chuckle that not only served to embarrass her further but infuriated her as well. She did not like being the continued focus of his amusement.

Almost as quickly as the color had drained from

her face, it returned a bright crimson. "But it is a promise I am more than willing to give."

"I don't doubt that," he said and his chuckle grew into hearty laughter. But when he saw how quickly she had tensed because of his teasing, he reached out and placed his hands on her shoulders.

Whether he was able to sense the strange sensations that had bolted through her before she was able to pull away from him again, she could not be sure, but she tried to appear unaffected while she hurriedly put some distance between them.

"I'm sorry," he said and made a visual effort to control his laughter by quickly withdrawing his smile.

With an almost somber expression, he added, "I didn't mean to offend you." But when he saw the way her eyes had narrowed while she watched him warily, he could not help but burst into laughter again. Clearly she did not trust him.

"Sir, I fail to see the humor in your apology," she said in as carefully controlled a voice as she could muster.

"I know." He nodded and again fought to bring a halt to his laughter. "And I apologize again."

"Your apology can be accepted only if you give it sincerely, sir," she said, still in a very low and controlled voice. Her fingers curled and pressed into her palms. The soft pain her fingernails caused her was almost a welcome relief.

"I was sincere," he told her and again the laughter came to an abrupt stop. "And will you please quit calling me sir?" he asked. Though he now bore a somewhat solemn expression, the bright glimmer in his blue eyes revealed that he continued to do battle with an extremely overwhelming urge to burst out laughing again. "I don't like to be called sir. It makes me feel . . . I don't know . . . old, I guess. Please, don't call me sir anymore. Anything but that."

"Anything? Well, then yes, *ma'am*," she corrected herself quickly. "Whatever you say, ma'am."

Daniel's brows lowered as if he suddenly had to struggle in order to keep control of his anger, but it was his need to laugh again that waged war inside him.

" 'Ma'am?' " he asked in disbelief. Then he could hold his laughter no longer and tossed his head back and roared.

This time Virginia could not help but laugh with him.

"You are far different from any woman I have ever met," he finally said when he had stopped laughing enough to be able to speak. He then stepped closer to her. "Why can't you just call me Daniel? It's really a simple name. I do wish you would use it. Because I fully intend to call you Virginia."

Threatened by his sudden movement in her direction, though there was no malice in either his expression or his voice, Virginia began to back away from him, her eyes wide with apprehension. "Are you sure it is wise for us to use each other's given names? After all, I am in your employ. I really should call you Mr. Pearson and you should refer to me as Miss Connors. It's only proper."

"I don't like hearing you call me Mr. Pearson," he stated emphatically. "I want you to call me Daniel. Try it. *Daniel*. I want to hear you say it."

She continued to back away, and for every step back she took, he reciprocated with a slow, forward movement of his own. She felt very much like a small, defenseless animal being stalked at leisure by an extremely hungry wolf. His glimmering blue eyes dipped downward to take in her feminine curves more than once while he gradually closed the distance between them.

"Come on, Virginia, surely you can say my name. *Daniel*," he urged again in a low, mellow voice.

He was close enough to her now that she realized she could reach out and touch him if she had a mind to, and for a brief second she actually considered it. Her heart slammed hard against her chest when she realized what had occurred to her.

"Daniel, don't," she said, her voice almost too weak to be heard while she continued to move away, her eyes transfixed on his.

"See, you can say Daniel," he pointed out with an appreciative nod. His lips spread into a pleased smile which formed long, narrow dimples in his lean cheeks. They were so appealing that she had another urge to reach out and trace them with the tips of her fingers.

"But my last name is not Don't, it's Pearson," he added, and his smile grew.

"I know what your name is," she stated coolly, but despite her outward appearance of calm and determination, her body rebelled at his continued approach. It was as if a tiny part of her wanted him finally to catch up with her just so she could find out what might happen, to see how she would handle it, but that notion was not only ridiculous, it was dangerous. She continued to back away.

"Then why did you follow my name with don't?" he wanted to know. His smile parted to reveal traces of his white teeth; his eyes sparkled with bedevilment.

Virginia tried to find a quick answer to his question, but could not. She was not quite certain what he intended to do, and because of that, she could not state exactly what it was she wanted to be sure he didn't do. Never had she felt so confused . . . never had she felt so afraid.

In a desperate attempt not to lose herself in the glimmering depths of his pale blue eyes, she pulled her gaze from his and looked down, only to become distracted by the nearness of his strong, muscular body, clad in extremely close-fitted black trousers. She continued to fight the urge to reach out and touch him, to see if those muscles were really as solid as they appeared. The lingering scent of the outdoors mixed with the rich smell of pipe tobacco was next to catch her attention.

"Do I make you nervous?" he asked with a meaningful raise of his brow; but even so, he continued to move forward, his gaze still trained on hers. Though his eyes displayed his amusement, his face remained expressionless.

"Yes, sir, you—" she started to answer but was quickly interrupted.

"Sir?" he asked in warning.

"Yes, *Daniel,* you do," she said in exasperation and released a deep breath she had held inside a little too long.

"I don't mean to," he said. Though his voice sounded sincere enough, the glimmer in his eyes was far from innocent.

Soon he had literally backed her against the wall. He smiled victoriously when she finally realized she was trapped; he stood just inches away from her and, although their bodies were not quite touching, she could feel the heat that radiated from him. Her heart beat erratically and her throat went completely dry, too dry to allow her to swallow.

"But you do. You make me very nervous," she somehow managed to say. Her gaze darted around the room to see just how far they were from the door and if it had been left open. She was relieved to see that it had.

"Why is that? What have I done to make you feel so ill-at-ease around me?" he asked while he lifted his right hand and casually ran a fingertip along the sensitive curve of her cheek. The gentle caress sent odd little shivers cascading down Virginia's spine and caused tiny bumps of anticipation to rise beneath her skin.

"Daniel, please," she said sternly and reached up to brush his hand aside. She pressed herself harder against the cold surface of the wall in an attempt to put even a quarter of an inch more distance between them. "You are not behaving as an employer should!"

"Oh? And how should an employer behave?"

"Not like this!" she assured him.

"Then how?" he asked softly, leaning forward so that his breath fell softly against her cheek and her ear.

Again tiny bumps rose just beneath the surface of her skin and delicate waves of tingling sensations scattered through her body. Daniel's heavily lidded eyes were now only inches away and she found herself mesmerized by their stark beauty.

"I don't know, just not like this," she tried again, but her voice was strained and had lost some of its earlier conviction. The close proximity of his lips to hers had caused her heart to pound furiously in her chest and her throat had tightened until she could barely breath, much less speak clearly. When his gaze then left hers to linger momentarily on her lips, all she could do was stand mutely before him, her eyes transfixed on his own slightly parted mouth, nervously anticipating his next movement.

He stared at her a long breathless moment. Then,

just as abruptly as he had started his little game of cat-and-mouse, he turned away and moved quickly to the desk. Then, as if nothing out of the ordinary had just occurred, he asked, "So, do you think this room will be suitable for your needs? Or would you rather have a room without so many windows? I'll warn you now, Mary shows an unusual fondness for staring out them for hours on end. They may prove too much of a distraction."

Oddly, his voice sounded strained, almost angry. She wondered it if was Mary's daydreaming that disturbed him, or something she herself had just said or done. Still dazed by the emotions that had so quickly overcome her, Virginia stammered a response, "Y—yes, the room will be just fine. And I think once Mary has other things to occupy her thoughts, she will spend less time staring out the window."

"I don't know . . . Mary is a strange child. She lets her mind wander until she's off into her own little world, and she stays there for hours on end. Just this afternoon she was almost run over by a wagon when she carelessly stepped off a walkway and out into the street. She wasn't even aware she'd done it. Scared me half to death."

He shuddered as he remembered the incident in town. "All because she was not paying attention. In fact, if she had not tripped over a rock when she did and kept going into the street, she would have been run over—the wagon came that close."

Virginia moved away from the wall, though not far in Daniel's direction, and considered what he'd just said. Finding that Daniel had a good reason for reacting as harshly as he had with Mary made her feel somewhat guilty: she realized she'd been much too quick to judge him. Even so, she did not like the way he kept referring to his own daughter first as peculiar and now as strange. Remembering how adept Mary was at eavesdropping, she wondered if the little girl had ever overheard her father's careless references to her unusual behavior.

"I think once Mary begins her studies, she will find she has little time for daydreams," Virginia assured him. "But right now she really has little else to do."

Daniel considered that for a moment, then surprised her by nodding in agreement.

She went on to explain, "Besides, after everything your daughter had been through this past year, what with the accident and the loss of her beloved mother, one would expect her to become at least a little withdrawn."

Daniel's expression darkened, then in an obvious attempt to change the subject, he ran his hand over the smooth surface of the desk and said, "I hope this desk will do. The only other desk I have is my own. It would take a week to clear it."

"It should do nicely," she responded, wondering about his odd reaction to what she had said about Mary. "It's large and has plenty of drawers."

Daniel's voice grew more nostalgic when he went on to tell her more about the desk, "Yes, it's a fine piece of craftsmanship. Caleb bought it because of all the drawers. He said it was easier to keep it neat when there were a lot of drawers to hide the clutter. Sometimes when I look at this desk I can almost see my uncle sitting there behind it, bending over his papers, his brow furrowed in concentration and his eyeglasses balanced precariously on the tip of his nose." He smiled at the fond memory.

"You said this was your uncle's house. Why was the house not passed along to his own children?" she asked, pretending not to know anything about Caleb in hopes of encouraging him to talk about the man.

"He never married."

"Never married? Why not?"

"Father once told me that Uncle Caleb fell deeply in love with someone way back when he was very young, but that whoever the girl was, she did not return his love. I think she may have allowed him to court her for a little while, or she was at least very close friends with him, but she chose to marry someone else. As I understand it, Caleb was not so wealthy then, and she chose to marry for money. Caleb never got over her, and because of that he never married. I guess he never found anyone else who made him feel quite the same way."

Virginia felt a sharp pang inside her stomach. "Did your father ever say who the woman was?"

"No, he never did. He knew Uncle Caleb would not want him to." Daniel paused a moment as he thought more about his uncle. "It was really a pity, too, because if anyone ever needed someone to love, it was Uncle Caleb. I never met a more kind or caring man in all my life."

Virginia was repelled to discover Daniel thought so highly of his uncle. How could anyone find anything so nice to say about such a cruel, heartless man?

"How did your uncle die?" she asked while she tried to conceal her hatred and resentment.

"His heart simply quit. He went out for a long ride one afternoon. When he came back home, he went directly up to his room, lay down on his bed, and quietly died. Lizzie said he was holding an old lace handkerchief next to his heart when he died." Daniel fell silent for a moment. "It was a sad way to die, all alone . . . without even any children to offer him a final comforting thought."

Virginia felt an unexpected twinge of sympathy but quickly forced it from her heart, for if anyone had deserved to die alone, it was Caleb Pearson. He deserved no sympathy; it was all his own fault. "But of course, he had at least one brother who loved him . . . your father. Did he have any other brothers or sisters?"

"No, just Father."

"And do you have any brothers or sisters?" she asked, trying to establish if there was anyone else out there who might think they had a claim to Valley Oaks and try to cause her trouble.

"I had an older brother, but he died when he was only eight years old, from a snake bite. I was only three at the time and don't really remember him, but even so, I find myself missing him from time to time. What about you? Do you have any brothers and sisters?"

"No, my parents were killed in a boat accident when I was eight," she answered, alarmed that he'd begun to question her past. Quickly she tried to turn the focus of conversation back to him. "Where did you live before you came here?"

He paused as if trying to consider his answer. "I roamed for a while, but I grew up on a large sugar plantation in South Louisiana."

"Is that where your mother lives?"

"No. Right after Father died, she tried to talk me into moving back and running the place, but I had too much on my mind. She eventually sold the plantation to her uncle and moved to New Orleans. It really was the best thing for her. In the city she can be closer to her friends and doesn't get so lonely all the time."

"Does Mary get to see much of her?"

"We visit."

"What about her other grandparents? Does she get to see much of them?"

Daniel's face hardened. "She has no other grandparents."

"That's too bad," Virginia said solemnly, realizing then that the only family Mary really had was an overbearing father and a grandmother who lived too far away.

"What about you? Your parents are dead, but are your grandparents still alive?" he asked.

"No, they're all dead," she answered, quickly swallowing back the bitterness that welled in her throat at having a Pearson mention them to her.

She hurriedly moved on to talk about something else . . . anything else. The last thing she wanted to discuss with Daniel Pearson was her grandparents. "It certainly is growing late. I really should get on to bed; I have a lot to do tomorrow."

Without giving him a chance to respond, Virginia headed for the door. Her words came out rushed as she spoke to him over her shoulder, "If you see Mary before I do, tell her I want to begin her studies by nine o'clock."

Daniel glanced around the room and wondered how Virginia had so suddenly become aware of the time. There were no clocks to tell her the hour; she had no watch. When he turned back and looked again toward the door, he said nothing but watched with a curious expression as she hurried out of his sight.

Chapter Six

In the weeks that followed, Virginia's daily pattern was quickly set. As requested, she spent most of her week teaching Mary during the daytime and keeping Daniel company in the evening. Though she'd wanted to visit with the Langfords on the two weekends that had passed so quickly, she discovered she had too much to do to prepare for her teaching to get away. Because of the trial terms of her employment for the first month, she worked extra hard to do the very best job she could.

To her own delight, Mary was learning at a far more rapid rate than Virginia had expected; keeping a step ahead of the child was not easy. With each day that passed, Virginia marveled at the girl's boundless curiosity and at how quickly she absorbed her lessons and yet still yearned to know more. Though at first Shirley Anne had been brought in and been made to sit beside Mary during her lessons, the doll was eventually forgotten and Mary came down to the classroom alone.

The more time Virginia spent with her student, the more she marveled at the girl's keen intelligence. And the more time she spent with Daniel, the more she grew to tolerate his company and the more infuriated she became over her unacceptable responses to him.

Virginia could no longer deny that she found him attractive, or that his mere presence made her stomach flutter in a ridiculous manner; but despite such strong responses, she staunchly refused to allow herself to actually like the man. She felt it was more than enough to tolerate him. After all, he *was* a Pearson. And because of this, she continued to try to keep a close guard over the strong feelings he evoked in her. The best way to do that, she found, was to spend as little time as possible in his company. When that proved difficult, she discovered that provoking minor arguments between them helped her not only to keep her budding emotions under control, but seemed to drive sufficient distance between them.

But even after she retired to her bedchamber and was at last alone, especially in the long moments just before she drifted off to sleep, Virginia found she could not completely rid herself of the man. Though sometimes her thoughts of him were repellent and at other times welcome, she was soon to discover he was a part of her thoughts more often than not—and at some of the most inopportune moments.

Finally, in hopes of finding something else to occupy her mind besides Daniel and Mary, something that would put less emotional strain on her, she decided to keep her promise to Jessie and Mark and go visit them, at least for a few hours. With every intention of doing so, she approached Daniel late one Friday afternoon to ask his permission to borrow a buggy the following Sunday. Though she knew she could walk the distance in an hour, she did not relish the thought of it. As the month of May grew long, the days had become increasingly warmer, at times uncomfortably so.

"This Sunday?" he questioned with a quick frown as soon as she had found the courage to ask for the buggy.

"Is anything wrong?" she wanted to know. "I promise to be very careful. I assure you, I do know how to drive a buggy."

"It's not that . . . I don't mind you borrowing the buggy for a Sunday drive, it's just that this Sunday I have company coming who I wanted you to meet."

Virginia was crestfallen. Why Sunday? In all the weeks she'd been there, not one person had stopped by for a visit; but then again, she had not expected there to be many visitors at Valley Oaks. She was well aware none of the local people cared to associate with a Pearson. Caleb had always had to import his visitors from other places. "I could stay long enough to meet them."

"They are coming for an afternoon visit and staying for an early supper. I was hoping you'd help keep them entertained the entire time. I know I don't have the right to ask it of you; after all, I have promised you your Sundays to do with as you please. But I would really appreciate it if you would do this one favor for me. I'll pay you extra."

"Who all is coming?" she asked, wondering how she would get through the entire afternoon of making pleasant conversation with people she did not know and would probably not even like.

"Amanda and William Haught," he told her. "Their father was a close business associate of my uncle's, and since I've taken over his shipping interests in Jefferson, he's become a business associate of mine as well."

Virginia was surprised to learn that Caleb had shipping interests because no one had ever mentioned them to her, but she was too busy trying to figure out why the names seemed so familiar to wonder about business for long. "Do they live near here?"

"Near Daingerfield," he informed her.

Virginia's frown deepened, for that was sixteen miles away. Why should she find the names so familiar? Then she realized why they had struck such a familiar cord: *Amanda*. Daniel's friend who had wanted to send Mary away to boarding school was named Amanda—the woman Mary claimed she hated. Suddenly Virginia was *very* interested in staying to meet the woman and decided her trip to visit with Mark and his family could wait one more week.

"What time do you expect them?"

Daniel shrugged. "When they come for Sunday supper, they usually arrive in the early afternoon."

Usually? That meant they came for Sunday visits often; Amanda was a frequent visitor. Virginia felt something tug at her insides. "Then I shall be ready to greet them shortly after noon."

Daniel smiled, revealing the dimples she found so dangerously attractive. "Thank you. And I promise to make it up to you next weekend. Not only will I let you use the buggy for the afternoon, I'll drive you so that you don't get lost. There's some lovely countryside around here. Maybe we could take a ride into Pittsburg. I hear their gardens are in full bloom."

Virginia felt a strange sensation she could not quite identify. She found Daniel's unexpected offer to accompany her on her Sunday drive as thrilling as it was frightening. And at the same time it was disappointing, because with Daniel along, she would not be able to stop by and visit with the Langfords. She still did not want him to realize she had such close friends nearby for fear he might be able to link that friendship with the past. "Daniel, that won't be necessary. I have a very good sense of direction."

She chose her words carefully, for she did not want him to guess she was already well acquainted with the roads and had been since childhood. In truth, there was very little chance she would get lost in Camp County.

"It will be my pleasure," he assured her, then dismissed the subject with a wave of his hand. His mind was set and, as usual, there would be no changing it. Virginia knew better than to even try.

The bright early summer sun threatened an unseasonably hot afternoon as it climbed effortlessly past its zenith in a cloudless blue sky. Though there was a slight breeze from the northwest, it did little to cool Virginia's anticipation, for neither she nor Mary looked forward to the visitors due to arrive at any moment.

Though Daniel had remained in the house since before lunch, under the cooling comfort of the ceiling fan, Mary and Virginia had chosen to wait outside in the shade of the tall oaks nearest the flower gardens. Both hoped Amanda would find the prospect of joining them outside on such a warm afternoon too unappealing but were disappointed when they noticed Daniel and his two guests headed in their direction only minutes after they had heard the carriage arrive.

"Virginia," he called out to her as he escorted his guests to the wide shaded area in which she and Mary had chosen to sit. "I want you to meet Amanda and William Haught, two very dear friends of mine."

Virginia reached up to smooth a rebellious strand of hair back into place when she noticed how beautifully Amanda's hair behaved. The thick black tresses had been pulled back and held in place by small silver combs, then allowed to flow in smooth shimmering waves down the woman's back and across her slender shoulders. A pert blue satin hat was perched atop the flawless coiffure and matched the deep blue of her wide, flowing skirts. To Virginia's complete dismay, the woman was absolutely beautiful, and despite the humidity that had caused the shorter hair to curl uncontrollably along her own hairline and to cling to her damp skin, Amanda looked as fresh as a morning flower. *Disgusting.*

"Pleased to meet you both," Virginia lied sweetly as she stood and stepped forward to greet Daniel's friends.

"Pleased to meet *you*," William responded eagerly and moved ahead of the rest to take her hand in greeting. He held her slender hand folded within his grasp a little longer than necessary. "Daniel, you didn't tell me Miss Connors was so beautiful. Oh, how I envy you, living in the same house with someone so lovely."

"Don't overdo it, dear Brother," Amanda warned with a smile that flattered her oval face but did not quite reach the depths of her overly large green eyes. "If you're not careful, you will frighten the poor girl off with your childish behavior."

William responded with a charming smile of his own, a smile very similiar to his sister's, as he finally released Virginia's hand. "And I certainly wouldn't want to do that."

Virginia did not like the way the young man's gray-green eyes studied the simple cut of the pale yellow cotton dress she had chosen to wear. The intensity of his gaze made her extremely uncomfortable and caused her to take a step back. She was relieved when Amanda decided it was time to gather everyone's attention to herself.

"I'm sorry we were so late, Daniel dearest, but I had such a hard time deciding what to wear." She paused at the appropriate moment to allow Daniel ample opportunity to compliment her final choice in dress, which he did lavishly.

"Oh, Daniel, how you do go on so," she said flirtatiously and prompted him further with a lively flutter of her long, dark eyelashes. "If you don't stop right now, you're going to make me blush." She reached into a pocket hidden away in the folds of her skirt and pulled out a dark blue silk fan, flicked it open, then began to flutter it about her face.

"But you do look lovely," Daniel repeated dutifully. "You always do."

Quickly tiring of Amanda's ridiculous antics, Virginia glanced back to see what had become of Mary and found the girl still seated in one of the cushioned lawn chairs, looking very bored with the conversation. Realizing the child was completely left out, she gestured to the chairs that surrounded her. "Shall we all make ourselves comfortable?"

"Yes, lets," Daniel put in and waited for everyone to settle themselves. "I'll have Lizzie bring out some lemonade."

"And have her bring a few of her cinnamon teacakes," Amanda put in. "We were running so late that we had to forgo lunch entirely."

"Of course," Daniel said with a smile and turned to leave.

While he was in the house, Amanda glanced around and realized that the only vacant places were near Virginia. She frowned. "William, wouldn't you rather sit near Miss Connors? You seemed so fond of her."

Eagerly William rose from his seat beside Amanda and took his sister's advice. "Of course. I'm very

100

eager to get to know her a little better. Beautiful women always fascinate me."

Mary's eyebrows lowered as she stared at Amanda, but she remained silent.

"So, tell me, Virginia—you don't mind if I call you Virginia, do you?" William asked as he leaned heavily on the arm of his chair toward her.

"No, of course not," Virginia said agreeably, though she would have been just as satisfied had he called her Miss Connors. She had to keep in mind that these were Daniel's friends and she was still under trial employment. She forced herself to smile.

"Good. So tell me, Virginia, whatever made you want to become a teacher?" he went on to inquire.

"I love children," she admitted readily.

"Fancy that," Amanda said, clearly not impressed by such a statement.

"Come now, Mandy, just because you don't care for them doesn't mean other people can't," William reprimanded her. "I think it is very commendable to care enough about children to want to teach them."

"Commendable, indeed," Amanda said with little enthusiasm as she rearranged an awkward fold in her satin skirt. "I just hope you don't find you have taken on more than you can manage, Miss Connors. Mary is such a difficult child."

Virginia came forward in her seat, infuriated that Amanda had said such a thing in front of Mary. "How can you say that? Mary is a very bright child, very eager to learn, and very eager to please."

Amanda opened her mouth to disagree, but at that moment she glanced across the yard and saw Daniel already on his way back. Suddenly, her face lifted into a genteel smile while she ignored everyone else present and waited for him to take the seat beside her.

"Lizzie will be right out with the lemonade," he informed them as he took the only seat still available that would allow him to be a part of the conversation. When he laid his hands on the arms of the wrought-iron chair, his fingers came within inches of Amanda's hand, and Virginia found she could not take her gaze from the tiny distance that lay between the two.

"And she promised to bring a plateful of teacakes," he went on to add with a reassuring nod. "In fact, she just made a fresh batch this afternoon."

"You are such a dear," Amanda said and reached over to pat his hand lightly, letting her fingers rest on the backs of his when she was through.

Mary crossed her arms and looked away.

Through the rest of the afternoon, Amanda managed to monopolize the conversation and as she did, Virginia caught her first real glimpses of hatred in Mary; but it was not until Amanda suggested Virginia leave to get them more lemonade that she was able to actually talk with the girl about it, because as soon as Virginia had stood to do as Amanda wished, Mary volunteered to go too and hurried to join her.

"She acts like a princess," Mary muttered in a low voice so that only Virginia could hear her while they walked together toward the house. "But all she really is is a spoiled brat." She grinned at having said that out loud but drew in her shoulders while she waited for the harsh reprimand which was sure to follow.

"I agree," Virginia responded with a light laugh, surprising Mary so completely that the child burst out in a fit of giggles. "But, sweetheart, we must keep in mind that she is a close friend of your father's, and because of that, we must try our best to get along with her."

Mary sighed. "I'd rather kiss a snake."

"Not much difference," Virginia pointed out, and again Mary burst out in giggles.

By the time the two of them returned with more lemonade, Mary's mood had lifted considerably. Occasionally, for no reason Daniel or Amanda could fathom, she would burst into a fit of giggles and have to cover her mouth with both hands in order to stop. Only Virginia knew what was behind her sudden outbursts, and because she did, they exchanged knowing glances more than once.

As expected, Mary was called to eat early and was already off to bed before everyone else gathered in the dining room for supper. Amanda took the seat to Daniel's immediate right, which was usually where Virginia sat, and did what she could to commandeer his attention throughout the meal. Though she allowed him to talk with William with little interference, whenever Daniel found he had something to say to Virginia or about Virginia, Amanda was very quick to interrupt and change the subject. It became clear Amanda was not at all happy that Daniel had decided to hire a live-in tutor for Mary, and she was especially not fond of his choice in tutors. She displayed little tolerance where Virginia was concerned and no patience whatsoever.

After they had finished their meal of roast turkey and brown rice and retired to the veranda for coffee and raisin pie, Amanda made the mistake of ordering Virginia to go into the kitchen and bring back a cinnamon stick for her. "Lizzie always keeps cinnamon sticks for me to put in my coffee, but she almost never remembers to put them on the tray."

Daniel was quick to come to Virginia's defense. "Amanda, Virginia is not one of the servants. If you want a cinnamon stick for your coffee, I'll get it," he said, rising from his seat beside her to do just that.

"Daniel, don't be silly. The girl is a hired nanny. As such she should be more than willing to fetch a cinnamon stick for one of your guests," Amanda argued.

Daniel paused in the doorway and looked back at her with a stern expression warning her that she was out of line. "She is not a nanny. She is Mary's teacher. She was hired to teach, not to fetch and carry. And even if that were not the case, today is her day off. She is here as my guest, the same as you are. So if you find you need something, anything, request it of me. I don't want you making demands on Virginia. I'll get your cinnamon stick for you."

"Oh, never mind, I'm no longer in the mood for coffee," she said with a pout as she set her cup aside. "Sit back down."

To Virginia's surprise, Amanda let the matter drop with no further comment, though she continued to cast disapproving glances in her direction during the rest of the evening and refused to address her directly.

The evening dragged on. It was well after dark before either William or Amanda mentioned leaving. William had been too intent on getting to know all he could about Virginia, and Amanda too intent on capturing Daniel's attentions. Virginia had started to believe the Haughts hoped to become permanent residents at Valley Oaks. Finally it was William who realized the hour.

"If we don't be on our way, it will be after midnight before we reach home. Mandy can sleep tomorrow away, but Father and I have a business appointment at ten. I dare not be late for that."

"So you can sleep in until nine and still make that meeting," Amanda quickly pointed out. "And you probably will . . . I'm not ready to leave yet."

Daniel reached across and caressed her cheek lightly, almost as he would a small child, "It is getting late, Amanda. I also have work to do in the morning. So does Virginia."

"Pooh, why is everyone so concerned about his work? Would the world come to an end if you neglected your work for one day?" When Daniel only laughed at her comment, she shrugged her delicate shoulders with defeat and pouted prettily. "You can at least walk me to the carriage."

"Of course," Daniel said as he stood and offered her his arm. "Come, William, let's see that your sister safely reaches the carriage."

"I'll be there in a moment," William said and did not make an effort to get up from his seat beside Virginia. "You two go on ahead."

Virginia did not miss the way he glanced up at his sister and offered her a knowing wink. He was purposely staying behind to give Amanda and Daniel a moment alone, and although it should not have affected her one way or another, Virginia found it made her very, very angry.

"It shouldn't be long before there are wedding bells for those two," William said as soon as the pair had disappeared into the darkness at the side of the house.

"Oh?" Virginia responded, hoping to sound unconcerned. In truth, the thought of Daniel marrying someone like Amanda made her want to scream out in protest. She thought of Mary and the misery the child would surely suffer at the hands of such a woman.

"Oh, to be sure, they've all but set the date," he went on to explain. "Mandy has been in love with Daniel for years. It broke her heart when he ran off and married Josie the way he did."

"How long has Amanda known him?" Virginia did not realize theirs was a long-standing relationship.

"Let's see," he answered as he reached up and rubbed his cheek lightly. "I think we first met Daniel back when I was about fourteen, which would have made Daniel and Mandy both about thirteen. It was nearly fourteen years ago." He shook his head as if amazed. "Mandy and I came with Father to one of Caleb's big annual picnics while Daniel was visiting. I think Mandy actually fell in love with him that very day."

"I see," Virginia said and wondered why it suddenly felt as if someone had spilled a vial of strong acid into her veins.

"Daniel paid court to her for a few summers whenever he was up here visiting his uncle, but then to everyone's surprise, about eight or nine years ago, he just up and married Josie Kilburn. True, Josie was one of the most beautiful girls around these parts back then, but no one had realized they were even seeing each other. Mandy was so heartbroken, she took to her bed for months after that. And I figure that's why she's never married. She could never find anyone she liked quite as much as she liked Daniel."

Virginia had heard enough. "Well, I really think they've had enough time alone for now. It's late; you really should be on your way. You mustn't miss your appointment tomorrow."

"Will you walk me halfway?" he asked eagerly, his gray-green eyes searching her face for any indication of interest.

"I'm sorry, but I must say no. I am very tired; it's been a long day and I do need to get to bed. Tomorrow is another workday for me and I'll have to get up early. I always start Mary's lessons promptly at nine." Without waiting any longer, she rose from her chair and stood expectantly until he had done the same.

"Why so early? That means you must have to rise by seven," he said, stunned by the revelation. It was obvious William was accustomed to a pampered life.

"I usually rise at six," she informed him. She wanted to laugh at the way his mouth sagged with surprise, but she chose not to offend him. "So you see, I really do need to get to bed." Then, in an effort to let him know the evening had come to an end as far as she was concerned, she smiled and politely offered her hand. "It was nice to meet you."

When he again tried to hold on to her hand longer than was necessary, she pulled it gently from his grasp. "Good night." Then without delay she turned and went inside. Relieved to be alone at last and away from William and his overly flirtatious sister, she hurried to her room to get ready for bed.

Quickly she took her hair down and brushed the tangles from it, then donned one of her cotton night-dresses, raised her bedroom windows, and was just about to climb into bed when there was a gentle knock at her door. She expected it to be Mary, wanting to talk more about her ill feelings toward Amanda, but just in case, she thought to put on her pink, floral-print robe before she answered the door.

"Daniel?" she asked in surprise when her gaze rose from where she had expected to find Mary's face to where Daniel's actually was.

"May I come in?"

When she did not immediately respond to his question, he added, "I'll only be a moment. I want to apologize for Amanda's behavior tonight."

"I guess it will be all right," she said, but hesitated

107

a moment before she finally opened the door for him to enter.

"I don't know what got into her today. I saw the way she kept staring at you—as if you'd done something wrong. And I wanted to explain that none of that was your fault. Amanda did not want me to hire a live-in tutor for Mary. She wanted me to send Mary to some fancy finishing school in Charlestown."

Not wanting to get Mary into any trouble, Virginia pretended that what he had told her was all new to her. "But, Daniel, Mary is too young to be sent away to school like that."

"I know, and I tried to tell Amanda that, but it seems her parents sent her to an eastern school when she was very young and she can't see that it hurt her in any way. She feels that if it was all right for her to be sent away to school at such a young age, it should be perfectly all right for Mary. She doesn't understand how insecure Mary is right now."

"I'm glad you see that, because she is insecure," Virginia told him.

"But you are already changing that," he said and smiled warmly. "And I want you to know how grateful I am for everything you've done for her. You don't know how wonderful it is to hear her laugh again. It's been months. You seem to work miracles. And I want you to know that although the full month is not yet up, I've already decided you should be a permanent part of Mary's life. I want you to know, I have no intentions of replacing you for someone with more experience. You have more than proved your worth to me."

After getting over her surprise at such unexpected words of praise from Daniel Pearson, Virginia felt a twinge of guilt in knowing she had no intention of making her teaching job as permanent as he seemed to think. "Thank you. I appreciate your confidence in me."

"And I appreciate all you are doing for Mary," he said, then reached out to take her hand in his. "You have made a world of difference in her."

Virginia stared at him in disbelief. It was the first real show of affection she had ever seen in Daniel, even when discussing his own daughter. Maybe there was hope for him yet.

"And you should know that Mary has made a world of difference in me," she responded honestly, because Mary had begun to make changes in her that she had not thought possible. She had started to dread the day she would have to say goodbye to the child. But it was inevitable if she was ever to get Valley Oaks back.

Daniel studied her for a minute, letting his gaze stray first to her shimmering hair, then back to her face. "I just wanted you to know that you were not to blame for Amanda's behavior."

"It was not just that I'm Mary's teacher. I'm afraid she's jealous that I live here with you. Absurd as it might seem, I believe she thinks you just might become interested in me as more than your daughter's teacher."

"That doesn't seem so absurd," he said softly and took a step in her direction. But before she could protest the threatening move, he turned and just as abruptly walked out of the room, leaving Virginia struggling to bring her rapidly beating heart under control.

Chapter Seven

When Virginia walked into the dining room for breakfast the following morning, she was surprised and a little disappointed to discover she would be eating alone. Mary had awakened earlier than usual and had already eaten breakfast with her father, who had also risen early. Daniel had left Valley Oaks right after sunrise for business he had in Pittsburg. Virginia felt it odd he had not mentioned anything about any business the day before and decided it probably had to do with pretty Miss Amanda Haught, who had mentioned that she frequented the shops in both Pittsburg and Daingerfield. It was probably something they had planned while alone together at the carriage.

The mere thought of Daniel stealing away to meet Amanda made her insides ache, but there was little she could do about it. Though Mary hated the woman, Daniel was apparently very fond of her—fond enough to want to marry her. And if the truth be known, it really was not any of Virginia's business, but even so, she wished there were something she could do to prevent Daniel from marrying a woman like Amanda Haught.

Though Virginia kept busy and tried not to think about Daniel or where it was he had rushed off to so suddenly, it was really all she *could* think about. Several times during the day, Mary had trouble catching her attention in order to ask questions, and half the time Virginia could not concentrate long enough to give appropriate answers. All she could seem to think about was Daniel, and to her chagrin it was late in the afternoon before he finally returned. When he did, he went directly to his library and stayed there until suppertime.

As was his custom, shortly after eight o'clock, he went upstairs to say good night to Mary, then arrived in the dining room just as Lizzie was setting the food on the table. Virginia was already seated and waited for him to settle into the tall chair across the corner of the table from her before she bothered to ask how his day went.

"Not so good," he stated frankly while he reached for his water glass and took several swallows. "It looks like I'm going to have to go to Jefferson for several days to straighten out some pretty serious problems the shipping company is having with their loading crew. I got a message from my supervisor asking that I come right away."

Virginia wondered if that was true or whether he had a far more personal reason for needing to be gone for so long to a town almost forty miles away. She seriously doubted he was going alone, and for some reason she felt angry because of it.

"Your goin' off there again?" Lizzie wanted to know while she set the last bowl of vegetables on the table between them, then placed the large serving spoon beside it. Daniel preferred to serve himself so that he did not have to chance too many vegetables being heaped upon his plate, so she was

111

finished with her serving duties and ready to return to the kitchen, but she stayed behind long enough to hear what Daniel had to say.

"Looks like I have no choice," he said and exhaled sharply to show his extreme displeasure. Though the words he spoke were directed to Lizzie, his gaze was trained on Virginia as if he wanted to encourage her to say what she thought about the matter. "I have to take care of this problem before it gets out of hand."

"I don't see why Mister James can't handle these problems hisself," Lizzie muttered and crossed her arms in front of her to show the impatience she had with the man. "That's what you pay him for."

"I pay him to see that the business continues to make a good profit and to keep me informed of any problems, which he does."

Starting to believe that Daniel's problems were indeed with his shipping company and not with Amanda, Virginia wondered why she should feel such a strange sense of relief yet at the same time an even stronger feeling of disappointment, just from having learned of his plans to be gone from Valley Oaks for a few days. In truth, she should be thrilled. Daniel's trip could finally afford her the opportunity to get into the library undetected and see if there was anything hidden away that would at last reveal exactly what it was Caleb had done to her grandfather all those years ago. Then she could finally do something about getting Valley Oaks back. Then why wasn't she more delighted by his announcement?

"That's too bad, Daniel. I know Mary will miss you," she finally said when she realized he was still waiting for a response from her.

When Lizzie marched off to the kitchen, still

muttering to herself, Daniel continued to stare at Virginia. Feeling awkward at having his gaze directed at her, Virginia also reached for her water glass, but more in want of something for her hands to do than because of thirst.

Daniel continued to watch her for a long, thoughtful moment before he finally spoke again. "I've already told Mary I have to go. She understands about my business trips." Again he paused while studying her face, then added, "It could take as long as a week to work out their grievances this time. I might not be back in time to take you for that ride through the countryside Sunday afternoon as I promised I would."

"That's all right; I understand. Your business is important. Besides, I already told you that it was not necessary for you to go with me. I can handle a rig." She looked away from him so he could not see the disappointment that surely had to show in her eyes . . . disappointment that should not even be there.

"Then I'll leave Pete with instructions to have the stanhope made ready for you while I'm gone just in case you do decide to try it alone. Just don't stray too far from here—we wouldn't want you to get lost."

"I'm not one to take unwarranted risks," she assured him, already knowing her destination. If Daniel did not return by Sunday afternoon, she would take the opportunity to go by and visit the Langfords. Even though she was not sure she liked the thought of Daniel being away for quite so long—which she felt had to be because of her deep concern for Mary, who would miss her father dreadfully and might allow her studies to suffer—Virginia was at the same time eager to see her

113

friends again, to let them know she was all right before they started to worry about her.

"Good—I'll hold you to that," Daniel said with a firm nod while he raised his water glass to his lips again. His eyes never strayed from hers; it was as if he wanted to see inside her. "I'd hate for Pete and Jack to have to spend their Sunday searching for you."

"Then you really do think you might be gone that long?" Again she felt a strong wave of something she could not quite identify, a hollow feeling of some sort.

"Could be. I never do know about these things. And here lately, I've been having to make a trip over there to solve one problem or another at least once a month, almost as much as Uncle Caleb used to. That's one of the reasons I finally decided to move in here at Valley Oaks, so I'd be closer to Jefferson, but still someplace where Mary and I could have privacy. Although I do have a good supervisor who oversees the shipping operation for me, there are certain aspects of the business he refuses to handle—and I'm afraid labor disputes are one of them."

"When will you be leaving?" She set her water glass back down and played idly with the narrow stem.

"Probably before sunup."

He would be gone before she woke up. Sadly, Virginia stared at the food that remained untouched before them and realized she was no longer interested in what Lizzie had prepared for them; she was not hungry anymore. She considered asking to be dismissed from the table but realized it was not what she really wanted to do. Though she did not particularly want to eat, she also did not care to leave just yet, either. Reluctantly she put a few spoonfuls of vegetables and a slice of roast beef on her plate and pretended to still have an appetite.

By the time the meal was over, Virginia had slowly come to realize why she felt so sad: she was actually going to miss Daniel, and not for Mary's sake, but for her. It surprised her. She had not realized how accustomed she had become to dining with him each evening, then retiring to the veranda so that he could smoke his pipe and she could enjoy a small cup of steaming chocolate before bedtime. Tomorrow night she would have to sip her chocolate alone.

"Are you finished eating?" Daniel asked as he looked doubtfully at her plate, still half-full. He had pushed his own plate aside now that it was empty and sat back in his chair, watching Virginia curiously as if still trying to read her thoughts.

"Yes, I'm through—I wasn't too hungry tonight. I guess I ate too much at lunch," she offered feebly, though she had barely touched her lunch, either. "You should have been here. Lizzie prepared a lovely meal of braised chicken and white rice."

"Then you are ready to go outside?" He obviously was not concerned with what Lizzie had served at lunch.

Rather than say anything else, she merely nodded while she pushed her chair back, then stood. She waited until he had come around to her side of the table and offered his arm, as had become his custom, then went with him to the veranda where kerosene lanterns had already been lit. Though they broke apart as soon as they stepped outside, neither moved to take their usual seats.

"Tell me, will you miss me too?" he asked casually. Though the question had been addressed to her, his gaze had gone to the dark shadows which lay beyond the soft island of flickering light that surrounded the veranda.

Virginia stared at him in surprise and when he turned to look at her then, his eyes glimmered with some new emotion. She felt her pulse quicken as she tried to devise something to say that would answer his bold question but not let him know how oddly her heart had responded.

"I imagine I will miss you a little, especially in the evening," she admitted hesitantly, then in an effort to cover her feelings, she quickly added, "After all, I hardly ever see you in the daytime anyway. I'll probably even miss the little arguments we always seem to have after supper. Whoever can I argue with while you are away?"

He moved closer. "I'm not looking forward to this trip. I'm really not. Just when I . . ."

Whatever Daniel was about to say became lost the moment Lizzie came bustling outside carrying the small silver tray that held Virginia's nightly cup of chocolate. "Here you go, Miss Virginia, a nice hot cup of chocolate to help you sleep."

It was the statement she always made when she brought her evening chocolate to her, but for some reason Lizzie's words irritated Virginia tonight and she found she wanted to snap at her. She managed instead to smile and say her usual thank-you.

"Pretty tonight, ain't it?" Lizzie asked as she set the tray down, stepped over to the railing, and breathed deeply the heady scents of honeysuckle and evergreen. Then, as if suddenly sensing she was not completely welcome, she turned back to Virginia and asked, "Is there anything else I can get for you before I go on up to my room?"

"No, thank you," Virginia said politely, and felt

116

her stomach flutter anxiously while she watched Lizzie gather up her volumous skirts and hurry back inside. She heard Lizzie pause just inside the door but waited until she heard the woman's footsteps well within the house before she looked at Daniel expectantly, ready to hear what it was he had been about to say before the untimely interruption. But instead of resuming where he had left off, he moved away from her and quietly lit his pipe as he usually did.

Neither of them spoke again until it was time to go inside, then it was merely to exchange an awkward good night and the usual wishes for pleasant dreams. Never had Virginia suffered such an unaccountable feeling of disappointment: Daniel left her just inside the back door, then went down the hall to the stairs, exactly as he always did, and from there on up to bed. When she returned to go to her own room, she knew she would not see him again until his return the following week. A week suddenly seemed an eternity.

Mary glanced up from the book that lay in her lap and stared across the yard. "Someone's coming."

Distracted from her thoughts, Virginia had also heard something from the road in front of Valley Oaks, and her heart swelled with hope that the traveler would prove to be Daniel, returning early. But when she saw it was a lo-boy wagon that had turned into the drive instead of an elaborately styled carriage, she knew she would be disappointed.

Mary closed her book, set it in the cool grass beside her, and raised her hand to her forehead in an effort to shade the bright glow of the late

117

afternoon sun from her eyes. She squinted as she studied the approaching vehicle. "It's a man; he looks to be by himself. I wonder who would be paying a call so close to suppertime?"

Suddenly Virginia knew it was Mark. Though the glare of the sun prevented her from being able to see either the wagon or the man clearly, she instinctively knew it was Mark. Her heart froze in mid-beat when she realized he was coming to see her despite the fact that she'd asked him to stay away. "I think it's a friend of mine."

"Really?" Mary asked, suddenly excited. "Is he coming for supper?"

"I imagine he's already eaten. He and his family have supper early." As she remembered, they had all their meals early. "Stay here. I'll go see what he wants."

Quickly Virginia rose from the lawn chair and headed for the front drive, where she knew he would pull to a stop just short of the carriage porch. Not about to be left behind, Mary hopped up from where she had sat reading on the grass and hurried to follow.

"Mark. It *is* you," Virginia called to him as soon as she had come close enough to see his grinning face.

"In person," he said and gave his chest a sound pat to assure her he was real.

"What are you doing here?"

"Came to see if you were still alive," he said with a raised eyebrow before he hopped down from the wagon and came forward to give her a large hug. He did not at first notice the wide-eyed little girl at her side. "I know; I know — you didn't want me to come visit until you were completely settled in. But mother was starting to worry about you. After all, it's been nearly a month since we've seen you. And as you might recall, I warned if you didn't come visit us I'd feel it my duty to come and visit you. Today I finished my chores a little early, so I decided to drive on over here and see why you've been neglecting us."

"I've been too busy," she said, and when he glanced skeptically at her, she frowned; then, realizing Mary had indeed followed her and was now listening to everything with keen interest, she decided to include the child rather than attempt to send her away—which would only serve to make Mary suspicious. Virginia decided she would wait until Mark left, then give the child as reasonable an excuse as she could produce for having already made friends in the neighborhood.

Smiling, she turned to Mary for reinforcement of what she had just said. "Haven't I been very busy these past few weekends?"

Mary nodded in agreement but did not actually back her with words. Virginia frowned, but not so much because Mary had not come to her defense better. Virginia's frown was because Mary had quickly stepped back to hide behind her. Virginia thought Mary had gotten over her shyness and it bothered her to realize the child had not.

"Busy? Even on Sundays?" Mark asked while he crossed his arms and looked from Mary to Virginia, still skeptical. "I thought you were supposed to have Sundays off."

"I do, but Mary learns so fast that I find I have to use my Sundays preparing more lessons just to keep up with her."

Mary grinned and again ducked her head behind Virginia when Mark looked at her then.

"Is that so? Got a regular little genius on your

hands, do you? Maybe you should bring her over to meet Jessie and see if any of that brilliance can rub off on her," Mark said with a laugh, having decided not to press the point that Virginia had not been by to visit: he was not there to start an argument.

"Who is Jessie?" Mary asked, letting her curiosity override her shyness for the moment. Slowly she came out from behind Virginia's skirts.

"My little sister. I'm afraid she doesn't take too well to schooling. She'd rather be outside climbing trees or catching crawdads than inside studying her times tables or memorizing her spelling."

"I can do my times tables," Mary said proudly. "All the way to the tens."

"Yep, no doubt about it—we need to get this girl over to our house and see about Jessie." Mark chuckled when he thought about what Jessie's reaction would be.

"I'd be glad to come over and help her. Where do you live?" Mary was so interested in what Mark was saying that when Virginia stepped aside, she did not try to duck back behind her. Instead, she actually moved closer to Mark and cocked her head back so she could better see his face.

"Not far," Mark said as he knelt beside the girl. He glanced up at Virginia. "Say, why don't you bring her over for a visit? Now that the Porterfields have moved, Jessie doesn't have anyone her age who lives close enough to play with. And Mother told me to remind you that it is her birthday Sunday. She fully expects you to come and have lunch with us. Surely you don't plan to disappoint Mother on her birthday. Why don't you bring Mary with you?"

"Oh, yes!" Mary's eyes sparkled with delight when she looked up at Virginia, then back at Mark. "How old is Jessie?"

"Nine, I think. But then, to tell you the truth, I'm not really sure."

"She's nine," Virginia put in and shook her head with disbelief. "What sort of brother doesn't even know how old his own sister is?"

Mark opened his mouth to offer a reply, but Mary interrupted him.

"She really *is* nine years old?" Mary exclaimed. Then of Virginia she asked, "May I? May I go with you Sunday? I don't have any friends my own age. I want to meet Jessie."

Virginia thought about it. In the three-and-a-half weeks she'd been there, not once had a child come to play with Mary. It really would do Mary good to have someone her own age to play with.

"I don't know. You know how your father feels about you overexerting yourself," she said, hesitant to make such a decision. After all, how would she explain having such close friends in the neighborhood? Would he believe a family who she'd met but once would care enough to invite her to dinner? And to invite both of them? Or would he suspect there was more to their friendship? She was not sure she could be convincing.

"But I feel fine! I do!" Mary responded hopefully. And to prove her point, she skipped around them both several times, then folded her hands together. "Please, please! Let me go with you!"

Mark stood and smiled defiantly at Virginia while he let Mary continue to skip about and plead with her. Aware of what he had done, Virginia cocked her head to one side and raised an eyebrow in warning, letting him know she fully realized how cleverly he had used Mary to help influence her decision. If it had been ten years earlier, she would have slugged him in the stomach for trying to outsmart her that way.

"I haven't said I'm going yet," she pointed out and tried to issue Mark a determined glare, even though she already felt a grin coming on. Despite the trouble he had caused for her, she could not stay angry with him.

"Could you disappoint such a sweet child as this?" Mark wanted to know while he pulled Mary to him and turned her so Virginia would have to look down into her hopeful face.

Finally Virginia had to chuckle and shook her head. "No, I guess I couldn't. Although I would dearly love to disappoint *you,* you conniving devil, I could never disappoint a sweet little angel like Mary. Besides, though I had forgotten it was your mother's birthday, I did have plans to come visit you on Sunday, anyway."

"Wonderful. Then it's all set. And Mother said to tell you to come early. Since it is her birthday, she thinks it is only fair everyone come in time to help. Mary, even you will be expected to help."

Mary clapped at the thought of it.

Virginia smiled, but then thought of Daniel again and frowned. For the first time since she had discovered there was absolutely no way to get into his library whether he was gone or not, she hoped he wouldn't return early. Not only did she now worry about his becoming suspicious of her friendship with the Langfords; she did not want to leave Mary disappointed. Mary was so eager to meet someone her own age. What if Daniel were to return early and refuse to let his daughter go with her? Mary would be devastated. But then, what if Mary did get to go and somehow learned from Jessie how she had spent her childhood in a house just down the road? Would Mary tell Daniel? Or course she would.

Suddenly Virginia wished she had refused to go. Daniel was certain to ask questions, questions she might not have believable answers for. Her only hope was that Mary would not find out about her past; that even when Daniel returned and learned of their trip, he would accept the story she would tell him and not become suspicious of her friendship with the Langfords. If he started to pry into her background and discovered who she was, or worse yet, who her grandparents were, he would surely discover her true reason for being there.

"I hear you had a caller today," Lizzie said when she brought Virginia a cup of chocolate later that evening. Because it just was not the same having her chocolate out on the veranda with Daniel gone, Virginia had asked Lizzie to bring the tray to her room, and she watched from the cozy comfort of her bed while Lizzie set the tray on the tiny bedside table and lifted the cup for her.

"Was it that same man who brought you here in his wagon?"

"Yes, his name is Mark Langford. He and his family live just southwest of here." She tried to sound casual, but it made her nervous to have Lizzie ask questions about Mark. She paused a moment before trying the same explanation she had given Mary and now planned to use with Daniel. "They're very nice people, eager to make me feel welcome in East Texas. In fact, Mark came by to invite me to have lunch with them on Sunday."

"So I heard. And I also heard tell that Miss Mary plans to go with you."

Virginia glanced up from her chocolate to see if

Lizzie disapproved of the decision, but she could tell by the woman's wide, toothy smile that she was deeply pleased. She felt relieved and hoped Daniel would prove just as approving of the idea. "I thought it might do her some good to get away from here for a little while and play with someone her own age. Did she tell you that Mark has a little sister who is just a little older than Mary?"

"That she did," Lizzie said with a laugh. "At least a dozen times—she can hardly wait. And I fully agree with you. It will do Miss Mary plenty good to get away." Suddenly, Lizzie's smile faded. "But I don't know if Master Daniel is goin' to be too pleased when he comes home and finds out these plans of yours. He's mighty protective of that little gal."

"Too protective, I'm afraid. He's got to start letting her lead a more normal childhood."

Though Lizzie did not come out and say she agreed with Virginia, she did not disagree. Instead, she merely said with a sad shake of her head, "That poor child has suffered enough."

Virginia wanted to ask her then about Mary's accident, but remembering her promise to Daniel not to speak of it, she kept quiet. Just as she could never go back on her promise to her grandmother to get Valley Oaks back, she would not go back on her promise to not ask about Mary's accident. She could only hope that one day either Mary or Lizzie would tell her on their own.

It was a beautiful Sunday morning. A cool breeze swept past Virginia as she made her way to the small carriage that had been brought out at her request and was waiting for her. Mary would be right down as soon as she finished tying her slippers, so Virginia climbed onto the carriage, adjusted her long cotton skirts, and took the reins into her hands to get used to their feel. While she waited, she brought her gaze up and slowly let it wander about the countryside, first to the elegant barn, then to the carriage house, then on to the outbuildings, and finally to the large orchard and the wide, rolling pastures beyond.

To the other side of the yard, closer to the house, she noticed the neatly planted vegetable garden and beyond that, more grassy fields, dotted with bright splashes of yellow and coral wildflowers and crisscrossed with narrow wooden fences that looked far too flimsy to hold back the large cattle that grazed there. She wondered when Daniel was going to make use of the barbed wire Jack had brought from town. But then, as she understood it, Daniel was reluctant to try anything that might injure his cattle.

To make the scene before her even more picturesque, a narrow stream wound lazily though the largest pasture's verdant thickness and, at one place, had been dug out and partially dammed to form a small, shimmering pond. The languid pool of crystal clear water was surrounded by deep green clover and grasses on all sides, and tall pink and red wildflowers speckled its far shore. Several massive oak and sweet gum trees shaded one end of the little pond, blocking part of it from her sight and forming a private little haven of natural beauty which might prove to be a cool respite from the hotter days of summer that lay ahead.

Although the present day was a cool one for so late in May, there was just enough warmth in the morning's sunshine to make the use of the canopy necessary and Virginia was glad it had already been placed into position overhead. Smiling at the thought that someone had been so considerate, she sat comfortably back against the padded leather seat and continued to stare out at the grounds which were very well kept by Rolly Sagan, who she knew lived in the little brick and stucco house near the main gate. It was Rolly's responsibility to keep the grounds neat, help with the vegetable garden, and see that the gates were always closed late at night but opened again just before sunrise. And as far as Virginia knew, Rolly never failed in his duties. She decided that when she took over Valley Oaks, she would keep Rolly on if he wanted to stay. She then thought of the other men.

Because it was Sunday and most of Daniel's men went into town on Saturday nights, staying out very late. The majority of them, including Rolly, were still in bed even at ten o'clock. Only Pete and his brother Jack were seen in the barn, and she knew they would not be up yet had she not needed the stanhope so early in the day.

It was Jack's responsibility to take care of all the equipment, including the carriages and wagons, and it was Pete's responsibility to take care of the stock, which included the horses and mules. Whenever it came time to hitch any of Pete's horses or mules to any of Jack's carriages or wagons, they both felt it necessary to be there and usually found it equally as necessary to argue about whatever it was the other did while accomplishing their single goal. Virginia loved to listen to their goodnatured bickering and wished she could hear what they were saying then, because Pete was clearly upset with Jack about something, even at that moment.

If Daniel was there, he would try to calm them

down, but would fail to do so. Pete and Jack would quickly remind him how they were brothers and had an inherent right to argue. Arguing was the one thing they *did* agree on and it was something Daniel found very amusing. The unexpected thought of Daniel made her heart jump. Although she was glad he had not come home early for fear he might spoil Mary's outing, she did miss him — dreadfully.

Virginia pushed the confusing thoughts of Daniel aside when she saw Mary hurrying across the yard toward her. Smiling, she scooted across the seat and extended a hand to help the girl up. She waiting until Mary was carefully situated before she lifted the wide leather reins high into the air and gave them a sharp flick. "Hee-eigh."

As the carriage lurched forward, she tried not to think about all that could go wrong. She intended to take Jessie aside as soon as she could to ask that she not tell Mary anything about her past, though she was not yet sure the reason she would give Mark's little sister for keeping such a secret. Virginia took a deep breath. If everything went just right, they would both have a lovely time that day, and Daniel would be none the wiser that the Langfords were actually friends from her childhood or that she was Essie Elder's granddaughter.

Chapter Eight

When Virginia turned the carriage into the small drive that led to Mark's two-story frame house, she noticed Jessie already outside, still dressed in her church clothes, watching eagerly as they approached.

"My, aren't you pretty!" Virginia complimented her when Jessie rushed to greet them. The girl scowled as she glanced down at her pink-and-white ruffled dress. Jessie was no more fond of having to dress up than Virginia herself had been when she was nine years old—back when donning a pretty dress for church had been considered one of the many necessary evils one had to suffer in order to keep peace in the family.

"We just got back from church," Jessie said with a disgusted twist of her lips. "I was on my way inside to get out of this thing when I first heard y'all coming up the road." When Jessie stepped closer and could see inside the carriage, she glanced sympathetically at the frilly turquoise-blue dress Mary had chosen to wear and then at the pretty yellow-and-white dress Virginia had on. "Looks like you two just got out of church, too. Where'd y'all go? Didn't see you at our church."

"No, we've come straight from Valley Oaks," Virginia supplied while she carefully looped the reins over the cross bar in front of her to get them out of her way. She did not bother explaining that Daniel did not believe in attending church, but instead studied the Bible in the privacy of his own home each Sunday morning. "These are not our church clothes."

Jessie's eyes widened, clearly alarmed by what Virginia had just implied. "You mean you *wanted* to dress like that?"

Mary looked down at her silk and satin skirts with a worried frown. "What's wrong with it?"

"Nothing, I guess. Just isn't the sort of thing you wear on Sunday afternoon. You can't climb a tree in a dress like that, or chase a 'possum, or even jump a fence."

Now it was Mary's eyes that widened. "Climb a tree?"

"Sure, haven't you ever climbed a tree?"

"No."

Jessie looked puzzled by such a revelation. "Never?"

Mary glanced down at the hands that lay folded in her lap. "Never."

Jessie's eyes narrowed while she studied Mary intently, and Virginia was suddenly aware of what thoughts had started to form in the young girl's mind. Quickly she pointed a finger at Jessie and wagged it in warning. "And you are not going to take it upon yourself to teach Mary how to, either."

"Who, me?" Jessie asked, her green eyes opened wide in a face that was suddenly a mask of such angelic innocence that it made Virginia want to laugh.

129

"Yes, you, Jessie Louise. Mary's been in an accident recently and she is not to be climbing trees."

"She couldn't anyway in those," Jessie conceded as she gestured at Mary's delicate kid slippers. "Gotta have a good pair of boots or be barefoot to climb a tree. *You* know that."

Virginia tensed, afraid Jessie was about to mention the stories she had heard about what an agile tree climber she had been in her youth, and how she had learned it to escape an angry Mark, who was not quite so agile and who could not risk the higher limbs because of his heavier weight. If Jessie was to mention such a thing, Mary would surely want to know how Jessie knew, and Jessie would have no reason not to tell her.

Just then Wyoma came out onto the front porch, wiping her hands on the raised hem of her white linen apron. "About time you came to pay us a visit," she admonished goodnaturedly, then smiled. "Hurry up and come inside ... both of you. There's still work to be done."

Jessie quickly disappeared to her room to change clothes while Mary was properly introduced to Mark and Jessie's mother. Then she was put promptly to work helping wash and chop the vegetables that were to be added to a large roast that had already simmered in the oven for several hours. The tantalizing aroma filled the house, whetting appetites just enough to make everyone willing to hurry.

When Virginia accepted the knife Wyoma offered her, she tried to think of a good reason to leave the room while Jessie was still gone so she could find her alone and ask her not to mention anything to Mary about how she had once lived only a mile from there. For the life of her, Virginia could not think of an excuse that did not sound contrived. To her chagrin, Jessie returned only minutes later wearing a more durable and far more comfortably cut muslin dress with a pair of well-worn leather boots and quickly began to help with the vegetables, knowing exactly what to do—unlike Mary. Drawing in a long, shaky breath, Virginia could only hope nothing would be said about her past before she could get Mark's little sister and Wyoma aside and warn them.

It was not until after they had scattered the vegetables over the roast, placed the huge iron lid back on the roasting pot, and gone outside to visit with each other on the front porch that Virginia had a chance to ask Wyoma not to mention to Mary that she'd known them since early childhood.

While waiting for the vegetables to cook and the rolls to finish rising, Jessie and Mary decided to find Mark and let him know lunch was nearly ready so he would hurry his chores and be finished in time. Their departure had left Wyoma and Virginia alone at last.

"Why not? Are you ashamed of us?" Wyoma wanted to know as soon as Virginia had made her strange request.

"No, of course I'm not ashamed. It's just that I was afraid to tell Daniel Pearson that I was Essie and Joseph Elder's granddaughter. I was afraid he wouldn't hire me if he knew too much about me, and I *so* wanted that job." She looked away as she spoke, because although what she had said was indeed the truth, it was not the whole truth and Mark's mother had an uncanny way of knowing when someone was intentionally keeping something from her. "If he found out about me now, he'd be angry enough at me for having kept such informa-

131

tion from him that he'd fire me. I can't risk losing my job."

"I see," Wyoma said quietly, and Virginia was afraid that she did see—far more than she wanted her to see.

"So, I'd prefer that Mary not know everything about me. She might tell her father, and then he would fire me for not having told him from the very beginning."

"Are you really happy working at Valley Oaks?" Wyoma wanted to know.

"Yes," she responded quickly and could look at her then because she now spoke the whole truth. "Mary is a little angel, so sweet, and so unusually bright. I'm very fond of her."

"And what about Mary's father? Are you also fond of him?" Wyoma's expression remained level while she waited for Virginia's response.

Virginia did not know how to answer that question: she honestly wasn't sure *how* she felt. After all, he *was* a Pearson: he just wasn't quite the ogre she'd expected. At times he proved to be almost likeable. In fact, if he were not a Pearson, and if he did not let his true colors show through now and then, she might find herself starting to like him— more than she really should. He was undeniably one of the most handsome men she'd ever met, and he could be very amusing at times; but at other times, he would do something in such a way that Virginia would be reminded that inside him lay the cruel, cold heart of a Pearson.

Luckily Virginia did not have to come up with an answer to Wyoma's question because at that moment Mark came out of the barn. Eager for the timely interruption, she stood to wave at him just when he began to run in her direction.

"I see you made it," he said with a broad smile as he scooped her off the porch into his arms and swung her around. He then pouted childishly when he gently lowered her back down as easily as he had snatched her up. "I understand you've been here over half an hour already. Why didn't you come out and tell me you were here?"

"Your mother put us right to work," she explained with a light shrug while she reached up and tried to pull the corners of Mark's frown up into a smile. "If you want to complain to someone, complain to her."

He pushed Virginia's hands away and scowled playfully at his mother as he took the chair between them and immediately joined in the conversation. It was just before they called the girls back from the barn that Wyoma quickly informed Mark of Virginia's request not to mention anything about her past around Mary, and although he seemed suspicious of the reasons she gave, he agreed to watch his tongue around the girl and to get Jessie aside and explain the situation to her as well. He managed to do so minutes later.

Lunch proved a festive affair. Wyoma's older sister, Jane Thomas, a widow who had only recently moved to Camp County from Louisiana with her eleven-year old daughter, Elizabeth, came from their new home near Cason to eat with them. Jane was much older than Wyoma and had the appearance of a very proper and well reserved lady, but she nevertheless proved to be quite a lively character. She kept everyone laughing with her unexpected quips about their childhood the entire time they were at the table. Afterward, because it was Wyoma's birthday, Virginia and Jane argued that she'd done enough work and volunteered to clean up while everyone else went back outside to enjoy the afternoon breeze.

Working quickly, Virginia and Jane were soon finished and had just put the last dishes away when Jessie, Mary, and Elizabeth burst through the back door, eager to get permission to go into the woods and wade along the creek. Though Virginia was reluctant to allow Mary to wander so far away, she remembered the fun she and Mark had had playing along that same creek as children. She finally relented, but demanded they all be back within the hour.

When an hour passed and the three girls did not return as promised, Virginia and Mark decided to walk down to the creek and remind them of the hour.

"Now don't you two get off down there and forget all about the time, like they did," Wyoma warned with a laugh as they set off toward the pasture. "You know how forgetful you both can be when it comes to such things."

"Who, us?" Virginia asked innocently, then looked at Mark as if they had been unjustly accused. But she could not keep the insulted expression on her face. She knew only too well how quickly an hour could slip by for a child off playing along the shallow creek that ran through the woods.

As she and Mark crossed the pasture, Virginia mused on her childhood. She remembered how if the two of them had not felt like splashing in the creek itself, they pretended to be U.S. lawmen, waiting to ambush whatever bad men might happen by on the narrow dirt road, or they made funny sculptures out of mud and left them out in the sun to dry. Virginia just hoped that whatever the girls had ended up doing to pass the time, Mary had

134

somehow managed to stay relatively clean. She'd hate to hear Lizzie's long tirade if Mary got that pretty dress of hers muddy. Pressing her lips together, she hoped Mary had shown some restraint.

Soon they entered the narrow strip of woods that surrounded the little creek for several hundred yards on either side. When they were fully out of his mother's sight, Mark casually slipped his arm around Virginia's shoulders and pulled her close. They walked together then, arm-in-arm, once again comrades of the closest sort—as if the five-year separation had never been.

"Brings back old memories, doesn't it?" Virginia mused as they continued along a still familiar path, getting ever closer to the shallow creek that had given them so many happy hours of play.

"That it does. We had lots of good times in these woods, playing along that creek," he said with a slight smile, then gestured to the narrow ribbon of water that had just come into their sight through the dense underbrush. They suddenly heard girlish giggles and turned in time to see the three girls hurrying along another of the many paths that laced the woods, headed in their direction.

"It hasn't been an hour yet, has it?" Jessie wanted to know as she came running up to meet them. She attempted to look sincerely doubtful.

"Almost twice that," Virginia said sternly. Though she was not angry about what they had done, she knew she should not let the girls know it. They had disobeyed, and because they had, they needed to be scolded. "You promised me you would be back within an hour. I trusted you to keep that promise."

By then Mary and Elizabeth had caught up with Jessie, and Virginia could see how happy yet worried the three were. Though Mary was just as muddy as Virginia had feared, the healthy glow in her cheeks and the bright smile on her face made it worth the tongue-lashing she knew Lizzie would give them upon their return. She was just glad Daniel would not be there to see his daughter like that.

"You three get on back to the house and wash off some of that mud," Mark said sternly, having also realized the need to be firm with the girls. "We'll be up directly to talk more about this. Until then, I imagine Mother and Aunt Jane will have a word or two of their own to say to the three of you."

Virginia looked at him questioningly. "And what is to prevent us from going back to the house right now?"

Mark grinned. "We can't get this close to the creek and not actually take our boots off and tramp through it, can we?"

Virginia glanced at the shallow creek, then back at Mark's dare-you-to expression, then laughed while she looked around for a good place to sit and take off her boots.

Jessie, Mary, and Elizabeth exchanged disbelieving glances while they watched Virginia and Mark come out of their boots, then their stockings. Then, as they had been ordered to, the girls hurried off in the direction of the house, eager to tell everyone what they had just witnessed, laughing with the sheer delight of having seen two adults behave in such a strange manner.

"Last one there is a mother skunk," Virginia said with a laugh as she lifted her skirts high and hurried barefoot off toward the water, leaving Mark still struggling to get his trouser legs rolled up.

"That's not fair!" he protested loudly. He decided to forget about his uncooperative trouser legs and took off after her. "You have on a dress!"

"And who said I had to be fair?" she shouted back over her shoulder just before she reached the edge of the water and splashed into the shallow depths well ahead of Mark. Not having braced herself for the sudden cold of the water, she squealed aloud from the initial shock.

"You think that's cold, wait until I set you down in that water," Mark growled as he splashed only half a dozen yards behind her.

"You wouldn't dare," Virginia cried, but did not care to take any chances; she had already started running downstream as fast as she could go. Though she held her skirts knee-high, the hem was rapidly getting soaked.

She frowned at how tender her feet had become in the past few years, but she did not dare slow down. Grimacing with each rock she stepped on, she continued to go as fast as her legs could carry her. "Mark, you behave yourself!"

"Cheaters have to pay for their crimes," came his delighted response.

Laughing and squealing, Virginia lifted her skirts higher and splashed her way toward the main road. She felt certain she would still be able to fit beneath the small wooden bridge that crossed the narrow creek, and she was almost just as certain Mark would never fit. She could then crawl to the center and be well out of his reach. Oh, how she would call out and torment him then!

"Stand still and meet your fate, you coward," Mark demanded, laughing between his deep draws of air.

"You'll never catch me," she called out boldly.

She saw she was nearly to the bridge and could tell by the loud splashing sounds behind her that Mark had not yet begun to close the gap between them.

Realizing the space below the bridge was just large enough for her to crawl through, she was certain she had it made; her victory was in sight, when suddenly she was aware of a rider approaching from the north. Just as suddenly she realized how foolishly they were behaving and what it might look like to a stranger passing by. She stopped just before she reached the narrow bridge and hoped Mark would show as much restraint when he noticed they were not alone. She would hate to have a stranger witness whatever it was Mark had in mind for her and what she would have to do to him in return.

While she still gasped for much-needed breath, Virginia felt her heart miss several beats, then come to a complete stop. Her mouth fell limp with horror the moment she realized just who the rider was. Wide-eyed and embarrassed by both her behavior and her bedraggled appearance, she quickly let go of her bunched skirt, not really realizing in time how the hem would fall into the water and become instantly soaked. Foolishly she brushed at her wet, wrinkled skirt, then attempted to smooth back her hair. She dropped her hand and smiled awkwardly when it became evident Daniel had spotted her.

She greeted him in a feeble voice. "Daniel. You are back early."

"Where is Mary?" he demanded angrily when he pulled his horse to an abrupt halt on the dirt road above where she stood. Dust rose in clouds at the animal's feet and slowly wafted over her.

When Mark appeared behind her, Daniel took his angry gaze off of Virginia and glared then at him. His

138

pale blue eyes widened noticeably when he recognized Mark was the same man who had brought Virginia to Valley Oaks that first day. But his eyes narrowed again, in a display of anger, when he directed his gaze beyond them and quickly scanned the surrounding woods. "Where is Mary?"

"She's safe," Virginia started to explain and began to move through the water toward the nearest embankment. Her skirts felt heavy and awkward when she stepped out onto dry land, and she found she had to lift them away from her to keep them from clinging to her legs and tripping her.

"That's not what I asked. Where is she?" His grip on the reins tightened until his fingers appeared almost white. His expression bordered on panic.

"She's at my house," Mark said. His own anger had flared to match Daniel's and was evident in the harsh tone of his voice.

"And where the hell is that?" Daniel demanded.

"It's just beyond the woods there," Virginia told him, gesturing in the direction of the house, though she knew he would not be able to see it from where they were. Hurriedly she climbed the narrow slope that led to the roadside and stood only a few feet away from him. "Not very far."

"Show me!" he demanded angrily.

Virginia glanced back in the direction she had just pointed then down the narrow road that lay ahead of them and decided the easiest way for Daniel to get there, since he would not be familiar with any of the different trails through the woods, would be the longer route. "Keep going down this road until you reach the end of these trees. There you will find a small carriage drive to the left. Take that. You'll find Mary at the house there . . . safe, I assure you."

"She'd better be," he warned her. The muscles in his jaw bunched, revealing the true fury that burned inside of him. Suddenly he stuck his hand out to her. "Climb up."

Rather than argue with him, she quickly accepted his hand and allowed him to pull her up and place her abruptly across the saddle in front of him. Though the saddle had not been made for a second rider, and the awkward shape of the thing forced her to lean her shoulder into Daniel's chest, she did not dare complain. Daniel then urged the horse into a brisk canter without offering another word to either of them, and Virginia cast Mark an apologetic glance, then turned to face the roadway and direct Daniel to the proper entrance.

"Hey, wait a minute. Come back here. You can't treat Ginny like that," Mark called out, but too late. Daniel had no intention of listening to anything he had to say. Realizing that, Mark turned and took off running as fast as his rage could carry him through the woods, determined to get to his house by the time they did, though he knew it was hardly likely.

"Daniel, Mary is safe," Virginia tried again, wanting to convince him of the fact before he saw how filthy and unkempt she was. Suddenly she felt ill.

"She'd better be," he said. His expression remained rigid, as if his face were made of rock, and his eyes were almost black from the many emotions that raged inside him. "She'd sure as hell better be."

The moment Daniel's horse was heard clamoring into the yard, everyone glanced up from the veranda and stared curiously first at the two of them, then at one another. Mary immediately recognized her father's intense anger and slowly stood from the rocking chair she and Jessie had been sharing and came bravely forward to meet her fate.

"Hello, Father," she said softly. Her gaze dropped to the planked floor beneath her muddied slippers when she spoke.

Daniel did not respond to Mary, but instead kept his voice low and spoke to Virginia.

"Who are these people?" Daniel demanded to know while he swung his leg over the back of the horse and dropped lithely to the ground. His eyes bore furiously into hers when he reached up and pulled her off the horse, then set her on the ground to stand beside him. He struggled visibly to control his anger and did what he could to keep his voice down. "How could you leave Mary in the care of strangers while you run off in the woods to dally with that man?"

"These people are friends of mine," she began, also trying to keep her voice down and remain calm, though aware that her heart beat in wild, erratic rhythm against her breastbone. "They invited me to have lunch with them."

"But why did you bring Mary?" he wanted to know.

Though he continued to speak in a low voice, she wondered how much what they said could be overheard by everyone else and what they all must think. "They invited Mary too."

"Mary doesn't even know these people," he countered. His voice began to get louder as his anger grew. "She has no reason for being here, and you had no right to bring her."

"I asked to come," Mary called out bravely.

Daniel looked then to his daughter. He paused, carefully studying her fearful expression, then said in a voice that defied further comment, "We will

141

discuss this when we get home."

Daniel then turned from Mary and the house. Virginia turned too, keeping a careful eye out for Mark while watching to see what Daniel was about to do. Her pulse quickened. Mark could be seen coming across the pasture in a dead run. His face was so contorted with anger he was almost unrecognizable, and Virginia feared what would happen once he finally reached them. Quickly she turned to Daniel and agreed to take Mary home right away, hoping he would mount his horse immediately. She signaled for Mary to start for the carriage.

But Daniel too had spotted Mark and watched with his legs set apart and his arms folded over his chest as the young man hurdled himself over the fence and continued across the yard toward him.

"Mark, we are leaving," Virginia called out in a determined voice, in hopes of stopping him from saying something they would all regret. Her blood felt as if it had turned to ice water, and she could sense her legs rapidly losing strength while she waited to see what would happen next.

Though she feared Mark would make a wild lunge at Daniel, he came to an abrupt halt beside her and turned to stare angrily at Daniel while he took several deep breaths. When he opened his mouth to speak his mind, he felt Virginia's restraining hand on his forearm and looked impatiently at it.

"Mark, we are leaving now," she repeated and looked pleadingly into his angry young face.

"He has no right to treat you the way he just did," Mark said. His green eyes flared with fury.

"Mark, don't, please. I have to go now." Then she turned to face the porch, where she found all eyes were upon her. She singled out Wyoma's worried face and tried to offer a cordial smile. "Thank you for the lovely lunch, but I'm afraid Mary and I have to be on our way."

"We enjoyed having you. Both of you," Wyoma answered, stressing her words. "We want you both to come back whenever you get the chance. You are always welcome."

Mary was almost at the buggy before Virginia fully realized the girl was no longer on the porch. Turning to see where the child had gone, Virginia hurried to join her, never once looking back to see if Daniel had finally remounted or if Mark had gotten a good grip on his temper yet.

It was not until they were both in the buggy and on the road headed back to Valley Oaks with Daniel following at a distance that Virginia's initial sense of panic subsided enough for her to realize the deep humiliation over the cruel injustice dealt her had of Daniel's behavior. Not only had he jumped to the wrong conclusion about why Mary was with her; he had refused to allow anyone to explain. He would not even let Mary speak in her own defense.

By the time they reached the house, Virginia's humiliation over the cruel injustice dealt her, had slowly turned into pure, unadulterated anger. She could not remember ever being so furious with anyone in all her life . . . not even Caleb. Nothing compared with the hatred and anger burning inside her.

"Get on in the house and find Lizzie. She'll know what to do with you," Daniel told Mary when he rode up. His gaze stayed on Virginia while he spoke. "Miss Connors and I need to have a little talk."

Virginia sat rigid while she waited for Mary to go inside. She looked forward to having that little talk. She was already imagining what she wanted to say.

"But Father, I wish you would listen to me. It was not Miss Virginia's idea to let me go with her. It was mine. I *asked* her to let me go with her to the Langfords. When her friend, Mark, came over here the other day to invite her to lunch today, I asked if I could go too." Mary then took a deep breath and, though she knew she risked angering her father more, added in a determined voice, "and I'm glad I got to go. I had a real good time."

Daniel looked at Mary for the first time since their return and studied her purposeful expression. His eyebrows rose with sudden interest as he quickly looped his reins to a hedgelimb and turned to face her. "What did you do?"

"I met two new friends, Jessie and Elizabeth, who showed me how to stir up crawdads from the bottom of a creek and catch them without getting pinched. Then we had races between the ones we caught, and my crawdad won!" Her eyes sparkled with what she obviously considered quite an achievement. "Did you know that crawdads aren't really slimy like they look? They don't smell too good, but they aren't at all slimy."

"You went to the creek by yourself?"

"No, of course not. Jessie and Elizabeth were with me the whole time. Elizabeth is eleven. She's the one who kept an eye out for snakes," Mary supplied quickly, then went on to tell him more. "Elizabeth and Jessie also taught me how to skip a stone. I can get five skips on a good throw."

Mary then looked at Virginia. "They wanted me to climb a tree with them, but I remembered how you told me not to do that." Her gaze went back to her father when she explained. "Miss Virginia was afraid I might hurt myself because I don't really know how, so I didn't even try. But you should see Jessie climb. Fast as a squirrel."

Daniel continued to study Mary's animated face. She went on to tell him about the pretty yellow flowers they had picked and given to Jessie's mother for her birthday; and how she had been allowed to help clean and chop the vegetables and had gotten to put the vegetables in the same pot with the roast. Slowly Daniel's anger gave way to amusement and a ghost of a smile played at the corners of his mouth, causing traces of his dimples to form in his cheeks. "I'm glad you had such a good time. Maybe you can show me how to get five skips out of a stone sometime; but at this particular moment, you are badly in need of a bath, young lady. You don't smell any better than those crawdads you stirred up. Go on inside and find Lizzie. And don't get out of that tub until you are perfectly clean. Hair, too."

"You won't be mad at Miss Virginia while I'm gone, will you?" Mary wanted to know, hesitant to leave if he was still angry.

"No, I won't be mad at Miss Virginia while you are gone," he said, and his smile grew as he reached out to stroke Mary's tousled hair. "Now that I realize you are safe and that your going was actually more your own idea than hers, I've calmed down—quite a bit. But if you don't go get that bath immediately, I might change my mind again."

Mary was still reluctant to leave, but did as she had been told and walked past her father toward the front door. It was not until after she had stepped inside and gently closed the door behind her that Daniel turned to Virginia to apologize. He held his hand out and helped her down from the carriage but did not let go of her hand immediately after she

145

stood on the ground before him.

"I'm sorry I overreacted, but you should have told me you had made friends nearby. When I came home and learned from Pete that you and Mary had gone off together all alone, headed away from the better roads, I set right out to find you. After all, you are not very familiar with the countryside or with my horses. I was so afraid you might have an accident and Mary would be hurt all over again that I was terrified. And then, when I came across you and your friend doing whatever you were doing, and realized Mary was not even with you, I panicked. I know I'm a little too protective where Mary is concerned, but I can't help it. She's all I have."

Virginia was deeply touched by his words, but not enough to completely dispel her anger. No matter what his reasons, he had treated her unfairly. "You might have shown some confidence in me. Don't you know that I would never put Mary in any situation where she could get badly hurt? And her going with me was just as much my decision as it was hers. I thought she needed to get away for a little while. You keep that poor child cooped up all the time—like some sort of prisoner."

She was aware his grip had tightened on her hand and that she had no right to talk to him in such a manner, but she was fighting for Mary's well-being, and that was very important to her. "Daniel, you have to give Mary more room to grow. You have to allow her to meet new people, learn new things, experience new feelings."

"And you are very good at making people experience new feelings, aren't you?" he muttered in a deep, throaty voice as he suddenly pulled her body hard against his. His lips came down on hers too suddenly to allow her to voice any protest or turn her face away in time. Unable to react quickly enough, she became trapped in a kiss that was so powerful, so overwhelming, that at first she could not even breathe.

Chapter Nine

Virginia's initial response was surprise followed almost immediately by outrage. Instinctively she began to struggle to free herself from Daniel's unwanted kiss, but his embrace and his determination proved too strong for her. Her next thought was to try to kick him with all her might, but she remembered she had left her boots and stockings beside the creek.

Quickly discarding the idea, she chose to clench her fist instead and pummeled his back as hard as she could with the one arm that was not trapped between them. Frantically she wriggled back and forth until she finally managed to work her lips free from his. But she could not seem to break his grip. Her brown eyes flashed with a strong mixture of fury and indignation as she brought her hand hard across the side of his face with a force that shocked both of them.

"How dare you!" she cried out. Her lungs refused to take another breath until Daniel's reaction was known. Her heart froze in mid-beat while she stared

148

into his icy blue eyes and waited for his response.

Though Daniel's cheek stung from his lower jaw to his temple and begged for his immediate attention, he did not release Virginia. Instead, he tighten his hold on her and brought his lips down to cover hers again, this time kissing her with even more force than before.

Infuriated that he dared try again, Virginia fought once more to free her lips from his, but found this time she could not break the kiss. His hold was far too secure and his mouth seemed able to follow hers no matter which direction she turned her head or how far she twisted her neck. She considered slapping him again, for at least that had gotten his attention; but she realized it might make him decide to be more aggressive, which was the last thing she needed.

Eventually, though it was not what she wanted, Virginia gave up her futile struggle against so powerful an opponent and allowed him his kiss, thinking he would tire of it quickly once he realized he would get no true response from her.

But a response had already started to form. A strange, unaccountable sensation of warmth had entered her bloodstream, spread slowly through her body, and attempted to take possession of her senses while she waited anxiously for him to give up his quest and finally pull away. To her horror, she felt herself starting to enjoy what he was doing to her and soon felt a curious urge for more. But the response was all wrong; a man she could barely tolerate had suddenly decided to force a kiss on her and she was actually starting to enjoy it: where was her reasoning? More than ever she wished he would tire of the unanswered kiss and pull away.

Yet Daniel showed no signs of lessening his ardor. If anything, the kiss intensified. Soon the strange warmth that had entered without warning and flowed through her body with languid ease caused her to feel a little lightheaded. Her thoughts became blanketed in a thick, lazy fog that made it hard to concentrate on anything but the wild rhythm of her heartbeat. Wishing she better understood what was happening to her, Virginia did her best not to surrender to the strange sensations. She was determined to ignore any of the feelings he stirred to life within her and prayed again the kiss would hurry and end.

But it appeared Daniel was not going to tire of his actions anytime soon. She felt the peculiar warmth that had so quickly overtaken her begin to mass in the vicinity of her stomach, then gently settle into her most intimate of places; Virginia was reminded of the true danger she was in and began to panic. Deeply afraid of these strong feelings that were so alien to her, she brought her hands up to his chest and tried once again to push him away. The effort only made him tighten his hold more bringing her body closer to his in the process.

It startled Virginia to feel her breasts suddenly flattened against the hard plane of Daniel's chest. No man had ever tried anything so bold with her. Mortified that he would dare attempt such a thing, much less hope to get away with it, she drew on an inner strength she was no longer sure she even had and finally managed to shove him away from her, though not far enough to assure an escape.

Breathing deeply in a hopeless effort to get

enough air to aid her rapidly beating heart, she glared angrily at him. Her eyes were dark with an unfulfilled passion she did not understand. Her blood raged frantically through her body while she considered what she should do next.

Still Virginia's reaction was not what Daniel wanted it to be, though it was a definite step in the right direction, for he had clearly brought her innermost passions to the surface. He pulled her back into another ardent embrace and kissed her yet again.

With her body again molded intimately against his, he put all he had into the next kiss. For the first time he could feel her body begin to relax. Gradually she allowed herself to relent to one brief moment of pleasure.

Though Virginia had sensed the extreme danger that lurked inside Daniel Pearson from the first day they met and realized he could prove more of a threat to her than most men, she had not expected the danger to be quite this great. She had found him far too enticing from the very beginning and had quickly become aware how charming he could be whenever he felt like it, charming enough to make her wish he did not have to be her enemy; but even so, she had not realized how deeply her feelings for the man went.

Foolishly, she had thought the kiss would not affect her. Kissing never had. But she was quick to realize that this man's kiss was far different from anything she had ever experienced before, the feelings he aroused in her far more powerful than any she had ever felt, and the moment her hands moved up to encircle his neck of their own volition, she knew she was in serious trouble, but now there was absolutely nothing she could do about it.

An unfamiliar hunger started to grow somewhere deep within her, an emotional awakening of some sort so strong, so completely overwhelming, it rendered her momentarily helpless—made her *want* to be helpless. The warm and gentle tide that had claimed her body without any warning continued to flow effortlessly through her veins and bathed her with still more of the beckoning sensations that now so completely possessed her—powerful beyond belief, urging her to give in to her newly awakened needs, weakening her desire to escape, yet all the while building a desire to explore these alien sensations further.

Although her strong, moralistic upbringing dictated she make another attempt to free herself before it was too late, her body rebelled against the idea—willing her not to pull away, but to lean against him instead, and in doing so, learn more about the strange and magical pleasure of his kiss.

Even when his hands moved down her back to come to rest on the soft curve of her hips, she was unable to do the right thing and push him away. His mouth was maddeningly sweet, alarmingly hungry, and as the kiss slowly deepened, she was no longer sure that pushing him away was what she really wanted. When his hands pressed her closer, a liquid fire spread through her and set her heart aflame, sending out a heat so sensual, so all-consuming, that it melted any last resistance she might have held onto which would enable her to eventually pull away from him. He had cast his evil spell over her. She was lost to his wondrous magic.

The frantic thudding of Virginia's heart grew stronger and her legs felt suddenly weak, though remained surprisingly strong, when one of his hands moved from the gentle curve of her hips slowly upward to first caress the sensitive area along her rib cage, then traveled upward again, slowly edging its way toward her breast.

Although she was terrified of the intense power he had over her and she could still sense the danger she was in, Virginia was helpless to stop him. Whatever his intentions were, even though the two of them were outside and in plain sight of anyone who might happen to peer out a window, she did not fight him. She could not; she was too unfamiliar with the passions that had so suddenly overcome her to know how to fight them, and she was becoming less and less sure they should be fought.

A moan welled deep within Daniel's throat when he realized he had finally found the response in her that he wanted. He could sense she was still hesitant, still unsure of what was happening inside her; but when he pulled her gently with him into the seclusion of a tall hedge alongside the house, he was relieved to be met with no resistance. When he brought his hand up to cup the curve of her breast, her only noticeable reaction was to gasp for air, and he was certain she was his.

It was not until his hand moved to take the entire breast into his grasp that Virginia's sanity finally struggled to return. The sudden feel of his hand as it pressed against the sensitive peak of her breast, coupled with the men's voices that could be heard in the distance coming closer, made her realize just how far she had allowed Daniel to go and how very close they were to being discovered. The reality of what was happening to her came crashing down around her and she pushed against him with all her might. When his hold broke with amazing ease, she quickly stepped back.

"Daniel, don't!" she gasped and brought her arms up to cross them protectively in front of her before she looked away, through the thick branches of the hedge, to see from where the voices had come.

Daniel closed his eyes and leaned heavily against the cold, hard surface of the house while he struggled to regain his composure. He had heard the voices, too, but had hoped Virginia would not notice. As he sucked deep breaths of air through his clenched teeth and felt the heavy rise and fall of his pounding chest, he could hear Virginia's padded footsteps moving rapidly away from him, and though he wanted to call out to her, he did not. He waited until he had heard the door close and she had time to reach her room before he slipped out of the hedge and went inside.

Virginia did not leave her room when it was time for dinner, nor did Daniel demand that she join him. Instead, Lizzie brought a tray to her room shortly before nine. Though Virginia was already dressed for bed and had tried unsuccessfully to go to sleep and leave her confused thoughts of Daniel far behind, she accepted the tray graciously and, as soon as Lizzie had left her room, tried to eat enough to calm her stomach. But she soon discovered food was not the cure for what ailed her; she could only hope sleep would help.

Lizzie returned for the tray within the hour, as promised, and frowned when she saw that Virginia was already back in her bed after having left much of her food untouched.

"I don't suppose you are any more willin' to tell me what went on between the two of you than he was," Lizzie stated matter-of-factly as she positioned the plate in the center of the tray before lifting it off the table. When no response came, she shook her head and puckered her lips into a curious frown. "First, neither of you showed up for supper when you were supposed to, then after I went to all the trouble to fix a tray for you both, neither one of you eats enough to keep a bird alive."

"Daniel didn't come down for supper?" Virginia asked, surprised. She knew why she did not dare go to the dining room for supper and why she had not wanted to eat much of the meal brought to her. But why should Daniel's appetite be affected?

"No, he went on up to his room right after the three of you got home and then never bothered to come downstairs again. I went up to see about him when he didn't show up to eat his supper—just to make sure he wasn't sick. But all he would tell me was how tired he was from that long trip and how he planned to go to bed early. He wouldn't tell me nothin' else. But then Master Daniel's always been like that. Whenever somethin' is botherin' him, no matter how bad it is, he keeps it to himself. And that's not good for him. That's not good for nobody."

Virginia could tell Lizzie was eager to find out what had happened between them and wondered what she would think if she was to be told exactly

155

what sort of man her Master Daniel really was; but Virginia did not feel like talking about it. She merely nodded her head and agreed with Lizzie's statement, "No, it isn't."

Lizzie exhaled sharply at Virginia's lack of cooperation.

"Miss Mary said it could be the two of you had a big argument. She told me how he went chargin' over to your friend's house and made you leave before you were ready." Lizzie then paused, in the hope that Virginia would decide to add something to what she had just said, but when it was obvious Virginia intended to be just as secretive, she continued. "I wish he had come on in the house and asked me about where you and Miss Mary had gone off to before he rode out of here to find you all on his own the way he did. I might have calmed him down a little. Might even been able to talk him into stayin' put and lettin' you come home on your own—because I knew you would. But then, Master Daniel's been real protective of that child ever since the accident. Maybe even too protective at times."

Though Virginia still did not say anything, Lizzie had her full attention. She sat forward in bed, her forehead drawn into a tiny frown, while she waited for Lizzie to continue. She may have promised not to talk about the accident with anyone, but she had never said anything about listening to someone tell her about it. She could sense that Lizzie was about to do just that.

"Poor Miss Mary," Lizzie went on with a sad shake of her head. "That poor little gal almost died from all her injuries. All I can say, God must have been watching over that sweet angel, because if she hadn't been thrown clear of the wreckage the way she was, into that field of freshly turned dirt, she wouldn't have come away with only broke bones and a crushed up chest. If she hadn't been thrown clear like that, she would have died right then, just like her mother did."

Virginia could feel the blood drain from her face when she realized what Lizzie had just said.

"Daniel's wife died in the same accident that nearly killed Mary?" No wonder he did not want anyone to talk about the accident. The subject was too painful to be discussed. Not only had the accident injured his daughter, it had taken his wife from him. And it had taken Mary's mother from her. Virginia stared up at Lizzie, her eyes still wide with sudden realization, her heart still too stunned to feel anything but shock.

"Didn't you know that?" Lizzie looked surprised, but then she nodded. "I guess not. Master Daniel don't like to talk about it much. Neither do Miss Mary."

"Well, that's certainly understandable." Virginia could easily sympathize, for she too had lost people she loved dearly. Such heartache was hard to put aside. Tears burned the edges of her eyes as her thoughts turned to her own loss, just as great as theirs—but one she could not reveal to anyone but Mark and his family. "It is probably very painful for both of them."

"I 'spect so. But it's somethin' they both have got to put behind them. Can't let the past keep festerin' up inside them. Sooner or later, they got to let it go."

Lizzie's words struck Virginia with a painful

force. "Sometimes that is too hard to do. Sometimes the past is all you have."

"That's a mighty strange remark," Lizzie said, and looked at her questioningly. "Everybody's got a future. How good that future is depends on what each person makes of it, but as long as you are movin' and breathin', you've got some sort of future ahead."

Virginia smiled at Lizzie's wisdom. How very true. One's future *was* what one made of it. She thought of her own future. If she was to ever get Valley Oaks back and avenge the terrible wrong done to her grandparents, she herself was going to have to do something about it. The future would indeed be just what she made of it. Suddenly she was aware she needed to stop procrastinating. She needed to quit allowing outside influences to distract her from her purpose. There had to be a way to get into that library, and the sooner she found it, the better. Her eyes were drawn to the door that joined her room with the room in question, but was never left unlocked. If she could just find a way to get that door open . . . if she could just get inside. . . .

"Would you like for me to bring you a nice steamin' cup of chocolate to help you get to sleep?" Lizzie asked just before she moved toward the hall with the food tray.

"No, I don't think chocolate is going to help me sleep tonight. I wish I had a good book to read, though . . . something that would really hold my interest, something I haven't read before."

"Master Daniel has plenty of good books in the next room there. I figure he's got more than a person could read in one lifetime," she said as she paused in the doorway and looked back.

"But he keeps the room locked," Virginia pointed out, frowning deeply. Her heart began to pick up its pace which caused her to breath a little harder, but she tried to sound casual when she asked, "You don't happen to know where the key is?"

"Sure I do. Master Daniel keeps it in his pocket."

"You mean you don't have a key? How do you get in to clean the room?"

"He don't like for me to bother with any of the things in the library. Fact, he don't like for anyone to bother with the things he's got in there. Every now and then he lets me go in to wipe the dust off the shelves and furniture, and he lets me sweep if the floor really needs it, but he don't like me rearranging any of the clutter. He's real particular about where he wants things in there." She grinned. "But I can't say I mind much. Just one less room for me to have to worry about." Lizzie paused and studied the disappointment on Virginia's face. "But I'll tell you what I'll do. I'll go upstairs and ask Master Daniel can I borrow the key long enough for you to pick yourself out a book to read."

Virginia thought about that, but realized Lizzie would probably stay right there with her until she'd chosen the book, then lock the door so she could carry the key right back to Daniel. "No, don't go to such trouble. I'll just reread one of my own books. I have a book of poetry that I'm rather fond of."

"Won't be no trouble. Besides, it would give me another chance to see how Master Daniel is doin'. It bothers me that he didn't eat hardly any of his supper. That man rarely lets anything upset him so that he don't eat."

Before Virginia could think of another reason for Lizzie not to, the woman had gone to get the key from Daniel. While waiting for her return, Virginia slid out of bed and into her robe. Though she would not be able to search the desk or cabinets with Lizzie watching her every move, she could get a better idea of the places to look whenever she did get the chance to explore. And she could get a closer look at the other side of that door to see exactly how Daniel had it locked. It occurred to her there might be a way to unlock the other side without Lizzie noticing, then she could slip in through the unlocked door after everyone else was in bed and no one would be the wiser. Her heartbeat quickened when she considered how easily accessible the room would be if she could secretly unlock the other side of that blasted door.

Virginia was so deep in thought that when the knock sounded at her door a few minutes later, it startled her. Eager now to be let into the library, she hurried to open the door, but to her surprise, it was not Lizzie. It was Daniel, dressed in only a pair of denim trousers and a hastily donned cotton shirt. Her gaze was curiously drawn to his bare feet.

"Lizzie said you wanted to find a book to read," he said, as if to explain why he was there. He held the key in his hand. "She also mentioned you did not eat very much of your meal and seemed to be having trouble getting to sleep. She said that was why you wanted a book, to help you get to sleep."

"Lizzie is not one to keep anything to herself, is she?"

"Not unless you actually specify that what you

160

tell her is to be kept a secret," he said with a half-smile. "I suppose she managed to inform you that I did not bother to come downstairs for supper tonight."

Virginia could not help but smile too. "And she also mentioned how you did not eat much of your own meal, either."

"I didn't have any appetite," he stated frankly. "I had too much on my mind to think about food."

Virginia was afraid to ask what that might be, but she wondered just the same. Did he have an attack of conscience? Was it possible that he actually regretted what he'd done? Or was he angry with her for not cooperating with him more, so angry it had affected his appetite? Or had he merely been too busy trying to figure out a way to get her alone again and elicit a repeat performance? Was that why he was at her door now?

"Daniel, you did not have to come down. I told Lizzie I had books of my own I could read. I just thought if she knew where there was a good book I hadn't read, she might let me borrow it for the night."

"I know I didn't have to come down. I wanted to. I wanted to talk to you."

"Oh? About what?" She could feel a nervous apprehension slowly building in the vicinity of her rapidly beating heart when he entered her room uninvited and quietly closed the door.

"About what happened earlier."

"I'd rather not discuss it," she stated firmly and reached for the sash of her robe, tugging it tighter as she stepped away from him, hoping fervently he would stay right where he was. "I don't even want

161

to think about it."

"I can't seem to think of anything else. And I not only want to discuss it with you, I also want very much to kiss you again." He took a step toward her.

Virginia's eyes widened with alarm while her heart jumped with equal anticipation. "Daniel, don't."

"Give me a good reason not to," he said and continued toward her.

"Because it is not right."

"What's not right about it?"

She wanted to say everything, but found she could say nothing. He continued to move in her direction. Her words had become lodged in her throat, unable to get past the sudden fear that had formed there. Her eyes widened with each heavy beat of her heart and her lungs could no longer get enough air. Part of her wanted to run from him, run for for dear life; another part of her wanted to run to him. Yet as he came closer, she found she could do neither.

Daniel's touch sent wildfire through her as his lips found hers with such passionate hunger that Virginia was at first too stunned to even consider fighting him the way she had thought she would.

By the time it did dawn on her that she should indeed be fighting back, her senses had already fallen prey to the unexplainable lunacy of her own passion and, just like before, her usual strong self-control and her staid common sense were snatched from her grasp and placed once again into the hands of this madman.

In the far regions of her mind, Virginia sensed that she was rapidly becoming Daniel Pearson's personal pawn, his own little plaything, and her brain fought to make her more aware of the foolish danger she was in, but her heart no longer seemed to care. All that seemed to matter whenever Daniel kissed her was the wondrous feeling that swept over her. Once again she was allowed to float in an endless sea of warm and tantalizing sensations—sensations she realized only Daniel Pearson had the power to arouse in her.

That tiny part of her that wanted her to give of herself freely and enjoy the intense pleasure he brought her grew larger, stronger. Rather than try to fend him off, as she knew she should, she found herself eager to explore the different feelings so suddenly brought to life within her, to find out just how far they could take her. She could always worry about the consequences later—and somewhere inside of her she was certain there would be consequences to be dealt with—yet it no longer mattered.

The wondrous kiss grew stronger by gentle degrees, and as it did, Virginia found herself falling further and further under Daniel's masterful spell. Whatever the demon that lurked so deep inside of him, it had somehow crossed over and taken complete control of her body too. She felt her legs grow increasingly weaker until she had to lean against him or chance crumbling to her knees. It was when she did at last lean into him and she was again able to feel his body molded so perfectly against hers that it suddenly seemed right to lift her arms up and encircle his neck. She wanted to somehow bring them closer still.

A sweet, sensual fog drifted over her, surrounding her, caressing her, until all that existed for her inside that warm sea of rolling mist were Daniel, the demanding kiss they shared, and the wild, erratic pounding of her own heart.

Suddenly, without warning, Daniel's hands moved to untie the sash of her robe and then quickly slipped inside, his touch warm and searching. Another alarm sounded from somewhere inside her head, warning her that this was not going to be just a kiss and demanded she break free of him before it was too late. It warned her to beware. Daniel was well on his way to accomplishing exactly what he had set out to accomplish, something he had probably accomplished with many women; and so far she had allowed him to get away with everything he had wanted, and without as much as a true struggle to prevent it. Did she truly want to be just another conquest of a man who had obviously conquered many?

If she allowed him to continue his quest, that was exactly what she would become—another Pearson conquest. She thought of her grandparents.

This time, Virginia heeded the staunch warnings that screamed from her brain and somehow managed to find enough strength to finally push herself away from such splendid pleasure. Taking several steps back, she jerked her robe securely closed again and stared lamely at him while she tried to decide what to do next. Her heart was in such a strong state of panic, she could hardly breathe.

The moment words were once again possible for her, she clenched her hands into tight fists and stated in a cold, determined voice, "Don't *ever* do anything like that to me again." Her nostrils flared with disgust and her voice shook from the horror of what had almost happened, but her resolve remained strong when she bluntly stated that which was uppermost in her mind: "I wonder what Amanda would have to say if she happened to learn anything about what you just tried to do."

"Amanda?"

"Yes, your future wife," she reminded him, her voice trembling from the emotions that still held her captive.

"Where'd you get that idea?" His brow drew into a tight frown as if he were confused by her words, but at the same time angered because of them.

"From her. And from her brother."

"What business is that of yours, anyway?" His jaw muscles hardened.

"It becomes my business when it concerns Mary."

"Mary?"

"Yes. Mary hates Amanda. She doesn't want you to marry her. Don't you know that?"

"I'm aware Mary does not care much for Amanda. And it is obvious she would not choose Amanda for a stepmother, if such a choice were left up to her. But it won't be. Even if I do decide to marry again, and I may not, I'm afraid I wouldn't feel it necessary to ask my daughter for her consent. She would just have to learn to live with whatever decision I made."

Virginia stared in disbelief as Daniel then spun on his heel and left her room. How could anyone who had claimed that very afternoon to be so deeply concerned about his daughter's welfare turn around and say something so heartless?

Daniel's worst problem seemed to be that he had no human heart to guide him, none whatsoever, not even where his own daughter was concerned. Oh, how she detested that man for being such a . . . a Pearson! She loathed him more than she had ever loathed anyone. But not only did she loathe Daniel, she also loathed herself—for the shameless way she had responded to his unwanted kiss.

Again.

Chapter Ten

That night Virginia did not sleep.

She was too angry and too confused to sleep. Although she had come to Valley Oaks with a strong and honest conception of what Daniel Pearson would be like, as time had passed, she had allowed herself to doubt the validity of that initial evaluation of his character. She had begun to consider she might have been wrong about him; but tonight she had witnessed the evil that lurked within him. She had seen Daniel for the man he really was: a man born with a black heart, ruled by the devil himself, just like every Pearson that had gone before him. No one mattered to the man but himself, and no one ever would . . . not even his own daughter.

When morning finally came, Virginia chose to stay in her rooms until it was time to begin Mary's lessons. Having come to fear the strange power Daniel seemed to have over her and probably had over all women, she did not want to give him the opportunity to catch her alone again. She knew she had to avoid him at all costs.

Later Lizzie came to see why she had missed breakfast. While she was there, she none-too-casually announced that Daniel had decided to return to Jefferson for a few more days, planning to leave that very afternoon; and Virginia could not have been more pleased.

Though she still found the abruptness of his decisions to go to Jefferson a little odd, she was not about to question anything that would put precious distance between them and would give her another opportunity to explore her surroundings without his presence. But she realized she needed to find a way to be let into the library before he left so she could try to unlock the other side of that door. She was still eager to see just what was hidden there and did not want to wait until his eventual return.

"How long do you think Daniel will be gone this time?" Virginia asked while she tried to think of a way to trick Lizzie into helping her get into that room.

"All he told me was that he'd be gone a few days, but with him that could mean just what it sounds like, a few days—or it could mean he'll be gone a full week or more. It always depends on what sort of trouble he runs into while he's there."

Virginia tried to look disappointed when she was actually very eager for the separation, especially if she could get that door unlocked before he left. "I wonder if he would let you borrow that library key before he leaves so I could go in and select a few books to read while he is gone."

"I can go ask," Lizzie volunteered.

"That would be wonderful. But please, don't let

him bother with coming down himself. He probably has a lot to do to get ready for his trip, and it might take me a while to select the books I'd like to read. I wouldn't feel right making him have to wait while I looked through all those books when he has so much to do."

"And it would give me the chance to dust and sweep in there before he leaves. It's been weeks," Lizzie said with an agreeable nod. "I'll go see if he will let me have the key."

Virginia could barely control the nervous fluttering in her stomach while she waited for Lizzie to return. It felt almost as if a swarm of bees had been let loose inside her. Far too apprehensive just to sit, she quickly stood and paced the floor of her sitting room, dividing her attention between the sound of her own rapid footsteps and the sounds immediately outside her room. She wondered if Lizzie would return alone with that precious key, or if Daniel would be the one to come down, hoping to force his way into her room again before he left. If he did, she prayed she would find the strength to fend him off this time.

When she finally heard loud footsteps approach her door a few minutes later, she brought her pacing to a halt. Her heart missed several beats while she waited for the knock. The blood that coursed through her veins at an alarming rate seemed to turn to icewater when the knock finally sounded, for it was a strong, hard sound, as if it had come from a strong, hard hand. To her relief, when she finally got enough courage to go to the door, she was met by Lizzie's broad smile—and the woman held the key in her hand.

"I told him I'd take it back up there to him as soon as we were through," she said with a happy nod of her head and thrust the key in Virginia's direction. "Here, you go on in there and start lookin' through all those books while I go fetch my broom and duster."

Virginia's heart soared with anticipation when Lizzie handed her the key, then turned away and headed down the corridor toward the kitchen. She realized that if she hurried, not only would she be able to unlock the other side of that door without being caught; she might have enough time to glance through a few of the drawers to see what sort of things were kept there.

Her hand trembled with nervous excitement when she first tried to put the key in the lock, but she managed to get the door open with little trouble. Hurriedly she stepped inside, frowning when she discovered the room dark. There was no window to admit sunlight, and none of the lamps had been lit. The only light came from the door behind her, which she had to leave open if she wanted to see anything at all. Even with the door left open, there was barely enough light for her to see her way across the room.

In her haste to get to the other door before Lizzie's return, she stumbled over a footstool and almost fell, but ignored the sharp pain at her ankle and continued to hobble across the room as quickly as she could. Relief flooded her when she discovered the door was only bolted, exactly like it had been on the other side before she had thought to slip that other bolt out of place. There was no padlock to worry with, no key to have to search for.

Carefully Virginia slid the bolt on this side back as well, then tested the door to be sure it would open. She felt giddy with delight when it came open easily. Quickly she shut the door back, made sure it stayed securely closed, then hurried to the other side of the room. She breathed a long sigh of relief when she had fully circled the large wooden desk and finally stood behind it. Though she did not care for the idea of being caught going through the desk, she had especially not wanted to be found anywhere near the door. She did not want to risk drawing attention to either the door or the fact that it was now unbolted.

Listening carefully for the sound of Lizzie's heavy footsteps, Virginia hurriedly began to open drawers to see just what Daniel kept where. To her disappointment, only the bottom drawers would open, and it was too dark to tell anything other than that there were papers of different sizes and textures inside. The upper drawers were all locked. Straining to see better in the darkened room, she leaned forward and began to feel around the top of the cluttered desk for a key.

"And what do you think you're doing?"

Virginia was so startled by Daniel's unexpected voice, she screamed aloud and threw her hand to her throat as if to keep her heart from bursting. Her stomach twisted into a tight coil while she tried to think of a sensible answer to his question.

"I'm trying to find matches so I can light one of the lamps," she said quickly, hoping he would not be aware of how her breath now left her in short, rapid bursts. "It's too dark in here—I can hardly see."

171

The only sound in Virginia's ears other than her own deafening heartbeat was the soft movement of his bare feet while he moved across the floor, which explained why she had not heard his approach. When Virginia realized he was headed directly toward her, she began to panic. She could not see his face and had no way to even guess what he planned to do to her, but her imagination supplied her with more than enough ideas, and she did not care to find out which of them might be his intention. Pulling in a deep breath and continuing to hold her hand protectively at her throat, she began to back away from him, relieved almost to tears when he stopped at the desk, lifted something from amid the clutter, then struck a match.

The simple sound of the matchhead scraping the side of the metal box Daniel now held in his hand seemed to fill the room with startling clarity, and soon he transferred most of the bright yellow flame to a nearby lamp. The glow instantly filled the room, casting shadows across his face. His eyes studied her while he shook the match out.

"Where's Lizzie?" he asked as he righted himself. Still staring at her, he crossed his arms impatiently across his chest and waited for an answer.

"Gone to get her broom so she can sweep while I look through your books." Virginia was relieved that her voice displayed none of the panic she felt.

He studied her a moment more, then his eyes slowly left hers while he dropped his gaze to the drawers of the desk. A notch formed in his forehead when he bent over and pulled out one of the lower drawers. His hand froze when he dipped it into the open drawer. Suddenly he looked back at her as if he had sensed something was wrong. Virginia shifted nervously when it occurred to her he might be able to tell she had tampered with the papers inside. Did she leave something out of place or move something important when she had groped inside?

"I came down to get something I'll need while I'm in Jefferson. Would you mind stepping outside for a moment?" His face revealed nothing to her.

"No, of course not," she stammered and went immediately to the door. As she closed it behind her, a strong surge of excitement overcame her still enormous sense of panic. She quickly realized that his desire to send her out of the room before he got whatever he wanted from that desk the way he just did meant the key to the desk drawers was indeed hidden inside that room; it had to be . . . possibly somewhere inside that very drawer he had started to reach into. With any luck, he would return the key to its usual hiding place when he was through, which meant she would be able to get into those locked drawers after all, because she was almost certain she would be able to find that hidden key.

Hoping to learn as much as she could by whatever sounds he made, she pressed her ear to the door and listened carefully. She could hear a drawer scrape open and the soft rustling of paper, then she heard the drawer close. She heard other drawers open and close, then she thought she heard a door close. Her heart seemed to collapse inside her chest, ceasing all necessary function while she tried to decide if that sound had come from the door to her room. Had he discovered it unbolted? If so, he would know she was the one who had tampered with it. But then again, the noise could have come from one of the cabinet doors. If only she could tell from which direction the noise had come!

Intent on trying to decide which the sound had been, the door to her room or a cabinet, Virginia ran the noise back through her head again and again. And because she was so deep in concentration, she did not at first notice Lizzie's footsteps.

"Can't you get the door unlocked?" Lizzie asked as she leaned the broom against the wall and held out her hand, palm up. "Here, give me the key. I can unlock it."

Though she still had the key in her hand, Virginia did not hand it over. Instead, she gestured toward the door with a slight jerk of her head and explained, "Daniel is in there."

Lizzie looked confused. "How'd he get in there when we got the key?"

"I had already unlocked the door. In fact, I was already inside searching around for a matchbox so I could light one of those lamps when he came in behind me. He asked me to leave so he could get something he needs for his trip."

Lizzie tucked her duster into the waist of her apron and crossed her arms over her ample bosom. She glanced impatiently at the closed door. "Did he say how long he was goin' to be? I got too many things I could be doin' to waste any time waitin' out here for very long. And you got to worry about gettin' yourself a bite to eat. After all, you hardly ate anything all day yesterday, and look at you now! You can hardly stand up on your own. Then, as soon as you've gotten yourself somethin' to eat, you'll have to be gettin' Mary started on her lessons.

It's already near nine o'clock."

"He didn't say how long he would be in there, but I got the impression it would be only a minute." Virginia felt a strong rush of relief that Lizzie had apparently not realized she had been trying to listen at the door.

"Then I'll wait," Lizzie said, but before she had quite finished her remark, the door swung open and Daniel stepped back to let them enter.

Virginia was aware that he openly stared at her while she crossed the room and continued to stare at her when she began to pretend to read the titles on some of the books that lined the walls. Uncomfortable to have him watch her every move, she wished she could afford a glance at the side door and see if it was still unbolted, knowing that if it was not, she would know exactly why he stared at her; but she did not dare chance his becoming suspicious of that door, if he was not already. If only he would say something that would let her know what he was thinking! The silence in the room was stifling.

"I appreciate your generosity, letting me borrow a few of your books while you are gone," she said politely while she casually took a book from the shelf and leafed through it, aware she had almost opened it upside down.

When he did not respond to her comment, she finally found the courage to glance back over her shoulder and felt an icy chill skip along her spine, then branch out to every bone in her body. He was gone . . . she had not even heard him leave!

Her gaze quickly swept the room. She was all alone. Her gaze went immediately to the hall door:

it stood wide open, empty. She then looked at the side door and felt a warm tide of relief to discover it still unbolted, and thus undetected. Her legs felt weak. She leaned against a bookshelf, for she realized she suddenly needed its support.

Lizzie stepped into the room at that moment, her broom again in hand. The mere appearance of someone in the door caused Virginia to gasp aloud, and she felt weaker still.

"It's just me," Lizzie said with a sheepish smile and a light shake of her head. She quickly set the broom in motion. "My, but you sure catch a fright easy. You're worse than my nephew, Odis Walls."

"I've always been the nervous sort," Virginia agreed, pretending to return her attention to the books, but there were too many thoughts buzzing inside her head for her to study their contents very thoroughly.

By the time Lizzie had finished sweeping and had dusted the furniture and the many shelves, Virginia had found several books that might interest her and she left to carry them to her room. Then she hurried to the kitchen to eat a quick biscuit so Lizzie would stop worrying about her. After that she went directly to the classroom and found Mary already busy with a chalk drawing she had started the day before.

Because Virginia was so very eager for night to come and for everyone to finally go to bed, the day seemed to drag at a snail's pace. Daniel left shortly after lunch, only moments after he stopped by the classroom to give Mary a brief, but seemingly loving hug and offer Virginia a terse nod. The cold indifference with which he treated her caused her a moment of unaccountable pain, but the feeling did not last . . . she had too much else on her mind.

Since Daniel was not to be at Valley Oaks for supper, Virginia dined early with Mary and retired to her room shortly after seeing that her little friend was properly tucked into bed.

Not wanting to arouse any suspicions, she waited until Lizzie had brought her evening chocolate and had returned for the tray before she even dared try the door to be absolutely certain it was still unlocked. She did not want to chance someone being near enough to hear, in case the door hinge should squeak, and she could only hope that nothing had changed, that it was still unbolted.

With the classroom almost directly across the hall from the library, she had been aware that Daniel had returned to the room at least twice just before he left and she was well aware he could have discovered the unbolted door during either of those visits. She was delighted and greatly relieved to discover the door still opened when she finally tried it. But, just to be perfectly safe, she closed the door back and went on to bed as if everything was normal. She planned to wait until there were no more sounds anywhere within the house before she actually dared enter the room.

It was shortly after midnight before Virginia decided the time was right. An hour had passed since she had heard anything stir on either of the floors overhead. Slowly and quietly she folded back her covers and slipped out of bed. Gathering her courage about her like a warm blanket, she lifted the small lamp from her bedside table and walked softly through the sitting room to the door that would finally let her inside the library. Carefully she turned the knob, eased the door open, and stepped inside.

The dim shadows cast by the small lamp she carried moved eerily across the walls and ceiling as she made her way further into the room, making her feel as if there was hidden life in the darkness that surrounded her. Pressing her hand against her throbbing throat, she searched those black shadows, praying she would not find a pair of uncanny blue eyes closely watching her, for suddenly she realized he could indeed have noticed the unbolted door and may have only pretended to leave Valley Oaks so he could hide in the room and wait for her to enter. Her lungs burned from lack of air when she lifted the lamp higher.

Nothing moved except the shadows.

Virginia released the air she had held in her lungs and lowered the lamp to her side again. Almost certainly she was alone now, for there were few places large enough for a man to hide, and so she moved on toward the desk. Finding nowhere to place the lamp on the cluttered desk top, she turned and set it on one of the bookshelves behind her. Quickly she proceeded to search the lower drawers for the key that would allow her to at last discover what secrets were locked away in those top drawers.

Unable to find the key hidden in among the papers which were piled into the two lower drawers, she decided to empty their contents completely and see if there might be a false bottom; there was. And beneath that false bottom lay two keys.

She smiled when the smaller key fit perfectly into the tiny lock that held the desk drawers securely closed. When she carefully turned the key, she could hear a rod move inside the desk and she was finally able to get into all three drawers.

The first drawer she opened, the largest of the three, held several ledger books and a leather pouch in which she found several hundred dollars. She glanced through the ledgers and found the information they contained of little interest to her. And money was not what she had come for; so she quickly returned those items to exactly where she had found them and closed the drawer.

In the second drawer she discovered more ledger books that looked as if they were older, and beneath them was a long wooden box which refused to open. When she lifted the box from the drawer and turned it over to examine it better, she noticed a large, narrow keyhole. With her lower lip pressed anxiously between her teeth, she tried the other key; it fit! Her breath held as she slowly opened the box and peered inside.

The folded papers she found there were yellowed with age, and when she opened them, she discovered they were letters to Caleb. Her heart pounded with eager anticipation, for she had just hit the mother lode. Some of the letters were signed by Daniel's father, some were from a supervisor of the shipping company in Jefferson, and some were from other business associates, but two of the letters were unsigned.

It was those two that caught Virginia's attention, for though there was no name on either, they were written in her grandmother's familiar scrawl.

Taking them closer to the light, she read the contents and found them both to be scathing letters, full of hatred and threats. In both, her grandmother denied her love for Caleb and repeatedly declared her love for her husband. Virginia frowned at the thought that her grandmother had decided it necessary to write these letters at all. Her grandmother had clearly felt very threatened by Caleb, threatened enough to make counterthreats ... threatened enough to openly declare her hatred over and over again. Virginia could feel her own anger tighten around her heart when she realized the suffering her grandmother had endured, suffering even beyond anything she had ever mentioned.

Though neither letter was dated, Virginia could tell by the faded paper and by the way they had started to come apart at the folds that the letters were very old. It seemed odd to her that Caleb had kept such hateful letters, letters that condemned him for the evil things he had done to her grandfather. But then again, the letters revealed nothing of what it was he had actually done, so there had been no real danger in his having kept them. That frustrated her; none of the letters inside the box was going to be of any help. In fact, the rest of the letters held only praise for Caleb. Disheartened, she continued to search the drawers for something else.

Her frustration grew when she discovered that nothing in any drawer contained the information she sought. She realized either Caleb or Daniel had been clever enough to destroy anything that might have incriminated him. They were not the fools she had hoped them to be, not so proud of their evil accomplishments to have kept reminders, evidently aware that anything they kept could one day be found and used against them. But still she had hoped. That both the room and the drawers were kept locked had given her great hope that something still existed which would reveal exactly what it was Caleb had done to Joseph and how he had gone about it.

She was so overcome with disappointment that she wanted to cry. Tears burned in her eyes. How was she ever going to prove to anyone what a cheat Caleb was with no tangible proof? She hadn't even found anything she could use to blackmail Daniel, nothing that would in any way bring dishonor to the Pearson name.

Sadly she pressed her trembling hands to her face and tried to think what to do next. How was she going to get Valley Oaks back if she had no proof Caleb had cheated her grandfather?

Shaking her head dismally, she wondered if there was anyone else who might know what Caleb did. Someone who was close enough to the man to be aware of his daily actions, his more personal decisions. She had to find out more about the man, find out who his friends had been. There still had to be some way to get to the truth. Virginia refused to give up.

Several times during the next few days, Virginia returned to the library in the quiet hours of the morning in hopes of discovering something she might have missed, but there was nothing to be found that would help her cause. Nothing. And until Daniel returned, there was no way for her to find out if there was anyone from the man's past who might have been privy to his secrets. Mary had never known her great-uncle Caleb, so she could be of no help; and Virginia was aware that Lizzie had

181

only known Caleb the last few years of his life. She needed to know who might have known him during his earlier years.

With no other source of information about Caleb, Virginia found herself anxiously awaiting Daniel's return. As the days turned into weeks, she slowly came to realize she actually missed him. Actually missed Daniel Pearson. Despite all that had happened between them, despite all his uncle had done to her grandparents, she missed Daniel more and more with each passing day. She missed his devilish smile, the long, narrow dimples that formed along his lean cheeks whenever he had something truly exasperating to say, and especially the way he looked at her sometimes late in the evening—a look so deep, so provocative that just thinking about it sent tiny little shivers up her spine.

And the more she thought about him, the more she realized she wanted him to come back as much as she actually needed him to return. She found herself slipping into long moments of ridiculous fantasies, dazed by such thoughts as looking up from Mary's studies while out under the oaks to find him riding up on a sleek horse to swoop them both into his arms and carry them away, one in each arm. When they reached wherever it was he took them, he'd confess he was actually a prince who had been stolen at birth by an evil witch and sold to the Pearson family, and in fact, had no Pearson blood flowing in his veins at all.

It was clearly the sort of thing children's stories were made of, and she knew it could never happen; but still she could not help daydreaming about it, especially the part where he turned out to be unrelated to Caleb Pearson. In some perverse way, the bittersweet thought of Daniel turning out to be someone else helped her get through the long, lonely evenings without him.

But soon, Virginia began to worry for her own sanity, for she was having fantasies about a man she actually loathed . . . a man with no heart. Yet the more long, lonely hours she was forced to suffer at the end of each day, the more she dreamed about his return. When Mark stopped by late that Saturday afternoon to bring her boots and stockings to her, she was so glad to see someone who'd help take her thoughts off Daniel that she begged and pleaded with him to stay for supper, even before she had arranged it with Mary and Lizzie. Luckily Lizzie had prepared plenty and had no complaints about having to feed an extra mouth.

During the meal, while Mark helped himself to seconds of sliced ham and cut corn, he mentioned the big Fourth of July picnic still held in Pittsburg each year. Mary's head snapped up at the mere mention of the word picnic.

"Is Jessie going to be there?" she wanted to know.

"She wouldn't miss it," Mark said with a laugh.

Mary then looked at Virginia, her blue eyes wide with hope. "Can we go? Will you please go to the picnic and take me with you?"

"I don't know if we should." Though Virginia clearly remembered Daniel's reluctance when it came to letting Mary go into town, especially when it meant she might be around other children who had proven to be cruel to her in the past, she also knew it would be something to help her push her worries aside, at least for a few hours. In the end, Virginia agreed, though reluctantly. "I guess there wouldn't be any harm in riding over for a few hours of the festivities."

"Great," Mark said with an eager smile, then quickly volunteered a ride. "Since we are going anyway, why don't we just stop by here on our way and pick you two up. The more the merrier, I always say."

"That would be fun," Mary put in quickly.

"Maybe too much fun," Virginia said with a laugh, knowing that Mark and his family would be there from the very beginning to the very end of the festivities. "No, I think it would be better if we went separately."

Looking from Mary's sudden frown to Mark's, she explained. "That way, we could return home if Mary should start to tire early and not have to worry about cutting your fun short. Besides, I have no intention of staying until dark. Mary and I have to get up early the next morning for her lessons."

"Even in the summer?" Mark asked, his brow raised skeptically. "None of the other children have to do lessons in the summer."

"Mary's catching up on eight months of lost time," Virginia reminded him. "And unless I do my job exactly as I'm told, I won't get paid."

"Well, as long as you come in for part of the fun," Mark conceded. "Mother's making enough fried chicken to feed the Confederate Army."

Virginia frowned. She had forgotten about food . . . they would need to supply part of the picnic lunch. Even if Wyoma did take enough chicken to feed them all and probably enough potato salad to sink a small ship, she would not feel right going empty-handed. "Tell your mother that Mary and I will make enough cinnamon teacakes for everyone."

Mary clapped her hands with delight. "I've never made teacakes before."

"Time you learned how," Virginia said with a laugh.

"And I've never been to a town picnic either," she told them just as excitedly.

"Time you went to one," Virginia and Mark said in unison, then Mark added in a thoughtful voice, "High time."

Chapter Eleven

The closer Virginia and Mary got to Pittsburg, the more Mary's excitement grew, until it finally burst from her in a loud fit of giggles about the time Virginia brought the carriage to a stop a few blocks from the festivities. Realizing they were not going to find a spot any closer, Virginia maneuvered the horse toward the right side of the street, where there was just enough room between two wagons for the small carriage. Quickly she climbed down to secure the animal to a post.

"Look at all these wagons and carriages," Mary exclaimed while she glanced first one way, then another. The streets and alleyways were lined with them. "Everybody in this entire county must be here today."

Virginia laughed at Mary's enthusiasm. "That's why it's extremely important that you stay near me. I don't want you to get lost in this crowd."

"How will we ever find Jessie in all of this?" she asked worriedly as her hand gave a sweeping gesture to the many people, so many that they had already filled the sidewalks and had started to spill out onto the dirt and gravel streets.

"They will be at the main park closest to the post office," Virginia told her. "And if I know Mark, he got here early enough to have one of the better spots beneath the trees at the far end."

"I hope so," Mary said sincerely. "Now that we've stopped moving, I'm starting to feel just how hot it really is." She reached inside the pocket of her light yellow skirt to be sure she had remembered to bring her fan.

Virginia glanced up at the cloud-dotted blue sky and wished she could count more clouds than there actually were. She too had noticed the heat, but Virginia had noticed it even when she had still been under the shade of the canopy and the carriage had been moving fast enough to keep a light breeze in their faces. Now that they were no longer moving at all, the heat had easily caught up to them and had quickly surrounded them, making it hard to breathe.

While Virginia secured the narrow tether strap to the post, tiny beads of perspiration started to form along her neck and forehead, causing the small ringlets of hair along her temple to cling to her face. Even though she had chosen a pale blue dress of a very light material, the garment seemed to trap the heat next to her body and she could feel a fine sheen of perspiration starting to form between her breasts and along the back of her neck. In imitation of Mary, she too reached into her pocket to be sure she had not forgotten her own fan, but instead of leaving hers in her pocket for later use, she slipped it out and held it ready in her hand. As soon as she had helped Mary down and gathered up her draw-string handbag and their food basket, she put the fan into rapid use. By the time they reached Main Street, where most of the festivities would be held, her flushed face had started to cool and she felt much more comfortable.

Mark spotted them as they walked along one of the boardwalks, even before they reached the largest of the three picturesque parks near the center of town. He moved quickly through the crowd to greet them.

"We're over there," he called to them as soon as he was close enough, gesturing toward the many trees that shaded the far end of the park.

"In the shade, I hope," Virginia said, still working her fan at amazing speed.

"Follow me and you'll find that I've gotten a prime spot, right in the very middle of all that shade," he said with a proud shake of his head. "And within full sight of the bandstand."

By the time Virginia and Mary finally worked their way through the crowd to Mark's side and he had offered his arms to them, Jessie appeared through the crowd, her face flushed with excitement. "They are about to start the pie-eating contest in front of the sheriff's office."

She looked hopefully at Virginia. "Can Mary go with me to watch?" Then to Mary, Jessie added with a delighted laugh, "You've got to see this. These people are so busy trying to gobble down all the pie they can, they get globs of pie all over their faces and even in their hair sometimes."

Mary's eyes widened with disapproval, but she turned to Virginia and asked with true eagerness,

"May I go?"

"Will you two promise to come back as soon as the contest is over?" Virginia asked, not knowing if there was any point in getting them to promise such a thing. She remembered how she and Mark had always had a hard time remembering they were supposed to go find the adults between the many events of the picnic.

"Of course, we promise," Jessie said with a disbelieving shake of her head. "Just as soon as they have handed the ribbon to the winner, we'll be on our way back." Then, without further comment, she took Mary's hand and led her through the crowd in the direction of the sheriff's office.

Virginia followed Mark to where Wyoma's quilts had already been spread smooth and were held down with several baskets of food and a stoneware jug of lemonade. He quickly took her basket and placed it beside the others, then adjusted his suspenders as he stood again.

"Where's you mother?" she asked, glancing around.

"She's entered her peach preserves again this year. The judging is supposed to be at eleven." He pulled out his watch and looked at it. "Eleven-twenty. She'll probably be heading back over here with another ribbon for her memory book anytime now."

"And are you entering anything?"

"Thought I'd enter the knot-tying contest at one-thirty. And then the horseshoe contest at three, over in front of Kesterson's Livery. Maybe even get in on the tenpin contest tonight at Little's Alley. What about you? Care to enter the three-legged race with me?"

"That's for children."

"Not necessarily. Some adults enter just for the fun of it."

"Well, I'm not one of them," she stated adamantly. "I don't happen to fall as gracefully as I used to."

"Oh, look, there's Mrs. Tucker," Mark said, easily distracted from such inane conversation. "Haven't seen her in years. She must have come back to town to visit with her sister."

Virginia glanced in that direction and smiled. Mrs. Tucker looked the same as ever—tall, thin, and tired. "I wonder if she still teaches school."

"Let's go say hello to her and find out," Mark suggested and started toward where the woman was already disappearing into the crowd.

Virginia panicked. Because she had changed so much over the past few years and had avoided telling anyone her full name, no one had really recognized her thus far, and she really preferred to keep it that way. The less often anyone realized who she was, the less chance Daniel would find out, even though she did not think he socialized much with the people of Pittsburg. Still, if anyone realized Essie Elder's granddaughter had returned and was actually living at Valley Oaks—working for a Pearson—the news would spread like wildfire. And someone might take it upon himself to go to special trouble to inform Daniel just who his daughter's new teacher really was.

"No, Mark, don't bother her . . . besides, if she was to remember you for the scamp you were back then, she might be inclined to take a strap to you right here in front of everyone. Using that strap on

190

you did seem to be her favorite way to pass the time, as I recall."

"As I recall, it seemed to be every teacher's favorite way of passing the time," Mark said glumly, but goodnaturedly. "What would you like to do?"

"Let's walk around and see what is going on. But I want to get back here before the pie-eating contest is over so I'll know if the girls actually did come back, as we asked them to."

"You wish is my command," Mark said and raised his finger to his forehead in light salute, then offered his arm to her again.

Virginia had forgotten what fun the Fourth of July picnic could be. Never could so many people find so much entertainment for so little money. The only contests that had any entry fees were the ones which sponsored a really good cause; otherwise, the only cost to any participants was physical.

By the time Virginia and Mark had walked the length of Main Street and had returned to the quilt, they both felt exhausted, and they had only watched the many games and contests; they had not participated at all. It was hard to believe the two of them used to enter one right after the other, so that by the end of the day their pockets were full of blue and red ribbons.

While they sat catching their breath, a pretty girl about nineteen years old casually made her way past them both. At first she frowned as she looked at Virginia, but when Mark glanced up to notice her, she smiled sweetly. "Hello, Ma-rk."

Virginia wanted to grin at the way the girl had said his name as if it had two syllables, but managed to keep a straight face while she watched the

191

girl stare adoringly at him.

"Oh, hello, Margaret," Mark responded with not quite as much enthusiasm as the girl had probably hoped. He acted as if her presence made him uncomfortable.

"Who is your friend?" she wanted to know and glanced only briefly at Virginia, for her eyes wanted nothing more than to look upon Mark's handsome face.

Virginia felt her stomach knot while she tried to place the girl's face. Did she know the girl? Would the girl recognize her as an Edler? She just hoped that Mark had the good sense not to introduce her too thoroughly.

"This is a friend of mine, Virginia Conners," he said simply. "Virginia, this is Margaret Cohen. She just moved here from Alabama. Her folks opened up a leather shop on the other side of Kesterson's Livery."

"Pleased to meet you," Virginia said with a sincere smile. Though Mark clearly revealed his discomfort at having the girl there with them, and the girl seemed just as uncomfortable being in his company, Virginia decided she liked her well enough to ask her to join them.

Margaret's eyes opened wide with alarm and her hand went instinctively to her throat to cover her quickening pulse. "Oh, I couldn't intrude; I just wanted to stop by and say hello to Ma-rk. Besides, I've got to be on my way. I promised Mother I would try to locate my two sisters so we can be finished eating before Brother Cannon gives his speech."

Virginia could sense Mark's relief and wondered

why he had been so opposed to the girl joining them. "That's too bad. I'd love the chance to get to know you better. If you find the time later on, why don't you stop back by for a short visit?"

"Yes; well, maybe," Margaret said, her cheeks turning bright pink as she turned and hurried away without offering a proper goodbye.

"I think that girl likes you," Virginia said, stating the obvious with a huge grin.

"She doesn't even know me," Mark muttered with a frown.

"But she clearly wants to know you better," she teased in a lilting voice.

"But she isn't gonna," he shot back.

"Why not? She's pretty enough."

"I know—she's real pretty. She's just not the girl for me, is all."

Virginia decided to let the conversation end right there, afraid that he might say something she didn't really want to hear. She was aware that Mark's interest in her ran deeper than it used to, and she did not know how to stop him from becoming even more interested. She still wanted him to be her best friend, but nothing more. She wondered why that made her feel so guilty.

Wyoma chose that moment to return. Jessie and Mary had found her just moments before and had asked if they could go back and watch Jessie's cousin, Elizabeth, participate in the beanbag toss scheduled to take place right at noon, after which Jessie was to enter the ring toss, and now Wyoma quickly explained to Mark that their lunch was going to be delayed. She did not want to eat until the girls had returned. Mark offered several reasonable protests when he learned he was going to have to wait too, but none swayed his mother from her decision.

It was almost one o'clock before the five of them finally settled onto the quilts for their belated noon-day meal. Mark was more eager to help than usual and quickly saw to it that everyone had a plate and that serving spoons were placed in both the potato salad and the carrot salad, and a fork in each of the pickle jars. When he then began to hand every-one a roll, pausing just long enough to take a big bite out of his own, Virginia had to comment, "You'd think this man was starving to death."

"What's your hurry, Marcus?" Wyoma wanted to know while she gave him one of her staunchest motherly frowns. "You'd think you hadn't eaten in a week."

All Mark could do was grin while he chewed hard. His mouth was too full of bread to allow him to speak out in defense of himself. It was not until he gulped down a large glass of lemonade that he finally commented, "My main concern is for you, Mother."

"Oh, is that so?" she asked skeptically and glanced at Virginia.

"Sure," he said with a worried frown while his eyes darted around at everything that lay before him, but then his face relaxed when an idea finally occurred to him. "I know how the hot sun affects your appetite, and if we don't hurry, we are going to find ourselves eating in the hot afternoon sun." He gestured to a large splotch of sunshine that had slowly been making its way from a neighbor's quilt toward theirs. "So, you see? My main concern really is for you."

"How noble you are," Wyoma laughed, knowing full well Mark had not noticed their shade was waning until he had needed to find a good excuse for his bad manners. "But if you think about it long enough, you'll remember that I brought my parasol for just such an occurrence. So please, son, don't be so worried for me. Slow down and enjoy your meal."

"Yes, ma'am," Mark said as he dutifully took a much smaller bite of his roll and munched slowly.

Virginia could not help but laugh, and once she had started, Jessie and Mary were quick to join in.

It was while they all laughed and Mark bristled uncomfortably, aware he was the brunt of their amusement, that Virginia first realized someone was standing behind Mark, just inches from the edge of their quilts, pointedly gazing down at them. She looked up to see who it might be, but the sun was directly behind him and all she could clearly make out was a tall silhouette of a man. Shielding her eyes with her hand, she squinted up at the man and asked, "May we help you?"

Even before he answered, she knew it was Daniel. There was something about the way he stood, the cocky stance he took, and the close fit of his clothes over an extremely masculine body that made her recognize him. Her heart froze in cold panic. Instinctively she reached out for Mary's hand and held it protectively in her own. She had taken Mary to the picnic without his permission, and Mary had eagerly gone. He was probably furious with them both. While she felt the strength slowly drain from her, she prayed he would hold his temper until they were away from the crowd.

"I was hoping someone would invite me to sit down," he said casually as he smiled at the group. But the manner in which his clenched fists hung stiffly at his sides belied his casual tone and sent Virginia's pulse racing.

"Why certainly, please sit down," Wyoma responded, her face twisted into a curious expression as she looked up at him.

Quickly everyone but Mark scooted over to make room for one more. Mark scowled angrily when he realized that the space they had so quickly provided for the man was between Virginia and Mary. Instinctively he moved closer to Virginia himself.

By the time Daniel was settled in and Mark had moved closer, Virginia discovered she had very little room to move. Daniel and Mark were both sitting so near to her that her skirts touched them both, but it was the fact that Daniel's knee was almost touching her own that made her feel the most uncomfortable. Tiny bursts of apprehension shot through her.

Smiling nervously, she handed her untouched plate to Daniel. "Here, have something to eat."

"I can't take your food from you," he protested and held up his hands, palms out, to prevent her from giving him the plate.

"There's plenty of food. I'll fill myself another plate," she insisted, knowing it would give her something to do with her hands; she felt a strong need to keep her hands as busy as her heart seemed to be.

"Well, if you insist," he stated amiably, finally accepting the plate. Lifting the fork from the rim, he dipped first into the potato salad and placed a large bite into his mouth, then realizing everyone was staring at him, he swallowed, smiled, pointed to the salad with his fork, and stated, "This is delicious."

Wyoma smiled too. "Thank you."

Daniel nodded and took another bite, as if to prove just how good it was. Then, realizing everyone still sat staring at him, he waved his fork to encourage them and remarked enthusiastically, "You don't know what you're missing."

After everyone had started to eat again and the girls began to tell Jessie's mother all about how close Elizabeth had come to winning second place in the beanbag toss, Virginia chanced a quick glance at Daniel. She had been so stunned by his sudden appearance and then by his asking to join them that she had not dared steal a good look at either him or Mark.

She was well aware Daniel did not like to come home and discover Mary gone, and she had also seen the instant flaring of anger in Mark's expression whenever Daniel's name was brought up in conversation. She knew that having Daniel there at her side, sharing their meal and their conversation, did not sit well with Mark; nor had returning to discover Mary had been taken off again without his permission sat well with Daniel. Both men were angry. What she did not understand was why Daniel was trying to be so nice.

"So, Virginia, aren't you going to introduce me to your friends?" Daniel asked as he accepted from Wyoma a quart jar filled to the brim with lemonade.

Virginia gasped at her thoughtlessness. "I'm sorry . . . I wasn't thinking!"

"Sure you were," Jessie piped in with a knowing nod. "My teacher, Mrs. Tucker, says that as long as you're awake, your brain is thinking for you. And even sometimes when you sleep, it does more than just dream . . . it works to solve problems for you."

Wyoma's eyes widened as she quickly nudged the child in hopes of hushing her, but managed a pleasant smile when she then extended her hand to Daniel. "I'm Wyoma Langford and that's my son, Marcus." She nodded toward her still scowling son; then, when she noticed how the two men's gazes had locked in silent battle, she quickly tried to take Daniel's attention elsewhere. "And this little chatterbox beside me here is my daughter, Jessie. I suppose you remember us from the other day. We have that small place that borders yours down by Cason Road, where we grow cotton and corn."

"Ah, yes," Daniel said with a charming smile. After accepting Wyoma's hand, he then turned and extended his own to Jessie. "Very pleased to meet you, Jessie. Mary has told me so much about you."

Jessie grinned and accepted his handshake. "Mary's my new best friend," she announced in earnest, and the two girls exchanged the smiles that proved it true.

"Wonderful," he stated in earnest. Daniel then turned to Mark and hesitated only a moment before extending his hand again. "And I'm pleased to meet you."

Mark's scowl deepened, but he accepted the handshake, though with far less enthusiasm than Jessie had.

Quick to bring his hand back once the handshake was over, Daniel returned his attention to Wyoma in an obvious attempt to let Mark know he was of little interest. "And I do want to apologize for my rude behavior that day, Mrs. Langford. It was just that Virginia had not told me she had made friends in the neighborhood, nor had she mentioned wanting to take Mary with her on a visit. When I came home and discovered she'd gone and taken Mary with her, I overreacted, I'm afraid. I'm so protective of Mary. But I am truly sorry."

"No harm done. And I can't say that you overreacted that much. I'm a mother . . . I know what it's like to have to worry so over my own children. They're too precious not to worry about." She reached over and tenderly stroked Jessie's braids while she spoke.

"Aww, Mother," Jessie complained, embarrassed by such sudden attention. Blushing slightly, she jerked her head aside so that she would be out of her mother's reach.

Finding Jessie's situation funny, Mary started to giggle behind a raised hand, and soon Jessie was scowling along with Mark, but the little girl's foul mood lasted only until Mary dropped the carrot salad on her fork into her lap, when Jessie could not help but laugh again. And, as it was with children so young, all was immediately forgiven.

But the adults were another matter. Virginia could sense that Daniel was forcing himself to be friendly, but what she did not understand was why. And the friendlier Daniel tried to be, the more sullen Mark became, and the more nervous she felt. It was as if she sat between two sticks of dynamite, each with a fuse burning, each ready to go off at any moment.

Shortly after everyone finished eating and the leftovers had been put away, Jessie and Mary asked if they could go watch some of the events that had been scheduled for the late afternoon. Daniel frowned as he thought about Mary's request to go off alone with only another small child to keep an eye on her, but in the end he finally nodded an agreement.

"But be careful," he warned as the two skipped off into the crowd toward the busier part of Main Street. He watched until they had completely disappeared from sight, and even then his eyes continuously searched for them.

Virginia could sense how hard it had been for Daniel to give Mary permission to go off with Jessie and could hardly believe he had agreed to let Mary go. She wondered if her little speech about giving his daughter room to grow and letting her do new things had had this strong an effect on him. She did not think Daniel had listened to a single word of what she'd said that afternoon and could not be more pleased to know that he had not only listened, but was now trying to change. But after only a few more minutes, he seemed to realize what he had done and turned to Mark and Wyoma. "Thank you for looking after Virginia and Mary today. I appreciate it. But the main reason I came was to see them safely back home, and I think we should get started back pretty soon. Mary is not used to so much excitement."

"But there are still hours of activities yet," Wyoma protested, knowing how Jessie wanted Mary to stay for as long as she could and how disappointed she would be to see her leave.

"I know; but Mary's had enough excitement for one day," he countered quickly.

"Still, that's no reason for Virginia to have to go just yet," Mark put in. "She loves the afternoon celebration. Let her stay with us . . . we can drop her off on our way home. It's not far out of the way."

Daniel's brows rose with interest. "That will be entirely up to her."

Virginia wondered what it would be like to breathe again, because she was certain her lungs had ceased to function forever. Mark had unwittingly indicated he knew her well enough to state what she liked and didn't like, and Daniel had obviously taken note of the fact. "To tell you the truth, Mark, I'm feeling a little tired myself. I think I will go on back with Daniel and Mary. I don't want to overdo it."

Mark scowled at the way Virginia had used the man's first name. "Suit yourself."

"But I do want you to know, I had a lovely time today; I truly did. And I hope you do well in the knot-tying contest," she said, hoping to ease his hurt feelings a little.

"I've already missed that and the horseshoes," he pointed out glumly. "And now I've got no partner for any of the races."

"You had no partner before," she quickly reminded him, a little angry that he was reacting so childishly. Turning to Wyoma, she smiled again and said, "The food was delicious and the company delightful. But I'm not used to such heat. The summers are not nearly so intense in Pennsylvania. I really am very tired."

"I understand," Wyoma said pleasantly as she handed Virginia her small basket. "Just remember where we are. Come visit us soon. Bring Mary, too."

Daniel stood first, then offered Virginia his hand. Mark stood at the same time she did and acted as if he planned to walk with them back to their carriage.

"Thank you again for taking such good care of Virginia and Mary, but I assure you, I can take it from here." Daniel's low tone of voice was just determined enough to cause Mark to hesitate.

"Goodbye, Mark," Virginia said and reached out to touch his cheek with her hand in a reassuring gesture. "I'll be by to see all of you soon."

Mark smiled, but his smile was short-lived when Daniel quickly suggested that he join her on that visit. "I hardly ever have an opportunity to get away from Valley Oaks, except when I go away on business," Daniel explained. "It would be nice to get out and pay a visit to some of my neighbors."

Wyoma had no choice but to extend her earlier invitation to include him.

Virginia was never so glad to leave a gathering as she was when Daniel finally led her away from Mark and Wyoma. Within minutes they located Jessie and Mary but agreed to stay long enough for Mary to watch Jessie take another turn in the slingshot contest. She had already won against two opponents and had only to win twice more to take first place. Mary held her breath when it came time for Jessie to take her final shot. When Jessie's rock hit its mark and the tin can clattered to the ground, Mary squealed with delight and jumped up and down from the excitement she felt. "Did you see that, Father? Did you see that? She never missed once."

"Well, you'd better go congratulate her for a job well done," Daniel said and allowed her to rush over to give her friend one last hug before he finally led her away on his arm. Virginia followed, smiling despite the strange sense of apprehension that lingered still.

"Where's the carriage?" he asked while he headed for the southwest side of town, knowing that was the direction of Valley Oaks and probably the direction of the carriage, but not knowing for certain where to find the thing.

Virginia's eyes opened wide with alarm. She had forgotten to note where she had left the carriage. Her face flushed with embarrassment, but before she had to admit her neglect, Mary piped up, happy to supply the information. "It's down the street that runs beside Jackson's General Store. Over in front of Cranford's Saloon."

Daniel's eyes widened as he looked back at Virginia.

"But don't worry. The saloon is closed. We didn't see anything," Mary quickly added. "Not that we would have looked, even if they had been open." But she had to grin at that last remark, because she knew full well she'd have tried to catch a peek of what went on inside had the doors been open.

Daniel remained thoughtful while they continued to walk in the direction of the carriage. Virginia worried that his silence reflected an anger he might be harboring from having returned home to find Mary gone again, and she waited nervously for the outburst that was sure to come. But when they reached the carriage, he helped them both up, then climbed in beside them without any show of anger. Even when he stopped to get his horse, which he had left at one of the liveries near the edge of town, he did not say or do anything to indicate the anger that surely boiled inside him.

It was not until he had tied his horse to the back of the carriage and they had started for home that Virginia decided it would be best to go ahead and offer an apology. "Daniel, I know how upset you must be with me for taking Mary off without your permission again; but you were not where I could ask and Mary so wanted to go."

Daniel stared at her for a moment, then glanced at Mary who sat between them. "Did you have a good time?"

"The greatest! I almost won a ribbon," Mary told him excitedly.

"You did? Whatever did you do?

"I jumped rope longer than nine other girls. If my rope hadn't gotten caught in my skirt the way it did at the last, I might have won."

"I didn't realize you were so good at jumping rope," he said and looked at Virginia to see if she was at all surprised.

"She likes to jump rope in the evenings," Virginia explained, but stressed, "after she has finished with her lessons and it is not so hot."

"How long has this been going on?" he asked.

"For several weeks," Mary told him. "Since Miss Virginia doesn't have anyone else to talk to in the

204

evenings anymore, I keep her company. She helps me keep count of how many times I can jump without making a mistake. Once I hit two-hundred-and-twelve. Do you want to see me jump when we get home?"

"Certainly. But only after you've rested."

"But I'm not tired!" she assured him.

Daniel studied Mary's smiling face a minute before he finally conceded, "Maybe you aren't at that."

Mary went on then to tell her father of the many things she had seen and done during the time they were at the picnic. Daniel never mentioned being angry with anyone for having come home to find his daughter gone again and listened attentively to everything Mary had to say, asking questions when her explanations were not too clear. Virginia soon wondered if there might be hope for a strong father-daughter relationship yet. She smiled with true contentment.

Later that evening, to Virginia's surprise and Mary's delight, Daniel announced that instead of Mary dining at seven and he and Virginia at eight-thirty, a compromise would be made: dinner would to be served at seven-thirty and the three of them were to dine together. When the time came for them to take their seats at the table, Mary seemed nervous, and when Lizzie first served her and she began to eat, her motions were awkward and self-conscious; but Daniel was quick to put her at ease by telling her some of the funny things that had happened while he was in Jefferson.

Virginia was stunned. While she watched Daniel and Mary slowly open up to each other, she wondered what had come over Daniel to change him so dramatically in such a short time. He was trying hard to get along with Mary . . . maybe too hard. Though she hoped it was because he'd finally realized what he was missing by excluding his daughter from so much of his life, somewhere deep inside Virginia could not help but wonder if there might be another reason.

Suddenly it occurred to her what that reason might be: it just might have something to do with Amanda. After all, he had openly admitted during the course of their conversation how Amanda had been in Jefferson while he was. Was Daniel actually preparing Mary for the announcement that he had at last asked Amanda to marry him? Did he hope to compensate for Mary's disappointment by pretending to be more of a father to her tonight? Virginia's insides coiled into a tight, burning knot at the mere thought of it, because there was nothing she could possibly do to stop him.

Chapter Twelve

Virginia went with Daniel to see that Mary was properly tucked into bed, fearing all the while that the good-night wishes he intended to offer his daughter were going to end with an unwanted engagement announcement; but the announcement never came. Daniel merely kissed his sleepy daughter's forehead and made sure she had her sheet pulled up to her chin. As hot as the nights were lately, there was no need for much cover, even with the ceiling fan that chugged and hummed high over her head.

Taking a step back, Daniel waited at the side of the pink, ruffled bed for Virginia to give Mary a good-night kiss too. Virginia smiled at the way Mary, who had stirred barely awake, offered her a sleepy smile just before she presented her now rosy cheek to be kissed, then curled into a new position, ready to go right back to sleep. Mary had had a long, fun-filled day that had not only seemed to bring more color to her fair cheeks, but had put a brighter sparkle in her vivid blue eyes. Yet all the excitement and physical activity had taken its toll: she was exhausted.

When Virginia smiled then, it was from more than the vision of the sleepy little girl who lay snuggled on the plump pink-and-white bed before them, or even because of how very much Mary had changed in just a few months. This was the first time Virginia and Daniel had visited Mary's room together to wish the child good night in all the time Virginia had been there, and it felt special somehow. It was a moment that seemed so easily shared between them, and that surprised her a little. When she quietly stepped away from Mary's bed, she could not help but turn her smile on Daniel.

"Come, let the angel sleep," he whispered and motioned toward the door. His expression revealed nothing to her. He neither smiled nor frowned, but still there was something very serious about him. "I want to talk to you."

Virginia felt her stomach tighten reflexively. Was it now that he planned to reprimand her for having taken Mary to Pittsburg? Had he held in his anger all this time just so Mary would not have to know of it? If that were so, she would have to give him credit for showing such restraint. It really was something that should not be discussed in front of the child.

After leaving the room quietly, the two walked in silence toward the staircase and for once Daniel did not put his hand at her elbow to guide her, as had become his custom. When they reached the stairs, she realized how his not touching her made her feel just as awkward as when he did.

"Daniel, I want to thank you for what you did tonight," she said, hoping to forestall his anger as they descended the stairs, only inches apart but still not touching; yet she was able to feel him beside her. The same tingling sensation flowed through her as when he had actually held onto her, and Virginia thought it strange.

"What did I do?" he asked innocently. For the first time since they'd left Mary's room, he smiled briefly. But the smile was so short-lived, Virginia had almost not glanced up in time to see it.

She knew then there was definitely something on Daniel's mind, something very grim. Her stomach tightened; there seemed to be pure ice water in her veins; but she tried to hide her apprehension. "Daniel, you know very well what you did. And I've never seen Mary so happy."

"She is happy because of all the fun she had at the picnic with you and Jessie," he put in quickly and smiled again, causing his dimples to deepen. This time the smile lasted a little longer.

"Mary is happier tonight because of the attention you showed her after she got home," she corrected him, studying that lingering smile and finding it most endearing. How she wished he would use it more often around her, and especially around Mary! It made his company so much more bearable. "And I want to thank you for that. A little added attention from you was just what she needed."

He paused at the bottom of the stairs and looked at her for a moment, gazing into the dark depths of her wide, expressive brown eyes before daring to speak what was on his mind. It occurred to him then, as it had several times in the past, how extremely perceptive and caring Virginia was when it came to Mary. The next thought to cross his mind was how impossibly beautiful she was. It was a strange combination in a woman: intelligence, compassion, and beauty. In most of the women he'd met, if one of those traits happened to be present, the others were not. "Instead of just thanking me, Virginia, I wish you would show your gratitude in another way."

Virginia felt her pulse beat erratically, and suddenly the blood began to push hard against her temples. In response to what she thought Daniel was about to suggest, she tried to take a step away from him, knowing distance would be her best protection, only to find she was blocked by the bannister: there was no room for her to back away. She considered bolting from him and running off to her room, locking her door before he could make his scandalous suggestion; but her pride just would not let her . . . her fear would be too obvious.

"Daniel, I think we, you . . ." she began, only to find herself immediately interrupted.

"Virginia, if you really want to thank me, there is a better way to do so. If you really want to thank me, agree to go with me to Amanda's party next week." The words came out rushed, as if they had been forced out of him in one mighty push.

Virginia could not have been more surprised and felt a little embarrassed because of what she had thought he intended to say—or do. "Amanda's party?"

"Yes—Amanda is having a lawn party next Saturday, on the fifteenth, and we've been invited." His voice remained calm, and his words came slowly again, but he still seemed curiously on edge.

"*We* were invited?" she asked, clearly doubting the fact.

210

"Well, I was invited, as I always am; but I insisted you be invited, too. You've been down here almost three months and haven't had a chance to meet any of my friends or business associates other than Amanda and William. I'd really like for you to meet some of them, and I'd like them to meet you."

"In other words, I was not invited until you made a request that they include me," she stated for verification, so that he would better understand when she gave him her answer, which was going to be no. She was not about to go where she was clearly not wanted unless there was something to be gained in doing so, and she could see nothing to be gained by going to Amanda's party.

"Amanda always invites the same people to her parties. It just never occurs to her to add anyone new to the list. I assure you, she was very happy to include your name once I suggested it."

"I can just imagine," Virginia said with a skeptical roll of her wide brown eyes. She wondered just what sort of threats went along with that suggestion and why he would bother in the first place.

"And William was delighted by the idea," he added encouragingly, though he frowned when he did so.

"That may be true, but still, I don't think I'd better," she began. "For one thing, I don't have a proper dress for such a party." And she knew such a frivolous dress—a dress she would rarely have occasion to wear—would probably cost her as much as two months' wages, as much as six or eight good, everyday dresses.

"But I've already accepted for the both of us," he said, then pressed his lips together as if he had not really wanted to reveal that fact.

211

"You what?" she exclaimed, unable to believe he would do such a thing without asking her first. But then, remembering he was a Pearson, something she seemed oddly prone to forget, it suddenly became easy to believe.

"I accepted for both of us; I already told them you would come. I'll buy you a new dress if that's all that's holding you back. I really don't want to go to the party alone."

Virginia stared at him a moment longer, studying his expression, and decided he was sincere. Even so, she was not at all sure she wanted to go. She also knew she should be angry with him for having been so highhanded and actually accepting the invitation for her the way he did without as much as mentioning it to her beforehand. But then, remembering how wonderful he had been that night with Mary, and how dreadfully she had missed him over the past few weeks, she found herself wanting to agree to go with him. Then, realizing she might meet someone at the party who knew Caleb and possibly discover just what it was he'd done to her grandfather, she knew she wanted to go. Despite Amanda and the terrible time that woman would be certain she had at the party, despite the fact she might have to travel alone with Daniel to get there, Virginia finally smiled and nodded her agreement.

"All right, I'll go. But you will have to buy me that new dress. I honestly do not have anything nice enough to wear to a party as grand as Amanda's will be, nor do I care to spend so much for a dress I will rarely have occasion to wear."

"Any dress you desire," he promised and placed his hand over his heart to dramatically seal the vow.

"But with the party barely over a week away, it'll

212

have to be a ready-made dress. There certainly won't be time to have a dressmaker make me one."

"There is, if I promise to pay her twice the price," he said encouragingly as he reached out to caress her cheek gently with his hand. "I want you to have the prettiest dress at the party."

Virginia could not help but smile at the sudden warmth his touch had brought her. "You don't have to be quite so extravagant. I'm sure I will find a lovely ready-made dress to buy."

"Nothing doing. First thing tomorrow, I want you to go into town and have the dressmaker of your choice make you a very special dress. Ask her to work day and night if she has to. Tell her I'll pay any price she asks."

"But I can't go tomorrow . . . tomorrow's Wednesday. What about Mary's lessons?"

"Take her with you. Teach her about the trees and the rocks and all those other nature-type things that you'll see along the way. She'll love it."

That was true enough; Mary enjoyed riding in the carriage. Still, Virginia felt hesitant. "Well, if you're sure it's all right."

"I couldn't be more sure. While the two of you are at the dressmaker's, have a dress made for Mary; have two, no—three. Four. Mary hasn't had a new dress in months, and since she's started to put some of her weight back on, she's quickly outgrowing the dresses she has."

Virginia wondered where this sudden generosity had come from, but she was not about to question it for fear he might change his mind. She was starting to look forward to the trip into town with Mary and helping the girl plan four new summer dresses, one of which would be suitable for climb-

213

ing trees and chasing butterflies. "Would you be averse to Mary having a pair of good boots?"

"If she wants them, buy them."

The next morning Virginia and Mary went back to Pittsburg, since there were very few dressmakers to be found in the smaller community of Pine and far fewer materials to choose from. They both selected fashionable new designs, the prettiest materials, and the most delicate laces they could find for all the dresses except one of Mary's four, which was to be durable. Though Mary was not going to be with them at the party, Virginia fully agreed that one of the girl's dresses should be a party dress also; they decided every girl should have a party dress. Fondly Virginia remembered her first real party dress while the dressmaker added up the bill.

Virginia recalled how her grandmother had scrimped and saved the money she'd taken in doing the minister's laundry and Mrs. Scroggin's sewing, and had added it to the money her husband, Joseph, had made doing odd jobs for the local merchants, then bought several yards of shiny blue satin and a whole card of lily white lace and made her the prettiest party dress Virginia had ever seen. When she and Mark went to the Harvest Dance that year and the next, Virginia had felt like a real princess.

But it saddened Virginia to realize how very much her grandparents had been forced to sacrifice just so she could have a more normal childhood — so she could have a few of the things the other girls had. Whenever she had openly protested the many sacrifices on her behalf, Virginia's grandmother would always toss her thin shoulders back and staunchly proclaim, "You are an Elder, and as such

214

you really deserve better—much better."

Such proud and loving people her grandparents had been! There was never an unkind thought, never a cruel word for anyone, except when conversation happened to bring around the name Caleb Pearson. Virginia shuddered when she remembered how hard and bitter her grandmother would suddenly become and how her poor grandfather would fall sadly silent and not speak again for hours.

Though she really did not want to think about them at that moment, the heartbreaking memories continued to wash over Virginia with vivid clarity. She could almost see the hatred that filled her grandmother's harsh expression when she would tell her, "Caleb Pearson is a vengeful, jealous man. When he learned I had chosen to marry Joseph instead of him and meant it, he proclaimed then and there that I would be sorry some day, but I had not realized that those words meant he planned to see to my misery personally. But he set right out to ruin us, and although he did manage to take everything of value from us, except for one little almost worthless piece of land, he was never able to take away the love we felt for one another. It was the one thing he could not destroy, and it turned Caleb into a bitter man. He began to try to make more and more money to prove what a poor choice I had made, until he eventually became very rich. I just hope he finds no comfort in living at Valley Oaks—only the heartache he deserves."

Whenever her grandmother went into one of those angry tirades, triggered by the mere mention of Caleb's name, her grandfather would usually sigh heavily and try to remind his wife that it was all in the past. There was nothing they could do to change any of it. Virginia could remember how her grandfather, such a kind and gentle man, had seemed to grow sadder, more despondent as he grew older, becoming a gray and bent man who kept to himself more and more.

It was clearly her grandmother who continued to make such a valiant effort to keep up appearances, so the neighbors would not realize just how poor they really were. And it was just that sort of sacrifice which got Virginia that first blue satin party dress. Sadly, Virginia realized her vivid memory of that pretty hand-sewn party dress was probably why she had chosen blue satin and white lace for the dress she was to wear at Amanda's party. Blue satin was a fabric she would always be fond of. Even Mary's party dress was going to be made of the very same blue satin, trimmed with a similar white lace.

"When will the dresses be ready?" Virginia asked Mrs. Akard while she watched the woman quickly take Mary's measurements and write them down. Virginia had chosen Mrs. Akard's dress shop because the woman was new in town and would not have any cause to recognize her.

"Since you say the party is Saturday week and are willing to pay so much, I'll get right on them. Yours should be ready for a final fitting early next week. The young lady's should be ready for her fitting by the end of the week," the woman said as soon as she made the last of her notations on her pad. Smiling, she slipped the pencil into her graying blonde hair and added, "I certainly want to please your husband so he will send you both back here again and again."

Virginia's eyes opened wide at the mistake the

woman had made. "Daniel Pearson is not my husband. He is my employer."

"Oh?" Now it was Mrs. Akard's eyes that opened wide. Though she clearly did not want to appear rude, she could not help but let her gaze sweep over Virginia's slender form appraisingly.

"She's my teacher," Mary put in, smiling proudly at Virginia when she reached out to take her hand. "Though I wish she was my mother; but my mother is dead."

"Oh?" Mrs. Akard said again, eyebrows arched while she committed the new bit of information to memory and connected it to the rest. Slowly her gaze was drawn to the child.

Virginia could not see any easy way to get out of what the woman was clearly thinking, and decided to simply let her think the worst. Eventually the truth would come out and everyone would realize just who she was and why she had been so willing to live at Valley Oaks, in the same house with a notoriously wealthy widower. And they would then see it was not at all what they had thought.

"I'll be in for the fitting on Tuesday then, if you are sure you will have my dress ready."

"It'll be ready," she said, her eyes still wide and her eyebrows so far up into her forehead that they had disappeared beneath her sweeping hairdo.

When Mary and Virginia then walked out of the dress shop onto the crowded boardwalk, Mary smiled up at Virginia and said, "I do, you know. I do wish you were my mother. Then you would be with me forever."

"No, I wouldn't. Eventually you will grow up, fall in love with some handsome young man, and marry. Then you will leave Valley Oaks in order to

217

live a life of your own with your husband."

Mary's face twisted into a definite scowl. "And spend the rest of my life living in the same house with some stupid old boy?"

"One day boys won't seem so stupid," she assured her with a half-smile, remembering she had said something similar to Mark once.

Mary thought about that, but shook her determined head with disbelief. "You aren't married," she pointed out quickly. "I think I'll be like you. I'll grow up to be a teacher. Then I can go places and do the things I want to do and not have to marry some stupid boy at all. I can live my entire life without ever having to worry with a husband who only *says* he loves me, or children who only get in the way."

Virginia's smile faded and a look of complete horror replaced it. When she wondered where Mary had gotten such a cynical view of marriage, she realized it had to have come from Daniel. Had he been so cold and so unfeeling in the past that he had led Mary to believe all marriages were only hardships?

"Why would you suppose that you would end up with a husband who did not love you?"

Mary looked at her, puzzled by such a question. "Why haven't *you* ever married?"

"Because I haven't found the right man," she conceded.

"Have you looked?"

"No," Virginia admitted hesitantly. She had been too preoccupied with her overwhelming desire to get Valley Oaks back to even consider getting married. That sort of thing would have to come later.

"Because you are too smart to let yourself get

218

tricked into such a thing," Mary put in, very serious in what she said. "You will never get married because you are too smart to be fooled by such a thing. You will never be bothered with children of your own."

Virginia's expression fell into a deep frown when she realized the implication of what Mary had said and she realized she was not getting any younger. Suddenly the future did not seem nearly so bright.

Though the party was to begin at five o'clock, Daniel did not want to arrive until after six and did not have the carriage made ready until shortly before three o'clock. As Virginia had feared, they were indeed to be traveling alone, and for the next three hours she would have to try to make pleasant conversation with Daniel. But then, she realized, as of late, having pleasant conversation with the man was not all that difficult. Ever since that second trip into Jefferson, he had returned a changed man.

Because she dearly wanted to look her very best, as much for Daniel as for herself, Virginia started to prepare for the party shortly after she had finished breakfast. Knowing how it would enhance the thickness of her hair, she curled and tied it a strand at a time with tiny strips of rags and left it tied while she took a long, hot bath so that when she was ready to take the narrow strips of cloth out, her hair would have far more curl than usual, which would make it appear fuller. The curls she wanted to fashion at the top of her head would not only be easier to manage, they would also last far longer.

When it finally came time to leave, Virginia was dressed in her new, shimmering blue gown, her hair

219

a fabulous array of curls. Just before leaving her room, she secured her new blue silk and satin hat in among the lovely curls, tilting it slightly forward, which was the style. Carefully she draped the thin veil that was temporarily attached to the pleated brim over the face and hair to protect her from road dust and insects while they traveled.

Daniel waited for her in the foyer and turned in time to watch her slowly descend the stairs in her wide, shimmering blue skirts, trimmed with gathered flounces and contrasted by a close-fitted bodice. When she finally came to stand before him, his gaze dipped only briefly to the modestly low curve of her neckline but quickly returned to peer into the dark blue veil that surrounded her, blocking her lovely features from his view. Without saying a word, he reached out both hands and raised the veil back to rest it on the curving brim of the hat.

"You are beautiful," he said with open admiration. Again his gaze dropped to take in the enhancing cut of her neckline and the perfect fit of her bodice. "Absolutely beautiful."

Virginia could feel a hot blush climb into her cheeks and wished she had not already put her fan away into her handbag. Because the skirt had been designed with no pockets—her own oversight, she was forced to carry both a handbag and a cumbersome parasol, which left her with only one hand to lift her skirts out of the way.

"Thank you. You look very nice yourself," she said shyly, wondering what was making her react so foolishly. She then glanced down at his attire, already knowing that she had greatly understated his appearance. Daniel was incredibly handsome in his close-fitted black trousers with their matching cutaway frock coat and a wide, dark gray sash which he wore over a gleaming white, lightly ruffled shirt. In his hand were a black silk top hat and white dinner gloves. It occurred to her then that she had never seen Daniel wear a hat or gloves, and she felt it would be odd seeing him in them tonight.

"I am going to be the envy of every man there when I walk in with you on my arm," he stated with honest admiration, and a smile slowly stretched across his face, causing those handsome dimples of his to dip playfully into his cheeks.

Virginia could not remember ever having felt so exhilarated. Never had anyone as handsome as Daniel been so openly affected by her, and she could not help but offer a little flirtation. "And I shall be the envy of every girl there."

His smile grew wider as he offered his arm. "The sooner we leave, the sooner we'll get there, and the sooner we can make all those poor people tear their envious little hearts out. Shall we go?"

"We shall," she said gallantly, then accepted his arm and smiled at him. He responded by wetting his lips with his tongue and then looked quickly away. Contented by such a response, Virginia allowed him to escort her quietly to the carriage which awaited them outside, under the carriage porch.

As she stepped up into the carriage and quickly adjusted her skirts so the folds lay right, it occurred to Virginia that having a little flirtatious control over Daniel, the way Amanda did, could someday be of use to her and decided to try her hand at it, if only a little. As soon as he had settled onto the seat beside her, he glanced in her direction, and just before she lowered her veil into place for the trip, she looked at him and lowered her lashes shyly, amazed at the immediate, eye-widening response she got. He stood long enough to accept the reins from Jack, and when he sat back down, he was a little closer to her than was necessary. He stayed that way when he urged the two gray horses into a lively canter.

The trip to Amanda's father's house just a few miles from the neighboring town of Daingerfield was made with amazing speed, for it seemed only a short time later that they were pulling onto the graveled drive of a large, three-story, elaborate French-roofed house. Though it was a style rather common to the Pennsylvania countryside where Virginia had spent the past five years, it was unique to this part of the country and seemed a little out of place surrounded by such common work buildings.

Though several guests had already arrived and could be seen milling about on the back lawn, Daniel pulled the carriage to an easy stop in front of the wide stone steps that led up to an intricately carved double door. A tall Negro dressed in fine livery stepped forward to take the reins from Daniel and waited patiently until Daniel had donned his hat and helped Virginia down. The man then waited until the two of them had stepped away before he quickly hopped into the carriage and drove it away to the shade of a nearby grove.

During the drive over, Daniel had told Virginia about the man who owned the grandly styled house, Amanda's father, who also owned several shipping interests in Jefferson, Shreveport, and New Orleans. Amanda's father had at one time been in a very lucrative partnership with Caleb, before they had decided to divide the company between them and go their separate ways. The business had been split for reasons no one ever knew, but it was clear they had parted as friends, for Lowell had been and continued to be a close friend of the family for as long as Daniel could remember.

Though the man was getting on in years, he was still very much alive and still tried to take an active part in his business. But because he was indeed getting much older, it was only a matter of time before the business would have to be turned over to someone else. And it looked like William was the only candidate at the moment.

Daniel had shaken his head sadly at the thought, because he felt William did not have a strong business sense and would surely lead the man's different enterprises to eventual ruin; it was the same feeling William's own father had. "Amanda would make a better businessman than William, if she were only inclined to do so," Daniel had told her, and the mere thought that Daniel felt Amanda possessed such business acumen had caused Virginia any amount of unreasonable discomfort.

Even as they neared the door, she still felt uncomfortable to know that Daniel considered Amanda clever and cunning enough to run a business. His admiration of the woman bothered her far more than it should. After all, she had been aware of his feelings for the woman for months now. It also made her wonder why he had invited her to come here with him in the first place. Was he playing a game? Was having her at his side just a ploy to make Amanda jealous? The possibility made Virginia's insides ache.

Just before they reached the wide double door, it was automatically opened by two young black boys outfitted in black knickers and spotless white shirts, and Virginia was temporarily distracted from her painful thoughts in order to take better notice of her surroundings. As Daniel escorted her inside, the doors closed soundly behind them and they were greeted by another Negro dressed in livery almost identical to that of the man who had driven away Daniel's carriage.

"Good to see you, Mister Pearson, sir," the elderly man said eloquently as he accepted Daniel's hat and gloves . . . gloves, Virginia noted, that Daniel had never bothered to put on.

"Thank you, Washington," Daniel responded with a smile before he turned to gaze proudly at Virginia. "Have the Haughts provided a room where Miss Connors can freshen herself? We've had quite a dusty ride."

"Yessir. The ladies are using the first two rooms at the top of the stairs," Washington said with a wide smile, indicating the grand, curving staircase with his gloved hand. "And the gentlemen who waits for them to do whatever it is they do up there are going into the front parlor for brandy." He gestured toward another room off to the right.

"Which is exactly what I shall do," Daniel said with a nod. Glancing then at Virginia, he smiled. "Go on up there and do whatever it is a lady does to freshen herself," he said, his eyes sparkling with the humor he had found in Washington's statement. "And I'll wait for you down here. But don't take too long . . . I'm eager to see everyone's reaction when I walk in with you at my side."

Virginia felt herself blushing again and hurried upstairs to detach her veil and wash away any dust that had managed to cling to her skin. When she came back down to accept Daniel's proffered arm, she had tidied her hair and adjusted her skirts, and she felt absolutely beautiful. The image she had seen in the mirror had hardly seemed her own. It was as if someone had cast a magic spell over her and made her into someone special, someone even a man like Daniel could admire. She felt absolutely giddy knowing she looked as nice as she did.

It was not until they had crossed through the house and entered the back lawn that they first saw Amanda. She had appeared out of nowhere, dressed in a beautiful gown of emerald green silk shot through with tiny traces of silver and white, with a daring neckline that showed off the three elegant strands of pearls she had chosen to wear.

When Virginia had first spotted Amanda moving gracefully toward them, with a drooping hand already extended for Daniel to take, which he did gladly, Virginia's self-confidence began to wither away into nothing. She realized that next to a beauty like Amanda, she was not much more than an awkward bumpkin.

"Daniel, I've been wondering where you were," Amanda said with the little-girl pout that looked absolutely adorable on her. "I was beginning to think you weren't coming."

"You know I'm always late for these things," he stated matter-of-factly.

"That's true. Always fashionably late . . . I think you learned that from me," she said with a playful laugh and moved ever so casually to stand directly between Daniel and Virginia, her back to Virginia and her pretty smile directed at Daniel. Catching his arm, she tugged gently. "Come, Father wants to speak with you."

"But I can't leave Virginia standing all alone," he protested, but was interrupted before he could finish his statement.

"She won't be alone," Amanda assured him, then called out to William, who was deeply engrossed in a serious discussion with three other men just a few yards away.

"William, be a dear and keep Miss Connors company while Daniel goes over to speak with Father. Introduce her around. See that she gets some punch," Amanda said sweetly as soon as her brother had joined them.

"Gladly," William responded with an eager smile and quickly offered Virginia his arm. "Shall we start with the punch? I'm sure after your long ride, you are very thirsty."

Before Virginia could speak in her own behalf, Amanda was again tugging on Daniel's arm and leading him away. He turned to glance one last time at Virginia, but said nothing.

"Punch or wine?" William asked, but found Virginia was not listening and he had to repeat his offer. "Virginia, would you rather have punch or wine? We have both."

"Whichever you prefer," she answered quickly, wanting to give her full attention to the effortless way Amanda manipulated Daniel, not to whatever the brother she had ended up with was saying to her.

"Wine it is," he said and led her toward one of the many tables which had been set up throughout the yard with large silver bowls of iced fruit punch and three different chilled wines.

Virginia accepted the rosé wine and held the glass in her hand without much thought to what it was until she absently took her first sip and found the drink to be appalling. She stared down at the wine in her glass, startled to learn that something that looked so pretty could taste so foul. But not wanting to be impolite, she continued to sip the beverage while she tried her best to keep Daniel and Amanda in sight as they flitted about from group to group. Finally the two came to a large gathering of older people seated about the shaded gardens near a splashing whitestone fountain a few yards away from another table of liquid refreshments.

Twice during the evening Daniel managed to return to Virginia's side, but both times he was immediately whisked away by Amanda, to meet someone else she wanted him to speak with or to help her do something else only he could manage. Even when dinner was served at nine, Amanda managed to seat Virginia at William's side and Daniel at hers, at opposite ends of the huge table.

As the night progressed and Virginia was forced to watch how easily Daniel was continually manipulated by Amanda, her misery grew to overwhelming proportions. Even the foul taste of the endless supply of wine William kept providing for her could not compare to the bitter foulness of her mood. By eleven o'clock she had had far too much to drink and far too much of Amanda, and she decided two could play at that game: if Daniel was so prone to a little flirting, she would do what she could to become better at it. Unwisely she decided to practice on William.

Imitating everything she had witnessed Amanda do for Daniel, Virginia looked coyly up at William and fluttered her dark eyelashes, laughing lightly at everything he had to say from that moment on, and bolstering his ego at every opportunity by making comments about how wise and clever he was. She even reached out and touched his arm from time to time.

It amazed her how readily William responded and she continued to sip her wine and flirt until she felt she was *almost* ready to try her newfound wiles on Daniel. The wine had given her just enough courage to go against Amanda head-to-head, and William had shown exactly how powerful this flirting business could be.

But somehow, before Virginia ever got to the point of feeling absolutely ready to take Daniel on, she found herself alone with William in the gardens at the far side of the house. She was standing behind a particularly tall hedgerow where there was hardly enough light to make out William's smiling face, much less the way out of the huge maze of greenery. Her thoughts had been too muddled by wine and too preoccupied with Daniel to understand the real reason William had taken her there. She had innocently assumed he wanted her to see the exceptional beauty of the secluded spot.

It was not until he pulled her hard against his thin frame that she realized exactly what his intentions were. Too late she saw they were entirely alone in the secluded gardens, and quite a distance from the rest of the guests. As she continued to scan the darkness around them in hopes of finding another couple who had decided to take advantage of the unlit gardens, Virginia became shockingly aware that there was not one other person in sight. There was no one to come to her rescue.

"William, don't," she said. Her words came out slurred, even to her own ear, as she tried to focus on William's face. But it was just too dark and her vision was too blurred for her to be able to see his expression clearly. She blinked hard; still she could not actually see the raw, open desire in William's eyes, but she knew instinctively it was there. "William, let me go," she cried.

"Virginia, I want you," he murmured in a low, husky voice, and instead of obeying her command, he bent low and kissed her long and hard, pressing his thin lips against her protesting mouth, making it hard for Virginia to catch her breath.

When he finally brought his mouth away from hers and lessened his hold a degree, Virginia found herself clinging to him, not because of any passion he had aroused in her, but out of sheer desperation to stay on her feet. The ground had suddenly come alive and rolled and pitched from side to side beneath her unsteady feet, causing her to stumble sideways whenever she tried to let go of him. Much more of this and she realized she would be seasick. She closed her eyes to stop the dizzy sensation from affecting her further, but it did not help.

William mistook her closed eyes and her sudden inability to let go of him for insatiable desire for more of his hungry kisses, and he quickly pulled her harder against his body, this time becoming bolder in his quest and bringing his hand up to cup her breast and fondle it lightly.

"William, don't!" she tried to say, but found her words muffled by his hovering mouth. She tried to push him away so that she could have more room to speak, only to discover she still needed him for support and could not let go. She leaned against him then, clutching his sleeve in a death grip, and tried again to tell him to stop, but he was too intent on continuing what he had started. Soon his hand was inside her clothing and groping under the soft fabric, edging ever closer to one of her breasts.

"William." Her voice was pleading with him, but before she could add the word "Don't," Daniel seemed to come out of nowhere.

"Don't!" Virginia slowly sank to her knees while Daniel made good use of William's left jaw. The last thing Virginia was fully conscious of before a peaceful darkness drifted over her was the sickening thud of a fist hitting sharply against something solid and the sound of some heavy object falling hard against the ground. She remained awake just long enough to hope that whatever it was that had fallen would not roll over on top of her and crush her, what with the way the ground rose and fell beneath her like a wave.

Chapter Thirteen

The next fully conscious thought to surface inside Virginia's muddled brain was that she was somehow once again in the carriage, headed back to Valley Oaks, no doubt, with a very angry Daniel Pearson at her side. She parted her eyelashes to look at him. Though his expression was rock-hard, his arm was around her, holding her, securely keeping her from sliding off the seat. She appreciated the gesture of kindness, especially when she considered how very angry he appeared. He looked as if he was about to explode. Still, he held her gently. There were so many contradictions in that man, so many things she did not understand. She tried to think about it more, but her brain did not want to bother with any deep thought at the moment.

"Are you awake?" he asked, his voice low and foreboding. He only briefly took his glittering blue gaze off the road ahead to glance at her. There was just enough moonlight to throw a silvery cast across his face, sending soft shadows beneath his hair, eyes, and nose that made him look almost demonic.

"No," she responded quickly and closed her eyes tight to prove it. Not fully understanding his anger in her muddled state of mind, nor wanting to, she snuggled next to him, rested her head against the warmth of his chest and was lulled back to sleep by the rocking of the carriage and the strong, rhythmic heartbeat that pulsed beneath her ear.

Daniel stared down at her, his expression still grim, yet at the same time a flicker of amusement had started to form in his eyes. He had a pretty strong hunch Virginia had never had any liquor before. She had not known when to set her glass aside—either that or she had deliberately set out to become quite inebriated. Whatever the case, he had to admit she made a most fetching sot.

Holding her close to keep her limp form on the seat beside him, Daniel could not help but enjoy the oddly peaceful moment. There were not too many moments of undisturbed quiet anymore, not with Virginia in the house. Either she and Mary were chattering away about something new they had found to discuss, or she was berating him for something he had done or arguing with him about something he hadn't. But at that moment, with Virginia sound asleep in his arms, it felt as if he was in possession of a precious angel—a very *intoxicated* angel—but an angel nonetheless.

His smile widened into a look of pure contentment while he watched the night shadows dance across Virginia's sweet face, now tilted comfortably against his shoulder. Able to look at her as long as he wanted without fear of being discovered, he could see how genuinely beautiful she was. He studied the perfection to which her high cheekbones had been molded, the thick dark lashes that fringed her closed eyes, the regal shape of her perfect nose, and the gentle curve of lips that were just right for kissing. Staring at the way her moist lips reflected the moonlight, Daniel wondered if any man would ever conquer this beautiful woman's heart and why none had.

Or was there someone already very close to doing just that? He thought then of Mark Langford and wondered just how close a friendship had developed between the two. There was no doubt young Langford would love to make Virginia his wife. But when Daniel thought of Virginia married to the young farmer, it made his insides tighten. He did not care to think of her as a poor farmer's wife, especially *that* poor farmer's wife. It was upsetting to him how damnably handsome Mark Langford was—he had the sort of smile women usually went for.

Next he thought of William and how apparently close his old friend had come to conquering Virginia. He felt a sudden chill fill his chest and surround his heart as he thought about what might have happened if he had not intervened when he did. William was not the man for her either, because although he might be able to provide well for someone like Virginia, he was not the type to make a good, stable husband. Sighing outwardly, Daniel glanced again at Virginia and wondered which of the two men she preferred, if either.

He felt envious of whatever man Virginia eventually chose to be her husband; Daniel had a feeling that Virginia Connors was the type to remain loyal to whomever she finally chose—*if* she ever did choose to marry. Though Daniel did not believe in undying love, for he had clearly seen just how

233

quickly sworn love could die, he knew Virginia was the sort of woman who would at least remain loyal to her mate, even after the strong physical attraction that was the cause of so many marriages finally wore off, which it so often did. She would stay with whomever she had chosen till death broke them apart. And that was the way it should be.

The coldness that had become a permanent part of Daniel's very soul grew strong and pressed tighter around his aching heart while he thought back to his own beloved wife. What a pity loyalty had never been one of her stronger traits! He could have lived with the fact that she no longer loved him, and he could have continued to love her despite her waning affection; but her heartless betrayal had been the harsh blow that had shown him what a farce love really was. Bitterness poured through Daniel's body like hot acid when he thought of all his wife had done until he literally burned with the hatred that still held his heart prisoner.

Never would he allow himself to be in so vulnerable a position again. Never would he leave himself open to such heartache. Without realizing it, Josie had done him one good turn: she had taught him just how deeply a man could be hurt if he allowed himself to foolishly believe in love—and Daniel had learned the painful lesson well. And because he had learned it so very well, he would be able to spare himself any such heartache in the future.

Daniel was now well aware of the truth: love was an unfortunate figment of the imagination. It was what children's fairy tales were made of—nothing more. And those who were foolish enough to believe in everlasting love, foolish enough to covet a ridiculous illusion created by the mind and heart, deserved to be hurt. Again he thought of Josie and how easily she had led him to believe in that which did not exist. Hatred surged through his body with unbearable force, burning like liquid fire through his heart right to his very soul, until he wished he could reach inside his skull and tear Josie's memory from his brain.

It was almost three in the morning before Daniel could see the pointed rooftops of Valley Oaks, and by then he had managed to put his hatred for Josie back where it belonged, locked carefully away inside the innermost chambers of his heart. When he finally turned the carriage into the drive, he was glad he had chosen to come home. Although Amanda had insisted he allow her father to provide them each a room for the night, he had decided it would be better to leave right away, before either William or Virginia came to.

Daniel sighed aloud his regret when he thought of poor William but felt only a small pang of guilt for having jerked him away from Virginia as he had, hitting him so hard against the jaw that he lost consciousness from one blow. But when he'd found the two of them and had seen exactly what they were up to, he just could not seem to stop himself.

After all, Virginia was his responsibility, and he'd been aware she was drinking far too much, and at William's encouragement. And because he also knew William for the true womanizer he was, Daniel had tried his best to keep a close eye on them throughout the evening. But when he had suddenly looked up from a conversation he was having with his friends to discover the two had vanished, and then found them in the gardens, something just seemed to overtake him. He not only saw a need to

235

stop the proceedings as quickly as possible; he had *wanted* to hurt William for having tried something so bold with Virginia, especially while she was obviously not sober.

Grimly, Daniel decided to send a letter of apology to William in the morning, for although he was glad he had broken the little tryst before it had gotten out of hand, he was not proud he had hurt his friend. It had just happened. He only hoped William would understand. After all, he and William had been friends for a long time, maybe not the closest of friends, but still friends.

"We're home," Daniel said loudly to Virginia when he had pulled the carriage to a stop. Realizing there was every possibility he would have to carry her inside to her bedroom, he wanted to pull up to the closest door. But first he would see if she could walk on her own.

"Wake up, Virginia; we're back at Valley Oaks."

"That's nice," she muttered happily with a slightly off-centered smile; but instead of sitting up, she merely snuggled closer to his warmth and went back to sleep.

"Virginia, we have to go inside," he tried to explain. A tiny smile tugged at his lips. She looked so childlike, sleeping up against him the way she was. He found he was sorely tempted to stay put and let her sleep the rest of the night right where she was, in the folds of his own arms. But, no, his better judgment told him he needed to get her inside the house and make her comfortable in her own bed. She was going to have a hard enough time of it when she awoke in the morning without adding an uncomfortable night's sleep to her misery. He next considered waking Lizzie and asking her help in getting Virginia awake enough to be put to bed, but decided Virginia might not want anyone else to see her in such an inebriated state.

"Come on, Virginia," he coaxed while he pushed her into an upright position on the seat beside him and held her in place with a firm grip.

"Hmmm?" Her eyes opened part-way as she attempted to focus on his face.

"Can you sit up?"

"Of course I can sit up," she said, suddenly frowning that he should ask such a ridiculous question.

"Good, then I'm going to let go of you and climb down, then I will hurry around to your side and help you down and into the house. Do you understand?"

"Of course I understand," she said. Her frown turned indignant when she tried to repeat what he had told her word for word. "I'm going to sit down and climb you into the house.'

Daniel grinned. "That's right. You just sit right there. You can climb me into the house just as soon as I get down from here and come around to your side to help you."

"Just as soon as you get around my help," she repeated with a firm nod that made her eyes roll from the resulting dizziness.

Testing, Daniel slowly let go of her shoulders and waited to see if she was going to slump forward and fall out of the seat onto the floor. When she did not, he eased himself out of the seat, careful not to jar the carriage, afraid she might strike her head on the iron cross bar in front of her or crack her chin on the hard, wooden flooring.

He was relieved when the carriage did not jolt as

his weight eased out of it. But while he rounded the back of the carriage, he noticed it move suddenly, and when he hurried on around to her side of the conveyance, he was relieved to find she had merely sagged sideways onto her right shoulder and had curled up on the narrow seat, using the padded armrest for a pillow. He wondered just how much wine she'd managed to put away! William must have kept himself extremely busy refilling her glass to encourage such a fine stupor.

"Virginia, sit up," he said while he tried to push her back off the seat into a sitting position.

"I am," she protested and stiffened her back momentarily, but continued to try to lie back down.

He chuckled as he again considered leaving her there. He would bring her a blanket, of course, and possibly a pillow. He chuckled a little louder when he considered what her reaction would be to wake up in the front seat of a carriage instead of her own bed. But he knew he could not do that. "Come on, Virginia. Sit up and scoot over here so I can help you down."

Slowly, Virginia did as she was told, blinking hard as she tried to stay awake and focus on Daniel.

"Come on, a little bit more this direction, then I can help you safely down."

Virginia smiled. "Thank you, Daniel."

He smiled back. At least she realized who she was talking to. "I'm going to lift you out now," he cautioned, so she would not be alarmed when he put his hands beneath her arms and pull her toward him.

"But I can get out by myself," she told him, and to show just how capable she was of doing just that, she stood up on shaky legs, bumping her head

238

against the top bar of the carriage. She grimaced while she rubbed the sore spot, then grinned again. "I think I grew."

Realizing she was not going to remember much of tonight anyway, he grabbed her by her waist and hauled her immediately out of the carriage, bringing her body firmly against his while he slid her slowly to the ground.

Virginia's eyes opened wide as she let her arms come to rest around his strong neck. "Thank you," she murmured again, but a tiny hiccup caused her to have to bring one of her hands away from his neck to lightly cover her mouth. " 'Scuse me."

They both waited motionless to see if she was going to hiccup again. Then, when she was certain another hiccup was not going to follow, she took her hand away from her mouth and put it right back behind his neck, an action that surprised Daniel. She smiled at him again, a comical smile that seemed to be connected to her lovely eyebrows somehow, because every time she managed to curl her lips upward, her eyebrows arched.

"You know what?" she asked. Her smile faded while she concentrated on whatever it was she had decided needed to be said.

"No, what?" he asked in return, finding that he was just as unwilling to break apart as she seemed to be. He gazed longingly at her parted, upturned mouth and at the way her dark hair had long since come loose and now fell in simmering soft curls about her neck and shoulders. With her eyelids lowered heavily — despite her ridiculously arched eyebrows — and with a faint blush to her fair cheeks, she looked incredibly enticing.

"Sometimes you are so nice that I forget not to

239

like you."

Daniel's brow furrowed at such an odd statement, but then his expression slowly relaxed; he realized the liquor was muddling her tongue as it had when she'd decided she was going to have to climb him into the house. Using her own phrasing, he asked, "And have you forgotten not to like me now?"

She stared at him a long moment as if his words had confused even her, then smiled and reached a finger to his lips. "You are so handsome for someone like you."

His hold tightened around her and her smile turned into a look of deep contentment, as if she had suddenly remembered having tasted something extremely satisfying, something she would always savor. He wondered if she might be remembering one of their previous kisses but quickly dismissed the thought, for she had quickly let her poor opinion of his kiss be known that night in her room. It was her bitter rejection of his kiss that had made him decide to go directly back to Jefferson before he did something to drive her right out of his life and out of Mary's life as well. He had not wanted to risk that.

Still staring curiously at Daniel's lips, Virginia slowly brought her fingertip away from his mouth and pressed it against her own, then closed her eyes.

Daniel could not bear the significance of that and immediately placed his lips on hers. With the hunger of a starved man, he tasted the sweet depths of her mouth, darting the tip of his tongue between her still parted lips as he carefully teased the sensitive inner edges of her mouth. Her shuddering response only made him want to show her more of

240

what he could do to please her and he pulled her closer.

Virginia's arms tightened instinctively around his neck and she returned his kiss with complete abandon, matching his hungry desire with her own deep hunger. His hands quickly moved to run an uncharted course over the gentle bumps along her slender spine, seeking and exploring every curve and contour he could find, from her feminine, soft shoulders to her rounded hips. To his delight she allowed her own hands a similar freedom.

Virginia was overcome with unfamiliar passions that she knew came to life only at Daniel's behest. Slowly her arms left his neck, seemingly under their own will—or maybe it was his. She caressed the strong muscles along his wide shoulders and upper back which moved wondrously beneath her fingertips; then she brought her searching hands farther down to explore the sturdy, hard curve of his back and his taut, lean, ever-so-masculine hips.

Even through his clothing she could feel the gentle warmth of his skin, the power and firmness of his body, so different from her own. She marveled at that difference and wondered at God's mastery.

Although the ground beneath her continued to move, she felt strangely secure in Daniel's arms and was able to give his ardent kiss her undivided attention as his body pressed against hers. How wondrous that body was to touch! How very different it felt from anything else she had touched before. Even Mark, who worked long, hard hours in the fields and in his small dairy, had not felt quite so strong or all-powerful.

The afternoon she and Mark went arm-in-arm to the creek to find Jessie and Mary, she realized how much sturdier he felt, now that he was all grown up; but even that realization seemed paltry compared to the incredible power she now sensed in Daniel. Never had she felt such intense, raw strength—and never had she wanted so much to fall prey to such an undeniable force.

The world continued to spin as Daniel's kiss deepened and his arms held her pressed against his body. But Virginia still sensed no real danger; in fact, she felt oddly secure. She knew that if her legs failed her again, she would not have to worry about falling to the ground, which she remembered having done before.

Though she was unsure just where she had been when she fell, she knew she was safe now. Daniel was seeing to it that she stayed on her feet. How odd to feel so very safe in Daniel's arms—in the arms of a Pearson. Odder still, the fact that he *was* a Pearson no longer seemed to matter. All that mattered was the devouring kiss he'd chosen to bestow upon her and the heavenly feelings aroused deep inside her—deep inside both of them.

Able to concentrate on but one thing at a time, Virginia did not bother to wonder what such a passionate kiss might eventually lead to or what the consequences would be. She merely savored the tantalizing sensations that rippled through her, teasing first her spine, then her legs, her fingertips, and toes, until it returned to circle through all over again. Finally the feeling began to settle in the center of her abdomen.

Her heart throbbed with such ferocity that she could feel it pulsating in her chest, along her neck, and at her temples. Any hostility she'd once harbored for this man seemed to be gone, washed away by a warm tide of passion. All she wanted now was to be kissed again and again. She wanted to know more of the pleasure that had so completely overtaken her senses — know more of the bewildering chaos only Daniel could arouse within her.

The same strange warmth she felt when he kissed her once again invaded her senses unannounced. It spread through her body like a hot mist and left her feeling even more lightheaded than before. She felt so weak that if he'd not had such a strong hold on her, she was certain she'd have fallen to the ground.

What *was* the strange power Daniel Pearson had in his kiss? she wondered as she leaned harder against him. How had he learned to use it so effectively? *Practice.* He had to have had years of practice. But for some reason that thought did not upset her; it only helped to make muddled sense of what she was feeling.

Slowly the pressure of Daniel's mouth and tongue grew more insistent, and Virginia felt her head tilt further back in response, giving him immediate access to the sensitive skin along her ivory throat. The tiny, nipping kisses he moved to place there brought her still more dizzying pleasure and sent a white-hot fire coursing through her until she was certain she would burst aflame with her own desire. Finally she felt compelled to moan aloud from the sheer tingling ecstasy that consumed her.

Virginia was filled with a burning desire, yet an icy little shiver darted downward along her spine whenever his tongue came into contact with the more sensitive areas along her neck and collarbone. The contrast of the shivers against the burning heat of her newly awakened passion caused her skin to prickle and come alive. She wanted more. She

243

moaned again.

While he continued to lavish kisses along her throat and collarbone, dipping lower and lower, his hand moved to undo the buttons between her breasts, buttons that had been placed more for fashion than function, for there were other, more useful buttons which ran along the back of her dress; but Daniel's interest was only in the tiny pearl buttons at the front, where her breasts were straining to be free.

One by one he undid the tiny, white fasteners until the bodice was open and he could see her lacy camisole. Beneath the sheer white fabric he could already make out the splendid shape of her jutting young breasts, and his desire for her grew until he felt he could not bear the heat of it. When he reached inside to caress one of her exquisite breasts with his hand, he marveled at the feel of her rapid heartbeat beneath his fingertips. And when she showed no resistance, he brought up his other hand and quickly slipped it beneath the satin of her dress to untie one side of the camisole, tugging the thin, white material down so he could finally see that which he had just touched.

He stared at her then, at the splendid shape of the straining breast in his hand, at the way her head remained tilted back, her lips still parted, her eyes still closed. She was at last overpowered by the many desires he had awakened in her, eager to know more, to experience more. Daniel knew then he wanted to bed her more than he had ever wanted to bed any woman. He wanted to carry her inside, undress her slowly and completely, then discover exactly what pleasures she might hold in store for him. But he was too aware of her innocence, too aware of the fact that she was responding with such inhibition because she had drunk too much wine. Had she been fully sober when he first kissed her, she would have pulled away by now, enraged with him for having tried to take the kiss so far; he was certain of it. And he knew it would be wrong to take advantage of her in her present state of mind — or lack of one. But still it was tempting. *Damned* tempting.

When his lips did not immediately return to cover hers, Virginia's face twisted into an impatient frown, but she did not open her eyes right away. Her breathing was very rapid, causing her breasts to rise and fall in a most enticing way. Her desire was still very obvious in the way she arched her back, as if she sensed that would help him to remember what it was he had been doing, but instead of continuing to pursue their pleasures, Daniel pulled her camisole back into place. He tugged the satin dress front together again but did not bother to button it, then gently scooped her into his arms.

She offered no protest while he carried her easily up the steps and across the veranda to the back door. He barely managed to get the door open without having to set her on her feet again, and then he carried her down the corridor to her room and her bed. Keeping a firm hold on his desire to take up where he'd left off outside, he quickly undressed her until all she wore were her drooping white camisole and bloomers, then quickly put her to bed. After gazing at her a moment more, aware her breathing had slowed back to normal — though his had not — he knew he had to get out of there. He kissed her lightly on her cheek, then again on her lips.

"Sweet dreams," he said as he gently lifted her hair away from her angelic face, then muttered something about her damnable state of intoxication just before he turned and left the room.

Virginia had heard his voice, but not his words. She smiled contentedly as she turned, hugging a pillow to her breast, and went right back to sleep, blissfully unaware of how close she'd come to losing her maidenly innocence to the man whom she was supposed to hate the most.

While Daniel strode down the corridor to go upstairs to his own room, he wondered just how much Virginia would remember, come morning. For both their sakes, he hoped it would prove to be nothing more than a blur, a faded spot in her memory that would never fully reveal itself to her. She would be outraged to realize the extent to which he had taken advantage of her inebriation and he knew she would have every right.

The fact that in the end he'd turned away without taking full advantage of the situation would not do much to quell her anger; he knew that. And in a way, he was angry with himself for having allowed it to go as far as it had. But he then had to smile, because at the same time he was angry with himself for what he'd done, he wished he'd not been so suddenly overcome by such a confounded stroke of decency. He'd loved to have taken her to the most lofty heights of passion and show her what being a woman was really all about.

Chapter Fourteen

The cheerful sound of a mockingbird chattering away just outside her bedroom windows brought Virginia slowly awake. Turning toward the sound, she breathed deeply the fresh scent of morning, then opened her eyes against the bright sunshine of another cloudless summer day.

Quickly she brought both her hands up and pressed them gently over her tender eyelids; they did not seem to bring her eyes much relief from the overwhelming glare. Slowly the sharp pain that had so suddenly pierced her head began to subside, until all that remained was a gentle throb. Reluctantly she took her hands away, then eased her eyelids open again, one at a time, until she could make out her surroundings enough to realize she was indeed back in her bedroom.

She forced her gaze back to the light streaming in through the window. Not only was it bright and beautiful outside; the birds were singing merrily and butterflies flitted about from fading flower to fading flower on the large, climbing rosebush which grew along a white trestle near her window. A gentle breeze brought with it the delicate scent of the roses still clinging to the bush, even though it was already mid-July, and along with it came the scent of freshly cut grass. It all seemed rather disgusting to a person who felt so near her death.

Massaging her temples and forehead with light circular motions, she continued to squint curiously at the window, thinking there was something decidedly wrong with what she saw. It was then that she realized how little direct sunlight spilled onto the floor, as was usually the case when she awoke. A quick glance at the clock revealed why: it was almost noon; the sun was already well overhead.

Moaning softly, Virginia laid her throbbing head back on the pillow and closed her eyes again while she tried to reason why she'd slept so late, and why the top of her head had started to pound the minute she'd tried to sit. Though she could remember going to the party with Daniel and having been pushed aside with Amanda's older brother, William, her actual departure from that party was very much a blur. But while she lay there thinking about it, she began to remember just enough to make her cringe with embarrassment.

She had acted like a wanton fool last night — first with William and then with Daniel. Everything was still a little hazy in her memory, but she clearly remembered having been kissed thoroughly by them both. Though William's kiss was the easier to recall for some reason, she was very much aware that

248

William's kisses had proved dull and lifeless compared with Daniel's, which were arousing. Her heart fluttered to life at the mere realization that Daniel had indeed kissed her again last night, though she was not quite sure when or where, and the rapid increase in her heartbeat caused her head to ache worse until she finally quit trying to remember so much.

It was bad enough just knowing she'd been caught in the garden alone with William. Suddenly she remembered where William's hand had been when Daniel had come bounding out of nowhere. Her temples pounded harder when she tried to recall anything else. But her next truly coherent thought was the fact that Daniel had been angry with her for what she had done—very angry—and with sound reason; but he had kissed her anyway. She wondered about that, then became horrified when she realized how he had probably hoped to take up where William had left off, since she had proved so willing. *Willing?* Misery overwhelmed her. *Drunk* is what she'd been; frogged out of her mind; no better than the trollops in the town saloon.

Mortified, she rolled her head to one side and looked down at where she remembered William's hand had gone. That was when she noticed she was not in a nightdress, as she should be—she was still in her bloomers and camisole, one side of which was not even tied. What had happened? She tried to remember, but everything after they'd left the party seemed to have a vague, dreamlike quality to it. She was sure Daniel had kissed her . . . but what else had happened? Just what liberties had he taken with her? She gasped; she sensed that whatever had happened between them, she had been extremely willing.

What must Daniel think? She covered her burning cheeks with her hands. She dreaded having to face him after her wanton behavior, to hear the cruel accusations that were sure to follow, along with her harsh dismissal, for a woman of such loose morals should not be a teacher of young children—and she fully agreed. She felt she should go to him immediately and tell him that, facing the consequences of what she had done. But she still was not sure exactly what had happened, and although she knew she would eventually have to face those bitter consequences, she could not bring herself to face Daniel yet. Not after what she had allowed to happen. Instead she decided to stay in her room, out of his sight, to nurse her throbbing head and tend to her shattered pride for the rest of the day.

It was Sunday, or so she hoped. She would not have to leave her room all day nor risk a confrontation with Daniel until she herself had come to terms with it all. Nor would she have to worry about teaching class until the next morning, that is, if she felt she still deserved to be a teacher. When Lizzie came to see why she had missed breakfast, which she was almost certain to do, she would explain that she was a bit under the weather and politely ask Lizzie to bring her meals to her room.

Virginia's stomach coiled into a tight knot and she tried to swallow back the rising ache. On second thought, she would skip that day's meals altogether. Turning her face from the window, she shaped the pillow beneath her head until she felt the least amount of pain, then took one of her other pillows and plopped it soundly over her head, burying herself in blessed darkness, praying sleep would quickly reclaim her, before she could remember more than she was ready to. But much to her chagrin, Lizzie's knock sounded just as she was about to drift off into sweet oblivion.

"Missy, can I come in?" she heard through the closed door.

"Yes," she responded, her voice almost a croak.

"When you wasn't in for breakfast, I started to worry about you," Lizzie said. "I've brought you a tray of buttered toast with blackberry jam and a cup of hot chocolate."

Virginia groaned at the thought of food. "Thank you, but I'm not feeling very well."

"What did you say?" Lizzie asked, lifting the pillow from Virginia's head just enough to see her tightly closed eyelids and hear her words more clearly.

"I said, thank you for thinking of me, but I'm not feeling very well."

"Where's it hurt?" Lizzie wanted to know as she reached beneath the pillow to feel Virginia's forehead: warm, but no fever. Lizzie frowned and crossed her arms while she studied Virginia's pale cheeks and compressed eyelids.

"My head . . . it feels like it's about to break wide open," Virginia said frankly. She tried to open her eyes, but the smell of food that now filled the room made her feel nauseated, and her arms moved to grip her churning stomach. "Please, just go away and let me die in peace."

"Can't do that," Lizzie said with a chuckle. She'd seen Master Daniel in just such a state many times and knew only too well that Miss Virginia had had herself a little too much to drink at Miss Amanda's party. "Got to keep you alive so Miss Mary can continue with her lessons."

"She can always get a new teacher after I'm dead and gone," Virginia moaned.

"Wouldn't be too easy for Master Daniel to get hisself a new teacher for tutorin' Miss Mary if it were to get out that the last teacher died tryin'," Lizzie said. She patted Virginia's arm reassuringly. "I'm goin' to go get you somethin' that will make you feel a whole lot better. You just lie there and take it easy till I get back."

"That's a promise," Virginia muttered just before she pulled the pillow back down over her head, savoring the darkness.

When Lizzie returned only minutes later, Virginia lifted the edge of her pillow and peeked out. The woman had a tall glass of something that looked suspiciously like dishwater in her hand and demanded that Virginia sit up and drink it down.

It was the last thing Virginia wanted to do. "Just set it beside the bed there. I'll drink it later." Weakly she lifted her hand and waved it toward the bedside table.

"Come now, Missy—sit up and drink this down."

"Lizzie, if I were to drink that now, it would not be likely to stay down, and you would have a huge mess to clean up."

"I'm prepared for that," Lizzie assured her. She

252

set a large bowl and a damp rag on the bed and slowly pulled the pillow off Virginia's head.

Virginia squinted up at Lizzie's determined face, then at the glass, then at the stoneware bowl that lay beside her. "Do I have to?" The question brought back memories of how her grandmother had had to cajole her into taking her medicine whenever she was sick as a child.

"Now!" Lizzie said sternly, holding out the murky concoction.

Surprised by her tone of voice, Virginia accepted the glass. Then, holding her nose, she drank about half of it.

"Can that be enough?" she asked in a comical voice.

"All of it," Lizzie said firmly.

With a contorted expression, Virginia drank it all down. When she let go of her nose, the horrid aftertaste struck her and she grimaced a protest as she ran her tongue across her teeth, hoping somehow to scrape the foul taste from her mouth. As she slowly sank back onto her pillow, she muttered, "I hope you realize my death will weigh heavy on your conscience for years to come."

Lizzie merely smiled, then moved the bowl to the nearest table. "I know you don't really want to hear this now, but you're goin' to live." Then chuckling softly to herself, she turned and left the room, the empty glass in her hand.

Whatever Lizzie had made Virginia drink, it had oddly enough settled her stomach and eased her throbbing head; it was possible for her to sleep peacefully for several hours. When she awoke again,

253

it was late afternoon, and this time when she sat up, the brightness outside her window did not hurt her eyes. Though her temples still seemed tender to the touch, she was amazed to discover she was pretty well cured.

She still had no intention of leaving the room. She decided to get dressed, knowing Lizzie would soon be in to try to get her to eat a little supper. As she brushed her hair and pulled it back with a brightly colored ribbon, she realized she was actually starting to feel hungry and just might be able to tolerate a piece of toast and a sip or two of cool tea.

She felt much better once she was dressed in a comfortable cotton blouse and linen skirt, her hair brushed and pulled away from her face. She went into her sitting room and settled onto a sofa near the windows to wait for Lizzie's return. Glancing at the clock, she realized it had been almost eighteen hours since she had eaten last, and then it was mainly to pick at food while she kept a keen eye on Daniel and Amanda.

Suddenly, at the memory of them together, her appetite was gone again. She tried to push all thoughts of last evening from her mind and searched for something that would do just that.

From where she sat she could view the gardens, the coach house, and one side of the barn. Giving her surroundings more of her attention in the hopes that last night's escapades would stop plaguing her, she smiled when she noticed Pete and Jack come out of the barn, headed for the coach house. They stopped halfway, flailed their arms about wildly, as

254

if in another of their heated discussions, then turned around and went right back into the barn. She wondered what the argument had been about that time and if Daniel was out there to help calm them down before it came to blows, as it sometimes did.

It was the sudden, unbidden thought of Daniel that brought another deep wave of humiliation to her. Though she was still not sure exactly what had happened between them, she was still not up to facing him yet; but knew she would have to before long. She knew she could no longer stay at Valley Oaks as Mary's teacher . . . not after last night. She should never have let things get out of hand — first with William, then with Daniel. Her actions were not only inexcusable; they had ruined everything. Without some link to Valley Oaks, she would never be able to find out what it was Caleb had done to her grandfather. And she would never get Valley Oaks back.

Saddened, she looked out the window again. As her gaze swept the perfectly kept grounds, she realized just how very much she was going to miss Valley Oaks and the people working there, like Pete and Jack, whom she had reluctantly come to accept as friends. She would also miss her nightly conversations with Daniel — even the bickering that was so often a result of those nightly discussions. But still she must leave, and it was her own fault. True, he was the one who had kissed her first; but she had not stopped him. She was the one who had drunk far too much wine. And, as she recalled her great-aunt telling her on more than one occasion, *it's the man's place to try and the woman's place to stop him.*

She could not remember ever having tried to stop him, and she was almost certain she'd encouraged him instead. The sooner she went and told him she would voluntarily resign, the better. That way she could at least spare herself the final humiliation of being told to leave, and having to hear him voice all the reasons why. Oh, how she dreaded facing him after what she had done . . . almost as much as she dreaded telling Mary good-bye!

But it had to be done.

Gathering her courage, Virginia stood and walked to the door. She paused after she had opened it and stepped out of her room, trying to decide where Daniel would be just now. Noticing then that the library door was partially open, she realized he would be in there.

On legs that felt as if they would fold beneath her, she walked toward that door, pressing her hand against it. Bravely, she walked through it.

Daniel had not heard her as he sat behind his desk staring idly at an empty whiskey glass. Both his hands lay curled on either side of it. Beside his right hand was a tall, angular, cut-glass bottle which was just half-full, the top lying at its base. With his head bent and his lost expression, it appeared that he might be wrestling with his conscience; Virginia could well guess why.

"Daniel?" she breathed, barely audible. She paused to clear her throat.

To her surprise, he seemed delighted to see her. With a quick wave of his hand he motioned to a leather chair opposite his desk. "Virginia . . . come in; sit down."

She stepped forward but did not know what to say. She had not expected such a congenial welcome. She felt suddenly wary of his good mood.

Daniel stood when she entered the room, and with a barely concealed grin he gestured to the bottle. "Would you care for something to drink? It doesn't have to be whiskey. Perhaps a little *wine?*" When Virginia stood frozen there with no retort, he shrugged and his grin widened, his dimples carved well into his cheeks. "No?"

"No," she replied flatly, then added in a sarcastic tone, *"Thank you."* He was obviously making sport of her, and though she had been prepared to hear his cold accusations—to be told how terribly unfit she was to be a teacher—she had not expected him to be so cavalier about her dismal situation.

"Come—sit down . . . make yourself comfortable," he went on as he came around the desk. He tilted his head to study her and his thick dark hair fell across his forehead, giving him a rakish appearance.

"If you don't mind, I'd rather stand to say what I've come to say."

"And what might that be?" he asked, then leaned forward as if extremely eager to hear it.

His nearness made it that much harder for her to speak. She looked away for a moment, but found the courage to face him when finally she spoke. "I've come to give you my notice. I'll be leaving in the morning. I just need enough time to pack my trunks."

"Why?"

"You know very well why. After last night, I—we—I—well, I simply can't stay on as Mary's teacher, that's all. After what happened between us, I think it would be better for everyone if I left."

"You were drunk," he stated bluntly, to which she sucked in a deep breath. But before she could comment, he went on. "And to be quite frank, I wasn't too sober myself. Let's just forget it ever happened."

"But what if something like that should happen again? I'm a single woman, and you—"

"Do you *want* to leave? Don't you care about Mary?" he asked suddenly.

"You know I care about Mary! I love her dearly! And I hate the thought of having to leave her."

"Then marry me," he stated, so calmly and casually that she felt certain she had misunderstood him.

"What?"

"Marry me. That way you'll have no reason to leave. My daughter needs you. She is just starting to open up to you, and as a result she is starting to open up to me. You've made all the difference in the world to her . . . you can't desert her now. She's suffered far too many disappointments in her short life. If you leave her now, I honestly doubt she'd ever get over it."

"Marry you? You mean be your wife?"

"That's generally how it works."

"You want me to be your *wife?*" Virginia was so stunned she had to reach out and grasp a chair for support. Marry Daniel? Marry a Pearson? Her? An

Elder? She couldn't. No, never . . . never would she consider such a thing . . . and yet. . . .

"Yes, Virginia—marry me. Become my wife. Make Valley Oaks your home forever. Just think of it: you'll be the wife of a very rich man, you will want for nothing, and you'll be mother to a little girl who loves you and needs you."

Make Valley Oaks your home. Those had been the magic words that caught her attention. Mary did seem to love and need her; and she, in turn, so dearly loved the child and worried about her. "But what about Amanda?"

"No, I don't think Amanda will ever love you, nor will she ever have any real need for you, especially now."

Virginia sighed with exasperation while she studied Daniel's half-serious, half-amused expression. "Isn't she supposed to be the one you ask to marry you?"

"She's not exactly what I want in a wife. Besides, you already told me how Mary hates her. Mary would much rather have you for her mother, and you'd be better for her. So: what do you think? I'd be a generous husband, I assure you. And I'd ask very little of you in return." He was solemn.

"But marriages aren't made like this. You don't simply jump headlong into something as permanent as marriage. It doesn't make sense." Her face was twisted in bewilderment.

"I assure you, it does. Lots of marriages are made with far less reason than a child's need. I suppose you would be happier if I offered you a lot of ridiculous talk about love; but I can't. Whatever else I may be, I'm not a liar.

"I'm incapable of feeling love. You may as well know that from the start. I will admit I desire you as I've desired no one, and I truly enjoy having you around; but love will never enter into it. I simply cannot feel love — not anymore."

Not anymore? Virginia wondered if having lost his wife eight months before had anything to do with such an angry and bitter attitude about love. Had he been more affected by his wife's death than he had let on? Was he really telling her that she could never hope to replace his first wife in his heart? Could she possibly marry a man knowing there would never be love between them?

Already it had occurred to her that such a marriage would fulfill her quest to recapture her stolen heritage: an Elder would once again call Valley Oaks home. And any future descendents of the Elder clan would have claim to what was rightfully theirs. Descendents? Children? Yes, of course, if she married him, he would expect that right. . . .

"I happen to feel a clear understanding is better than all that romantic nonsense," he stated, cutting into her thoughts.

He waited expectantly, but when she seemed too lost in thought to reply, he asked, "Don't tell me you are hesitant because of that farmer of yours. You and Langford haven't discussed getting married or anything like that, have you? Because even if you have, he might not feel the same way about it once he learns about what almost happened between us last night."

Almost? Relief washed over her, but at the same time she could not help but wonder how close "almost" was in this case.

"No, Mark and I have not discussed marriage," she answered honestly, though she knew that was what Mark had been hoping for ever since her return. "But I know this is going to hurt him deeply."

"Then your answer is yes?"

She paused, thinking about Mary. By marrying Daniel she would prevent Amanda from ever being able to manipulate a proposal from him. She thought of her vow to get Valley Oaks back and of how she had failed to do that; then she considered the passion she felt for Daniel and how it would mean never having to leave—something that was becoming more and more important to her. And there was more: as Daniel's wife, no rooms would remain locked to her. She would know about all the secret drawers, all the hidden safes. If there was some sort of information that would finally reveal what Caleb had done to her grandfather, she would have a better chance of coming across it as Daniel's wife.

Finally Virginia closed her eyes, fully realizing that she was about to commit her entire life to a man who clearly could never love her. It destroyed any hope of ever having the type of marriage she'd always dreamed of. Yet she clearly spoke the words he seemed to want to hear.

"My answer is yes." She did not open her eyes again until she had taken a long, deep breath.

Daniel smiled and clasped his hands. "Good. Sit down and let's talk about this further."

Feeling numb, Virginia took the chair he had

indicated and sat, still somewhat dazed, while he began to discuss their plans, as if they had just struck some sort of business agreement. She found it difficult to listen to what he had to say.

"And I promise not to try to consummate the marriage in any way without having discussed it with you first and secured your verbal agreement."

Virginia could feel herself blushing, but said nothing. Though she wanted children and wanted Valley Oaks for them, she did not want to think about the intimacy she would have to share with Daniel in order to have those children. Nor did she want to consider the fact that her children would have the hated Pearson name. Not now . . . not when her resolve was still a little too shaky, her nerves a little too taut.

Daniel did not seem to sense her discomfort. "Although I do hope to have more children one day, it will happen at your discretion. But in return for such a consideration, I will want you to agree to do what you can to make the marriage appear as normal and proper as possible to outsiders. No one is to know of the circumstances that led to our marriage . . . no one."

Virginia agreed readily. Not only would it assure her that he would not force his affections on her; she would not have to worry about what people might think of it all. As far as she was concerned, it was better that people thought their marriage normal, and she quickly told him so.

Daniel's voice remained emotionless while he continued to shape their agreement into something practical, something they both could live with. If not for the glimmer of excitement in his pale blue eyes, she would never have guessed he was actually pleased with their agreement.

"I will provide you with the finest clothes, furs, jewelry, and whatever else you feel will make you happy, and in return you will fulfill the duties of official hostess to any business dinners, picnics, or special parties that are held here. You are to act as a wife should whenever *anyone* else is present—even Lizzie. In turn, I will behave as a doting husband should. It will mean we will share the same bedroom, but once we are alone, whether we use the bed as husband and wife will be up to you." He bent forward to get a better look at her stunned expression. "But most important, you will treat Mary as if she had been born your own daughter."

Virginia reassured him. "Becoming a mother to Mary is the best part of the whole bargain."

Daniel frowned at her use of the word *bargain* but made no disagreeable comment. "Then it's settled. We'll be married the first weekend in August."

"But that's only weeks away!" she protested, wishing to delay the inevitable as long as she could. "Don't you think it would seem more appropriate to have a longer engagement?"

"And give you time to back out? No. The bargain, as you put it, has been struck. I see no reason not to continue with our plans."

He glanced, then, at the clock on the bookcase behind him. Virginia's gaze followed; she was surprised to see that two hours had passed since she'd first entered the room.

"I see we've both missed supper." He frowned

thoughtfully. "Mary will be in bed by now. Shall we go on up and tell her the good news, or wait till tomorrow?"

"She's probably asleep," Virginia answered quickly, hoping to put off anything that would make this sudden decision seem so . . . final. There were things about it she still wanted to think through more carefully. "Let's wait until morning."

Sensing her reluctance, Daniel's eyes narrowed. "In the morning we *will* tell her." Then he crossed his arms defiantly, making his intentions all the more clear.

Chapter Fifteen

That night, by the time Virginia had left the library, Daniel seemed satisfied with the plans they had made and everything appeared set for a small wedding the first weekend in August. But after she'd returned to her bedroom and gotten ready for bed, she became acutely aware she did not feel the euphoria a future bride was supposed to feel, none of the giddiness she had always hoped to experience. Instead it felt as if she were suddenly facing her doom, as if she had unwittingly sentenced herself to a life of bitter imprisonment.

Though she wanted nothing more than to lose herself in sleep, slumber evaded her for most of the night. Her thoughts twisted and tumbled over everything that had transpired in the library hours earlier. Nothing about any of it really made sense to her, now that she was away from him, though she wasn't sure it had made sense even when she had been with him.

Why would Daniel want to marry someone he did not love? Was Mary's happiness really so important to him, important enough to sacrifice his own? Or could it be he actually did care for her and felt they would be happy enough? At least he had said he enjoyed her company. And she already knew how much she enjoyed his—even when they were arguing or finding fault with one another. She had missed him dreadfully those weeks he'd been away . . . that accounted for something; but it wasn't love, nor was it enough to base a marriage on. Now she wondered if getting Valley Oaks back and avenging the wrong done to her grandparents made it worth entering into a loveless marriage. Why had she been willing to agree to such a thing?

Virginia continued to try to make sense of his sudden decision to marry her and of her own sudden agreement to the plan, but the more she tried to reason it out, the less sense it made. Although she did finally manage to drift off to sleep in the wee hours of the morning, she awoke tired and with a heavy heart, wondering if she should not save them both a lot of grief and simply call the whole thing off before anyone else could find out about it.

For though the marriage might benefit Mary in the long run, and should they ever have children, Virginia would be getting Valley Oaks back into the hands of the Elder clan, she was going to

266

ruin her life, forever tied to a man who could never love her. She had always hoped she'd fall hopelessly and endlessly in love with someone someday, finding the sort of love that made women swoon and brought men to their knees . . . the sort of love they wrote books about. How she wished there could be that sort of love . . . but there couldn't; not if she married Daniel. He'd made that clear. Besides, he was a Pearson; she would not allow herself to fall in love with a Pearson. It would be the same as renouncing everything that her grandmother'd ever done for her.

Virginia lay in bed unmoving. The more she thought about it all, the more she wanted to convince Daniel to forget the whole thing. Glancing at the clock and seeing it was almost time to wake Mary, she hurried to get dressed. She needed to speak to Daniel before Mary came out of her bedroom. She must explain to him that she had changed her mind. Marriage to a man who could never love her, who she was not in love with, was out of the question, despite the attractive benefits.

Quickly she slipped into a mint green cotton dress with a fitted bodice and wide flouncing skirts and took only enough time to brush her hair back away from her face. She had no time to put it up into a neat twist or even to find a ribbon and tie it back. Mary would be coming out of her room any minute now, she had to hurry.

Virginia had just set the hairbrush down on her dresser and turned to leave the room when her door burst open and Mary came bouncing in, so completely thrilled about something that she'd forgotten all about knocking.

"Miss Virginia! You're going to be my mother!" the child squealed, excited to tears while she rushed to throw her arms around Virginia's slender waist. "I can hardly believe it! I am so happy."

Virginia felt her insides ache. She pulled Mary's arms away from her and knelt down with every intention of explaining her change of heart, only to have the child's arms flung quickly around her neck instead. The embrace touched her heart. When she could finally speak, her voice was weak, barely audible, even to herself. "I gather your father has already told you."

"Oh, yes!" Mary said as she lifted a hand away from Virginia's neck to wipe a shining tear from her bright blue eyes, eyes so very like her father's. "Yes! Yes! I can't wait until you are married, until you are my very own mother. I love you. I really do!"

Virginia closed her eyes and hugged the child to her, pressing her cheek against the girl's soft, light brown tresses. While she held Mary she realized she would never have the heart to tell the child she'd changed her mind—not after seeing such a precious glimmer of joy in her wide blue eyes. Virginia could never destroy the girl's sudden hope of finding true happiness again, and she smiled as love radiated from the girl, warming her to the depths of her heart.

Virginia knew then that she would go through with it; she would marry Daniel. She knew she would never receive any love from her husband, but she was certain to be awarded ample doses from Mary. She would be also getting Valley Oaks for her children. And she would have a better opportunity to discover what it was Caleb had done to her grandfather.

It was also mostly for Mary's sake that Virginia acted the part of the blushing bride-to-be during the busy weeks that followed. With no show of resistance, Virginia let Lizzie and Mrs. Akard fuss all they wanted over her gown, and she allowed Mary to help with the planning of both the wedding and the small reception, at least as much as Lizzie would allow. Lizzie was so intent on seeing to everything herself that she unwittingly left everyone one else out of the planning — Virginia's opinions were rarely sought and Mary's opinions were usually ignored.

Virginia was content to stay out of it; it didn't really feel as if it was her wedding, anyway. The wedding was for Daniel. He was the one who had insisted on a proper ceremony . . . he and Lizzie. And they were the ones who made all the decisions, even about what flowers to use. When, the following Friday, Lizzie had come to her with Daniel's approved wedding list to ask for her approval, it surprised Virginia a little.

"I thought Daniel had already decided these were the people he wanted to attend," Virginia said quizzically.

"He has, but you are the bride," Lizzie stated, as if Virginia might somehow have forgotten. "You need to approve the invitation list as well."

"I'm sure the two of you have thought of everyone who should be included," Virginia said with a shrug, not really caring. But she took the list and looked at it anyway.

To her dismay, it was rather long. She had expected a small ceremony, since it was to be held at Valley Oaks. Daniel had actually used the word *small* whenever he referred to the reception.

"Can we fit all these people in the main salon?" she asked doubtfully while she quickly tried to calculate how many names there were.

"Oh, sure, once most of the furniture has been moved out, there'll be plenty of room. 'Course, only the ladies will sit; the men will stand," Lizzie explained. Then, to reassure her mistress further, she added, "Master Caleb used to have a fancy ball once a year, and more people than that would come."

Virginia raised an eyebrow. She'd never been aware that there'd been any balls at Valley Oaks. It was odd that such a rumor had not gone around. Curiously she looked at Lizzie and tried to judge how old the servant would have been back when Caleb had cheated her grandfather. It was hard to judge Lizzie's age. Whenever she laughed, she looked barely thirty, but when she frowned one of her deep, scowling frowns, she looked fifty. Virginia supposed she was somewhere between.

"Did you know Daniel's uncle very well?"

270

"No, he was a man who kept to hisself most of the time. Occasionally he would talk about things he thought needed to be talked about, but not often. He was a nice man, though, generous to his servants, but he was not very outgoin'. Liked to stay to his room a lot."

The moment Lizzie had said Caleb was a nice man, Virginia decided the woman must not have known Daniel's uncle even as much as she wanted to pretend, so she decided to drop her questioning. Any information Lizzie happened to give her about him would be unreliable . . . but then, Virginia was aware that until just before Caleb died, Lizzie and her mother had only been the man's housemaids. Another woman had been his main housekeeper.

She was also aware that there had been a cook and valet in Caleb's employ as well. She wondered why Daniel did not feel he needed as many servants. He could certainly afford it, but then, remembering Lizzie's attitude toward other people's meddling in what she clearly considered her affairs, Virginia could well guess why.

She glanced back at the long list. Most of the guests were people she'd never heard of, a majority of them from Jefferson and Shreveport and a few from New Orleans. One of the latter was Iris Pearson, no doubt his mother. Only a few other names seemed even vaguely familiar, but she could not quite place them. Perhaps she had met them at Amanda's party.

It embarrassed her a little to realize such people she could not recall would probably remember her

271

quite vividly. They would not likely forget how Daniel had come to her rescue in the garden. It would make for fine gossip once it was learned the two of them planned to be married.

"Does the list meet with your approval?" Lizzie asked, growing impatient with Virginia's lengthy perusal. "Moses is ready for Master Daniel to get the invitations made out so he can start delivering them."

Virginia shrugged. The only people she really knew personally were the Langfords. That's when she realized Amanda's and William's names were noticeably absent. She wondered about that and decided Daniel did not want to hurt her any more than he had to, though Amanda was undoubtedly going to be upset. In fact, she would be furious when she learned about the sudden wedding plans.

Still, Daniel probably felt there was no sense rubbing her nose in the fact he had not decided to marry her. Virginia wondered then what Amanda's response *would* be. A cold chill darted down her spine. Amanda was not going to sit idly by and let Daniel slip away from her again; Virginia was certain of it. There would be trouble from her. And if Virginia weren't so against his marrying Amanda, she would almost hope the woman *did* cause trouble—trouble enough to stop the wedding.

"Are there any names you wish to add?" Lizzie asked, breaking into Virginia's reverie again.

"I have no one to add," she answered honestly, almost regretfully. The truth was that many

272

people in town hardly knew her. She no longer wore her hair in tousled braids; her chin had long since healed of its numerous scrapes and bruises; her freckles had faded. Almost no one realized who she was—although a few had tried to decide why she looked so oddly familiar. And because they had not realized who she was, there was no reason to invite any of them. They were the same as strangers to her now, and if she married Daniel, they would have to remain strangers to her. They treated Daniel with the same contempt and abruptness they had shown Caleb.

Virginia realized, as she agreed to the list and handed it back to Lizzie, that she was to be married to a man who would never love her, in the company of a hundred and twenty people who did not know her. But at least the Langfords would be there. She felt a twinge of wonderment that Daniel had thought to include them. After all, he was clearly not fond of Mark, which was why she had not sought to invite the Langfords herself. She suspected he had done it for Mary's sake.

But the Langfords were still blissfully unaware of her decision to marry Daniel. Because the proposal had been sudden and unexpected, the plans had to be made quickly. Her gown was fitted and refitted to perfection, while Mary had to be kept occupied with her lessons to keep her well out of Lizzie's way. Virginia had barely had time to sleep and eat, much less think of Mark or how her marriage was going to affect him. Knowing the invitations were due to go out the very next day,

Virginia realized she could no longer put it off. She immediately rushed outside to find Daniel.

As she flew down the steps, she saw him in the yard, coming out of the wide barn door, going in the direction of the coach house. As he glanced up and saw her running toward him, her skirts raised enough to allow him a glimpse of her delicate ankles, he smiled curiously. The bright sunlight favored her shimmering dark hair, bringing out its amber highlights.

"Daniel, I have to have a carriage made ready right away," she said, breathless as much from her worry over Mark as from the physical exertion of having run so far so fast.

"Why?" His forehead furrowed with suspicion.

"I must go over to the Langfords, to explain to Mark about this marriage before their invitations are delivered."

"That won't be necessary; your farmer already knows all about it. I knew how busy you were, with all those fittings for you and Mary. So I went over there and explained the situation to him late yesterday."

"You *what?*" she gasped, infuriated that he'd taken it upon himself to do such a thing. Though she'd tried to stay on his good side these past few days, she could not help but show her outrage. "How dare you!"

"I felt he should know," Daniel said matter-of-factly, crossing his arms insolently.

"The Langfords are my friends. *My* friends," she said. She emphasized the fact by pressing her hand to her chest, which brought his attention to the moderately low cut of her turquoise dress. She bristled to realize where his gaze had so boldly gone. "And because they are *my* friends, you could have let *me* be the one to tell them about this in my own way. I can just imagine how you handled it — abrupt, to the point. I would have at least tried to explain it to them."

"And tell them what?" His eyes were back on her face, now narrowed with a dark undercurrent of emotions. "That you are actually marrying me for Mary's sake? No! I won't have anyone know that. And I *won't* have you going to visit your old beau, no matter what reason you come up with." He slammed his fist into the hard muscle of his thigh as his voice rose with a burst of fury. "You are going to be my wife. And because you are going to be my wife, you will leave your past loves behind. I know it was not discussed, but that has to be part of the bargain."

Virginia had never seen anyone so angry. His eyes narrowed to slits; they were cold as ice. The muscles in his jaw jumped from the fury he was barely able to contain. Fully fearing what he might do next, she pressed her hand to her throat in a reflexive action and carefully stepped away from him.

"And you are damn well not to see Mark Langford again." He stared at her, his angry gaze piercing right through her. He waited for a response, but when none came, he realized the fear evident on her face. He lowered his voice, then amended, "Unless I am at your side. Occasionally, we might pay a neighborly visit to your friends, because they are also Mary's friends, but we will do it as a family . . . do you understand?"

"Yes, sir," Virginia said with an indignant toss of her head, though her first inclination had actually been to tell him to go straight to hell. She continued to step back until she was several feet away, well out of range of whatever he might want to do to her. As the distance between them grew, she felt her courage returning.

Daniel's brow rose.

"Sir? You call the man you are about to marry *sir?"* he asked, a warning in his voice. "What if someone should overhear? Do you really think it sounds appropriate?"

"No," Virginia conceded, and for the first time in days, a smile played at her lips.

"No, what?" he prompted, just as she had expected him to.

"No, *ma'am,* I guess it is not appropriate. I shall try to refrain from the use of the word *sir* in the future."

Daniel's anger melted into amused laughter, which surprised Virginia.

"That's better," he said agreeably. Then, as if nothing had happened, he looped his arm around her shoulders and began to escort her back to the house. "Tell me . . . did Lizzie find time between her bickering with Mrs. Akard and deciding what to move out of the salon to prepare lunch?"

"I really don't know," Virginia admitted, then ventured to ask, "Daniel, don't you think we are asking an awful lot of her? Having her arrange everything for the wedding and still keep up with her regular duties, too?"

"As I recall, no one asked her anything," he said, still amused. "When she heard the word *wedding,* she just shoved everyone else aside and took over. I've offered to hire temporary help, but she refuses to let anyone have a hand in the actual planning, nor does she want anyone else tampering in her kitchen in the meantime. If she knew much about sewing, she'd probably have demanded to put together your dress as well. At least she has agreed to let a few girls come in the day before the wedding to help get the food prepared and assist with the serving, but she doesn't want anyone around trying to interfere until then. Lizzie can be pretty stubborn about such things."

"But it is too much for her," Virginia continued to protest. "She can't possibly do everything for the wedding *and* keep up her regular duties, which are already too much for one woman to handle."

"I imagine our stomachs will suffer a few undercooked meals over the next week or so, but there's nothing I can do to slow that woman down once she has gotten up a full head of steam. Believe me, I know."

It was true. Even Virginia could not slow Lizzie down, and she tried on more than one occasion by offering to help in some way. But each time, Lizzie flatly refused her assistance and even became upset that Virginia seemed to have so little faith in her ability to get the job done on her own. Finally Virginia gave up and simply let the woman do whatever she felt she had to. She tried her best to merely keep herself and Mary out of the woman's way—which was really the wisest course of action.

Lizzie never complained about the extra work . . . not even when, just two days before the wedding, Lizzie's work was at its most complicated, and Daniel returned from a trip with news that two guests would be arriving a little early.

"When are they coming?" Lizzie wanted to know, not bothering to ask who they were. It was as if she already knew.

Daniel flinched. "Seems they will arrive this very afternoon." He flinched again. "Lillian hopes to be able to help in some way."

"Who's Lillian?" Virginia asked.

"The wife of a business associate. They planned to arrive early so Lillian could help out."

"I don't need no help," Lizzie repeated for what had to be the dozenth time.

"I'm sure there's something you can find for her to do. She so wants to give you a hand."

"Maybe," was all Lizzie would concede. "How come they waited so late to let you know they was comin'?"

"The message reached Pittsburg days ago, but as usual, it was never dispatched to Valley Oaks. That seems to be a courtesy only allowed people who were born and raised here. Newcomers don't seem to get the same consideration . . . or at least, I'm having an unreasonably hard time getting them to send important messages out to me. I hope you have time to make the guest room ready. If not, I'm sure Lillian will understand."

"Won't be nothin' *to* understand. I'll have the room ready in plenty of time," Lizzie said. She now had to get one of the guest rooms ready, yet already she had a full afternoon of work ahead of her, still she refused to allow Virginia to help. "Miss Virginia, you know you is the bride-that's-to-be. You shouldn't be bothered with the doin's for your own weddin'," she insisted. She hurried back to the storage room to get her broom, the lemon oil, fresh linen, and several rags so that she could freshen up the larger of the three upstairs guest rooms.

Virginia followed in hopes of finding something she could do anyway, but Lizzie refused even to let her into the room. Eventually Virginia went back downstairs defeated.

Just before six, Daniel's friends arrived. To Virginia's amazement, Lizzie had the guest room completely ready and a proper meal prepared. Even the dining table had already been set with Daniel's finest china and silver, for this was not just a business associate and his wife, Virginia had learned. James and Lillian York were very, very close friends of Daniel's. And James had even been a friend of Caleb's . . . information Virginia felt would be well worth remembering.

When Virginia heard a carriage drive up, she jumped up to open the door for them. Lizzie would be too busy keeping an eye on her many pots and pans to bother greeting them, Virginia reasoned; but to her astonishment, when she came down the corridor, she discovered Lizzie there, quickly tidying her skirt and blouse while she waited for the knock. Never had Virginia known such superior qualities in anyone.

The moment Lizzie had the door open, she stepped quickly back. A slender woman, elegantly dressed, with lovely gentle features entered, followed by her husband, who seemed somewhat older and very authoritative.

Lizzie rushed over to attempt the proper introductions. "Mister James, Missus Lillian, I imagine you done guessed who this is." Lizzie beamed when she nodded proudly at Virginia.

"I do have my suspicions," Lillian said with a lovely laugh as she presented her gloved hand to Virginia. "Hello, Virginia, I am Lillian York. This grouchy old coot at my side is my husband, James."

"Grouchy old coot?" James challenged as he plopped his gloves into his upturned hat, then handed it to the grinning Lizzie.

James tossed back his head defiantly. "Just because I would not make a stop in Daingerfield so you could spend more of my money, you call me an old coot?" He extended his hand to Virginia. "Hello, Virginia, I'm very pleased to meet you."

Lillian laughed again, a rich silvery laugh that was pleasant to the ear and made everyone in the room smile—Virginia especially.

"Don't mind him," Lillian stage-whispered. "Believe me, no one else does."

"Least of all you," he muttered with a boyish pout. Then, glancing around as if suddenly aware something was missing, he asked, "Where's Daniel? I want to find out how on this earth he ever

280

convinced anyone as pretty as you to marry him."

Although Virginia had been dreading their arrival all afternoon, she found she actually liked both Lillian and James. He was obviously the "Mister James" who supervised Daniel's shipping company in Jefferson, the man Lizzie insisted turned to Daniel far too often for advice. Because he was a man of such importance, Virginia expected him and his wife to have high opinions of themselves, to be rather like Amanda and William. But they weren't—not at all. What a relief! The next two days did not look so dismal anymore.

"Daniel should be down in a minute." Virginia turned to guide the two into the salon, trying to guess their ages by their appearances. Though James looked to be nearly fifty, Lillian, she thought, was probably in her late thirties. She wore a fashionable frock of blue and silver which brought pleasant highlights to her blue-gray eyes. Her dark blonde hair had withstood the long trip admirably.

"Why don't you two come into the main salon and make yourselves comfortable," she went on as they fell into step beside her.

Virginia began to wonder whether it was up to her to offer them refreshment, but as they entered the room, Lillian went immediately to the well-stocked cabinet where Daniel kept his supply of whiskey, scotch, and rum, opened the doors wide, pulled a glass from the cabinet shelf, and poured it about half-full with a dark liquid. Then she quickly returned to hand the drink to her husband, who had taken a chair near the empty fireplace. Evidently Lillian was used to playing hostess in Daniel's house; Virginia decided it was probably because Lillian was a frequent guest and there had been no true hostess in Daniel's household . . . at least not yet.

"There, maybe that will satisfy you," she said while she made herself reasonably comfortable on the arm of James's chair.

"Satisfy me, eh? I guess it'll have to do," James responded with a meaningful gleam in his hazel eyes. "At least until I can get you alone."

Lillian feigned annoyance and batted him playfully on his lightly balding head. "Hush, before you give Daniel's bride the wrong impression." Then, in an effort to change the subject, she glanced around the room. "I see most of the furniture has already been removed to make room for the ceremony."

"Yes, Lizzie has been busy deciding what must go and what can stay. She's decided to leave these chairs near the fireplace until that morning so we can still use the room. Then, as I understand it, the folding chairs will be brought in and set in their proper places."

"I imagine Lizzie has been very busy. This was all so sudden," Lillian said, her wide blue-gray eyes curiously studying Virginia. "It was only a month ago, Daniel was in Jefferson. . . ." Lillian paused as if trying to find a delicate way to put something. "And well, quite frankly, though he talked of you often and it was clear he admired you for all you'd done for Mary, he never mentioned any intention of asking you to marry him.

I really am a little put out with him for having kept such a secret from us. After all, we've been friends for years."

Virginia felt an odd little flutter at realizing Daniel had talked about her to his friends, and in a way that led them to believe he admired her. But the sudden joy melted quickly when James thoughtlessly added, "The way Amanda clung to him those three days she visited with him, I thought she—" Then, as if suddenly realizing what he was about to say, he cleared his throat and abruptly changed the subject of his conversation. "Well, let's just say I was surprised to receive the wedding invitation and see your name on it. But pleasantly surprised. Never cared much for Amanda Haught. Any more than I cared for Josie Kilburn."

Lillian began to pale, realizing the sensitive subject her husband had unwittingly broached. Rising quickly, she came forward and grasped Virginia's hands, holding them in hers while she let her gaze sweep approvingly over her. "Yes, Daniel has made a lovely choice in his bride. I imagine Mary is delighted. Daniel told us how fond of you she is, and what a change you made in the child. I'm *so* glad."

Virginia blushed at such open compliments and found herself at a loss for words. Luckily Daniel chose that moment to enter and take up the conversation.

"You won't believe the change in Mary," he said with a beaming smile as he moved to embrace Lillian, placing a platonic kiss above her temple.

He went to shake hands with James just as the man pushed himself tiredly out of his chair. After a few pointed remarks were exchanged between the two men, remarks Virginia realized must have meaning only for the two of them, he came to stand beside Virginia and asked proudly, "Isn't she everything I said she was?"

Virginia felt her mouth drop with astonishment but quickly decided his glowing words were to trick his friends into believing they truly cared for each other . . . to make the marriage seem more reasonable to them.

"And more," James agreed wholeheartedly. "I still don't know how you convinced someone so gentle to marry a man with your temperament."

"Don't let that sweet smile fool you," Daniel said with a laugh while he casually brushed a knuckle against Virginia's cheek. It sent a scattering array of tingling sensations through her body. But Daniel seemed unaware of the effect his touch had had. "Behind that politely upturned mouth lies a tongue as sharp as a rapier and as quick as lightning. And she's not afraid to use it on anyone she feels deserves a proper tongue-lashing, so beware. And Lord help you if your opinions differ from hers!"

Virginia's eyes widened with horror at what the Yorks must think. For he had spoken the truth, and she could not very well deny it. Her barbed tongue had managed to place distance between them when distance was most needed. And she had become so accustomed to causing him as much annoyance as possible that she had grown to enjoy it.

But what she did not understand was that Daniel had come to enjoy it as well. He had never had a woman openly defy him before, or even state her own different opinions. Josie had in fact been very secretive while she went about her evil deeds. Most other women, though, bent themselves to please him, probably because they were aware of his wealth. But Virginia had never changed herself in any way to try to please him, and he realized once they were married, she probably never would. Still he felt it was better to be openly defied than secretly rebelled against. Largely because of his experience with his former wife, Daniel detested people who kept secrets from him. He especially detested those who felt it necessary to lie.

"Wonderful," James said, laughing at the thought of someone besting Daniel in an argument. "Maybe she'll use that sharp tongue to cut you down to size."

Lillian shook her head, exasperated at the two. "She'll need a sharp tongue, and a quick tongue as well, if she's to survive around the two of you."

Daniel and James looked at each other, raised their eyebrows, then turned to Lillian with such indignance that Lillian drew her mouth into a flat line and turned her back to them. Extending her hand to Virginia, she nodded toward the door. "Come, my dear . . . they are impossible to be around when they get like this. It is better to simply ignore them until they decide to rejoin polite company."

Virginia suppressed her strong desire to laugh, not knowing how Daniel or James would take it.

"Come upstairs with me so I can change out of these dusty clothes before supper. I want to get to know you a little better. I must find out why such a lovely, intelligent girl would agree to marry such a spoiled, arrogant man."

Virginia could not seem to hold back the retort, "Possibly for the same reasons you did." She then bit her lip, stunned she had actually said it aloud.

Lillian looked at her a long moment, then back at the two men. There was a glimmer of mirth in her blue-gray eyes. "Oh, I like her, Daniel. I like her very much."

Chapter Sixteen

The next two days passed quickly for Virginia, largely thanks to Lillian. The woman's lively and constant chatter and her uncanny ability to say the most unexpected things helped Virginia keep her mind off the enormity of what she was about to do. And by the morning of the wedding, Virginia and Lillian had become good friends. Good, but not so close that Virginia felt she could confide in her. Nor so close that Virginia felt she could admit her growing fears to her.

And there was really no one she could turn to. Because of that, she had to keep her apprehensions to herself, she realized as she began to dress. The lovely bridal gown was made of gleaming white cambric lawn, with a wide double ruffle around the high, curved neckline. The bodice was fashionably pleated across the front, the pleats tucking into a delicately banded waist. Her wide skirt flowed in soft, luxuriant folds to the floor.

Because the gathered and flounced overskirt of

her gown was made of an intricate lace beset with tiny white pearls, Virginia had to remain standing while Lizzie climbed up onto a footstool and worked with her hair. Though Virginia had not thought much about a coiffure, she realized how important it was to Lizzie and so allowed the busy servant ample time to work her magic. The woman wove a tiny strand of gleaming pearls into the elaborate array of curls she had fashioned, and Virginia was more than pleased at how lovely she appeared.

"You are the most beautiful bride I ever did see," Lizzie said a little tearfully as she stepped down from the stool to view the results of her two hours of effort.

Virginia spun on her slippered feet in front of her, making her shimmering white skirts billow and swirl about her. She realized she felt beautiful, truly beautiful. "Why, thank you for your compliment, and for all your help. But I don't see how you can possibly devote so much time to assisting me when you have all those other preparations to see about."

"Done seen to them," Lizzie said proudly as she reached out to test a particular curl. "Everything's done but the lightin' of the candles and the placin' of the food in the dinin' room. Food's already on the trays, but I won't put those out till just before the guests arrive."

"How'd you possibly manage to get everything done?" Virginia asked.

"I worked through the night," Lizzie told her with a light shrug.

"But you shouldn't have . . . you must be exhausted."

"*Am* a might tired, I suppose. But I'll have plenty of time to rest once you and Master Daniel is gone off on your wedding trip and Miss Mary done left for her visit with her grandmother," Lizzie assured her. "Besides, weddings don't happen in this house very often." Lizzie frowned as she thought about that. "In fact, as far as I know, this is the first wedding that's ever been held here. And it deserves to be special."

A knock at the door brought an immediate halt to their conversation.

"Who is it?" Lizzie asked with sudden apprehension. Her eyes cut to the closed door.

"It's me," came Lillian's response. "May I come in?"

Lizzie's sudden frown lifted. "Thought you might be Master Daniel," she said as Lillian stepped quickly inside, just barely able to clear her skirts before Lizzie had the door closed again. "Can't let him see the bride before the weddin'. Don't want to bring no bad luck to *this* marriage."

Virginia thought it a rather ludicrous remark, considering the odd circumstances that had brought about the marriage in the first place, but she realized neither Lizzie nor Lillian was aware of the circumstances.

"Virginia, you are stunning," Lillian said admiringly. She came forward to take Virginia's hands into hers and lift them away from her dress so that she could admire the gown. She smiled and there was a glimmer of tears in the corners of her eyes. "Daniel is a very lucky man. I'm not at all certain he deserves someone like you."

Then, as if she had suddenly remembered something, Lillian turned to Lizzie and pointed at her, but only frowned. Finally, she said, "Someone told me to tell you something. What was it? Oh, I know. One of those girls Daniel hired to help you in the kitchen wanted to know if she was supposed to put the wedding cake out yet. The guests are already starting to arrive and there is still much for the girls to do."

"Already? But it is early yet," Lizzie protested. "I'd better get in there before those silly girls decide to take it upon themselves to put the trays out. They'll probably put them in all the wrong places—if they don't drop them first."

When she opened the door she came to an abrupt halt. Virginia felt her heart skip a beat as her eyes stretched wide . . . was it Daniel? Though she did not believe in superstition, she was not ready for him to see her yet. Just in case, she stepped away from the door and waited for Lizzie to shoo him away.

"May I help you?" Lizzie asked curiously.

"I'm looking for Virginia," the feminine voice said politely.

"May I ask who wants to see her?" Lizzie asked just as politely, as much out of her growing curiosity as any propriety.

"Daniel's mother."

"Oh, yes, ma'am, sure . . . go on in. We was wonderin' if you was goin' to make it here in time. Sort of thought you'd be in last night. I'm Lizzie,

Daniel's housekeeper." Lizzie's words came out in an excited rush as she stepped back into the room so that the woman could enter.

"Daniel's mother is here to meet you," she said, her dark eyes wide with excitement.

Iris Pearson was older and far more fragile than Virginia had expected. When she stepped forward to meet the woman, Virginia found that though she herself was not tall for a woman, she was still several inches taller than Iris Pearson. It made Virginia feel like an awkward giant. She wondered, somewhat amused, how such a small, frail woman had borne such a tall, powerfully built son.

"Hello, Mrs. Pearson," she said awkwardly while the little woman gazed up at her with a studious expression on her pale, weathered face.

"So you are Virginia," she said as she tilted her gray head.

"Yes, ma'am, I am," Virginia responded nervously. Her gaze went from the tiny woman to Lillian, who was more her own size, then back to the tiny woman.

"You're sure pretty enough," Iris conceded while her soft blue eyes studied her closely. "But tell me, do you love my son?"

Surprised by the woman's directness, Virginia began to stammer, "W-what a question to ask!"

Lillian then came to her rescue. "Of course she does. Why else would she have agreed to marry him? A woman would have to be very foolish or very much in love to be willing to marry a man with Daniel's obstinate temperament."

Virginia thought it a very profound statement

and knew instantly in which of the two categories she fell.

Iris blinked several times as she thought about what Lillian had said, looking from one to the other. Then she turned back to gaze at Lizzie, who had forgotten all about leaving. Because Virginia was not at all sure how the woman would respond to Lillian's bold remark regarding her son, she was pleased when Iris's thin lips curved into an appreciative smile. "I just wanted to be sure. Daniel deserves a wife who loves him." Then, as if she had just really noticed Lillian, she twisted her face into a wrinkled frown and peered questioningly up at her. "Who are you?"

"I'm Lillian York. We've met before, but that was years ago," Lillian said, politely extending her hand. "My husband is supervisor of Pearson & Company in Jefferson. Perhaps you remember him. James York?"

"Oh, yes, now I remember," Iris said, and for the second time since entering the room, she smiled. "Caleb always thought the world of your husband. Claimed he was a bright lad with a very good business sense about him. Daniel seems to think so, too."

"Though I doubt Daniel quite considers him a lad," Lillian added in amusement.

"Maybe not, but Daniel mentions him often in his letters," Iris went on to say, then glanced back at Virginia, still smiling. The longer she smiled, the more at ease Virginia realized she was starting to feel. "And my son mentioned you a lot, too. He likes the progress you have made with Mary.

292

Says you're responsible for the change in her. He just never let on that he was so fond of you that he hoped to marry you. The wedding invitation took me quite by surprise."

"As it did all of us," Lillian supplied with her silvery laugh. "I guess Daniel has a good head on his shoulders after all and did not want to chance letting her get away."

"Maybe," Iris agreed. "It just seems hard to believe that someone managed to get that poor boy to be so willing to take another chance."

Virginia considered the odd statement, but decided Iris was referring to the terrible heartbreak he had suffered upon his first wife's death. She probably felt her son would worry about risking a second heartbreak. Little did his mother know that he had in no way risked his heart—in fact, that he was unwilling to let his heart be any part of this second marriage. His wounds had never fully healed from the overwhelming devastation of having lost his first wife. Suddenly Virginia felt a twinge of compassion for the man and realized how deeply he must have loved his first wife, how painful the loss had been for him—and obviously still was.

"His willingness to take that second chance won't be so hard to believe once you get to know Virginia better," Lillian said, giving Virginia a reassuring wink.

"But I won't get that chance to know her better, will I? Daniel plans to whisk her away right after the reception. I won't get to talk with her at any length until I return with Mary in three weeks."

"By then that stormy disposition of his may have run her off and you won't get a chance to know her at all," Lillian said, laughing at her own outrageous remark; but when she realized no one else had responded in kind, she quickly brought her laughter to a halt.

"He'd better not," Iris said, then turned to Virginia. "You don't let him."

"She doesn't let him do anything she doesn't want him to do," Lillian assured him. And this time, though that had been said in all sincerity, Iris laughed.

It was clear the three women were going to get along. Lizzie remembered she had been about to leave and did so. Iris soon followed, wanting to find her son and have a word with him before the ceremony began, knowing there would be little time for them to talk afterward.

"Looks like you came through that unscathed," Lillian said with a light laugh as soon as the door closed behind Iris.

"Thanks to you," Virginia said gratefully. "Is she always so blunt and forthright?"

Lillian nodded. "She's always reminded me of my own mother. *Always* says what's on her mind. But she means well. Daniel is her only son and she worries about him . . . we all do."

Virginia thought that a strange thing to say. Daniel was one of the wealthiest men in East Texas, a man who could get anything he wanted and usually did. Why would anyone worry about a man like that?

Lillian seemed unaware she had said anything in

the least bit odd. She glanced at the clock and drew her lower lip between her teeth. As she looked back at Virginia, she pointed out unnecessarily, "Barely an hour to go before you have to march out there and become Mrs. Daniel Pearson. Are you starting to get nervous?"

"No," Virginia answered honestly, then grinned. "I've gone way beyond nervous. I'm nearing hysteria."

"Good, just so long as you aren't nervous," Lillian said, and followed her absurd statement with another pleasant trickle of laughter.

Virginia grimaced at first, but then joined in Lillian's laughter. It felt good to laugh; it relieved some of her tension and helped take her mind off the enormity of what was about to happen.

In less than an hour, she was going to have to walk out of that room, down the hall, into the gaily decorated salon to join hands with a man who was still so desperately in love with his first wife that he had openly proclaimed he could never love again—a man who could never be the sort of husband she had always thought she would marry—and she was then supposed to promise to spend the rest of her life with him.

Shortly thereafter, they would leave as husband and wife for a week-long trip to only Daniel knew where. When they returned, her things would have already been moved upstairs into his room. From that day on, she would be expected to share not only his room but his bed as well. She would be a Pearson. Eventually, if she ever hoped to have children of her own to nurture and love, to become rightful heirs to Valley Oaks, she would have to. . . . The thought of it sent prickly shivers of apprehension through her and made the tiny hairs stand out along the sensitive nape of her neck.

All too soon the time came for Virginia and Daniel to be wed. A soft hum of voices could be heard from the front rooms and piano music drifted lightly through the house. Lillian had stayed by Virginia's side during that final hour and smiled as the hour finally came for her to open the door.

"It's time," she said gaily, her eyes misting while she watched Virginia step out into the hallway.

Only a few minutes later, the two of them stood in the corridor near the foot of the staircase where they could see the main entrance hall and hear the clamor of voices inside the front salon more clearly. No one lingered outside the door besides the two elegantly dressed ushers, who to Virginia's surprise turned out to be Pete and Jack. She had never thought anyone—not even Daniel, who they both obviously admired—could get those two into any attire quite so formal. She smiled at them when they finally realized she was there behind them and had turned to look at her.

"Look there," Pete said, grinning as he jabbed Jack sharply with his elbow. "If that ain't the loveliest sight I've ever seen, then I don't know what it coulda been."

Jack tugged at his gray vest, looking very uncomfortable at the close fit of his clothing, but still managed to smile at Virginia. For the first time she could remember, he agreed with his brother wholeheartedly. "Yep, she's sure the prettiest bride I ever seen."

"Are they ready to begin?" Lillian asked, going forward to peek into the room. Virginia could not help but follow, though she stood far enough back so the guests might not notice her.

"I guess so," Pete replied. "The women's all seated and the men's all standing up along the walls."

Virginia tiptoed to peer over the shoulders of the other three and felt her apprehension grow tenfold. The room was filled with strangers, all dressed in their finest silks, satins, and brocades, all seemingly eager to see Daniel Pearson wed.

The salon had been elaborately decorated for the occasion with several fabulous arrangements of white flowers trimmed with pale blue ribbons and bows. At the altar were two tall candelabra laced with fresh greenery and blue and white ribbons, each holding sixteen lighted pale blue tapers. Near the altar, a tiny raised platform covered with white velvet, was Daniel, already in place, carefully avoiding everyone's gaze. The minister at his side was speaking softly to him.

She could not help but smile at how elegant Daniel looked. He wore a three-button cutaway of black satinet cashmere, well stitched kip boots, and black trousers that were not quite so snug as he ordinarily wore. His thick hair, which usually fell loosely forward across his forehead, had been brushed back from his face, perfectly parted to the side. He stood, slightly bent, still listening to whatever it was the minister had to say, his hands clasped behind his back, but turned only a moment later to say something to his mother, who was seated behind him.

That's when he first noticed the shadows in the hallway and glanced then to the clock. He said something to his mother, then whispered in the ear of the minister, who hurried into place at the front of the altar. He nodded then to a rather plump lady in an outrageously fashioned feather hat who had sat patiently at the piano—which until now had been in another room of the house—and within seconds the traditional wedding music began to play.

Lillian went first, dressed in a lovely gown of pale blue silk, holding a modest bouquet of white flowers.

All eyes turned to watch while Lillian moved gracefully toward the altar. Then, when Virginia stepped into the doorway, Lizzie appeared out of nowhere to straighten her train and James came forward from where he had stood just inside the room, took her trembling arm, and placed it into the crook of his own. The music grew suddenly louder.

"Ready?" he whispered in a low voice.

"Not in the least," she whispered back.

Though James had clearly been trying to uphold the appearance of dignity, he could not help but laugh at such a remark. "Too late to back out now."

Was it? she wondered. *Was it really too late?*

She turned from James's smiling face and saw how Daniel had craned to watch her entrance, a pleased smile on his face. Finding that smile disconcerting to say the least, she quickly pulled her gaze away and glanced next at the guests who were all carefully watching her while she and James continued to move slowly down the narrow aisle. It occurred to her that they were all smiling too. Why was it that everyone had found something to smile about except her?

That was when she caught sight of Wyoma's curious half-smile, and beside her, Mark's deeply glowering expression. Well, at least there was one other person in the room who shared her apprehension and understood that this just possibly might *not* be the greatest thing that could happen to her. How she wished she could go to Mark and talk with him, tell him everything she was feeling. He would listen and, though he would surely tell her what a fool she was for going through with such a harebrained scheme, he would still offer her a sympathetic ear. That's the way Mark was; that was one of the reasons she cared so deeply for him. Unable to bear the anger and confusion on Mark's stricken face, she looked down at the carpet beneath her.

As James had said, it was too late to consider changing her mind now, even if she wanted to. With each step she took, she moved that much further away from her girlhood, away from her greatly treasured freedom, yet at the same time closer to making Valley Oaks her home and the home of her children. Behind her now were all her hopes and dreams of how marriage was supposed to be. Ahead of her was . . . who really knew what? Bravely she lifted her eyes and looked at Daniel, who was still smiling, still so incredibly handsome, yet more than a little frightening. Her heart raced out of control, begging her to quickly reconsider, but her feet continued to move forward.

Feeling very much like a marionette whose strings were being pulled by some unseen hand, Virginia remained at James's side until they reached the altar, then she allowed him to gently hand her over to Daniel.

James's words played over and over again in her mind as her arm was linked with Daniel's. *Too late to back out now. Too late to back out now.* And just when she was about to cry out that it was not too late, that she simply could not and would not go through with it, that she could not enter into a loveless marriage for any reason—not even for Valley Oaks—she suddenly caught sight of Mary, who had come forward to stand beside Lillian. Smiling proudly, Mary held the pillow on which the wedding rings lay. And during the same moment Virginia became aware of the child's joyful tears, she felt Daniel place a reassuring hand over hers.

Though her heart continued to beat its fearful message beneath her breast, her breathing slowly relaxed and her determination took hold again. She would go through with it. Despite all her misgivings, despite the fact she felt she was in some way betraying her grandmother by actually becoming a Pearson—becoming part of the family she had been taught to hate—she *would* go through with her marriage to Daniel. She would make Valley Oaks her home. And she would become a mother to Mary.

When she then turned and glanced at Daniel's deeply concerned expression—looking as if he had somehow sensed her reluctance and was concerned about it—she felt oddly happy to know he had indeed worried. Though he would never love her, nor would theirs ever be the sort of marriage she'd always longed for, he was at least concerned about her.

That realization startled her so that she did not hear the first sentences the minister spoke. It was not until she heard her own name that she was able to bring her thoughts back to what was actually happening and could say "I do" at the appropriate moment. When the time came for him to do the same, he gave an immediate response, which assured her there had been no hesitation on his part.

In a matter of just a few minutes, the vows were spoken, promises made that were fashioned to last a lifetime; and there, before a room filled with strangers and a handful of her own friends, Virginia Elaine Connors became Mrs. Daniel Edward Pearson—exactly as she had agreed to do. A lingering kiss sealed the pledge.

Virginia was still responding to that kiss long after the ceremony was over, even while all the guests clamored around them both, wanting to introduce themselves to Virginia and wish them both well. Then, just as Virginia was getting her wits about her, little Jessica appeared out of nowhere to offer her older friend a piece of sage advice, advice that brought an immediate blush to Virginia's cheeks and a peal of genuine laughter from Daniel.

"I'm going to tell you what Mother told both my sisters when they got married," Jessica said, quite serious about what she had to say. "Try with all your strength not to argue with your husband, but if you do find yourself in some kind of argument with him—no matter what it is you have found to disagree with him about—don't ever go to bed angry." Jessica delivered her speech with much aplomb and grinned proudly at how she had held everyone's attention with it.

"Sounds like good advice, all right," Daniel said, still overcome with laughter. He reached an arm around his new wife, and pulled her closer to his side. Then, leaning close to her ear so only she could hear, he brushed the side of her face with a light kiss and added, "But why do I have a feeling it is advice that will go unheeded?"

Virginia's cheeks remained a flattering crimson, not so much from the embarrassment of having been given such odd advice from a nine-year-old as from the agitation she felt at what Daniel had just whispered.

"Thank you for that advice," Daniel said to Jessica, his tone deeply grateful while he bent forward to chuck Jessica lightly under her chin. "I'll see that she is reminded of it often."

Virginia bristled but remained smiling while she watched Jessica and Mary skip off into the crowd, knowing the two were going either to the dining room or outside to play away the hours. How she wished she could go with them! She felt uncomfortable accepting so many congratulations and warm wishes for a long life and for a large and happy family, especially from people she did not know. She felt just as uncomfortable hearing Daniel thank them all sincerely while continuously teasing her with affectionate little kisses and husbandly hugs.

Finally the well-wishers began to thin out, venturing at last to the dining room, where a wide assortment of food had been set on large silver trays and ruby-red punch filled several huge cut-glass bowls. It was not until then, when there was hardly anyone else left in the room, that Mark and his mother came forward to offer their good wishes for the couple, who still stood in the middle of the room. Daniel's arm was draped ever so casually across Virginia's shoulders.

"I hope you have many years of happiness," Wyoma said, trying to sound gay, but she was clearly as confused as Mark about all of it when she reached forward to caress Virginia's cheek with her hand.

"I just hope she knows what she's doing," Mark muttered, his green eyes narrowed meaningfully.

Virginia felt Daniel's arm stiffen around her. "I know it seems a little odd. After all, it did happen rather quickly," she responded hurriedly as her heart picked up its already frantic rhythm.

"Very quickly, indeed," Wyoma said with open-eyed concern, still trying to present a pleasant smile.

"Yes, it still makes my head spin a little to realize just how quickly it did all come about. But once the decision was made, we did not see any good reason to delay the wedding." She felt Daniel's arm relax a little, but Mark's expression turned even darker. There was a clear message of hatred in her friend's green eyes as he stared at Daniel and a look of deep hurt when his gaze finally moved to take in Virginia's pale features.

"Well, I hope you will be happy," he muttered as if he thought it was expected of him, then turned abruptly away and stalked out of the room.

Virginia's hand went to her mouth as tears filled her eyes and an unforgiving pain swelled in her throat, making it impossible to call him back. She had not wanted to hurt Mark; he had to know that, but she had no way of telling him.

"He'll be all right," Wyoma assured her as she leaned forward and placed a brief kiss on Virginia's cheek. "It'll take him a while to adjust to this sudden marriage of yours, but he'll finally make that adjustment. Just give him time . . . he'll come around." While she was still so near to Virginia's ear, she quietly added, "And if you ever feel you need someone to talk to, remember: you can always come to me."

Virginia closed her eyes to the swirling tangle of emotions that now raged wildly within her. Wyoma was obviously concerned about the decision that had led her to become Daniel Pearson's wife. How Virginia yearned to explain all to her, and to Mark—explain to them the *real* reasons she had agreed to marry Daniel. How it was not only going to benefit Mary, but had gotten Valley Oaks too, which was still very important to her. Yet, oddly enough, she also wanted Wyoma to understand that it was not going to be as bad as it might seem because, although Daniel would never love her, there was every chance she already loved him. But she knew she could never speak of those things with Wyoma. She could never speak of those things with anyone.

Chapter Seventeen

The reception was an extravagant affair, with trays upon trays of food and four large bowls of bright red fruit punch set about the room. One of these had been spiked to include a goodly amount of rum, and as a result it seemed to be quite popular with all the men and many of the women.

Virginia was handed a plate of tasty tidbits when she first entered the dining room and was immediately surrounded by several women, none of whose names she could recall. It did not take her long to discover she had little appetite for the food — or for such inane conversation. She looked around for Lillian to come to her rescue, but could not find her new friend's face among the crowd. Finally she realized she would have to devise her own escape.

After a suitable amount of time, she politely excused herself from the talkative circle, claiming she wanted to tidy her hair. But what she really wanted was to step onto the back veranda and get a bracing breath of fresh air while enjoying a brief moment of blissful solitude.

She had not seen Daniel since they had first entered the crowded dining room, when he had been instantly swept from her side by a pair of overly jovial friends. She hoped he would not be too angry with her when he returned to discover she had left his guests to fend for themselves. But even the thought of Daniel's anger did not prevent her from slipping quickly down the hallway and outside. Still, she did not want anyone to know where she had really gone, so she continued on out into the yard and around to the back of the classroom, knowing she would be well out of everyone's sight once she had rounded the corner.

In the less elaborate gardens just outside the classroom she leaned heavily against a small rail fence to rest, not really caring if the rough wood would pull at the delicate lace of her gown or not. The dress had already served its purpose and she was tired—bone tired. All that mattered was taking some of the weight off her tightly slippered feet. If she'd been certain she'd later have found the strength to stand up again, she'd have knelt down to loosen the ribbons of her slippers and enjoy a moment's relief from the bindings.

Sighing aloud, she lifted her aching face to the late afternoon summer sky, enjoying the soothing warmth of the breeze against her cheeks. She closed her eyes to revel in the way it seemed to gently caress her skin, lifting her hair so that it might cool her better. Because the sun was low enough to cast long shadows, the oaks further away into the yard had reached out to offer her their comforting shade, and she felt almost like thanking them out loud for such a refreshing respite.

It was while she leaned heavily against the fence, braced with a hand on either side of her, her eyes closed, and well out of everyone's sight, that she first heard voices: a man's and a woman's. She frowned when she realized one of them belonged to Daniel. Not wanting him to catch her outside, so obviously trying to avoid his guests, she quickly stood and looked around for a place to hide, but there were no hedgerows tall enough, and she was not sure she had the time to scurry around the corner unnoticed.

Judging by the sounds, Daniel was but a few yards away, just around the side of the classroom, but further away from the veranda and all that was going on inside than even she was. It occurred to her that he, too, had sneaked out of the house unnoticed by all except one, and so would not want to be discovered any more than she did. She was no more guilty of avoiding the crowd than he was. Having realized that, she started to listen to the voices with interest. That's when she discovered the female voice belonged to Amanda. When did she arrive? And why was she there? Had Daniel decided to invite her after all?

"Amanda, don't cry," she heard him say, though

without much sympathy in his voice. "It's too late now, anyway. The deed has been done; I am married."

"But it can be easily annulled. Nothing has happened to actually seal the marriage. Just go in there and explain to everyone what a dreadful mistake you have made. Tell them how you really love me." Amanda pleaded with him. There were strong, tearful emotions choking her voice.

"A-man-da," he said, obviously annoyed. Virginia could almost see him cross his arms in that insolent manner of his.

"No, Daniel, don't turn away. I love you . . . you know that. And *you* love *me*. You have said as much more than once. You have admitted it to William—he told me. And until that little trollop entered your life and trapped you into marrying her, you were planning to marry me. *You know you were.*"

Virginia's hands curled into fists at her side. How *dare* that woman call her a trollop! How *dare* she intimate Virginia had somehow trapped Daniel into getting married! No one could get away with saying such things about her . . . no one!

Taking a deep, angry breath, Virginia stood, gripped her white skirts, and moved toward the voices with every intention of telling that wench a thing or two in her own defense; but to her amazement, just before she reached the edge of the classroom wall, Daniel came to her defense for her.

"Don't try to pretend that I've actually said I

309

love you, because I haven't," he cried. "Those are words I'll *never* speak again. I can love no one. And don't you dare call Virginia a trollop." His voice was low with warning. "She is nothing of the sort. You don't even know her. She is my wife by *my* choice, and that is something you are going to have to come to terms with. I am now a married man."

Virginia stopped just a few inches from the corner of the house, mouth agape, and listened carefully for Amanda's retort to that.

"It won't last," Amanda put in quickly. "It won't last because you *don't* love her, and I doubt very much that she loves you. All she cares about is your money."

"Maybe," he conceded. "But for Mary's sake, I'm going to give this marriage a real try."

For Mary's sake. Those words pierced Virginia with an unaccountable force as did the fact that he had as much admitted to Amanda that he had not married for love. But why she should feel such pain, she did not know. She had known from the start that Daniel was marrying her for Mary's sake, and only for Mary's sake. He had said as much to her at the outset. So why had she not come to accept it yet? Why did hearing him say it to Amanda hurt so deeply that it brought tears to her eyes?

"Is *that* why you married her?" Amanda asked with open disbelief. "Don't you think *I* would have made a good mother for the child?"

"Mary doesn't like you," he replied bluntly. "And as far as I can tell, you don't particularly care for her, either. No, Mary needs someone who truly cares about her—someone who can help change her life—and Virginia is just the one to do it. She may not love me, but she cares deeply for my daughter."

"Does that woman ever have you fooled!" Amanda cried out angrily. "All she cares about is herself. And when you come to realize that, when you finally see what a mistake you have made by marrying her, I want you to know I *won't* be waiting for you. Not this time." Her voice had begun to tremble from the anguish she felt, then when she spoke again, the bitter anguish turned to open sobs of misery. She wailed. "Oh, Daniel, that's not true. I'll be waiting for you. You know I will. When you finally come to your senses and discover what a mistake you've made by marrying someone else, I'll be waiting for you. I promise."

"I think you'd better leave," Daniel said quietly, his tone of voice low but noncommittal, "before someone sees you."

"Do you mean besides the two groomsmen who took my carriage?" she asked tartly. "And the guests who were milling about out front when I arrived?"

"Yes, before someone else sees you."

"Who else? Virginia?"

"Exactly. Now leave."

There was a pause, as if Amanda actually considered defying him, but in the end, she said softly, "Okay, Daniel, I'll go quietly—if you'll promise me that when you finally *do* realize what a horrible mistake you have made, you will come to me . . . you will let me be the one to console your broken heart."

With her eyes pressed closed, ready for the humiliation, Virginia waited for him to remind Amanda how his heart could not be broken because he had never allowed it to become involved in their marriage proposal, but to her amazed relief, he did not speak the words. He did not go into the strange terms of their marriage agreement at all; he kept it to himself. All she heard after Amanda's tearful plea was the quiet rustling of footsteps as he obviously led her back the way they had come. Both were unaware anyone had overheard their conversation, much less that it had been Virginia.

Waiting until she could no longer hear the footsteps, knowing they would then be out of earshot of her own, she hurried back inside. Rather than return to the dining room, where she would be forced to make polite conversation with all those strangers, she turned just as soon as she entered the house and hurried to her bedroom.

The moment she was inside the room, she closed the door and leaned heavily against the cold, hard surface. Overcome by anger and humiliation, and something more she could not even clearly identify, she felt very much like crying, yet she refused to let the tears fall. She had to keep a tight rein on her emotions if she was to keep her sanity. She must not let them have the control they sought.

Barely ten minutes later, while she still struggled to keep back the tears, there was a knock at her door which caused her to jump

"Who is it?" Her voice came out amazingly strong. Quickly she wiped at the moisture in her eyes while she waited for the response.

"It's me, Daniel. May I come in?"

Panic struck her heart as she pressed her hands against her hot cheeks and made a last inner appeal for strength. To her amazement, she managed to place a sweet smile on her lips just before she opened the door. "I was just coming out. Is it time for us to leave yet?"

"Just about. It's going to be dark when we get there as it is," he told her while his gaze swept over her, his brow drawn with concern. "Are you all right?" He reached out to feel her cheek, then her forehead.

"I'm a little tired," she admitted, but that was all she planned to admit. She had no intention of telling him she had overheard him out in the garden with Amanda, nor would she tell him how deeply hurt and emotionally drained that conversation had left her. "Where is it we are going? Now that we are about to leave, you can tell me. I won't tell anyone."

"And spoil your surprise?" he asked, suddenly smiling, obviously pleased that she was so curious. "Never."

Virginia was in no mood for any more surprises, but did not want to argue with him about it, either. She decided to let him have his little secret if it made him happy. She could certainly wait until they got there to find out. Where they spent their wedding night was of little interest to her, anyway. All that mattered was that when they got there, she would be provided a comfortable bed and several hours of uninterrupted quiet. She was very glad she had agreed to be the one to decide when and if they should ever consummate their marriage. At least she did not have to worry about such as that tonight of all nights.

"You can enjoy yourself for a little while longer, if you'd like, but you'd better think about getting changed soon," Daniel went on to say, wishing he could tell what thoughts were passing through that pretty head of hers. "I would prefer to leave here as quickly as we can."

"Then I'll change now," she said, just as eager to be away from all these well-meaning strangers. "It shouldn't very long. My clothes have already been laid out."

Barely half an hour later, after having bid the final farewells to the wedding guests—who would stay on and eat and drink until the wee hours under the watchful eyes of Iris, Lizzie, and Lillian—Daniel guided Virginia out to the awaiting carriage. Their things had been loaded earlier that afternoon, and a driver sat waiting patiently on the front seat. All they had to do once the time finally came was to say one last good-bye and climb in.

As they reached the gaily decorated carriage, which sported ribbons, flowers, and a colorful array of satin bows, someone presented them each with a tall glass of champagne and demanded there be a special toast before they left. In the spirit of things, Daniel nodded jovially to the crowd and waited with Virginia while James tried to get the crowd to hush long enough so he could make the official toast.

Holding his own glass high, James called out in a deep, eloquent voice, "We can't let them leave here without toasting to their future together."

A cheer went up in the crowd, and those who had thought to bring their glasses with them raised them high, the others merely pretending to do so.

Daniel cried out a sincere agreement, letting his gaze scan the cheering crowd, "To our future." Then, with a cocky raise of his brow, he drank down the champagne in three large gulps.

Everyone cheered louder, then looked expectantly at Virginia. Realizing they were all waiting for her to do the same, she lifted her glass in toast, then pinched her nose and drained it empty. Everyone cheered again, thinking she had also just drank a toast to their future together. But Virginia had purposely neglected to state the words "to our future" out loud, because in her heart, she had just raised her glass in sad farewell to her past. Nothing would ever be the same for her; never had she felt more determined to be miserable.

When they were both finally seated in the carriage, just as it pulled into motion, Daniel leaned and waved happily to his friends, then glanced back at Virginia to see if she wanted to do likewise. Knowing she'd better, she leaned forward over him and waved too, very aware of the fact that her leg had come into hard contact with his;

it had sent a bone-jarring jolt through her. When she looked out over the sea of faces which were smiling merrily back at them, she was surprised to see Mark still there. She thought he'd left right after the ceremony, but he'd actually stayed to see them off. What did not surprise her, though, was the stricken expression on his face.

She sent him a special farewell look that she hoped would help ease his present torment, though she knew it would do little toward easing his confusion and hurt. One day, shortly after they returned from their trip, she would find a way to talk with Mark. She would try to explain her decision to marry Daniel as best she could without actually breaking her promise to keep the true reason they chose marry a secret. She just hoped she could find a way to make him understand . . . she did not like seeing such a painful expression on her friend's handsome face.

Soon they were on their way, headed east, and Valley Oaks was long gone. Still unaware of their destination or how long it would take them to get there, Virginia leaned back into the padded seat of the carriage and made herself comfortable. All she really knew was that Daniel expected them to arrive after dark.

The sun had already dipped behind the distant trees. It had been a long and tiring day, one that had been preceded by a long, sleepless night, and the strain she had been forced to go through quickly took its toll on her exhausted body. Not twenty minutes into the ride, Virginia started to nod sleepily at Daniel's side and soon found herself drawn into the warm, comforting circle of his arm.

Hours passed and Virginia slept, her cheek pressed against Daniel's chest, her arms folded together and snuggled between them. It was not until the carriage turned off the main road onto a much smaller one that Daniel gently nudged her awake.

"We're almost there," he whispered.

"Where?" she asked sleepily, but not moving from her comfortable position.

"At River Ridge," he said proudly.

"Where?" she asked again and her eyes at last came open. When she realized she was lying within Daniel's embrace and that he held her close against him, his hand gently stroking her hair while he spoke, she pulled quickly away.

Wondering just how long she might have slept in his arms, she leaned forward in the seat and looked out into the darkness, able to make out the shadowy silhouette of a huge house in the distance. It would have looked spooky among such tall trees if it weren't for the golden light that glowed from many of the windows, beckoning them forward. Tall torches had been lit along the edge of the drive.

"River Ridge," he repeated, nodding at the apparition before them. "It's called that because just beyond that huge ridge of trees is the Little Cypress River."

Virginia stared ahead with interest. Now that he had pointed it out to her, she could see the silvery reflection of moonlight on the rippling water

317

through the thick branches of the dark trees that encircled the house. "But where are we?"

"A few miles outside of Jefferson," he told her.

Virginia's attention was again drawn to the house itself, which lay just ahead at the end of the drive.

Although the house was smaller than the one at Valley Oaks, it was in no way less grand. There was enough moonlight aided by the flickering torchlight for her to make out the dark, sharp-angled, sloping roofline that capped off a tall, possibly three-story, blue-gray structure which appeared to be made of lapped wood.

Next she noticed the well-kept grounds that surrounded the house on all sides, though they were not so vast nor so well-decorated with ornamental gardens as the grounds at Valley Oaks. And as they drew closer to the house itself, she noticed a small Negro boy dressed in cutaway pants and an open shirt. He waited just a few feet from the drive, his hands behind him, and watched them approach. He looked to be about ten, thin as a rail, with a wide smile that could be seen even from where they were.

"Whose house is this?" she wanted to know, turning to look at Daniel then. If they were about to be someone's guests, she'd at least like to know their names ahead of time.

"Our house," he responded with a light shrug. "Like it?"

"Yes, I like it. It's beautiful." She also liked the thought of not having to stay at a hotel where they would surely be expected to share a suite of rooms, which she'd dreaded. But what she liked even more was how Daniel had included her as one of the owners without giving the matter any thought. What was his was now hers, too. She smiled.

"Actually, this was one of Uncle Caleb's houses. After he realized how often he had to be in Jefferson to take care of business there, he decided to have a house built nearby so he'd not have to stay at the hotel or impose on friends."

"How could he manage two such extravagant houses?" she asked, still a little surprised. She had known Caleb was wealthy, but had no idea of the extent of his wealth. She wondered who else he'd had to cheat in order to get all this.

"This house was just a place for him to stay when he had to be in Jefferson. He was not here too often . . . and when he was not using the house or letting friends use it, the Edmonds took care of it for him."

"The Edmonds?"

"An elderly couple—freeservants—who as I understand it had worked on the plantation that was here before Caleb bought most of the land and built this house. The two came as part of the land purchase agreement. If he wanted to buy the land, he was to provide a livelihood for the Negro couple who had been born and raised on the land and had served the previous owner loyally."

"Do they still live here?" she asked, hopeful to be told that she and Daniel were not going to be in such a secluded house all alone.

"Well, they don't actually live in the main

319

house . . . they have their own cottage down river a ways. Caleb had it built for them years ago. He wanted to make it easier for Ruby as she got older. With a smaller house to go to, she could simply close up the main house when it wasn't needed and not have to worry about keeping so many rooms clean. Sometimes the place was vacant for months at a time."

Virginia felt her hope change to despair. "Does anyone actually live in the main house?"

"No . . . it is still kept closed unless I need it or one of my friends asks to use it." Realizing her concern, he smiled a truly lecherous smile. "Just think . . . we'll have it all to ourselves. You won't even have to worry about Mitchel there being around to spy on us. He's the Edmonds' grandson. He and his father live with them."

"I see," she said none-too-cheerfully and gazed at the house once again. Suddenly it didn't seem nearly large enough.

"Not afraid to stay there alone with me, are you?"

"Of course not," she lied, then turned to look at him and asked. "Should I be?"

"Yes," he answered quite honestly.

Suddenly she felt very afraid . . . afraid he might conveniently forget his promise to let her be the one to decide when he could take his husbandly rights. Afraid he actually intended to do so that very night, when no one else was in the house, and there would be no one to stop him from doing just that. But then, she realized, they probably wouldn't do anything to stop him anyway. After all, he was her husband, and those were his rights. Her heart slammed hard against her breastbone at the mere thought of it—and harder still when she heard him chuckle beneath his breath.

The carriage pulled to a gentle stop in front of the young boy who had waited so patiently, and Daniel called out to him in a cheerful voice, "Hello, Mitchel."

"You're much later than we 'spected, Mister Daniel," the young boy replied as he moved to greet them. "Grandma thought you'd be comin' 'bout dark. Had your supper all fixed and on the table waitin' for you."

"I'm sorry, things happened that prevented us from getting away as quickly as I'd expected." He climbed down from the carriage and hurried around the back to assist Virginia.

Virginia cringed, knowing exactly what unexpected happening had managed to delay their departure . . . Daniel had obviously not thought Amanda would have the audacity to come to his wedding uninvited. Though she suddenly felt like making some sort of comment about his deeply heartbroken visitor, Virginia wisely remained silent.

"This here your new wife?" the boy asked, staring up at Virginia unabashed, still smiling his wide smile.

"That's her. What do you think?" Daniel wanted to know.

"Pretty," he said with an approving nod. "Real pretty."

"Isn't she, though?"

Virginia was getting tired of being talked about as if she was not even there but could not seem to find a large enough gap in their ridiculous appraisal of her to say anything.

"She's much prettier than any of the other ladies you've brought here," Mitchel said thoughtlessly, tilting his head to admire her more.

"Thanks a lot, there, Mitchel," Daniel said with noticeable exasperation and glanced apologetically at Virginia. She had turned her interest to gathering her skirts about her, a task which seemed to be taking far more effort than necessary. Frowning, he turned back to Mitchel and added briskly, "Why don't you help Steve get our things inside?"

"Want it all up in your room?" Mitchel asked.

"Of course," he responded quickly, hoping to interrupt before the boy could manage to add anything terribly incriminating to his question, like the words, "as usual." "Then you can help Steve get the horses and coach put away. Once that's done, why don't you see that he gets something to eat before he beds down for the night?"

"He's stayin'?" Mitchel asked, surprised.

"For tonight. I've got errands for him to run in Jefferson tomorrow," Daniel explained. "Then he'll have his choice of staying around here and helping with odd jobs, or heading on back to Valley Oaks and doing his regular work until we return." Turning then to Virginia, he reached out a hand to help her down, smiling at her sheepishly, for Mitchel's comment still caused him some discomfort.

"Amusing child," Virginia commented drily as she allowed him to assist her, but once she was on the ground, she pulled away from his grasp. She turned and headed for the house, staying just far enough ahead of him to make it impossible for him even to place his hand at her elbow. Though she had known Daniel had had lots of women in his lifetime, it made her unreasonably angry to know that he had brought some of them there.

Shortly after entering the house, her anger subsided as she was introduced to Ruby and Rufus Edmond, both slender in build and starkly gray-headed. Ruby wasted no time assuming her duties and led Virginia up the stairs to see the room she evidently was to share with Daniel during their stay at River Ridge. Then, while Virginia waited for Steve and Mitchel to see that everything was taken upstairs and placed in the room, the elderly couple left for their own cottage.

Daniel explained the Edmonds' absence when Virginia came down to discover them already gone. He had made arrangements to warm and serve the meal they'd prepared, telling them to go on to bed and get their rest. Even Mitchel, who eagerly wanted to stay behind and help, was told to go on to bed just as soon as the horses were taken care of, the carriage was put away, and the driver had been fed.

"It's late," Daniel told the boy. "You'll need all the rest you can get if you plan to ride into Jefferson with Steve in the morning."

Suddenly included in the trip to town, Mitchel left willingly. And within an hour Virginia found herself very much alone in a strange house with no one for company but her newly acquired husband. The realization of that sent nervous tremors through her, and a cold apprehension climbed upward to claim her throat in a painful grip. She could only guess what would happen next.

Chapter Eighteen

"Would you like to go back upstairs and freshen up before we settle down for supper? Maybe you'd like to change into something more comfortable. Ruby is supposed to have left you a pitcher of hot water and a cake of soap on the washstand," Daniel told her. He pulled his coat off and tossed it over the nearest chair, then quickly unbuttoned his white ruffled shirt to reveal a narrow span of his bronzed chest to her.

"No, what I am wearing is just fine," she said. She glanced away from the opening in his shirt to the fawn-colored brilliantine trimmed in light salmon silk that she had chosen to wear for their trip. Because she had not been sure of their destination, she had chosen something fairly formal, just to be safe. And though she had dresses that were far more comfortable, she did not want to risk changing into one of them with no one to prevent Daniel from coming in on her while she did. She knew she would eventually have to risk dressing behind bedroom doors that had no bolts, and she was more than willing to put it off for as long as possible. "I've already run a wet cloth over my face and neck to get some of the dust off."

"Well, then, I guess you're ready to eat," he said and turned toward the kitchen. "Go on into the dining room and sit down. I'll get the food."

Virginia thought she should volunteer to bring in the food for him, since that was considered a woman's task, but she did not feel like it; she was not even hungry. Even though she had not eaten a solid meal since lunch the day before, her appetite was absent. She felt that sitting down to supper would be a waste of time; but when she considered what alternative Daniel might have in mind, she decided it was the safest waste of time she could hope for.

She wandered into the open door he had indicated just before he disappeared into another door further down the hall. Inside the room she discovered a large dining table with twelve chairs spaced around it and six matching chairs lined against the wall. All twelve places had been set with a full placement of china, silver, and gleaming dinner glasses, making her wonder if Daniel had originally planned for company or if Ruby always set a full table no matter how many were expected to eat. To Virginia it seemed wasted effort, but then she was not accustomed to the lifestyle of the elite. Maybe to the wealthy, a fully set table was important. She had to admit it did look nice.

She walked further into the room and noticed two tall, richly carved sideboards against the walls on either side of her. They had been hand-rubbed until the entire room seemed reflected on their dark surfaces. The floor was carpeted and from the high ceiling overhead hung a huge chandelier dripping with sparkling crystal.

Only every other candle in the chandelier had been lit, but even so, it illuminated the room. Virginia could well imagine what it was like when all the candles were aglow. Glancing around in a full circle at her luxurious surroundings, she decided the room was quite elegant, if somewhat pretentious for a house that was rarely used. She wondered how many days Ruby had spent rubbing and polishing to get the house to look so grand.

Choosing a chair at the end, knowing Daniel would choose to sit at the other end, Virginia settled into the surprising comfort of the tall-backed chair and waited for Daniel to return. While she rested her elbows on the arms and locked her fingers together in front of her, her eyes were drawn across the wide room to the lace curtains that billowed slightly with the evening breeze and to the glimmering moonlight which bathed the yard beyond. The delicate scent of fresh mint drifted in through the tall windows and blended with the aroma of food. She breathed deeply the pleasing scents and let herself relax just enough to enjoy them.

But Daniel's sudden appearance through a swinging door she had not noticed startled her from her reverie. Though discovering a door where there did not appear to be one had caused her heart to lurch, it was the realization that he was back in the room that set her senses reeling. Self-consciously she raised a hand to cover the telltale pulse she could feel beating at her throat.

"I had hoped Ruby would have fried us a large platter of catfish," Daniel said when he first entered the room carrying two plates. "But it looks like we'll have to make do with roast turkey."

"Turkey is fine," she assured him. He removed the service plates and put the already filled plates in their places. To her dismay, he chose to set his own in front of the chair directly to her left instead of at the far end of the table. There would not be very much distance between them after all.

"I'll see if I can't persuade Rufus to do a little fishing tomorrow. You haven't tasted heaven until you've had Ruby's fried catfish and hush puppies. I don't know what she puts in them, but they're better than any I've ever had."

Virginia knew what fried catfish was, for her grandmother had prepared it on occasion, but wondered what hush puppies might be. She did not want to sound ignorant of such delicacies, so she merely agreed it would be nice to try Ruby's special recipe.

Daniel returned to the kitchen and came back with a tall pitcher of chilled water and filled their glasses. Virginia took note of the linen napkin carefully draped over his arm and his stiff manner; she realized he was trying very much to act the proper waiter. She could not help but produce a smile when he nodded curtly, clicking his boot heels together, and asked if there would be anything else for "Madame."

"No, Madame is just fine," she said, wanting to laugh at his ridiculous behavior and feeling some of the tension drain from the tired muscles of her body.

"Well, then, if you are certain there will be nothing else, I shall go tell the gentleman of the house that supper has been served."

"Gentleman?" She could not resist her own retort. "I'm afraid you'll find no gentleman in this house."

Daniel twisted his mouth at the remark but remained in staunch control. "Then I shall see if there is anyone else around here who might be interested in the food that fills that other plate. Gentleman or no."

He then disappeared through the side-swinging door and when he reappeared only seconds later, the napkin was gone from his arm and his lazy, long strides had returned.

"I was told by a very handsome and extremely gallant waiter that supper was ready," he said with an endearing smile as he pulled out the chair to her left and sat down with lithe ease.

Virginia responded to his comment with a laugh. "I wonder how *he* knew? I guess that awkward, rather pompous man who was just in here to bring in these two plates of food must have told him."

"No doubt," Daniel said with a raised brow, as if she had just offended him deeply, but the grin tugging at the outer corners of his lips and pressing in on his dimples let her know that he was not so very offended that he couldn't see the humor in her comment.

To her delight, Daniel continued to be charming while they ate their meal, and once she finally began to eat, though the food was barely warm and the turkey had lost most of its moisture, Virginia's appetite returned. She ate most of what was on her plate. When they were finished, Daniel suggested they retire to the back veranda for a while so she could see the remarkable view of the river. She was feeling very relaxed, relaxed enough to allow Daniel to sit in the porch swing with her and not offer any protest.

"When did your uncle have this house built?" she asked while she looked out across the glittering dark water. The slow moving river ran several hundred yards from the house—far enough to prevent any bother with flooding, but close enough to make it easily accessible. The gentle movement of the moonlight sparkling across its surface had a tranquil effect on her and she leaned back into the swing smiling.

"I'm not really certain when. Long before I was born. I remember coming here in the summer and staying with him for weeks at a time when I was still young. I used to love to spend those long, hot summer days swimming in the river." He laughed lightly at the memories that the conversation had stirred. "Uncle Caleb used to swear I was part river turtle. I'd go swimming just as soon as I had my chores done and stay until dark."

"He made you do chores?" she asked, finding that odd, but then deciding Caleb was just the sort to take advantage of his own nephew like that.

"The chores were my father's idea . . . Father

330

did not like the thought of me staying with Uncle Caleb without at least trying to earn my keep. But Uncle Caleb pretty well let me choose my own chores. Of course, I picked things that could be done in a hurry so that I'd have more time to play." He laughed. "I remember how Louis used to hurry with his chores too so that he could join me."

"Who's Louis?"

"Louis Edmond—Mitchel's father. You'll probably meet him tomorrow . . . he's the handyman around here. That man can do anything he sets his mind to. He was like that even when we were kids. I remember, one summer he decided we were going to build ourselves a fancy pirate ship, but what we ended up with was more like a large raft with shallow sides. But it was a sturdy thing. We played with that for two entire summers before it fell apart."

Daniel laughed. "We made fine pirates, too. Our only problem was that when we'd go looking for buried treasure chests or other ships to loot there were none to be found. And Uncle Caleb refused to let us take the raft out of his sight. Made being a successful pirate in these parts next to impossible. But we sure had a lot of fun pretending." His eyes sparkled with the memory. "Had fun building our special hide-out, too."

Virginia enjoyed hearing about Daniel's childhood. It seemed strange to learn he had done many of the same things she had as a child. It left her eager to hear more. But when she continued to ask about himself, he began to ask about *her* childhood. Well aware that she needed to stay as

331

far away from the subject as she possibly could, she finally offered what had started out to be a feigned yawn, but had quickly taken hold and developed into the real thing.

"I'm tired, Daniel. I think I'd like to go on up to bed, now."

"Me, too," he said agreeably as he leaned forward in the swing, a response which sent the swing swaying from side to side and her pulse racing out of control. "I think I'm about ready to catch a little shut-eye too."

Virginia did not know what to say next; she had hoped to be allowed to go up without him. "Please, don't think you have to turn in just because I'm so tired."

"I'm tired, too," he assured her. "It's been a long day." Then, as if he suddenly realized her discomfort, he leaned back in the swing again. "But then, I haven't had a chance to smoke my pipe in two days." Quickly he reached into his pocket and took out his tobacco. He felt inside for the pipe, then took out a hefty pinch of tobacco to fill it. "You go on up and get ready for bed. I'll be up in a few minutes."

Virginia did not waste any time, not knowing how long it would take him to smoke the pipe. Rising quickly, she hurried back inside. Taking the carpeted steps as rapidly as she could, she returned to her room and quickly closed the door behind her, wishing there was a bolt to be put into place. With no time to lose, she turned to search the room for her trunk and her valise, but her eyes were immediately drawn to a wide pool of shimmering white that lay across the bed awaiting her.

Moving cautiously toward it, almost as if she thought it could jump up and bite her, Virginia quickly realized it was a nightgown—a nightgown made of some ridiculously flimsy material edged at the indecently low neckline and along the wide hem with two rows of delicate French lace. When she reached out to touch the garment, she discovered the flimsy material was so thin that it was practically useless. Such material would be put to better use as mosquito netting.

Next she noticed the matching wrapper that lay just to the side. Lifting it up, she decided it would prove to be just as impractical. And by the lavish way the two garments had been displayed on the bed, it was obvious Daniel expected her to wear them. Panic constricted her throat. Did he plan to break their agreement? Did he plan to take his husbandly rights? A shiver of fearful anticipation wafted over her, causing her legs to grow numb. Knowing she did not have much time to ponder the situation, for a pipeful of tobacco did not last forever, Virginia decided to compromise.

Knowing Daniel could now come in at any moment, she hurriedly slipped into the gown, but quickly searched her valise for her own flannel wrapper. She stuffed the flimsy outer garment deep into the side of the valise so that it would not be out in view and continued to hurry as quickly as she could.

Tying the sash of her wrapper tightly, lapping the front edges as far as she could in an effort to be sure she was properly covered from her neck to her ankles, she hurriedly blew out all the candles and the lamp on her side of the bed, which left only the lamp on his side of the bed burning when she climbed into bed. Shivering beneath the three layers of sheets, she tried to pretend to be asleep when he came into the room less than twenty minutes later.

Though Daniel had opened the door noisily, after he had caught sight of her with her eyes pressed closed, he shut it again very quietly, then tiptoed over to the bed to undress. He fought the urge to smile at the way she looked, curled up like a kitten, obviously hoping he would believe she was already asleep. He was disappointed the gown had not made her feel more comfortable in his presence. Obviously it had worked to do the opposite, because it was gone from the bed and Virginia had the covers pulled up to her neck. She held the blanket firmly in place by two white-knuckled fists. She was clearly terrified of what might happen next. His heart went out to her when he realized exactly how vulnerable she really was. For a woman who always seemed to be in control, she really was as vulnerable as a kitten.

Though she had not yet opened her eyes, Virginia could hear the movement of Daniel's hands on the satiny material of his shirt. She tried nobly not to peek, but unfortunately she lay facing him, and by the time he had tugged off his shirt, she could see him through her squinting eyelids.

He sat down to tug off his boots, then stood again and reached for the opening of his trousers. She felt a sharp intake of air and clamped her eyes shut again, but as the sound of the material moving against his skin reached her, beckoning her, she found herself peeking through barely opened eyelids once more. She was relieved to discover he had his back to her.

Never having viewed a naked man before, Virginia was startled to see what perfectly molded beasts they really were: the muscles in Daniel's back, shoulders, hips, and thighs moved with such grace while he removed the last of his undergarments that it made Virginia want to open her eyes a degree more. She didn't dare for fear he would turn around and realize she had watched.

After he was undressed, she wondered if he had bought *himself* something special to sleep in on their wedding night. Resisting the urge to bite her lower lip while she waited to find out, she wondered if it would prove to be as flimsy and worthless as her own gown. Her breathing grew more rapid and increasingly shallow when, instead of looking around for his own night garment, as she had expected him to, he moved quickly into the bed. The man had no intention of putting on a nightshirt of any kind!

Petrified, Virginia lay still as he arranged the covers about him, then reached over to the small lamp and slowly turned it out. Aware he could no longer see her because of the darkness, she drew her lower lip between her teeth and bit down hard in preparation for what was to come.

With each movement that came from his side of the bed, her heart beat a little louder in her ears, until she was afraid she would not hear him start to slide toward her when the time finally came. But to her surprise, Daniel did nothing to try to wake her. She lay beside him wondering about the fact that he didn't even attempt a simple good-night kiss.

The next thing Virginia knew, she was waking up to a bright flow of sunlight that streamed into the windows and a loud knock at the door. Blinking rapidly awake, instantly aware of where she was, she sat up in bed, the covers still clutched to her throat, and looked around the bedroom. Why didn't Daniel respond to the knock? Oddly, her first thought was of how very different the room looked in the daytime, bathed in sunlight, with the happy sounds of larks singing just outside her window. Realizing Daniel was already gone from the bed, and gone from the room, she called out, "Who is it?"

She waited to see if it was Daniel, but at the same time wondered why he would bother to knock. It was when she bit her lip that she discovered how very sore it was, probably from having gone to sleep with it still held firmly between her teeth.

"It's Ruby, ma'am. I've brought you some breakfast." The craggy voice was cheerful.

"Come in," Virginia called out, relieved it was not Daniel; but she continued to clutch the covers to her throat. She realized she still had on her flannel wrapper and knew how odd that might look to the servant. Since she had promised Daniel not to make the marriage seem in any way out of the ordinary, she decided to keep the sheet drawn tight.

"You must have been very tired from everything that went on yesterday," Ruby commented, trying to hide an amused smile as she entered. "It's already after ten o'clock, and you look like I might have awakened you with my knock."

"Ten o'clock?" Virginia repeated incredulously. She saw a clock far across the room, on the fireplace mantel, but it was too small for her to make out the time. "I guess I must have been far more tired than I realized."

"Doesn't matter," Ruby went on to reassure her. "Mister Daniel had a feeling you'd be sleeping in. He's already eaten his breakfast and gone off with Louis to see the latest improvements to the pier. He told me to let you sleep undisturbed for a while, but if you weren't up by ten, to bring you a tray. So here I am." Ruby placed the wooden breakfast tray beside Virginia and smiled as she shook the folds from the napkin and handed it to her. "Is there anything else I can do for you while I'm here?"

"No, thank you. This is fine," Virginia told her as she eyed the steaming mound of scrambled eggs, a half dozen strips of bacon, several bowls of colorful jams, and two incredibly rich buttered biscuits. Until the aroma reached her, she thought she wasn't hungry. But from the moment she broke off a tender piece of the biscuit and put it in her mouth, she knew she was famished.

"You just enjoy the meal. I'll be back for the tray directly," Ruby told her. "Because you both ate such a late breakfast, lunch won't be much; but for supper we're having fried catfish, hush puppies, and fried potato hash."

Virginia felt as if it was a warning to eat light, and after Ruby left the room, she decided to do just that by eating only half her food. But she realized that even that precaution would not yield

337

a sparse meal, for the plate was filled to abnormal proportions. She decided then to try just a few bites of each item and put the rest aside. But even the best-laid plans proved they could quickly go awry, for before she realized it she'd eaten almost everything on her plate.

It was not until she'd put the tray aside and stretched back into her pillows that she let her thoughts wander from the awesome repast into areas far more forbidding. She remembered how Daniel had gone directly to sleep once he had come to bed, and she knew she should be relieved; but when she thought more about it, she had an odd sense of disappointment. It didn't make sense.

So far, nothing she considered truly disappointing had happened, for Daniel had been the perfect gentleman. They were to spend their wedding trip in a beautiful place, yet still she felt disappointed. She realized that Daniel had *not* tried to take what was lawfully his. Was he truly so honorable?

Suddenly Virginia began to feel self-doubt: it was hard to believe Daniel was so noble. Did he not want to make love to her because she was perhaps not appealing enough? But no, that could not be it—he had made it plain how much he desired her the afternoon he'd proposed. So it was not because he did not find her desirable. Then what? Had he been too tired? He had openly said he was; but then, he had not really acted very tired.

Never had Virginia felt more confused. And when Daniel did not try anything intimate with her again that evening after they had enjoyed a delicious meal of catfish and hush puppies, her confusion grew even more. Later he climbed into bed exactly as he had the first night, turning out the light and going right to sleep. She'd again felt a deep sense of relief, but also a strange foreboding, a sense of disappointment.

The following morning she awoke to discover him once again gone from her bed. He'd left word that he planned for them to go on a picnic together somewhere nearby, along the river. Virginia felt a fluttering of excitement: the two of them would be alone out among the beautiful flowers and trees that lined the wide, slow-moving river. But she quickly attributed the feeling to the fact that she had been so lonely and completely lost for something to do the day before.

Shortly before noon, Virginia, dressed in a pale yellow cotton dress, waited downstairs in the front parlor. Daniel suddenly appeared at her side with a huge wicker basket. With little need for conversation, they walked side by side to a small, picturesque cove, where he quickly spread out their quilts and served the lovely lunch Ruby had packed. To her growing confusion, he did nothing to try to touch her, even when they lay on the quilts to rest after lunch. When the time came for them to return to the house, he did not once even try to touch her elbow, as he used to do. She began to feel frustrated.

That night, Daniel again stripped and climbed into bed. Because she had not tried to feign sleep this time, but had only averted her eyes while he undressed, he bent forward and kissed her lightly on the forehead—but did nothing to try to seduce her before leaning away from her, then dropping off into a sound sleep.

Virginia, on the other hand, did not find sleep so readily attainable and lay awake beside him until the wee hours of the morning.

On the third day she overslept once more. The morning ritual of breakfast in bed continued. Smiling as usual, Ruby was quick to inform her that Daniel had just left for a walk along the river, but would return before lunch.

Feeling a growing sense of restlessness, Virginia picked at her food; but when she thought about it all, she set the food aside, hurriedly dressed in a pretty pink cotton dress, and went downstairs to find out where Daniel had gone. Learning that he was probably headed for the same cove where they had picnicked the day before, she wasted no time in attempting to follow him.

She was surprised at the light mist that clung to the ground in places, and at how cool it was beneath the dark shade of the tall, elegant cypress trees that grew in such abundance near the river. She wished she had thought to get her shawl; she never would have expected the morning to be quite so chilly in the month of August. But instead of going back, for the day would quickly warm, she wrapped her arms about her shoulders and continued her search for Daniel, eager to catch up with him and share his walk.

Though she was not certain of the path she should take and knew there were several to choose from, she felt the one she had chosen once she neared the river was the right one. She began to hurry along, her heart alive with anticipation. As she entered the woods she wondered how she was going to explain her sudden appearance to him without letting him realize her eagerness. If Ruby was correct, he had been gone only half an hour. He could not have walked very far in that short a time.

The deeper she went into the surrounding woodlands, the denser became the undergrowth; and the less sure she was that she had taken the right path. Finally she paused and looked for anything that looked familiar. She frowned with uncertainty and called out Daniel's name. When there was no answer, she decided it would be better to turn back than chance getting lost.

Though the mist still clung to the darkest areas of the woods, she realized it was slowly clearing, and the air was tinged with just enough warmth for her to be comfortable even under the trees. She dropped her arms to her sides. Knowing she was headed *back* in the right direction, she relaxed and became more aware of her surroundings.

She noticed for the first time a large clearing off through the trees, in the opposite direction of the river. Beckoning her from the sunshine of that clearing were several tall patches of bright yellow daisies and a lush sprinkling of lavender primroses. Unable to resist the flowers, she turned off the path and hurried to pick a colorful bouquet.

As she entered the clearing and felt the sun against her skin, she noticed a tall rock-and-mortar fireplace with chimney; the clearing had to be the result of an old homeplace. Lured forward to see what else she might discover, she went to stand in front of the fireplace. As she looked around, she tried to imagine what sort of house had once stood in that spot.

There were several pieces of rusted metal, a few planks of weather-worn lumber, and a wide, solitary stone step, but nothing besides the chimney to indicate that a house had ever stood there. She wondered how long ago the house had been brought down and what might have claimed it. She shuddered at the thought of a tornado having come through to snatch it away but felt there would have been noticeable damage to the surrounding trees. Her next thought was housefire, because scorched trees had been known to survive seemingly unscathed. But there was no real way to know. With her curiosity stirred, she decided she would ask Daniel about it, and turned to go back the way she had come. Quickly she stepped across a few planks of wood that had been carelessly left behind and continued to study her surroundings, wondering if she would be able to find the place again so she could show it to Daniel.

That's when she heard a splintering crack from the wood: it broke beneath her weight and she felt herself tumbling into a deep, dark hole. She screamed as she went down and again when she struck her head on the side of something hard, but once she had landed in the icy water at the bottom of the narrow opening, she found herself stunned into silence. Though she could not see what lay around her, she felt solid ground beneath her, she stood waist-high in chilling water. It was several minutes before she had her bearings and realized she was in an old abandoned well.

Glancing up through the boards overhead at the patches of August sky, she began to call out for help. Far more frustrated at having been so careless than over the fear she would never be found, she did all she could do to call out Daniel's name again and again at the top of her voice—until she heard something move in the black water beside her.

Chapter Nineteen

"Did she say when she would be back?" Daniel asked. He pulled back the curtain and looked out toward a path that cut through the recently mowed grounds, winding its way toward the river.

"No, she didn't." Ruby shook her head to emphasize the point. "I got the impression she planned to catch up with you, so I didn't think to ask her about it. She wanted to know which path you might have taken and I told her you was probably headed for that pretty little cove a little ways upriver, that being your favorite spot and all."

"That's where I went, all right," he said with a nod, wondering how they could have missed each other, then realized Virginia might have asked about where he'd gone not so that she could join him, but so she could avoid him altogether. Though he had tried his best to make her feel more at ease she still was very nervous when she found herself alone with him. He was well aware that when he climbed into bed beside her, though he made no move other than once to kiss her forehead, she tensed visibly and then did not manage to fall asleep for hours.

She was terrified of being alone with him. And having realized that, Daniel had started to wonder if Amanda might have been right about their marriage; maybe it was a mistake. He had hoped that by getting her alone at tranquil River Ridge he could break through the barriers between them and at last become her good friend. He was not foolish enough to hope for anything more, though he longed to make much better use of their bed. But even if their relationship never reached such an intimate stage, they at least needed to become better friends and feel more at ease in each other's company—or people were going to realize their marriage was not at all what it should be. Soon Mary would realize it, too.

"She must have forgotten the way and taken off on the wrong path," Ruby put in worriedly as she set her paring knife aside and peered out a window. "There are several she could have taken. Even so, you'd think she'd be back by now. Sun's high up in the sky. It's time for lunch. Surely she realizes that."

"I'm sure she does," he commented coolly, then turned away. "She'll probably be along shortly. Put off serving the meal until one. If she hasn't returned by then, I'll eat without her."

When Virginia did not return, Daniel sat down at the table to eat his noonday meal alone, but found he was not any too hungry. After a few bites he pushed his plate aside and rose from the table. With a look of pure agitation on his handsome features, he entered the kitchen and headed straight for the back door.

"I think I'll go look for her. Though she does not seem to be the mindless type, there's still a possibility she's lost. If she should return, ring the emergency bell so I'll know to quit looking for her."

Ruby released a sigh of relief. "I hope you find her quick. I'm worried. If she intended to be gone this long, surely she would have thought to tell me."

Daniel nodded; though Virginia could be the most argumentive and exasperating woman on this earth, she was usually very considerate. As he stalked past Ruby, he automatically reached for his rifle, kept on a rack near the door, and headed down the path toward the river.

After he was well away from the house, he began to call out her name every few dozen yards and stopped occasionally to listen for a response, but heard nothing.

When he cut through a small wooded area to where a path wove its way into the dense woods, he started calling her name again; still no answer. After trying the third trail for some distance, he returned to the main path and began to try the trails that actually did lead in the direction of the cove. As time edged away from him and still he failed to find her, he started to worry.

Daniel continued to stop often to call out Virginia's name, each time listening carefully for a response. It was only after he had gone several hundred yards further that he heard footsteps hurrying through the woods in his direction.

"Mister Daniel, come quick," Mitchel called to him, breathless from having run so fast. Daniel was able to hear the boy's strained, panic-filled voice even before he could see him, and he turned to peer into the underbrush for sight of him.

"What is it?" Daniel asked, feeling a prickle of fear rise along his neck while he watched Mitchel hurriedly push his way through the dense brush. Blood trickled down the boy's legs; he'd run right through briars and berry vines. "Does it have to do with my wife?"

Mitchel nodded, his dark eyes wide. He continued to gasp for air. "She's fallen . . . into a well!"

Daniel felt as if he had received a blow to the stomach. "Is she hurt?"

"Says she's not, but there's snakes down there with her, Mister Daniel."

"Snakes? How'd snakes get in there?"

"Don't rightly know, but there's lots of them. She's staying still like I told her to, but you know how snakes are. Sometimes they stay plumb clear of you. But sometimes you don't even have to make a move and they strike."

Mitchel planned to go into further detail, but Daniel had already bounded forward, his eyes wide with horror and his nostrils flared wide. Suddenly it felt as if a white-hot fire had become trapped in his lungs. Never had he felt such intense fear.

"Where is she?" he cried, scowling when he discovered Mitchel had not yet moved to follow him.

"The old Hitt homeplace," Mitchel called back. He had turned to watch as Daniel tore through the woods. Drawing in another long breath, the boy finally set his lanky legs into motion, though he could not hope to keep up with Daniel, who raced like a madman through the dense underbrush.

"Virginia!" Daniel began calling out as soon as he had the clearing in sight. He knew right where the old well was; he had been there when they'd replaced the rotting boards just four years ago. He ran directly to the gaping hole, his heart lodged in his throat as he slid to his knees.

Peering inside, all he could see beyond the first few feet was darkness. Swallowing back his fear, he called out to her, "Virginia? Are you all right?"

He heard a light splashing sound, but there was no verbal response to be heard. Quickly he reached into his pocket, jerked out his tobacco pouch, and flung it hard across the ground to get it out of his way, then found his matches. As soon as his fingers could single one out, he struck it. His whole chest pounded furiously while he laid his rifle next to the broken boards, bent forward, and held the burning match down inside the hole as far as his arm could reach so that he could see. His heart willed her to still be alive. He did not think he could stand it if she was dead.

First Daniel felt relief, for the flickering light, dim though it was, revealed that Virginia was indeed still alive . . . still standing . . . frozen to the spot. But he was suddenly besieged with as many as six snake heads protruding from the dark waters that surrounded her. Water moccasins.

All that moved besides the snakes were Virginia's eyes: she looked at the slithering creatures, then peered skyward into his terrified face.

"Damn," he cursed as the match burned to the nub, scorching his forefinger and thumb before he thought to drop it. Ignoring the pain he lit another.

"Don't move," he said unnecessarily, for she was barely breathing in her effort to be stone-still. Mitchel arrived in the clearing at that moment. "Come over here, Mitchel," Daniel cried.

The boy's eyes widened with concern but he did what he'd been told. Carefully he stopped closer to where Daniel lay. Over the hole where Missus Virginia had fallen. In the same hole with all those snakes. Mitchel shuddered.

"Find something to make a torch," Daniel told him, barely taking any time to glance up at Mitchel's terrified face. *Hurry.*

Minutes later, Mitchel returned to Daniel's side with a long, stout limb. Daniel quickly tore off part of his shirt and wrapped the material around the leaves, then lit it.

"Hold this down in the hole, where I can see . . . off to one side, so you don't set fire to me. I'm going to try to pick off those snakes one at a time without hitting Virginia."

A tiny noise that greatly resembled a puppy's yelp came from deep inside the well, but Virginia voiced no real protest while Mitchel slowly lowered the torch into the hole. Tiny pieces of flaming leaves broke away and drifted down over her, but she did not move. Now that there was enough light, she could see just how many snakes there were—far more than she had thought—some were bold enough to swim up against her waist. She could also make out their blunt noses and realized they were indeed poisonous.

Though her legs had already grown numb from

the extreme cold of the water, she could still sense that her knees and thighs were weakening. Brief flashes of light went off inside her head, yet she suffered no real pain. Still, she realized that in another few minutes she might faint.

Alarmed by all that could happen to her if she did, her brain cried out for Daniel to hurry, but her lips remained pressed together to prevent her from uttering another sound.

"Don't move," Daniel called out, and she discovered she was becoming a little annoyed at having to be told not to move; she was certain she had not even breathed since he had mentioned his decision to shoot the snakes.

While Daniel lifted his Winchester and scooted on his stomach as close as he dared to the ragged edge of the hole, he prayed there would not be more than fifteen snakes down there altogether. He had not thought to grab extra ammunition; all he had was what the rifle held. He realized he would have to aim carefully: not only did he not wish to risk a bullet ricocheting recklessly off a rock; he did not want to waste even one of his fifteen shots. Holding his breath deep in his pounding chest, he leaned into the hole. The burning torch was close enough to his face so that he could feel the heat against his skin. He took careful aim at one of the snakes furthest from her.

The shot echoed off the walls and nearly deafened him, but he saw the slithering reptile go down. The others began to swim about in a frantic manner, which would make it almost impossible to get a good shot at another.

"I've got to wait for them to calm down," he

told Virginia, hoping she would prove to be understanding. "I don't want to waste my ammunition."

Oh, no, of course not, she thought bitterly, wildly, unaware that Daniel was concerned because he only had fifteen shots in all. *Let's not waste any of your precious ammunition. After all, these are only poisonous snakes swimming around me.* She felt her legs grow weaker still. Finally, she realized that she was going to have to break silence in order to get this stupid man to understand the true seriousness of her situation.

"Hurry, will you? I think I'm going to faint," she said softly through her firmly gritted teeth. Just as she'd feared, the sound of her voice stirred the creatures again and they slithered through the water at an even faster rate.

"Damn," she heard him mutter again as he returned to the hole and took immediate aim. He fired the second shot, but this time missed. "Damn, damn, *damnation!*"

Virginia found that though she usually did not abide by such obscene language, she was in no way opposed to them now; the exact words had occurred to her. She took her pleasure in hearing him say them again and again.

Daniel rose from his position over the hole to cock his rifle again. But this time he had failed to pull back far enough and the empty casing fell onto the boards; before he could catch it, it rolled into the hole. He heard a thud before he heard a splash and realized it had hit her on the head. Despite the extreme seriousness of the situation, he could almost see the expression on her face and had to grin when he called down his apology.

351

Ready for the third shot, he leaned back out into the hole, bending further down than he had before, and again took careful aim, letting the barrel of his rifle follow the movement of one of the calmer snakes.

He fired—again one of the creatures went down. After thirteen shots, and only two of them misses, there was no other movement from the water.

"I think that's all of them," he called out to her, but continued to watch in the fading light of the dying torch. He knew there had to be a way the snakes were getting in and out, and knew more snakes could appear at any moment.

"Are you certain?" she called out in a tiny voice.

Daniel waited a moment longer, listening and watching. When there still was no movement, he said with finality, "That's all of them. Are you all right?"

"I've been better."

He grinned. "I mean were you bitten?"

"No."

Sitting up, relieved to hear she had not been bitten, Daniel laid the rifle aside and began to worry next about how he was going to get her out of there. Whatever he did, he needed to hurry.

He thought of a stout tree limb, but realized that it might not reach her, not as far down as she was; and after such a terrifying ordeal, she just might not have the strength to climb out on her own anyway. Finally he realized he would have to lower himself into the hole and haul her out. He looked at Mitchel, who stood stock-still, bent slightly over the hole, still holding the torch in place. Daniel felt a perverse twinge of amusement at how the boy resembled a statue, so frozen with fear that he did not move, though the most terrifying part of their dilemma was pretty well over. "Mitchel, go back to the house and get a long piece of rope. Get Louis, too, if you can find him."

When the boy did not immediately respond, Daniel reached out to touch him. "Mitchel, go back to the house and get a rope. *Hurry.*"

Mitchel looked at him then, pulling the torch out of the hole as he did, blinked twice, opened his mouth to speak; then fainted dead away.

"What next?" Daniel cried out in exasperation. He reached first to beat out the flames of the torch, then moved toward the boy, hoping to hurry and bring him back awake. The answer to his question came just seconds later, when he heard a loud splash in the well and realized that Virginia had fainted too.

"Virginia?" he called out. There was no answer.

Aware she could drown, Daniel wasted no time. He left Mitchel and quickly lowered himself into the hole until his shoulders were level with the ground, then let go of the boards and dropped. With it now dark in the hole again, he hoped he would not accidentally land on Virginia and injure her, knowing she'd probably already injured herself enough during the fall.

Groping for her in the dark, he found her floating just below the water's surface and quickly lifted her head and shoulders out of the water. Patting his hand against her cold, wet cheek, he called out her name again and again, wishing he could see her face to know if she was responding. Finally he heard her moan.

"Virginia," he called out once more, relieved, and hugged her to him. "You had me scared half out of my mind." Immediately his voice turned angry, while she stiffened her body and tried to stand. "What were you doing, breaking through those boards like that?"

Virginia's brow rose with warning, but Daniel was unable to see the angry expression in the darkness; yet when she spoke, he could hear her irritation.

"Falling, mostly," was her angry reply.

She felt Daniel's grip tense while he continued to hold her tight against him, though she was now partially standing on her own two feet. But his grip gradually relaxed and she heard a light chuckle come from deep inside him.

"Did you hurt yourself when you fell?" he asked, most of the anger now gone from his voice.

"Some, but I did far more damage when I landed," she said, this time serious in her answer, because although she had scraped her arm on the jagged boards as she fell through, her head and shoulder had slammed hard against the side of the well just before she landed in the water. She twisted her lips into a tight scowl when she heard Daniel respond to her comment with a short burst of laughter.

"I'm glad to know that my injuries bring you such undeniable pleasure," she muttered with annoyance.

"They don't. I'm sorry. Are you badly hurt?" He reached out to run his hand over her damp face, brushing the clinging strands of hair aside so that he could feel her skin for injuries.

"I'm not telling you," she said stubbornly. She jerked her face away from the tender touch of his hand, mostly because it had started her heart to fluttering too soon after she had finally gotten it calmed again.

By now Daniel's eyes had started to adjust to the dark just enough to make out the shape of her. He bent forward, his nose just inches away from hers. "Well, then, just as soon as I get you out of here, I'm going to have to look for myself. Aren't I?"

Despite the cold water, and the fact that they were both trapped down in a well with almost a dozen dead snakes, Virginia felt her fluttering heart flower into excited apprehension. "You wouldn't dare."

"A complete and thorough examination," he stated and brought his nose closer until it actually touched hers. "From your pretty little head to your dainty little toes."

Virginia could see a faint reflection where his eyes were and knew that if she had a little more light, she would see an expression that would bring her hammering heart to a standstill.

"My head and my toes you can examine to your heart's content, but don't you dare touch anything that lies in between."

Daniel chuckled. "Then you'd better tell me now where your injuries are."

Virginia sighed aloud, realizing it would be to her own advantage to surrender this battle early on. "I've hurt my head and my right shoulder.

And I've scraped my arm and possibly my leg. But I have no serious injuries—no broken bones."

"You never can be too sure about broken bones," he said, and she could almost hear the leer in his voice when he added, "Maybe I should examine you anyway the moment we get out of here—just to be sure."

"And, when, pray tell, *are* we getting out of here?"

There was silence, as if Daniel had not given that problem much thought. "Good question. Why is it teachers always ask such darn good questions?"

"It's in our training. Why is it poor students always avoid giving answers?"

"It's in *our* training."

This time it was Virginia who could not help but laugh. Then she asked, "Do you have a plan to get us out of here or not?"

"At the moment—not," he admitted. Then, suddenly remembering that other snakes could appear at any moment, he called out, "Mitchel! Mitchel! Are you awake yet?"

"Mitchel went to sleep?" Virginia quizzed and looked skyward for a moment.

"Mitchel fainted," he grumbled, then chuckled. "Toppled over like a felled tree."

"Mitchel!" he shouted at the top of his voice. It echoed off the sides and rang in his ears. There was no response.

"I need something to toss out of here to try to get his attention," he finally said. "Help me find something."

"What about these dead snakes?"

Daniel chuckled. "That sure ought to get his attention."

"You toss one dead snake out of that there hole and I'm leavin' here for good," they heard Mitchel's voice call just as his head moved to peer cautiously at them.

Within moments Mitchel was on his way to get the rope and to find his father.

"How are you holding up?" Daniel asked after several minutes.

"I'm not," she said simply. "In fact, if you weren't helping hold me up the way you are, I would probably by lying at the very bottom of this well, right along with most of those dead snakes. My legs are very, very numb."

"Are you sure you haven't injured them too?" he asked, suddenly concerned.

"No. I felt them grow gradually numb from the cold. This well must be fed by spring water."

"The cold?" he asked, sounding bewildered.

"Yes. Aren't you cold?"

"I hadn't really noticed," he admitted, but now that she mentioned it, he did feel cold—awfully cold. The water had to be forty degrees or less. He could not imagine why he had not noticed it before, but he certainly noticed it now. By the time Mitchel returned with his father twenty minutes later, Daniel's teeth had begun to chatter and his own legs had started to feel a little numb.

"Mister Daniel? Missus Virginia? You still down there?" Mitchel called out.

Virginia sighed heavily, shaking her head with exasperation. She spoke so that only Daniel could hear her. "Will you tell me what is it about being up there and looking down here that makes people want to say and ask such stupid things?"

Daniel laughed softly, then called out to Mitchel, "We are still here. We talked it over while you were gone and decided not to leave until you got back."

Mitchel was too worried about their predicament to realize the intended humor; he turned to his father to announce, "They're still down there."

"Thanks, son," they heard Louis say. "Now will you unwind the other end of this rope while I tie it onto that tree over there?"

Virginia listened for several minutes before finally admitting the dismal truth: "Daniel, I don't think the rope will do any good. I honestly don't think I can climb out of here. My shoulder is too sore and my legs are too numb."

"That's okay . . . I plan to carry you."

"How?"

At that moment the rope dropped into the hole and landed on top of them in a wadded heap, bringing mutterings of complaint from both; and because Daniel had first thought it was a fresh covey of snakes, he nearly jumped out of his skin.

"There's the rope," Mitchel called to them a little late.

"Thanks, Mitchel," he said for again having delivered his obvious piece of information five seconds too late. Quickly, he reached up to pull the tangled rope from their heads.

"Can you stand?" he asked Virginia, and when she answered that she could, he let go of her, wrapped the rope around his own waist twice, then tied the end off to the lead piece.

"Ready for me to hoist you?" Louis called down, understanding exactly what Daniel had in mind.

"Just a second," Daniel called back, then quickly scooped Virginia into his arms and held her tightly against him. "Okay. Now!"

As the rope tightened, then began to pull them slowly out of the water, a gradual inch at a time, Daniel put out his legs and began to use them to walk up the side of the wall. Unable to really see, he could only hope he would not place his boot into the hole where the snakes entered the well and were probably resting.

"Comin' up easy," Louis told them and Daniel felt more relieved with each tug of the rope.

Though Virginia had yet to meet Louis, she knew his son Mitchel and could not imagine the two of them being able to pull Daniel and her both up as easily as they were. She was amazed they proved so strong. But when they finally reached the top and she was able to pull herself out onto solid ground and roll away from the well, she saw that Louis was huge . . . he had to be at least six-six and his weight was probably in the vicinity of three hundred pounds. The man reminded Virginia of an oversized oak. He was frightening to behold, and Virginia felt herself wanting to move away from him with fear until a wide, gentle smile broke his dark face. Suddenly he looked like an overgrown boy, and she realized he was harmless as a pup.

The moment Daniel had pulled himself out, Louis dropped his sturdy hold on the rope and came forward to see if he could help them. Mitchel hurried to stand beside his father.

"*This* is your pretty new wife?" Louis asked skeptically and glanced at Mitchel with a worried expression, as if he suddenly suspected the boy had rocks for brains.

Daniel laughed and explained, "She's seen better days."

Slowly Virginia looked down at her ragged wet dress. It had become caked with mud, and spattered with dried grass and broken leaves. The skirt was not only filthy but badly torn, and it revealed much of her mud-spattered legs.

Self-consciously she pulled the largest of the tears closed, then reached up to her hair and felt the wet, tangled mass that had also collected its fair share of grass, dirt, leaves, and splintered wood. Awkwardly she glanced up at Louis, who towered between her and the bright August sun, creating such a shadow that she could not see his face. Slowly she offered a sickly smile.

"You want me to carry her back to the house?" Louis asked as he started to reach down with only one hand, as if that were all he would need.

"No, I'll carry her. You gather up the rifle and the rope and bring them along," Daniel said as he pushed himself off the ground and quickly stood. He, too, had collected his fair share of grass and dirt, but for some reason he did not look so unkempt.

Now fully aware of her horrible appearance, Virginia wanted to crawl back into that hole. She decided she could at least keep Daniel as far away from her as possible until she had had a bath and could put on clean clothes.

"I can walk," she assured him, hoping he would come no closer, and pushed herself first to her knees, then tested her wobbly legs one at a time until she was indeed standing on her own two feet. "See there?"

Daniel frowned as if disappointed she had not broken both her legs.

"I told you my legs were fine," she added, and then, to prove the fact, she took her first step. Her legs folded and left her staring sheepishly up at him.

There was so much devilish mirth in Daniel's eyes when he knelt to catch her along, that Virginia wanted to punch him in the nose.

She opened her mouth to protest the way he was silently laughing at her, but he refused to let her speak.

"I know; I know . . . your legs are fine. And quite frankly, I agree. You have a fine pair of legs. But at the moment they aren't doing you much good."

"Daniel," she tried to interrupt, still eager to protest his decision to carry her.

He shot her an exasperated look while he lifted her up off the ground and held her against his chest. "Virginia. I am your husband. I want to carry you. It would give me great pleasure. For once, would you just humor me?"

"Yes, sir," she answered meekly, but when she saw the immediate raise of his brow, she quickly corrected herself, "I mean, yes, *ma'am.*"

Daniel's brow fell back into place as he smiled, obviously pleased by her remark.

"That's better," he said, then headed off toward

the house with Virginia balanced in his arms. He did not look back to see the curious glances Louis Edmond and his son exchanged while they gathered up the rifle and the rope, then quickly moved to follow.

Chapter Twenty

Mitchel raced ahead of the rest after they had reached the grounds and were all headed toward the house. He wanted to open the back door for Daniel. Stepping back as soon as he had the handle in his hand, he held the mesh door wide. A broad grin crossed his face when he heard his grandmother's instant demand that he close that door before he let flies into the house.

"I can't, Gran-ma. I'm holdin' it for Mister Daniel," he called out to her. He was delighted to have a good reason to disobey.

Daniel never paused in his long strides while he carried Virginia through the open door directly up the main stairway and into their bedroom.

Mitchel, Louis, and Ruby followed him only as far as the foot of the stairs, where they stopped to discuss what all had happened, knowing it would be inappropriate for them to go on up and intrude upon the newly married couple. But aware Virginia would be needing a bath, Ruby went back to the kitchen to start several pans of hot water just as soon as she had heard all her son and her grandson had to tell. Her brow drew into deep lines as she wondered why Daniel would want his wife to call him ma'am. White folks could certainly be strange at times.

Only seconds after they had entered the bedroom, Daniel kicked the door shut. Glad to have been left alone, he carried his shivering wife on across the floor and gently deposited her on the side of their bed, not really caring that she was still soaking wet and splotched with mud and grass; the satin coverlet was the last of his concerns. Instantly he parted the ragged tear in her skirt and began to examine the scrapes and cuts along her legs, glad to see that the cold water had done wonders toward stopping any bleeding.

Virginia trembled from having been cold so long while she watched Daniel carefully search her legs for further injuries. When they had first come out of the woods and into the bright summer sunshine, the warmth had been a welcome relief. But the moment they had entered the house and were out of that wonderful sunshine, she had become instantly cold again and her teeth had begun to chatter so violently that she could not speak.

"You have to get out of those wet things before you catch your death," Daniel said matter-of-factly. Immediately he bent over her and began to undo the many buttons of her dress.

Virginia thought to protest, but the words did not find their way past her trembling lips as she watched, mesmerized, while his strong, masculine hands deftly undid the buttons along the front of her dress. His fingers felt pleasantly warm against

364

her icy skin. Soon he was tugging the wet material back and down, pulling her arms out of the cold, clinging garment one at a time. It was not until he had the dress off her, had dropped both the dress and the underskirt to the floor in a sodden heap, and had then turned back to untie the straps of her camisole that she finally found her voice.

"That's well enough," she assured him, though her teeth still chattered so hard, it was very difficult to tell what she'd said.

"No, it's not," he said with determination and set about doing exactly what he intended. Though Virginia's arm went up to protectively surround her breasts just as he tugged the wet camisole up and over her head, he seemed doggedly unaware that she had a legitimate reason to be concerned with his actions. He seemed concerned only with getting her out of her wet things.

It was not until he'd reached for the waistband of her bloomers and she'd actually screamed out his name that Daniel finally seemed to realize she lay there on the bed before him, nearly naked — and by the force of his own hand. When he did finally realize what he had done, his hand hesitated in its task to remove the last of her wet clothing, hovering only inches away from her waist, as if still undecided as to whether he should proceed or not.

"Virginia, I-I—" he began to say, but was so startled by what he had done that the proper words failed him.

Still clutching her breasts to her, she stared up into his strained expression and realized he had been so concerned with her welfare that he had not stopped to think through what he was doing. She could not help but smile at his heroic intentions. It had not been enough for him to rescue her from the well; he had wanted to see that she was again warm and dry.

"I think I can manage the rest by myself, thank you," she told him with no trace of anger.

"I-I'm sure you can," he said, quickly turning around. "I'll find you something dry to put on while you wash some of the mud off." He then set about searching the drawers of her dresser for clean underclothing.

Deciding he was trying his best to do the honorable thing, Virginia slowly sat forward and cautiously scooted off the bed. She paused to run a still quivering hand through her hair to get the wet mass to stay away from her face while she continued to clutch her breasts protectively.

It did feel much better to be out of all that wet clothing. And it would feel even better to run a warm, soapy washcloth over her body and put on something clean and dry. If only Daniel would continue to be noble and keep his gaze averted.

Slowly and bravely, though keeping a keen eye on Daniel while he continued to select the clothes she would need, she let go of her breasts and began to peel off her wet bloomers. They were cold and clung to her pale skin like icy fingers when she pulled them down over her legs and let them drop to the floor. Glad to be rid of the last of her wet clothes, she stepped away from the sodden mass, then again clutched her breasts to her with one arm. She moved the other to cover the dark patch of femininity that she wanted to be absolutely sure he did not catch a glimpse of, should he suddenly decide against such a fine show of integrity and turn around.

Awkwardly, while still keeping a wary eye on Daniel, Virginia inched her way back toward the washstand with every intention of quickly washing away the mud that clung to her skin, then immediately wrapping herself in the nearby bedcovers — not wanting to take the extra time to cross the room and get her wrapper. She worked as quickly as she could, yet just when she finished rinsing the last vestige of soap from her body, Daniel turned around with her clean undergarments in hand. His eyes widened when he realized what had happened while his back was turned. She now stood before him totally naked, with nothing more than a wet cloth to cover herself. The last of her wet clothing had joined the rest on the floor.

"I-I—" he started to make excuses, but all he could think to say was, "You are beautiful."

Funny, she did not feel very beautiful, with her hair still a wet, tangled mass and her skin almost blue from the cold.

He took a step toward her, his eyes full of admiration for what he saw. "I knew you would be beautiful, but in all my wildest dreams, I never realized just how very exquisite you really were."

The chill that had claimed Virginia's body melted beneath his appraising gaze. He honestly found her to be beautiful, even with her wet, tangled hair. Slowly her hands fell away, dropping the wet cloth in the process, and she stood before him shyly but proudly, while she watched his glittering gaze turn to hungry, open desire. He took another step in her direction, and although she knew his intentions, all fear of him was gone. It warmed her to her soul to know that although Daniel would never love her, he did indeed desire her. All the doubts and confusion she had suffered the past few nights vanished the moment she realized it.

With emotions still running high, her heart began to race out of control while he continued to slowly move toward her. Gazing expectantly into his shimmering blue eyes, she made no effort to cover her nakedness or back away. Although it occurred to her that she could stop him with mere words, and knowing full well what was about to happen, she merely stood motionless, her face turned upward, watching him with breathless anticipation as he finally brought his lips down to meet hers.

Slowly her arms lifted to accept him willingly, to make him aware she was ready to know him on a more intimate level. She was ready to allow Daniel the most important of his marital rights. Daniel—the man who had just saved her life—the man who had curiously wanted to marry her, though he claimed he could never fully love her. Daniel, her husband.

It was strange that she no longer thought of him as a Pearson. She no longer considered him cold-hearted. A cold-hearted man would never have come to her rescue with such vigor and concern. Suddenly she was glad she had fallen into the well, for the incident had proved something important to her; that although he might never come to truly love her, he did indeed care for her—very much. As much as she cared for him. *Loved* him.

Overwhelmed by the sudden revelation that she did indeed love Daniel Pearson and probably had for some time, she felt a strange and sudden need to be close to him. She wanted to let him know what she felt for him at that moment and pressed herself against his hard body. Her nipples came alive when they moved against the warm, damp material of his shirt.

There would be no pulling back this time; they both realized that—there was no longer any reason to. This time when he brought his lips away from hers, she would not try to prevent them from returning to claim her mouth for yet another kiss.

"I want you," he said huskily in the seconds he was able to tear his lips away from hers. He waited only a brief second more to give her a chance to protest, if that should be her intention; but when no protest came, he quickly dipped down for another hungry kiss. He had given her a chance to stop him, and she had not.

When his devouring kiss returned to her parted lips, Virginia tiptoed in an effort to bring his mouth closer still. To her ever-growing delight, he dipped his tongue into her mouth, going deeper and ever deeper with each tiny thrust. Her heart soared; her need to be closer to him increased. All that seemed to matter was her husband's wondrous desire to kiss her and the strong, heavenly feel of his embrace while he held her so close—but she wanted it to be more—something more. Eagerly and willingly she sought to find out exactly what it was she had so long denied herself.

While Daniel continued to dip his tongue ever deeper into her mouth, one gentle degree after another, Virginia could not help but return the favor in kind. She savored the tantalizing taste she discovered when she allowed her tongue to follow and enter his mouth.

It was like nothing she had ever experienced. And when she felt his lightly shuddering response, it only made her want to discover more about him. She brought her mouth harder against his, dipped her tongue deeper, and pressed her body closer, all the while knowing there was something more, but not really sure what that something was. She knew a little about the process of coupling, but had been innocently unaware how powerful a thing it really was.

Daniel realized the passions in Virginia had fully ignited and now raged deep within her and knew he could take her then and she would let him, but he chose to move very slowly. He let his lips linger on her sweetly demanding mouth while he eased his hands down the curve of her back and began to explore the gentle swell of her hips, then slipped around to the curve of her rib cage. He was well aware that her breathing became more and more labored with each movement he made, and it delighted him to realize he was finally able to bring about a passionate response in her.

There was a beautiful sense of accomplishment in knowing he was able to provide her with such true and basic pleasure. He struggled to hold back his own response while he worked to bring her to one new height of arousal after another. Unhurriedly he moved his hand ever upward along the smooth surface of her skin in a slow but hungry prowl of her soft body, savoring the feel of her delicate skin, until at last he was able to feel the gentle undercurve of her breast. Sliding his hand between their bodies, he cupped his fingers around the precious find, then gently played with the tip until he felt it grow rigid with desire.

Virginia had become lost in the deep, swirling torrent of emotions that Daniel had so effectively brought to life inside her. Liquid fire coursed through her veins as her arousal spiraled ever higher, quickly possessing her entire being.

Every part of her yearned for more. Why did he not try to remove his own clothing? Didn't he want to know how it might feel to stand just as naked against her as she was against him? Unable to bear the rapacious flames which burned deep into the very core of her, she considered removing his clothing herself, but could not seem to find the courage to actually do so.

Finally Daniel brought one of his hands to his own buttons and at first tried to work with them as he had hers earlier, but then suddenly gave the material of the already torn shirt a hard yank and let the contrary buttons spill to the floor. All the while his other hand continued to play with the swelling curve of her breast, which sent more delicious waves of pure ecstasy and eager pangs of anticipation through her body.

She closed her eyes and trembled with expectation when he stepped away just enough to slip his shirt back over his shoulders. While he then worked to unfasten his trousers and quickly remove them, he allowed himself a leisurely view of her thrusting breasts. He ached to return to her by the time he had dropped his own wet trousers to the floor and had kicked them well out of his way. He found that Virginia's body was perfect in every way and stood staring at her quivering beauty only a moment more before he bent down to gather her into his arms.

While he carried her the short distance to the bed, his eyes grew darker with desire. His lips sought hers once more before he gently lowered her onto the soft mattress, careful to place her well away from the dampened area where he had laid her before, while she had still been in her wet clothing. Then he stood again and stared at her another long moment, watching her breasts heave with each labored breath.

Her eyes drifted open and she looked at him expectantly. Slowly he reached down and removed his final undergarment in one lithe movement, revealing his splendid body to her. This time she did not press her eyes closed; she had no desire to. As he moved toward the bed, she openly admired his lean, strong body and found herself almost breathless with approval. Slowly, she lifted her arms to receive him. Daniel . . . her husband. The man she loved.

Lying on the bed just to one side of her, he bent over and brought his lips down to claim hers once more and gently let his hand slide over her now-warm bare skin, eagerly exploring anyplace he may have missed before. He wanted to leave no curve, no valley untouched. It took more and more effort for him to put her pleasure before his needs, especially knowing he could take her at any moment and find complete fulfillment.

As if to purposely torment her, Daniel's finger-tips teased and taunted Virginia, coming ever closer to the sensitive peaks of her breasts in slow circular motions, but staying just out of reach.

Unable to bear the gentle torture of having him come so close but not actually touch the places that desired his touch the most, Virginia arched her back and thrust her breasts ever higher in the hopes of somehow accommodating him better, wishing frantically that his hands would hurry and reach their obvious destination.

When his mouth broke free of hers in order to gasp for the air he needed and to gaze down at her writhing form once more, Virginia moaned aloud her impatience. How could he bring her to such a fine state of madness and not fulfill her needs? She moaned again and reached out for his neck, wanting to bring his mouth back to hers.

Daniel obliged her with another long, plundering kiss but then brought his lips away again, only this time to trail tiny feathery kisses ever downward until at last he reached her heaving breasts. Deftly his tongue teased the hardened tip with short, tantalizing strokes, nipping and suckling until she cried aloud with the pleasure it brought her. Then, when she thought she could bear no more, he moved to take in the neglected breast. Again he brought a cry of ecstasy from her lips.

Virginia was not certain how much longer she could endure the tender torment and began to pull on his shoulders in an effort to make him stop this delicate torture and do whatever was to come next, whatever would bring her the relief she sought. But his mouth continued to bring her breasts wave after wave of unbearable pleasure. She shuddered from the delectable sensations that continued to build inside her, degree by degree, until she was certain she would burst. A delicious ache centered itself somewhere low in her abdomen and had reached that same unbearable intensity as the rest of her. Her body craved release from the sensual anguish that burned within her.

"Daniel!" She called out his name, only vaguely aware she had said it aloud.

Realizing the time had come at last, Daniel drew first on one breast, then the other, one last time before moving to fulfill her. Carefully, he eased through the barrier that proved he was her first and with smooth, lithe movements, brought their wildest longings, their deepest needs to the most ultimate heights. When release came for Virginia, it was so wondrous and so deeply shattering that she gasped aloud with surprised pleasure. Only a moment later, the same shuddering release came for Daniel.

Once their passions had been fully spent, the bonds of marriage made complete, they lay perfectly still, listening to the steady rhythm of each other's heartbeats, still bound together in each other's arms as if afraid to fully let go. Slowly they sank together into the warm depths of satisfaction, both still in awe of what had happened between them, for it was like no other experience in their lives. There was nothing that even closely compared.

Lying contentedly at Daniel's side, Virginia marveled at the fact that this exquisite man was her husband. Such joy was to be hers forever! She refused to let any other thoughts enter her mind, refused to worry about Amanda and the woman's open invitation for him to come to her whenever he needed her. She also refused to concern herself with the fact that Daniel would never love her in the way she now loved him. It seemed enough at the moment that he cared for her and that the two of them could share such pleasure.

For the time being, all she wanted to do was bask in the warm aftermath of their lovemaking and enjoy the feel of her husband close at her side. For the first time in Virginia's life, she felt blessed, truly blessed, and did not want to consider that it might not last . . . that if he should ever discover who she really was and how she had purposefully kept that identity a secret from him, he would no doubt be angry enough to leave her.

And if he ever found out that the main reason she had come back to East Texas was to find a way to get Valley Oaks back into the hands of the Elders and avenge what his uncle had done to her grandfather, he would surely realize the reason she had originally agreed to marry him was so she could do just that. It worried her to know that if she should continue to pursue the mystery of what Caleb did in order to take Valley Oaks away from her grandfather, she could be creating even more trouble. But did she dare give up the search? Could she betray her grandmother like that? Could she betray her grandfather?

Virginia knew she would not be able to give up the search yet, but at the same time almost hoped that when she did finally find out what happened all those years ago, she would discover Caleb innocent—for Daniel's sake. But that was ridiculous . . . Caleb was not innocent. And for her grandmother's sake, she should still try to prove it.

If only she had not come to love Daniel! It would have made her quest so much easier. Because if she did find out the truth, and Daniel found also out, it would hurt him deeply. Daniel had truly loved his uncle and he would hate her for having discovered the truth, just as he would hate her when he discovered her real reasons for having married him.

He would never believe that she had actually come to love him in the meantime. It was hard enough for her to believe it herself. No, if he learned of her quest to find the truth, it would destroy this wondrous happiness . . . she knew that. Still she had promised herself—and her grandparents—that she would eventually uncover the truth.

Frowning, Virginia refused to think about it. She pushed the bleak thoughts aside and turned to gaze at Daniel only to discover he was carefully watching her.

While she looked tenderly into his glimmering blue eyes, she could not resist expressing the feelings that had surfaced inside of her. "Daniel, I want you to know that although you may never come to truly love me, I love you with all my heart. I was not even aware of it until today, but I'm very aware of it now."

Her words surprised even herself, but she was not sorry she had stated them. He might as well know.

Though she had not known what to expect Daniel's reaction to be to her sudden admission of love, she had not expected him to explode into a fit of anger. Leaping from the bed, he turned to stare down at her, his eyes dark and menacing, his nostrils flaring with rage.

"Don't you dare tell me you love me. I don't want to hear it." His voice vibrated with anger.

"But why?"

"Words of love are petty and senseless. They only serve to make a man vulnerable. What you feel for me isn't love. Don't try to convince yourself that it is. All you are really feeling right now is an appreciation for lovemaking. And lovemaking *should* be appreciated. You should openly admit that you appreciate it, that you enjoy making love with me. But you are not to ever say that you love me. You are not to try to manipulate me like that. I won't allow it."

"Whatever did she do to make you feel this way?" Virginia asked bravely, fighting back the tears his angry words had caused to rush forth.

"Who?"

"I don't know who. But someone has done something to make you feel the way you do. Who?"

Daniel stared at her for a long moment, then stormed over to the dresser to jerk out a pair of clean trousers. "My dear first wife," he said, his voice cold with hatred while he stepped into the trousers and then tugged them on without bothering with any underclothing.

"What did she do?" Virginia prompted before she slid off the bed and started to put her own

377

clothing on. Now that he was partially dressed again, she felt uncomfortable with her nakedness.

When Daniel looked at her then, his eyes became almost black with the rage that had so suddenly consumed him. A muscle in the side of his face pumped in and out of his jaw while he fought to control his mounting hostility. "What did she do? What didn't she do? First, she made a complete fool of me, with her lies and clever deception, then casually let the whole world know just how big a fool I really was. She got a good laugh out of it. Everyone seemed to." His eyes suddenly narrowed with remembered pain.

"And you think I'm going to do the same thing?"

"Maybe; maybe not. I don't intend to give you the chance. And I really don't want to talk about it." Abruptly he grabbed a shirt and stalked out of the room, calling back to her that he would see her at supper.

Virginia sat on the edge of the bed wearing only the undergarments Daniel had gotten for her earlier, stunned by what had just happened. One minute they lay peacefully in each other's arms, content with what had transpired between them, and the next minute, after she had boldly declared her love, he had become livid with rage, demanding that she never mention the word to him again.

So *that* was Daniel's demon. That was what prevented him from ever giving his love to her, or to anyone.

She wondered just exactly what his first wife had done to cause him such intense, unforgiving pain . . . what sort of lies and deception were involved. It was hard for Virginia to imagine anyone being able to make Daniel appear like a fool. But if his wife had somehow managed to do just that, why had it marred his view of love so very drastically?

A cold chill ran down her when she again remembered her own lies and deception. Now she really *did* worry what might happen if Daniel ever learned just who she really was and that one of the main reasons she had agreed to marry him had been vengeance, pure and simple. What Daniel had just told her made her earlier conflict about whether she should continue to try to find out what Caleb had done that much harder to deal with. Part of her wanted to forget Caleb Pearson had ever existed, while another part of her felt she should not go back on her promise for any reason. She did not want to do anything to betray her grandmother. Yet she should not continue to deceive her husband. The situation was impossible.

That night, after a very placid supper, Daniel retired to the veranda with Virginia as usual, but did not sit in the swing with her; he chose a chair several yards away from her. He remained extremely cordial, but distant. Even when they returned upstairs to the very bed in which they had made love, he kept his distance. Finally Virginia could bear it no longer and as he reached to turn out the light, obviously ready to go right to sleep, she openly apologized.

"Daniel, I'm sorry for what happened this afternoon. I apologize for having asked so many questions. I didn't mean to make you angry; I just wanted to know why you did not want me to tell you how much I have come to love you."

Daniel turned back to stare at her, his face hard, his anger evident. He narrowed his eyes suspiciously.

"And I promise not to mention my love for you again." Gently she reached out and stroked a fallen lock of his hair away from his forehead. "I just want things to be back the way they were this afternoon. Daniel, I swear, I'll never mention the word love to you again, if you'll just stop this brooding. I did not mean to hurt you."

Virginia was never really aware when Daniel's anger had turned into desperate passion, because both emotions raged black in his eyes; but within seconds he had pulled her hard against him, his mouth hungrily seeking hers. Sensing he needed to be reassured somehow that they could still enjoy the pleasure of lovemaking without the verbal commitment getting in the way, Virginia wrapped her arms tightly around his neck and returned his kiss with a passion she had not known until he had introduced her to it that very afternoon.

Daniel moaned aloud, the sound lost to the hungry depths of her mouth, as he brought his hand up to cup her breast through the soft material of her nightgown with such surprising gentleness and playfulness that it made Virginia wish she had never put the garment on. Her heart thrashed wildly inside of her when his fingers closed over the covered fleshy mound and claimed it once again as his.

Daniel's passion grew instantly frantic when he felt her heartbeat throbbing with such force beneath his fingertips. And when she showed no resistance to where his hand had gone, he brought his other hand up to undo the two tiny buttons that held the opening in the back of her nightdress closed.

Virginia felt no fear when he quickly undid the garment, letting his fingertips gently brush against her back, sending delicious little shivers of delight and hopeful anticipation coursing through her with each contact his fingers made against her delicate skin. While her body continued to absorb the deep pleasures of his passionate embrace and the wonderful feel of his mouth on hers, Daniel carefully worked the gown up over her head until he had it in his possession and was able to toss it to the floor.

He then pulled her naked body hard against his and pressed her firmly to him. His kiss became immediately more demanding and she responded by rolling over on her back, letting him come to rest on top of her. The gentle pressure of his body on hers made her wild with need and she wrapped her arms tightly around him, pressing hard into the taut flesh of his back with her fingertips.

Daniel responded by bringing his mouth away from hers, stilling her immediate protest for the sudden neglect with tiny intermittent kisses, then began to trail similar kisses down the column of her neck, making a heated trail ever lower until his mouth finally moved to cover one of her straining breasts.

Virginia gasped aloud at the intense responses that shot through her as Daniel masterfully brought spasm after spasm of pure ecstasy. Eagerly, she arched her back, pressing her softness higher, to give him easier access to do what he wanted, eager to lose herself in the wondrous sensations he created for her. And Daniel did not disappoint her. While his mouth continued to bring one of her breasts undeniable pleasure, his hand moved to first bring the other breast the same delicious sort of pleasure, then moved ever downward—seeking and finding.

Then, when Virginia again called out his name, unable to bear the exquisite torment his wondrous administrations had caused her, he again moved to fulfill her. This time the moment of release came quicker for both of them, almost frantically so, but was in no way less earth-shattering, no less satisfying in the end.

And when it was over, and they again lay in each other's arms, marveling over what had just occurred between them yet a second time, Virginia again realized exactly how much she had come to love Daniel. Only this time, she very carefully and very wisely chose to keep those thoughts to herself.

Chapter Twenty-one

Daniel and Virginia spent the next two days getting to know each other better, though Virginia was careful to make sure he did not get to know her too well. Whenever their conversation turned even vaguely in the direction of Virginia's past, she quickly found something else more important to discuss.

Daniel had gradually become aware of the evasive action and found it both annoying and intriguing; but he did not try to force her to tell him anything about her childhood that she did not want to. He hoped she would feel eventually confident enough to share whatever it was about her past she was so obviously ashamed of. He felt he needed to give her more time to decide he could be trusted.

All too soon the moment they both had dreaded came and it was time for the newlyweds to return to Valley Oaks. Since Mary was not to come home for two more weeks, it seemed to Virginia there was little reason to leave their private haven at

River Ridge, but Daniel finally convinced her he had to return to the working world if he did not want his businesses to suffer. Though he trusted James York with his shipping business and Pete and Jack Pilgrahm with his ranching concerns, he still felt he needed to be readily available to them; and at River Oaks, he felt readily available to none.

It was while Virginia was reluctantly repacking their clothing that she heard someone ride into the yard on horseback, crying out Daniel's name in a near-panic. Curious, Virginia stepped over to an open bedroom window and looked out into the yard below. She watched Daniel bound out of the barn.

"What is it?" she heard Daniel call out while he quickly closed the distance between himself and the frantic young man who had just now thought to climb down from his horse.

"Trouble," came the grim reply, but then as Daniel came closer, the man's voice dropped so that Virginia could not longer hear what was being said; but she could see by their expressions that the trouble was serious.

Daniel's countenance grew suddenly grim; while he studied the messenger's animated face, he listened carefully. Abruptly, after he had heard enough, he turned away. He marched directly into the house, while the young man stood in the yard holding his horse's reins and running his tongue along the lower corner of his mouth, obviously awaiting his return.

Virginia heard her husband's brisk footsteps, and she turned in time to see him enter. His brow was drawn into such a serious, scowling frown that she first thought something terrible had happened to Mary.

"What's wrong?" Her breath caught in her throat.

"Trouble in Jefferson," he stated somberly.

Relief washed over Virginia. She reached for the back of a chair in order to steady herself. Though she was not fond of the idea of trouble with his business, she was grateful the trouble had not involved Mary.

"What is it?" she asked curiously.

"Stupid trouble," he muttered. "I'm going to have to go to Jefferson right away. This will take a while. You will to have to go back to Valley Oaks alone. Steve will see that you arrive there safely."

"But why can't I go with you?"

"There's no reason for you to. Besides, I don't know how long it will take me to get this straightened out. I'll be along as soon as I can."

Giving her no opportunity to ask questions, and offering no further explanation, Daniel grabbed up one of his valises, looked inside to see that it held enough of the things he would need, then hurried out of the room.

Virginia hurried to follow, but Daniel was too preoccupied to realize she was behind him. When he entered the kitchen, he quickly explained to Ruby that he was leaving and that Virginia was to return to Valley Oaks with Steve just as soon as she had everything packed. Ruby's eyebrows perked when she looked back at Virginia curiously, but she asked no questions.

Without another word, Daniel snatched up his

385

rifle and went outside to take the saddled horse away from the young man, who looked as if he had half expected it, yet at the same time was at a loss about what to do next.

"Have Steve or Louis saddle one of my horses," Daniel told him as he urged the tall roan toward the roadway. Then, finally spotting Virginia on the veranda, he smiled reassuringly. "I'll see you in a few days," he called to her.

Then he was gone.

For two long days Virginia searched the house for information concerning Caleb; then, when she realized there was none to be had, she began wandering aimlessly through the house—with only Lizzie to keep her company when she could. Virginia decided she had to do something to keep from going stark raving mad. She thought about going to see Mark and Wyoma and trying to explain why she had decided to marry Daniel, but did not feel up to such a confrontation just yet. Her promise to Daniel not to reveal everything about their marriage was going to make her explanation difficult, if not impossible, and she had enough problems right now.

Instead she strolled out to the barn to see if she could find Pete or Jack, hoping either could spare a few moments. . . . Anything to fight the deep loneliness she felt. But when she entered the barn, she discovered they were both too busy arguing over some ranch matter. Realizing what poor company the two would make even if they did have time for her, she decided to see if she could find someone else to talk to. She next sought Rolly Sagan, the groundskeeper, but as it turned out, he was nowhere to be found.

Finally she decided to take a long walk. It was a beautiful day; the sky was a vivid blue, filled with white, fluffy clouds. The light breeze that curled down from the northwest caused the grass and trees to dance at leisure and kept the bright summer sunshine from becoming unbearably warm. The birds in the trees chirped endlessly while big yellow-and-black butterflies flitted about and grasshoppers sprinted in the grass.

Wanting to enjoy all nature had to show her, she set out across one of the pastures. She wanted to avoid any well-traveled paths for the moment, yet hoped to link up with the main road eventually.

It was twenty minutes before the main road came into sight, and even though there was a tall, newly strung barbed wire fence blocking her way, she decided against turning back. She had never contended with barbed wire before, but was sure she could find a way to master it.

When she reached the fence, she first considered climbing over the wire; but quickly decided against that when she discovered how resilient the wires were. She feared they might snap up and catch her. Finally she stretched the wires apart as far as she could and carefully eased through, only snagging her wide, mint-green skirts once. She thought of Mark again when she realized it had been her hem that had caught and torn; she knew that if he were there, he would tease her about the many skirt hems she had worn to tatters in the past.

Thinking of Mark reminded her yet again of how he had looked at her after the wedding and she felt pangs of both guilt and something akin to homesickness. She knew that while she was out, she should walk on over there and try to explain the situation as best she could, but she was too afraid of hurting him further. If she told him the truth, he would be disappointed in her, and if she lied, he would surely know it. She did not want to do either.

As soon as she was on the other side of the fence, with the smooth, hard surface of the road to walk on, Virginia picked up her pace. The exertion slowly eased some of the tension that had been building inside of her ever since Daniel's sudden, unexplained departure.

What could have been so terrible that Daniel could not have taken even a few minutes to offer her a proper goodbye? Virginia became so lost to her melancholy thoughts that she did not hear a horse approach from behind. When she did finally notice the clomping sound of shod hooves, her first thought was that Daniel had finally returned and she spun about to see if it was true. Her hopeful expression fell when she realized it was only Mark Langford, but was quickly replaced with a brave smile, for she knew Mark would want an explanation concerning her marriage. She realized she might as well get it over with.

"What are you doing out here?" he asked as he drew his horse to a halt just a few feet away from where she stood.

"Taking a walk," she said with an apprehensive shrug, quickly aware he did not return her smile.

"Why?" He pushed his hat back with his thumb, then tilted his head as if trying to judge her expression better.

"Because I'm bored!" she admitted with a childish pout.

"Mary isn't back from New Orleans yet?"

"No. And she won't be for almost two weeks. And Daniel is not back yet either."

"Where's Daniel?" His face finally displayed true interest.

Virginia's pout turned into a instant scowl. "He's off in Jefferson attending to some sort of business problem that suddenly came up." Anger she was not even aware she felt quickly began to surface. "Within minutes after some young man had come to tell him there was trouble, he was on a horse and gone. He sent me back here alone. He didn't even offer me any explanations; he just left."

"You were still on your wedding trip?" Mark asked, also showing definite signs of anger by the time he slid down from his horse and quickly looped his reins around the saddle horn. "And he left you?"

"Easy as you please," Virginia retorted, her nostrils flaring with humiliation.

"Obviously his business is more important to him than his marriage." Lowering his eyebrows with sudden concern, Mark stepped over to where Virginia stood sadly watching him and gently placed his hands on her shoulders. "Virginia, why did you marry him?"

Virginia tried to look away from the deeply anguished, handsome face, but Mark put a fingertip below her chin and forced her to look back up at him. "Virginia? You have to tell me . . . I deserve to know. Why did you marry Daniel Pearson? Why, when you know how very much I love you? Don't you know that I had hoped to be the man you married?"

Something inside Virginia twisted painfully. She had already hurt Mark deeply and she was about to hurt him more. "And I love you too, Mark, but surely you must know that I love you like a brother."

Mark pulled her against him and held her tight. "That could have changed. I, too, used to love you only as a brother might a sister, but after you left, I started to miss you more than I ever thought I could. While we continued to write to each other, I realized I had begun to love you in a different way. You became more important to me. Then, when you returned and I saw how beautiful you had become, I knew I loved you. I had hoped that in time you would come to realize that same sort of love for me." A sob broke low in Mark's throat and she heard him try to swallow.

"I'm sorry" is all Virginia could say. Tears filled her eyes when she realized just how very deeply she had hurt him.

Mark then pushed her away to hold her at arm's length. His eyes were moist from unshed tears, but his voice was deceptively calm. "You never did answer my question."

Virginia stared at him, puzzled, because she had forgotten there had been a question.

"Why did you marry Daniel Pearson? What did he do to make you marry him? I know now that you don't really love him. I could tell that by the way you just talked about him. Did you marry him for his money? Is that it? Is money so important to you?"

Virginia's mouth fell open, ready to protest such a cruel remark, but found herself too angry. Clenching her hands into tight fists at her side, she thought of punching him in the stomach, but instead she turned and stormed away.

"Well, what then?" she heard him call out to her. "Was it Mary? Was she why you married him?"

Though he had hit upon one of the reasons, Virginia did not answer. Confused, angry, and hurt, she kept walking as fast as she could.

"If that's the reason, don't stay," Mark cried out desperately. "He'll destroy you. That's the kind of man he is."

Virginia did not want to hear any more. Quickly lifting her skirts out of the way, she began to run.

"Virginia, I love you! I'm the sort of man you should be married to!"

Nearly out of earshot and still running as fast as she could, she'd still managed to hear his last words. She winced with misery, because she too thought that Mark was the sort of man she would want to marry. She wished Daniel could somehow be more like Mark—deeply caring and always concerned for others. She wished there were some way to rid Daniel of his demon and free his heart forever. Then maybe he could grow to love her as much as she loved him.

Virginia could not get Mark's hurt-filled expression or his open declaration of his love for her out of her mind. As she restlessly paced the house, she almost wished she *had* fallen in love with Mark and had chosen to marry him instead of Daniel. Mark would never be so inconsiderate of her feelings; Mark would have explained any reasons he had for abandoning her, especially if he found he had to do so during their wedding trip. Mark would have made certain she understood, and even then he would have taken the time to offer a proper goodbye. She winced as she thought how freely Mark would have given of his love. Daniel was incapable of that.

Teetering between a growing anger for Daniel and the deep concern she felt for Mark, Virginia could not seem to get a tight hold on her emotions. No matter what she found to do, her thoughts seemed to be drawn to one man or the other. Finally, in an attempt to still her troubled mind, she sought Lizzie's company.

She found the woman sitting on a tall stool in the kitchen, busily chopping vegetables for supper.

"Come on in and join me, Missus," Lizzie said. Virginia stood in the doorway looking forlorn. Smiling, Lizzie gestured to a nearby stool, "That is, if you don't mind sittin' with the likes of me."

"I'd be grateful for your company," Virginia answered honestly.

"Feelin' a little lonesome with Master Daniel still gone?" Lizzie asked, pausing with her knife in mid-air, her hands chalky white from the mound of potatoes she had just cubed.

"Why do you call him 'Master' Daniel?" Virginia asked, for it had bothered her from the very first.

"He does not own you, nor can he. You have no masters; you are no man's property. Certainly you realize that he is in no way your master."

"I know that; it's just what I call him—always have. He don't seem to mind," Lizzie said with a shrug of her large shoulders as she resumed her work. "Besides, I don't call him master 'cause I think he owns me. I call him master 'cause he's the one who owns this place and is the man in charge. He became 'lord and master' of this property now that Master Caleb is gone, and since I consider Valley Oaks my home, too, that makes him the master."

Virginia was not certain she understood the logic, but knew she did not want it explained again. But the way Lizzie had referred to Caleb as Master Caleb had caught her attention, and she decided to find out exactly what Lizzie did know about the man. "How long did you work for Caleb Pearson?"

Lizzie reached for a tall glass of water and took a long drink before answering. "Don't rightly know. My mother came to work here as a housekeeper back when I was still too young to be put to work. But as soon as I was old enough, Master Caleb found work for me, too. He let me help my mother and Miss Mattie with the housework, and in the summer, he sometimes let me help Mister Stracener, the groundskeeper back before Mister Sagan was hired on."

Virginia's eyes widened with sudden interest. "I know your mother died several years ago, but is this Mattie who you worked with still alive?"

"Oh, sure. She lives in a small house Master

393

Caleb give her through his will. He give her the land around it, too . . . up toward the Porterfield place."

Virginia leaned forward. "What about Mister Stracener? Is he still alive?"

"No—he died just before Master Caleb did. He got hisself snakebit while diggin' in a flower bed near the road. Tried to make it back to the house for help, but collapsed in the yard. No one saw him right away and he died where he fell." Lizzie and Virginia both shuddered at the thought. "He was pretty old—didn't have no family left. Had him buried over to the Crossroads cemetery."

"But Mattie *is* still alive," Virginia said, hoping to discuss the woman further.

Unaware Virginia had more than a passing interest, Lizzie continued, "Sure, Mattie Williams is still alive. Every once in a while she comes over for a visit, but now that her legs are so stoved up, it's getting harder and harder for her to get around."

Lizzie suddenly had Virginia's full attention. Realizing Mattie Williams just might be the critical link to the past, and realizing that it would be better to explore what Mattie might know while Daniel was gone, Virginia decided to ask more about her. "You say this Mattie Williams' house is out toward the old Porterfield place?"

Lizzie looked at her curiously. "You know where that's at?"

"I've heard the name mentioned. I believe it's north of here."

"No, it's over to the west. Her little piece of land takes a tiny chunk out of the boundary line

394

off west of here. Used to be a rent house. Master Caleb had several of 'em at one time. Some along that western boundary, and a couple down to the south. But in his will, he give all but one away, and that one was destroyed by a tornado only a little over year after he died."

Virginia could feel her blood turn cold. "So I understood."

"The woman who was living there was killed," Lizzie continued and started to put the chopped vegetables in a bowl of water to keep them fresh. "It was terrible. Though she never once paid her rent after Master Caleb died, I hear she was a real nice woman, but it seems she didn't have no family. The folks around here pitched in and bought her a headstone after she died. They even cleaned up the destroyed house for us while we was still waitin' for word from Master Daniel or his mother about what to do—burn it on down or rebuild."

Tears burned in Virginia's eyes. She had to get off the subject of her grandmother before Lizzie began to suspect something. "Does Mattie Williams allow strangers to visit?"

Lizzie grinned. "Mattie loves visitors, strangers or not. She's got no children—never married—so, except for a few friends, she doesn't have no one to call on her. I go over from time to time to be sure she's all right. Sometimes I take her a cake or a loaf of fresh-baked bread."

"Would you bake a fresh loaf for me to take in the morning? I think I'd like to visit with her. It would help me pass the time until Daniel returns."

"Mattie would like that," Lizzie nodded agreeably. "Maybe I'll put aside some time and go with you."

Virginia felt her heart jump; if Lizzie went with her, she would have to be careful about what she asked. But to her relief, Lizzie remembered how much mending she had to do and declined to join her.

Virginia climbed into the carriage early the following morning with a freshly baked loaf of bread and two jars of Lizzie's strawberry jam. Lizzie came outside to explain for the third time exactly how to get to Mattie's house.

"Now are you sure you know how to get there? 'Cause if Master Daniel was to come home and discover I'd let you run off and get yourself lost, he'd have my hide stretched out on stakes."

"Yes, your directions were very clear," Virginia assured her, though she had known which house had to be the one given Mattie almost from the start.

"Are you sure? It sits off the main road a piece. You can't really see the house until you done turned off. But if you come to a big house made out of big brown rocks, you've gone too far. That is the Porterfield house," Lizzie explained, then went on to give her more unnecessary information. "A Ewan family moved in there for awhile about a year ago, but they moved off to Daingerfield only a few months after they had moved in. Place is vacant again. Looks it, too. So, if you see that house, you've gone too far and need to turn back."

"I understand," Virginia assured her.

"And you understand which road to take off this road?"

"Perfectly," Virginia said while she took the reins into her hands. "I'll be back by early afternoon."

"See that you are. Otherwise, I'll send Pete and Jack out lookin' for you," she said, then grinned. "I'd send Moses, but I'm afraid my husband is just as likely to get lost as you are. Man has no common sense at all. Maybe that's why he married me."

"I'll be fine," Virginia said, shaking her head in exasperation, ready to be on her way.

Finally Lizzie stepped back to watch her leave and Virginia was quickly on her way. Knowing she had to pass in front of Mark's house, she thought about stopping by for a short visit and a chance to try to straighten out her relationship with Mark again, but decided she should save that for the way back, just in case her visit with Mattie Williams should last too long.

Judging by what Lizzie'd said, Mattie was getting on in years, and Virginia knew that older people sometimes took a long time to remember things. Virginia hoped Mattie knew enough of what she wanted to know so she could indeed remember it all. She wondered if the woman would be reluctant to talk about it.

"Virginia!" She heard a voice and turned, startled out of her deep thoughts, in time to see Mark running toward her.

She had been so lost in thought that she had not noticed he was in one of the roadside fields working the plow, turning under a cornfield that had long since yielded its harvest.

"Virginia! Stop!"

She pulled hard on the reins until the horse had

slowed to a walk, then led the carriage off onto a shaded patch of grass at the side of the road. While she waited for him to hurdle the wooden fence and cross the road, she drew her lower lip between her teeth and wondered if he intended to toss more harsh words at her. Or was he just as eager to make amends as she was?

"Where are you headed?"

"I'm going visiting," she answered, sitting stiffly erect because his voice had revealed neither anger or friendliness and she still did not know what to expect.

"Who? Us?" he asked hopefully.

"Among others, yes," she said. Then upon seeing the honest concern on his face, she smiled. "I'm on my way to deliver a loaf of bread and two jars of jam to a neighbor who used to work at Valley Oaks . . . a Miss Mattie Williams. Do you know her?"

"Sort of. We've spoken a word or two when I was out working near the road and she passed by on her way to town."

Knowing Mark's next question was going to be "Why," she decided to save him the trouble of asking. "Well, she's a good friend of Lizzie's and Lizzie wanted her to have this bread and jam." That was true enough. "Seems this Miss Williams is stove up and does not get around too well."

"Gets around well enough," Mark assured her. "I see her pass by here on her way to town at least once a week, and I don't think she ever misses church on Sunday."

"Does she go to your church?"

"No, to one in Pine, but she always leaves very

398

early, almost always carrying flowers for the altar, so I usually see her pass by long before we leave for our own church." Then, as if the thought had suddenly occurred to him, "Why don't you come to church with us next Sunday?"

Virginia thought about that and felt a strong yearning to, but she realized the people at the church would be the most likely to remember her, especially if she sat with Mark and his family. "Daniel should be back by then," she said, knowing it would eliminate Mark's interest. His expression grew instantly gloomy.

"I see," he said and looked away.

"Mark, don't be like that," Virginia pleaded. "Just because I'm married doesn't mean we can't still be friends."

"Friends don't keep secrets from one another," he said bluntly and turned back to look at her again.

"What secrets?"

"I don't know; I just feel as if you're keeping secrets from me."

She looked at his hurt expresion for a long moment, wanting to tell him everything, but not sure how much she dared reveal. "Okay. I'm really going to visit Mattie Williams so that I can find out if she knows what it was Caleb did to my grandfather all those years go. Mattie was Caleb's housekeeper, hired the very day he moved into Valley Oaks. She should know as much about him as anybody."

"Why?" Mark wanted to know. "You yourself said all that was in the past. Why dredge it up now? Who could possibly benefit from such information? Certainly not you, and certainly not your grandparents. Not even your children, since they'd be Daniel's children, too. I think you should just leave it alone. No good can come from it."

"I have to know exactly what it was Caleb did to my grandfather," she stated in a cool, determined voice.

Mark's brow drew inward while his gaze studied her hard expression. "Let it go, Virginia."

"I can't," she told him honestly. "I have to find out if Mattie knows anything. I'm too close now; I can feel it. I'll stop back by if I have time."

Mark's nostrils flared with disgust when he stepped back to let her go. "Don't bother. I'm not interested in what happened forty years ago."

Angered that Mark had managed to make her feel so guilty, Virginia flicked the reins hard and hurried on her way, leaving a trail of dust to settle over Mark.

Virginia was at first disappointed to discover Mattie Williams was not at home; but then, when she realized she would not have the opportunity to talk with the woman after all, she felt oddly relieved. She placed the bread and jam on the front porch, where it would easily be found, and came to the surprising conclusion that Mark had been right—for once. Now that she the same as had the land back in the family, she no longer had any real reason to dredge up the past. He was also right about the fact that no one would benefit from knowing the truth: not her grandparents, not any future children they might have, and *especially* not Daniel. The thought of Daniel having to know the truth caused her heart to ache.

No, if she was to be perfectly honest with herself, and it was about time, she would probably do far more harm than good by dredging up the past now. Although she was still very curious and knew she always would be, she decided it would be in everyone's best interest if she followed Mark's advice and left it alone.

Feeling better about herself than she had in months, Virginia quickly returned to the carriage and headed back to Valley Oaks. She thought about stopping off to tell Mark of her decision to accept his advice, but was too afraid they would end up in another argument, and she was in too good a mood at the moment to want to risk spoiling it.

That afternoon Daniel finally returned home. As soon as Virginia heard his horse, she ran outside to greet him. He had just handed the reins over to Pete and was turning to go to the house. Virginia was already on her way to him when he noticed her and he barely had time to drop his valise and throw his arms open wide before she flung herself against him and hugged him close.

After a long, hard embrace, she finally pulled away, suddenly shy. "I missed you."

"And I missed you," he responded warmly, then bent over and patted the valise while he picked it up off the ground. "I brought you a gift to help make things up to you."

Virginia's heart soared, but not so much because he had bought her a gift: it was the fact that he realized just how terribly he had treated her and wanted to make amends that caused her heart to want to sing out for joy.

"When do I get to see it?" she asked eagerly.

"Well, if you would like to come upstairs and help me unpack, I'll show it to you right away," he told her. He put his arm around her and guided her toward the house.

Virginia felt giddy; it was wonderful to have Daniel back home, wonderful to have his arm around her again. She had missed him so much that she felt a strange urge to openly weep over his return.

Chancing a quick glance in his direction when they approached the back steps, she was delighted to see that she had his full attention. His gaze roved over her approvingly, and she could tell by the way that hungry gaze lingered on the curving lines of her bodice that they would do more than unpack his valise once they got upstairs. Much more.

Chapter Twenty-two

The next few weeks were happy ones for Virginia. Mary returned the last week in August eager to continue with her lessons, and Daniel found more time to spend with them in the late afternoons and evenings. The three of them gradually grew closer as a family, and Virginia began to feel much more a part of both their lives, until she actually started to believe that someday, if she remained patient and very, very careful, she might be able to break right through the emotional barrier Daniel had placed around his heart. More than anything, she wanted to rid Daniel of the cruel demon that held both his heart and his ability to love captive.

Virginia was amazed at how contented she was. Every day began and ended in Daniel's arms, and in the hours in between, they found more and more time to be together. Virginia could not remember ever having been so happy or having had so much hope for the future.

Then, late one afternoon, Daniel returned from

a trip into Pittsburg with a murderous expression on his face. There was such dark fury in his blue eyes that Virginia actually feared him when he stormed into the classroom, grasped her by her arm, and physically forced her down the corridor, then up the stairs into the privacy of their bedroom. Mary had been horrified by the cruel way her father had grabbed Virginia and tried to come to her stepmother's aid, pleading with her father to let her go; but she had been promptly ordered into her own room, where she was to remain behind closed doors until told otherwise.

"What is the matter with you?" Virginia demanded as soon as they were behind their own closed door. He had let go of her arm with such suddenness, it had caught her off guard and she stumbled sideways, almost falling. Her brow was drawn with concern while she studied his rock-hard expression. A cold feeling came over her, but she did what she could not to reveal it.

Daniel looked at her a long moment with dark, loathsome disgust before he muttered sarcastically, "Such youthful innocence you display. And to think it was that very youthful innocence which attracted me to you in the first place. That and your warm, *virtuous* nature."

"Daniel, what are you talking about?" she asked. Tiny bumps of apprehension formed under her skin. "What is wrong with you?"

"I ran into Mark today," he said, as if that should answer her question in full.

Virginia's stomach tightened and a constriction moved to quickly claim her throat, making it hard to force out the single-word question: "And?"

"And we had a long, friendly little talk," he told her. Quickly he raked his fingers through his thick hair. His eyes were livid with the rage that continued to grow inside of him.

"What about?" she asked weakly. Already she had guessed, yet she was unable to believe Mark would betray her; and at the same time she wondered what Mark was doing in Pittsburg during the middle of the week.

"About you, mostly," he said. His eyes narrowed when he added, "Amazing how loose your farmer's tongue becomes after only a couple of drinks."

"Could you be a little more specific?" she asked. She too was starting to get angry, or was it a reflexive reaction to her fear? Whatever the emotion, it was profound and caused her heart to hammer fiercely beneath her breast.

"Well, seems your dear friend Langford was in town calling on some girl, probably in an effort to get over what you had done to him. He had just left her house dressed in his Sunday best and was headed back out of town when I crossed paths with him. Wanting to mend any hard feelings he might have about us getting married, I hailed him down and offered to buy him a drink so we could talk."

Daniel crossed his arms and shifted his weight to one leg in that insolent manner of his. "Langford seemed a little reluctant at first, but eventually agreed to join me for one drink. But once we started to get on better terms with one another, he agreed to a second drink, then a third."

Virginia felt her heart fill with despair: Mark

was hardly a drinking man; he could never hold his liquor. Fear sent an icy chill racing through her veins.

Offering a sardonic smile, he went on. "That's when the conversation started to get really interesting. Langford began talking about how he knew you back when you were both kids — a fact I found a little astonishing, considering I thought you'd been raised in the north. But I didn't tell him that. He then mentioned how you two had seen each other since the wedding — since I told you not to see him again. He *next* let it slip just who your grandparents were and how they were connected to Uncle Caleb's past. Imagine how surprised I was to learn that you were brought up *not half a mile from here!* Now, I wonder why you never told me any of that yourself." Daniel's voice came deep in his throat while the muscles in his face jumped rhythmically in a display of pent-up rage.

"I didn't think that sort of thing was very important," she offered feebly. Her mind raced frantically for an excuse he might understand, but in the end she could not seem to focus on thought other than the fact that Daniel had found out.

"Important enough for you to keep it a secret," he pointed out. "But then I guess I would want to keep that sort of thing a secret, too. I sure wouldn't want it getting out that I was the grandchild of such a truly wicked, vengeful old woman."

Virginia's lips pressed hard against her teeth in response to what Daniel had just said, because he had attacked the woman she held dearest in her heart. "My grandmother was not a wicked, vengeful old woman."

"Yes, she was," Daniel replied quickly. "The more Mark had to say, the more I came to realize that she is the same heartless witch who ruined my dear uncle's entire life, all because of her petty jealousies."

Virginia's voice climbed as the anger and frustration she had harbored all these years rose quickly to the surface. "Your *dear* uncle, as you so blindly put it, cheated my grandfather out of his home. Cheated him out of Valley Oaks. All because my grandmother chose to marry my grandfather instead of him."

"My uncle never cheated anyone out of anything. There wasn't a dishonest bone in his body," Daniel shouted back, eager to defend his uncle. "He was a good man. I never knew anyone more honest and decent than Caleb Pearson."

"Then I'd hate to meet the rest of the people you know. If they couldn't even measure up to the likes of your black-hearted uncle, then they must be a pack of thieving cutthroats. Caleb Pearson cheated my grandfather out of his land and his home simply because my grandmother refused to marry him. If anyone should be called wicked and vengeful, it is him. He took what rightfully belonged to my grandfather without a twinge of regret or the slightest remorse. He was cold and ruthless, and I never hated anyone more in my entire life than I hate that man!"

Daniel's blue eyes widened with sudden comprehension. "When you came here, your only hopes were to find a way to get Valley Oaks back, weren't they? That was your *true* goal all along. That's the reason you agreed to marry me, isn't it?" It was all starting to come together in his mind. Angered at the realization that he had been duped yet again, his nostrils flared while he waited for her response.

"Yes, but—" she started to answer, eager to try to explain; but she was interrupted before she could finish.

"But nothing!" he bit out angrily. "I could strangle you for what you've done! When you came here, you had every intention of deceiving me. It was all carefully planned, wasn't it? You lied to me about who you were, led me to believe you were from the north, just so you could get the job and maneuver yourself into our lives. How long did it take you to lose your East Texas accent? How many long hours of practice, just so I would believe you were from the north? You even pretended to care about Mary in order to get what you came for. *And I fell for it.*"

"I *do* care about Mary!" she cried out, her fists clenched at her side. "The rest of what you condemned me for may be true, but that part is not."

"You are no different than your grandmother. You are a vengeful, deceitful, wicked witch, full of lies and hatred. You are exactly like my first wife. You came here with every intention of humiliating me, of using me in any way you could in order to get what you wanted—didn't you? All you ever cared about was getting your unjust revenge." His blue eyes narrowed into glittering slits of rage. "You deliberately set out to make a fool out of me and get Valley Oaks back in the process!"

Virginia winced at his words, for he spoke the truth: she *had* come to Valley Oaks to do all those things, but that was before she had met him . . . and that was *long* before she had fallen in love with him. Never had she felt so ashamed of herself; he had every right to loath her. Having heard her horrible intentions spoken with such disgust from his lips, she now loathed herself.

"And you did a dandy job of it, didn't you?" He spoke through teeth gritted with such force that the muscle in his jaw flexed. "Not only did I fall easily into your trap and prove to be the biggest fool ever to hit East Texas; but by getting me to marry you, you actually managed to get Valley Oaks back. And what about Mary? Let's not forget how easily she allowed herself to love you."

Daniel slammed his fist against the cheval dresser, upsetting his shaving mug, which fell to the floor and shattered into tiny pieces. The sudden noise fueled his anger. He stepped over to stand directly in front of her, his cold expression only inches from her fearful one. "Damn you, Virginia. That is all that matters to you—getting Valley Oaks back. You didn't even care who you hurt in the process. Well, not only did you hurt me, but Mary is going to be devastated."

He was so furious by then that he realized he had to get out of there. Angrily he reached out and pushed her out of his way. The unanticipated force of the shove caused her to stumble over a chair and fall to the floor, knocking her forehead against the foot of the bed. He never looked back to see what damage he'd done but stalked to the door with every intention of getting as far away from her as he possibly could.

Quickly Virginia got back to her feet. Although she was still afraid of his explosive rage and feared what else he might do to her if she should anger him further, she tried to explain. "Yes, Daniel, I did come here with those intentions. Your uncle plotted and connived against my grandfather until he was able to ruin him. Then he took what was rightfully my family's—Valley Oaks. And along with Valley Oaks, he took my grandfather's pride. He caused my grandparents to be poor for the rest of their lives. Contrary to what you believe, they were good people; they did not deserve what he did to them. Your uncle was an evil, spiteful man. He did not deserve to own Valley Oaks."

"He was not evil!" Daniel had spun to face her again, only a few feet short of the door. His thick brown hair had fallen across his forehead and his blue eyes blazed with the fury that consumed him, making him look all the more frightening. "My uncle was a good man, and there's no way you can convince me otherwise. There was nothing that man wouldn't do for me or any of his friends, and there is nothing I won't do for him, even now. And I refuse to allow you to talk about him that way. I don't even want to hear his name cross your lips again. It disgusts me."

Virginia, speechless, watched him turn away from her again and stalk out of the room, his hands curled into tight knots at his sides. She felt a vibration in the floor when the back door slammed shut as he stormed out of the house. She could not believe that he had refused to give her a chance to explain, to tell him how although her motives had at one time been purely vengeful, somewhere along the way she had fallen in love with him. But her misery grew when she realized he would have gotten angrier still if she had dared mention the word love again.

Stepping back and sinking onto the mattress of their bed, she sat massaging her swelling forehead in stunned silence while she tried to figure out what she should do.

Daniel had ridden away in a rage, leaving everyone in the house curious about what had happened between him and Virginia. They had all heard the shouting; it would have been impossible not to. Because the windows had been open at the time, even Pete, Jack, and several of the workhands had heard the shouting all the way out in the barn and had stopped to stare at the house, concerned. But no one had caught exactly what was being said.

By the time Lizzie knocked at Virginia's door just a few hours later, everyone at Valley Oaks had already discussed it at some length, hoping that by putting their heads together they might be able to figure out what could have caused such an argument; but no one had a clue.

"Missus, you in there?" Lizzie asked when there was no immediate response to her knock. Her voice was filled with worry.

"Yes, Lizzie, come on in," Virginia finally answered, wondering how much of what they'd said had been heard by the others, and blissfully innocent of the fact that even those outdoors had caught parts of it.

"I guess you know Master Daniel rode out of here a little while ago," Lizzie said, trying to approach a sensitive subject as delicately as she knew how. "He didn't say where he was going."

"I heard him leave," Virginia admitted, and glanced up to see the look concern on Lizzie's dark face as the woman stared, brow drawn, at the swollen area that had risen along the side of Virginia's forehead.

Aware she should not be staring, Lizzie looked away, noticing then that except for the rumpled bed, the room was in order. Nothing had been thrown or knocked over; nothing was broken. That's when she surmised that Daniel had actually struck his wife and she felt herself grow furious with him; but she thought better of allowing those angry emotions to show.

Rubbing a plump hand over her face, Lizzie decided to go ahead with the speech she had rehearsed several times before daring to knock. "Well, ma'am, it seems before he left, Master Daniel told Miss Mary to go to her room and stay there until she was told otherwise, and . . . well, ma'am, it's now past her suppertime. Should I take her a tray, or will you be givin' her permission to come on out of her room? Seein' how you are the one in charge when he's away, I felt it would be up to you if she stayed any longer or was allowed to come out. I realize she talked up to her father, but maybe she's been in her room long enough to make up for that."

Virginia closed her eyes with the realization that

412

she had been so caught up in her own misery that she had forgotten all about Mary. "Is the supper still on the table?"

"Yes, ma'am, it is."

"Then, please, tell her she can come out of her room. In fact, tell her I will be joining her for supper in just a few minutes. I just want to tidy up a little." She reached up and felt of the hair that had pulled loose from the rest during the fall.

Lizzie smiled briefly but was unable to hold the expression for long; she was again reminded that Master Daniel had actually struck his missus during the argument, and Lizzie could never condone such behavior. Even if it meant risking her job, she intended to give Daniel a piece of her mind when he got back. "I'll do that, Missus. I'll tell her you'll be right down."

When Virginia turned to the mirror to repair her hair, she saw just how grotesque the lump on her forehead was. Not only was the large area swollen, it was red around the edges and starting to turn blue in the center. That's when she also caught sight of the deep concern that had so quickly returned to Lizzie's face. She decided the woman needed to be reassured somehow.

"Lizzie, Daniel and I had our first real argument this afternoon," she said, though she had a feeling she had not yet imparted any information the woman was not already aware of. Then, although she had only intended to tell Lizzie just enough to satisfy her curiosity, Virginia ended up pouring out her heart to her. She told her everything. With tears spilling down her cheeks, she rushed into Lizzie's waiting arms and wept openly.

413

"What am I going to do, Lizzie? I love him so much. And now he hates me."

"Give him time to get over it," Lizzie advised wisely. "I think, by the way he talked about his first wife, that you have opened up old wounds that will take an awful long time to heal, but eventually they *will* heal. I just know it."

Virginia closed her eyes and pressed her damp face into the softness of Lizzie's shoulder. How she prayed that would prove to be the truth! She could not bear to think what her life would be like without Daniel.

Lizzie held her a moment longer before gently pushing her away. Offering a wide, reassuring smile that was almost convincing, she patted Virginia on the arm. "Things have a way of working themselves out for the best; you'll see. I'll go tell Mary she can come out now."

Having heard someone else voice such strong optimism, Virginia felt much better. By the time she had restyled her hair and had come downstairs to join Mary for supper, she was able to put a fairly convincing smile on her face. She realized Mary had to have heard their angry voices and wanted to do what she could to reassure the child that everything was going to be all right—much as Lizzie had done for her a few minutes earlier.

During supper Virginia continued to put on a brave front and did what she could to cheer them both by keeping up a lively conversation; but despite her efforts, Mary remained subdued throughout the meal. Virginia worried then that Mary had actually heard the exact words they had exchanged. If that was so, Mary was now aware of all the deception and the terrible secrets she had kept from them both. Virginia felt she should try to explain everything to the girl and apologize, but she did not know exactly how to go about it. She was not absolutely certain the girl had heard what had been said. Just the fact that there had been an argument and her father had stormed away in a rage could be enough to make her become so withdrawn.

Still they needed to have a talk. Mary needed to express her own feelings about what had happened. By the time they had finished eating and had risen from the table, Virginia had decided not to put off their talk any longer.

"Mary, would you mind coming outside with me for a while? I need someone to keep me company," she asked just before they walked away from the table.

Mary didn't answer, but shook her head to show that she did not really mind. Glancing up at Virginia with huge, sad eyes, she took Virginia's proffered hand and went with her outside.

"Would you rather take a walk or sit in the swing?" Virginia wanted to know.

Mary shrugged; it didn't matter.

"Well, then, let's sit in the swing. I want to talk to you about something."

After they were comfortably seated, Virginia went right to the heart of the matter. "I guess you heard the argument your father and I had this afternoon."

Mary nodded as she bent her head and studied her folded hands.

"Did you happen to hear what it was about?"

Mary shook her head that she had not, and glanced briefly at Virginia.

Virginia was relieved; Mary was really too young to fully understand. Then again, Virginia wasn't too sure she understood it herself anymore. What had seemed so clear to her before, so very important, now made little sense.

"But you did hear us shouting at each other?" Virginia went on to ask.

Mary nodded again.

"Does it worry you that we had an argument?"

Tears filled Mary's huge eyes and shimmered in thick pools near the edges of her heavily fringed eyelids. In a quivering voice, she asked, "Is he ever coming back?"

Virginia's mouth fell open when she realized what had been going through Mary's mind. "Whyever would you think he might not be coming back?"

Mary closed her eyes; the tears were pressed out onto her cheeks. "Because when he and my mother had a real bad argument like yours one night, mother left him and never came back; Father never saw her again. But I don't think he wanted to. They stayed mad forever."

Virginia pulled Mary close. "This is your father's home. He'll be back." She closed her own eyes as she prayed that what she had just told the child would prove to be the truth. But when she thought about, she realized if Daniel was indeed angry enough to want to put her out of his life as he had his first wife, when he did return, he would immediately send her away. Suddenly her heart felt as if it was made of lead.

Virginia and Mary talked a little while longer, until Mary began to yawn. Aware it was over an hour past the child's bedtime, Virginia went upstairs with her and helped tuck her into bed. Mary was almost asleep by the time the covers were properly arranged. But because Virginia knew her own sleep would be impossible, she returned to the back veranda.

When she passed through the hallway just moments later, she noticed it was only a little after eight o'clock, but to her it felt like midnight. The sky was just beginning to turn dark outside when she settled into the swing once more.

Only a few minutes after that, she heard the rattling of a carriage as it pulled into the drive. Her first thought was that Daniel had returned, but then she realized he would not be returning in a carriage when he had left on horseback.

Unable to see the drive and aware someone would be knocking at the front door within minutes, she rose and went back inside. She was in no mood for visitors, but she could not very well send them away. She paused in front of a mirror to check her hair, then proceeded to the front door.

To her further dismay, when she opened the door, she discovered William Haught standing before her, dressed in his finest, an overly concerned expression on his lean features.

"Virginia, I came as soon as I heard," he said melodramatically and stepped forward to embrace her without bothering to close the door behind him. He frowned when she immediately pulled away.

417

"Heard what?" she wanted to know.

"That you and Daniel are having problems."

Virginia paused to think: how on earth had William heard about the argument so quickly? Barely seven hours had passed, and no one from Valley Oaks had left in all that time except Daniel himself. "What makes you think Daniel and I are having problems."

"He sent word for Amanda to meet him somewhere, saying that she had been right about you. She left immediately to go to him," he said as if Virginia should have guessed as much while he reached out to gently stroke her silken hair. When he did, some of the hair pulled away from her face and revealed the dark injury on her forehead. "My God! He's beaten you!"

"I fell!" she responded quickly, then realized that must be what Lizzie had believed as well.

"You don't have to lie to me," he said sympathetically. Again William wrapped his arms around her in an awkwardly consoling manner. "I'm here for you, Virginia."

"I am not lying, and I am fine," she assured him. She tried again to pull away, but found his hold on her too strong.

"How could he do something like this to you? How could he strike someone so beautiful and helpless?"

Virginia could almost hear Daniel's sardonic laugh to such an outrageous remark.

William stared longingly into her eyes until she felt compelled to look away then he reached out to stroke her hair again. "The man must be insane, I'd never treat you like that. A woman like you

418

needs tenderness, not force—and never violence."
He reached down to lift her chin and draw her
face up so that he could gaze longingly into her
eyes once again. "Daniel is a fool. How can he
choose Amanda over someone as beautiful and
kindhearted as you?"

William's mention of Amanda stung enough to
cause Virginia to close her eyes; and when she did,
he took immediate advantage of her responsive
reaction: he brought his mouth down against hers
in a searing kiss. She shrugged again to push him
away, but his kiss only became more ardent. When
he finally paused to declare his desire to help her
through her time of need, she took advantage of
the momentarily distance and screamed out his
name in outrage.

Wide-eyed, he reached up to cover her mouth
with his hand. "Please, Virginia, let me help you
through your difficult times; let me help you to
forget. If Daniel feels free enough to turn to my
sister so soon in your marriage, then you should
feel just as free to turn to me. I can help you
forget your pain, if only for a little while."

He then let go of her mouth in hopes of resuming his earlier pursuit, only to have her scream out
again.

"William! Let go of me!"

William's face tightened with anger. "I'm just
here to help you, to comfort you. Can't you see
that?"

"I don't want that sort of comfort," she told
him in definite tones while she continued to try to
free herself from his grasp. "And I think it would
be best if you left now. Before I decide to scream

again, this time loud enough to bring everyone at Valley Oaks bounding to my rescue!"

Tossing his head back indignantly, William looked very insulted when he voiced his response to her threat. "Very well, if you insist on being so ungrateful, I will leave. But later on, when you go upstairs to face that bed of yours all alone, do remember that I tried to help make the night an easier one to bear."

He then spun on his heel to leave, but thought of something else he felt was worth saying and paused just long enough to say it. "Just keep in mind that Daniel will not be so alone when *he* goes to bed tonight — if he isn't already there."

On that cutting remark, William left.

Chapter Twenty-three

Virginia found sleep impossible while she waited for Daniel to return. She tossed and turned restlessly until her bed was a jumble of twisted covers and dented pillows. In her mind she rehearsed exactly what she wanted to say when he finally did come back and prayed he would give her the opportunity to speak in her own defense before he locked himself away in his library or ran off to the barn.

Afraid to think of any other possibility, she tried to focus her thoughts on making things right with him again. She tried not to worry about what Daniel was doing that kept him away for the entire night. The image of Daniel with Amanda caused her unbearable pain, and she did all she could not to dwell on the fact that Daniel had sent for his former lover so readily—much less why he may have wanted her to come. William's insinuation that the two were probably sharing the same bed hurt so that Virginia could not ignore it. Yet she refused to think about it for very long at one time; instead she tried to concentrate on what she would say and do to set things right again, if he ever came home.

Daniel's anger and his parting words haunted her, playing over and over in her brain, until she began to realize how important his opinion of Caleb was.

If only she could convince Daniel of Caleb's evil crimes, then he might realize why she had felt so compelled to do what she had done. He would understand how cruelly the man had treated her grandparents, how he had caused them to suffer needlessly, all because of his own spiteful jealousy.

The more she thought about it, the more she realized getting Daniel to see his uncle for the blackheart he really was might indeed help her husband to better understand the reasons for her actions. She realized how painful it was going to be for him to have to face the truth about his beloved uncle at last, and she really did not like the thought of hurting him in such a way; but she could see no other way out of her dilemma. Once Daniel was made aware of the truth, he would then be able to see why her own hatred had grown to the intensity it had and why getting Valley Oaks back had become so important.

Though Virginia wanted to be home when Daniel returned, she realized if she could somehow obtain undeniable proof of what Caleb had done, it would help Daniel see what had made her try and avenge all the terrible things done to her family. And the sooner she could make Daniel understand, the better.

Only moments after the sun made its first efforts to turn the bleak, night sky into a pale, dusty blue, Virginia quickly dressed in a simple yellow cotton summer dress, then arranged her hair to make the ugly bruise less apparent. There was little she could do about the bluish sunken areas beneath her eyes which her fretful night without sleep had caused. Quickly she donned a wide-brimmed hat and thought to grab up a pair of gloves before heading downstairs and then outside to find someone to prepare a carriage for her.

The sun had not yet risen above the towering trees that blanketed the gentle slopes of the distant hills before she was well on her way. She dearly hoped to find Mattie Williams at home this time and prayed the woman would know something—anything—that could help her convince Daniel of the truth.

Thirty minutes later, when she pulled onto the small carriage drive leading to Mattie's small frame house, she found the woman sitting on her front porch with a heaping bushel of peas at her side and a large metal pan in her lap. The woman was busily running her withered thumb through the plump, dark-purple shells, letting the peas fall into the bowl, then tossing the empty hulls into a bushel basket. She looked up just as Virginia pulled her carriage to a halt in the front yard.

"Hello," the old woman called out as she set the bowl atop the bushel of peas and slowly pushed her slight frame up out of the chair. She squinted in an effort to recognize her early morning caller while she wiped her stained hands on the corner of her bleached white apron.

"Hello," Virginia returned with a friendly smile,

then waited until she had gathered her skirts and stepped down from the small carriage before bothering to explain her presence. "I'm Virginia Pearson, Daniel Pearson's wife. I was by to meet you earlier, but you weren't home."

The old woman's lily-complexioned face relaxed into a pleasant smile and the pale green in her eyes seemed to brighten. "So *you* are the pretty little lady who managed to get our Daniel to marry again!"

That comment gave Virginia a moment's pause: it had not occurred to her that the woman would know Daniel, too, but of course she would. Daniel had come to Valley Oaks often in his youth and had obviously stolen this woman's heart just as he'd stolen the heart of every other female he'd ever met. There was something about the man that women could not seem to resist—herself included.

"I'm the one," Virginia said, trying to sound cheerful. She gave her hair a self-conscious pat to make certain it still covered the ugly bruise on her forehead before she moved across the yard to greet the woman.

"Come, sit down," Mattie said happily. She pulled out a tall, ladder-back chair so they could talk. "I'll make us some tea."

"No, thank you. It's too early in the morning for tea," Virginia said quickly, unwilling to admit her stomach was twisted into too many knots to allow her to drink anything.

"Then, please, sit down; I must get to know you. I've been wanting to meet you ever since I heard you and Daniel were to be married," Mattie began.

After the usual introductory conversation between strangers, Virginia was finally able to arrive at the subject she wanted to talk about the most: Caleb.

"How curious that you should mention him," Mattie said with a fond smile as she leaned her silvered head back against the top rung of her chair and stared up into the bright blue morning sky. "I was just thinking about him this morning. But then, I think about the man quite a lot."

"Oh? Was he a nice man to work for?" Virginia asked. It was a ridiculous question, but one that might encourage Mattie to tell a few stories about the man. Virginia then prepared herself for a long accounting of all the evil, wicked things he had done to her over the years and was surprised when instead, the woman virtually glowed while a shy little smile stretched across her thin mouth, causing a fine display of dimpled creases in her weathered cheeks.

"Caleb was a wonderful man, a kind man—and generous with his employees, even in death. He gave me this house and five acres of land in his will," she said proudly and gestured over her shoulder to the small, single-story frame house, then out to the surrounding vegetable gardens and orchards. "And fifteen dollars a month until my death to help me get by."

Virginia's brow dipped with disappointment at the woman's remarks. Obviously whatever evil the man had ever done her had been instantly undone in this woman's mind by what he'd left her in his will. It was going to be hard to get the truth out of her; but still she had to try.

"Do you miss living at Valley Oaks?" she asked, hoping to approach the subject of how Caleb had gotten her grandparents' home from them by talking first about the place itself.

"I miss having so many people around me . . . it gets lonely here at times," Mattie admitted with a sigh. "But I keep busy." She paused a moment while she reflected. "I particularly miss Caleb."

The way Mattie kept referring to him by his first name made Virginia wonder if the woman had not at one time actually been secretly in love with the man; but she quickly dismissed the thought as absurd. How could anyone love a man like Caleb?

"I understand you went to work for Caleb the very day he moved into Valley Oaks. I imagine it was an exciting day for everyone."

Mattie's forehead wrinkled. "I was certainly excited about starting to work in a house so grand, and for a salary so generous—very excited indeed; but as I recall, Caleb acted kind of sad that first day. He kept to himself most of the day, letting me and Mister Gelbman pretty much handle all the moving-in chores. When I asked Caleb if anything was wrong, he started talking about ghosts from the past. Spooked me something awful to think there might be ghosts lurking about, but soon I came to realize there were no ghosts. I think he just felt bad because the house had belonged to a friend of his. Fact is, it was his friend's family home. It had first belonged to his friend's father."

The very subject Virginia wanted to hear about! Eagerly she leaned forward, wanting to know more. Her heart began to hammer rapidly when

426

she asked, "If the house belonged to his friend and was the family home, then how did Caleb come to own it?"

Mattie shook her head as if the answer she had to give was unpleasant to remember. Virginia's breath held.

"His friend needed money in a bad way. Seems the man was prone to taking trips from time to time that were supposed to involving ranching business, but in fact involved a lot of heavy gambling, where he had lost ungodly amounts. After one such unfortunate trip, the man went to Caleb and asked him to help him out. One of the men he owed money to had threatened both him and his family harm if he did not come up with the money quick. He desperately wanted to sell Valley Oaks to Caleb."

Mattie shook her head slowly. "Caleb didn't want to but it at first, and offered to simply lend him some money, but his friend's pride wouldn't hear of it. So Caleb finally gave in and bought the house, mainly so that when his friend was back on his feet, he could be sure to buy it back at a fair price. Caleb stipulated that his friend was to stop gambling as part of their loan agreement. But I don't think the friend ever fully gave up his gambling ways; the man never did get back on his feet."

Virginia did not believe a word of what the old woman was saying and desperately wanted to cry out that it was all a string of lies, but something made her remain quiet while Mattie continued with her tale. "In return for his promise to give up gambling, his friend made Caleb promise never to tell anyone the real reason he had bought the place. The man was afraid his wife would hear tell of it and would be so disappointed in him it would break her heart. He was afraid she'd leave him."

A look of deep-seated pride lifted Mattie's expression. "And Caleb never did tell anyone the truth—except me, and he wouldn't have told even me if he hadn't gotten himself miserably drunk one night and let the whole story slip. That next day, when he realized what he'd done, he made me promise not to tell anyone, especially not the man's wife, and I promised. Not really knowing the man's wife, it was an easy enough promise to keep. And not knowing anyone else who really knew her made it easy, too."

A wistful look misted the woman's pale green eyes and she looked down at her folded hands when she added, "But I don't guess it matters now who I tell, not now that they are all dead."

"You didn't even know the man's wife?" Virginia questioned further. She was not at all satisfied with the woman's story.

"Oh, I knew *of* her. Caleb had provided them with a house on a little part of his land, down to the south. And with them living so close, I had occasion to catch glimpses of her from time to time. She was a pretty woman, but always looked so tired, and so sad. Because I knew the life she could have led if only her husband hadn't gambled it all away, I kind of felt sorry for her. Just like I felt sorry for Caleb."

"Caleb?"

"Yes. Caleb loved that woman with all his heart

. . . loved her to the very day he died. She's the real reason Caleb provided his friend with that house." Mattie frowned, closing her eyes to the untold pain—as if jealous for some reason of the memories she had. "Why do I keep calling the man his friend? That man allowed everyone around these parts to think Caleb had cheated him out of that house . . . let them all think Caleb was the reason he had gone broke. He let his wife think so, too. She never even knew how Caleb was the one who had provided that house for her, though it wasn't anything grand. It was a lot like this house, but it was plenty enough to keep her and her family warm and dry. Caleb had also seen to it that food was provided at times when they might not have had any—through his *friend*."

Mattie frowned again and placed a withered finger to her chin. Virginia noticed the hand started to tremble slightly when the woman spoke again in a voice tinged with anger. "I wish I could remember that man's name so I wouldn't have to keep calling him Caleb's friend. He was no friend to Caleb."

Mattie fell silent, then lifted her pale white brows. "Joseph, that's what his name was . . . *Joseph*. Whenever rumor got back to Caleb, from the men he always had keeping up with what went on over there, that the family was doing particularly poorly, he would have one those men catch Joseph alone and hand over a supply of food. Or sometimes Joseph would come right out and ask him direct. And Caleb always gave him the food he needed, yet Caleb was careful never to give him money whenever he came asking for help, for fear he might gamble it away. Still, Caleb was always seeing to it the family had enough to eat, and medicine, too, if one of them was to get real sick."

Virginia thought back and remembered how her grandfather had often insisted he be the one to go into town to get their stores and would come back with more than her grandmother felt they could afford; and on occasion he would not have mentioned that he was going into town for food at all, but had returned with plenty. He always claimed he'd done odd jobs for the merchants in return for their food and medicine, which was why he was able to stretch their dollar so well. But when asked, he sometimes could not remember exactly what sort of job he had gotten rewarded for.

Her grandmother had told her that was probably because they had not been the jobs he had claimed them to be, like cutting wood and repairing roofs. She decided the jobs he had done were jobs he felt ashamed having had to do, like shoveling out stables, cleaning privies, and the like. Now Virginia wondered if his inability to remember the exact jobs he had done was really the result of his strong sense of pride or because he could not think quickly and creatively enough. Still Virginia did not want to believe what the woman was telling her.

"I don't know why I'm going on about this," Mattie said, reaching out and patting Virginia on the arm with a cool hand, interrupting Virginia's thoughts and bringing them back to what was being said. "I guess because while the three were still alive, I was sworn to secrecy. And I so wanted to tell the world everything I knew about this. But they're all three gone now . . . last of them died in that awful storm we had last year. His beloved Essie can't be hurt none at all by me telling anyone about it now. Nobody's left. She didn't even leave any family in these parts. Town had to bury her."

Mattie sighed softly, then smiled. "You know? It feels good to finally be able to tell someone about all the suffering Caleb put himself through because of that woman. To finally tell of all the things he did for her without her ever even knowing it. And all that poor man ever got in return was her scorn. The woman loved spreading those lies about Caleb and did just that whenever she found a willing ear; but then, in all fairness, she didn't know they were lies. Only Caleb and Joseph knew the truth. And of course, me."

Virginia sat in stunned silence while the woman drifted into her own private thoughts. Virginia wondered if it could actually be true. In a way, it all made sense—it fit things the way they had been: the fact her grandfather could always seem to come up with food or medicine when they needed it most; the fact that her grandmother had discovered the house they had lived in did indeed belong to Caleb. But still she did not want to believe it. Because if it was true, she had returned to East Texas seeking revenge on a man who in no way deserved revenge. If what Mattie had just told her was true, it was her own grandfather who was at fault, and not Daniel's uncle. If Mattie spoke the truth, the only thing Caleb deserved was her gratitude. She had a sinking feeling in the pit of her stomach.

"How do you know that Caleb told you the truth, that he was not making up a story which would make him seem innocent of all those rumors?" She was still reluctant to believe a story that went so completely against everything she had been told by her grandmother.

"Because I was there in the room one day when Joseph paid a call on Caleb; he begged Caleb for money to buy his granddaughter a fancy party dress for a big dance that was coming up. Caleb was hesitant to do so until Joseph broke down and started to cry, claiming his granddaughter did not deserve to suffer for all the foolish mistakes he'd made. He pleaded with Caleb to give him the money. In the end, Caleb gave in. He always wondered if Joseph did indeed use the money to buy that dress, or if he went directly to a gambling table and piddled it away."

Virginia felt her heart twist painfully. She wanted to tell the woman how he had indeed spent the money on material for a beautiful party dress . . . the finest dress she had ever owned, until Daniel had bought her the one for Amanda's party. Tears came to Virginia's eyes. It *was* true. It was *all* true. Instead of proving that she had been right about Caleb, that he had cheated her grandfather out of his land and his home, she had discovered just the opposite: her grandfather had cheated Caleb. He had cheated Caleb out of the friendship and respect of his neighbors, cheated him out of his good name. And Caleb had let him . . . because he was in love with her grandmother.

The tears spilled down Virginia's cheeks, and

when Mattie's attention returned from her own straying thoughts, she noticed the deep sorrow in the girl's face.

"I didn't mean to make you cry, dear. Indeed, it is a sad story, but I didn't mean to make you cry. My, but you have a tender and compassionate heart! Daniel is lucky to have found someone like you," Mattie said sincerely while she reached her hand around Virginia's wrist and gave it a reassuring squeeze. "He and Mary are lucky indeed."

Not so lucky, Virginia thought with deep misery. Suddenly she was filled with self-loathing, appalled by what she had set out to do. She had maneuvered her way into Valley Oaks, then had stolen into Daniel's library with hopes of finding information to use as blackmail if necessary. She had been willing to go so far as to marry a man who did not love her just to get the land back.

No, Daniel was not lucky to have found someone like her; nor was Mary. Poor Mary—how Virginia hoped the child never learned that she had become her stepmother for all the wrong reasons.

Suddenly Virginia had to get away, to be alone to think about all she had learned, to see just how well it did fit with the way her grandfather had behaved all those years.

"Thank you for such a lovely chat," Virginia quickly said before she stood to leave. "I would love to come back and talk again. I want to learn more about my husband's uncle. But for now, I'd better be getting back home. Mary will wonder what is keeping me. I promised to read to her this afternoon."

"Yes, do come again. I have tales to tell you

433

about that husband of yours when he was a young scamp," Mattie said in earnest before she pushed herself out of her chair and walked Virginia to her carriage. "And warn Daniel that many of the stories I intend to tell will get back at him for some of the stunts he pulled on me during his many visits to Valley Oaks. Remind me to tell you how he switched the salt and the sugar in the kitchen cannisters the day a very important business man was due for supper."

"I will," Virginia promised. It sounded as if it might prove an interesting story indeed. But for now she had enough to think about.

A few minutes later, Virginia was on her way back home, her head spinning with thoughts that went against everything she had ever been led to believe. At first she did not notice Mark outside, working a field close to the road. Not until he shouted her name for the fourth time did she finally pull the horse to a stop. Because she had taken so long to hear him, Mark had to cover quite a distance to join her.

"Where have you been?" he asked, a little out of breath.

"I went to visit Mattie Williams," she answered simply, trying to make her thoughts focus on Mark instead of on the astounding realization that she had been wrong, that they all had been wrong about Caleb.

"Oh, Ginny, you didn't," Mark responded, disappointed. "I had so hoped you'd given up that notion by now. I was relieved to learn she was not home when you first tried to visit her. I don't think you realize the trouble you'll cause if you continue to try to find out whatever it was Caleb did to your grandfather. After all, knowing about it is not going to change anything now." He paused a moment, studying her serious expression, then shrugged as if defeated by his own curiosity. "Well, was she home?"

"Yes, she was."

"And did you find out exactly what Caleb did to trick your grandfather out of Valley Oaks?"

Virginia's eyes closed to the sharp pain that struck her heart. When she was finally able to open them again, she was not surprised to find Mark on the seat beside her, his face drawn with concern.

"I told you you were only going to make matters worse," he said, but his voice was filled with sympathy. "I guess you opened up some pretty painful old wounds. Do you want to talk about it?"

She shook her head adamantly for fear she would burst into tears. Her hair moved just enough for Mark to see the ugly bruise on her forehead; he reached out, snatched her hat off her head, and pushed the hair back.

"The bastard! I'll kill him," he shouted angrily, his eyes turning dark with fury.

Remembering William had assumed Daniel had struck her, she quickly responded, "No, Mark, it isn't what you think . . . I fell."

"I'll just bet," Mark said, his lips curling in against his teeth. "And I was starting to think he was a nice guy after all. We had a long talk in town and he tried to convince me how much he cared for you. And I drank it all in like a complete idiot."

435

"You drank it in, all right," Virginia cried out, bursting into tears, unable to hold her tangled emotions in check any longer. "Mark, how could you?"

"Me?" Mark asked, clearly confused. "What did I do?"

"You told Daniel who I was. You told him about my grandparents. I realize you had been drinking, but still, how could you do that to me?" Her shoulders began to shake while she reached for her handbag in search of a handkerchief. "He was furious with me for having kept such secrets from him. He called me a liar, accused me of having married him just so I could get Valley Oaks back."

"Ginny, I thought Daniel knew. After all, he is your husband now. I figured you must have told him everything about you, and that he decided it didn't matter." Mark reached out to touch her, but decided against it and placed his hand on the back of the seat behind her. "Ginny, I never intended to cause any trouble. You've got to believe that. I wouldn't do anything to hurt you in any way." He paused a moment, watching her as she buried her face in the handkerchief. "Ginny? *Was* vengeance the reason you married Daniel? Did you marry him to get Valley Oaks back?"

Virginia pulled the handkerchief from her face and looked at him. Her eyes pressed closed while her body trembled with shame. "It was part of the reason. I wanted to get back what I thought belonged to me." Her eyes flew open when she sought to plead with Mark to understand. "But there were other reasons, too. If you only could know how happy we were becoming, how very, very happy. We were becoming a real family. Now it is all ruined!"

"Don't cry." Mark drew her into his arms, pressing her damp cheek against his shoulder. "You never would have been completely happy with him, anyway. I told you from the beginning, he was not the man for you. There are too many differences between you . . . too much from your past prevents you from ever truly loving him."

"You're wrong," Virginia said, pulling away to look into his face. "Daniel is the man for me, the only man for me. I love him, Mark. I love him with all my heart."

Mark stared at her in stunned silence.

"And I've indeed found out about the past. It can no longer work to drive us apart. I was wrong; my grandmother was wrong. Caleb did *not* cheat my grandfather out of Valley Oaks. My grandfather gambled it away." Virginia then told Mark everything Mattie had revealed to her.

Mark listened quietly until she was through. "No wonder I never saw him doing any of those odd jobs," he said as he thought back. He sat silently beside Virginia for a long moment before finally saying what he felt had to be said.

"Ginny, you need to go back to Daniel and tell him everything you've just told me. You have to get all this straightened out before it gets out of hand."

"Mark, you're the best friend a girl could ever have," she cried softly and hugged him close.

Mark closed his arms around her, embracing her for what would be the last time, and spoke, trying to sound like his old, cavalier self. "I could have told you that if you'd just asked."

The sound of a horse galloping along the hard-packed road caused them to break apart, though their arms remained loosely around each other. Not bothering to wipe away her tears, Virginia glanced in the direction of the sound and was horrified to see Daniel close enough to have witnessed their embrace. He pulled to a stop only a few feet from the carriage and gave them both a devil's glare, then prodded his horse into a dead run, leaving behind him a thick trail of dust.

"Oh, Mark, what must he think!" Virginia cried when she finally found her voice. Her eyes were filled with horror.

"Go after him, Ginny; explain it all to him," Mark said as he quickly jumped down from the carriage. He looked sadly into her fearful expression. "If he doesn't believe you, send word and I'll speak with him."

"What must he think?" Virginia repeated and flicked the reins hard, her heart frozen in her chest.

Virginia ran the horse as hard as she dared on such a deeply rutted dirt road, bouncing off the seat at times whenever a wheel hit a particularly deep hole or a large, unavoidable rock. She had seen Daniel's horse hurdle the roadside fence and knew that he had cut across the pasture in order to get home as quickly as he could. She wished she could take the same shortened route, but she had no other choice than to follow the road. It seemed as if she would never get there.

Chapter Twenty-four

By the time Virginia had brought the carriage to a complete stop and hurried into the house, Daniel had already gone. Lizzie told her how he had quickly packed a valise, ordered her to see that his remaining clothes and personal items were packed into trunks, and set waiting downstairs first thing the following morning. Then, without another word, he left as quickly as he'd come.

"I don't want to worry you more than you is already worried," Lizzie added hesitantly, then paused a moment to let her teeth pull nervously at the corner of her mouth. "But I feel you should know he was still very upset. I'd say he was just as upset today as he was yesterday when he left."

"Did he say where he would be until tomorrow?" Virginia asked hopefully.

"No, just told me to have his things together and waitin' downstairs tomorrow mornin'." Lizzie shrugged, obviously wishing she had more to tell.

Turning away before Lizzie could see just how close she was to crying, Virginia fled the stairs to go to their bedroom. But upon entering and seeing how Daniel had left drawers open, with clothing spilling out of them in his haste to get packed and out of there before she returned, she turned and fled right back down the stairs. She went to the bedroom she had occupied before they married, collapsed face forward onto the bed, and wept bitterly for hours, then spent the rest of the afternoon and all that night trying to decide what she should do.

The next morning, Virginia returned upstairs to dress in one of her prettiest frocks, a pale-pink lightweight dress edged with rose-colored satin ribbon and white lace. It was one of Daniel's favorites. Working quickly, she used similar rose-colored ribbon to style her hair—careful to hide the bruise, yet at the same time still shape it to be attractive. There was nothing she could do about the darkened semicircles that had sunk deeper into the hollows beneath her eyes—evidence of another long night without sleep.

Though she felt it was almost hopeless, she made every effort to look as appealing as she could and went directly to the entrance hall to stay with his trunks until he came for them. She did not intend to allow him to leave before she could have a talk with him. If she had to sit on his very trunks before he would listen to her, she would.

Twisting and rubbing the palms of her hands nervously, Virginia paced the hall and listened carefully for the distant sound of a carriage or a horse. Since he had not left word for a man to hitch up one of his own wagons, she assumed he would bring another with him, probably one from River Ridge, which is where she thought he'd gone. She just hoped he did not have his rendezvous with Amanda at River Ridge; the thought of them together in the same bed she'd shared with him was too much to bear.

Finally, after several long hours, she heard the clatter of a wagon. *Daniel.* At last. Virginia hurried to the window only to be instantly disappointed: it was not Daniel at all ... it was a young man she had never seen before.

She watched while the tall, lanky youth climbed down from a large wagon and ambled slowly to the front door, taking time to glance around at his surroundings approvingly.

Virginia opened the door just as the boy raised his hand to knock.

"May I help you?" she asked curiously.

"I'm here to get Mister Pearson's things," the boy said as his hand moved from where it had paused in mid-knock to quickly remove his hat. He nodded politely.

Virginia's heart plummeted. "Why didn't Mister Pearson come for them himself?"

"I don't rightly know," the boy admitted, looking past her to the three large trunks which sat in the middle of the foyer floor. "All I was told was that I was to come out here to get the man's things early as I could and carry them over to Jefferson. Are those Mister Pearson's trunks?"

"Yes," Virginia answered weakly and watched through tear-filled eyes when the boy plopped his hat back on his head while he carefully eased past her. Instead of asking for assistance from someone, as she expected him to do, the young man took a rope and began to make a harness which he attached to the side handles of one of the trunks. Soon he had the trunk hoisted onto his back, secured by the rope, which he had looped around his chest and shoulders, and was headed back out the door. After two more such trips, he was ready to leave.

Virginia had followed him outside after he had carried the last trunk, and she stood aside watching helplessly while the boy dropped it beside the others in the back of the wagon.

"Are you Mrs. Pearson?" the boy asked while he pushed the trunk as far up into the wagon as it would go.

"I am."

"Good. I was told to give you this just before I left," he said. He reached first into one shirt pocket, then the other, until finally he pulled out a folded piece of paper.

Fearing the message penned inside, Virginia reluctantly accepted the paper and waited until the boy was on his way before daring to unfold it. Knowing the impact Daniel's words might have on her, she returned to the veranda and slowly lowered herself into the closest chair.

A tear blurred her vision, but as she carefully opened the paper and gazed down at the message Daniel had written her, she was still able to make out the words. With an aching heart, she read:

Virginia,

I have decided to leave while I still have at least part of my pride intact. And I do not intend to return until you have left Valley Oaks, which you will start preparing to do immediately. You have one month to find somewhere else to go, somewhere far away. Meanwhile, I am making arrangements for Mary to travel back to New Orleans to stay with my mother. See that she is ready to travel by the weekend. If she asks about my sudden absence, I want you to tell her I had to go on a long business trip. I will wait until you've gone before trying to explain any of our problems to her.

I don't intend to ask for a divorce, mainly because I feel the mistake was partly mine for having believed your lies to begin with. But although lawfully we will remain husband and wife, in reality we have always been strangers and will remain strangers. As long as you do all that I say and leave Valley Oaks within the month, and agree not to tell Mary any of what is going on, allowing me to explain it to her in my own way later, I will supply you with a generous amount for living expenses, plenty to help you find another place to live. And I will continue to see to it that you have enough to continue to live comfortably, but I want it understood that I never want to have to see you again. You will no longer be a part of my life, or Mary's life. You have one month.

Daniel E. Pearson

When Virginia finished reading the letter, she crumpled the page and pressed it to her heart. Tears scalded her cheeks. Daniel was pushing her out of his life forever. His mind was already set never to see her again. She was not going to be allowed the opportunity to explain anything to him. A pain incomparable to any she had ever felt swelled deep inside her and slowly spread until it left no part of her untouched.

Wanting to hurry to her room before someone happened by and saw her crying uncontrollably, realizing there would be no way for her to regain control of the tears this time, Virginia quickly rose from the chair and blindly headed for the front door. But the closer she came to the door, the further away it seemed. The planked floor began to move back and forth beneath her feet, causing her weakened legs to fold at the knees. Darkness enveloped her before she struck the floor.

"Help me get her upstairs." Virginia heard Lizzie's deep voice long before she managed to open her eyes. Blinking hard, she looked from Lizzie to whoever had gently lifted her off of the floor, and saw an equally worried expression on Moses' face.

"What happened?" she asked while she glanced around and wondered what she was doing outside on the veranda. She frowned when her memory flatly refused to cooperate.

"You fainted," Lizzie told her. "That boy had just drove out of here with Master Daniel's trunks and you must have been on your way back to the house when you fainted. You was right near the

444

door when I found you. I went lookin' for you, after Miss Mary came into the kitchen wonderin' where you were. She looked so sad, I thought I'd help her find you. I found you all right. Lying out here, passed out and barely breathin'."

Virginia could feel the crumpled paper still clutched in her hand and suddenly her memory returned, striking full force against her heart. She quickly glanced around, her pale brown eyes wide with concern. "Where is Mary?"

"She went out back to see if she could find you maybe out in the garden. I don't want her havin' to worry none about you when she already has so much else to worry about, so I haven't sent word I found you yet. I called upstairs to Moses for some help. I wanted to get you inside and to feelin' better before I let Mary know where you are." Lizzie then looked at her husband, who was starting to show evidence of muscle strain. "Carry her on up to her room."

"No," Virginia stated adamantly, "I'm fine now. I guess I shouldn't have allowed myself to miss so many meals these past two days. It must have finally caught up with me—made me feel a little dizzy there for a moment, but I'll be all right now."

Moses looked from Virginia to his wife, clearly not knowing who to obey on the matter.

Lizzie saved him from his dilemma after she felt Virginia's cheek and studied her determined expression. "I guess you can put her down. The color's back in her face. I think the best thing for her is to come into the dinin' room and let me get her

445

somethin' to eat. Lunch is almost ready anyway."

Virginia stood on precariously weak legs, determined to walk under her own power, while she followed Lizzie inside. Never having been prone to swooning, she decided it would be good to eat. She knew she would need her strength when she left to search for Daniel. Because as soon as she had eaten, she intended to pack a valise with enough clothes for several days, have a carriage made ready, and then head directly to Jefferson to find Daniel, making River Ridge her first stop.

By the time she had eaten, packed her valise, and gotten the money Daniel had always insisted she keep hidden away for emergencies, she felt much stronger physically; but emotionally she was still as weak as a kitten. She had to find Daniel; she had to try to set things right again.

Neither Lizzie nor Mary tried to talk her out of her quest, nor did anyone else. And though Pete and Jack and several of the other workmen pleadingly volunteered to drive her, when Virginia finally set out to find Daniel she was alone.

Following a map Pete had quickly drawn for her, she had no problem staying on the correct roads. As she had planned, her first stop was River Ridge; she knew that would most likely be where Daniel would be spending his nights.

When she discovered all three doors to the house locked, the windows shut tight, and the curtains drawn, she went in search of one of the Edmonds. She discovered Louis and Rufus several yards out into the shallow water near the riverbank, working with a seine only a few feet from the end of the short pier. Both seemed surprised to see her and quickly disappointed her with the news that neither had seen Daniel since the day he'd left her to go into Jefferson.

Virginia thought to ask Louis for directions to Daniel's shipping company, and when she felt River Ridge only minutes later, that was to be her next destination.

Both Rufus and Louis tried to talk her into waiting until morning, but Virginia knew she would go completely out of her mind if she had to wait any longer. Although it was after sundown when she turned the carriage onto the main road in the direction of Jefferson, and there was still an hour's drive ahead of her, Virginia did not once doubt her decision to go on.

Because there was no one at the shipping office by the time she had finally located it among the many crowded streets of Jefferson, Virginia was forced to wait out the night anyway. Disappointed and teetering on exhaustion, Virginia chose to stay at the Irvine Hotel.

She had paid little attention to the luxurious appearance of the hotel's street front when she entered just after ten o'clock and asked to have a room for the night. Appearance had had nothing to do with her selection of a place to stay; she was concerned only with location. It was the hotel closest to the shipping office, where she wanted to be first thing the following morning, to see if anyone there might know where Daniel had gone. She prayed she would find Daniel himself when

447

she finally entered those office doors.

The night dragged on forever, and despite the luxury of her room and the undeniable comfort of her feather-stuffed bed, Virginia slept very little. She was too full of nervous apprehension, too afraid to hope, yet determined not to fall into despair.

When she finally did enter the shipping office the following morning, Virginia was a jumble of nerves. She was disappointed not to see Daniel anywhere in the large, crowded front room, but relieved to find James York standing just inside the door, talking with one of his clerks. When James glanced to see Virginia, he hurried to greet her.

"Virginia! What brings you here?" he asked, his brow drawn with instant worry. "Where's Daniel?"

Virginia's face paled. "I was hoping you could tell me that. I am looking for him."

"I don't understand," James said, giving his gaping employees a stern look while he directed her toward the back of the room. He waited until they were inside his office and the door was closed before he asked, "Why would you be looking for Daniel here?"

Bravely holding back her tears, Virginia admitted, "Daniel and I had an argument . . . a terrible argument. In fact, he got so angry with me that he left Valley Oaks. He returned just long enough to toss together some of his clothes and order the rest of his things packed for travel. Then he sent a young man out the next day with a wagon to get his trunks and carry them to Jefferson. I assumed he meant to River Ridge; I went there first, but when I found out he hasn't been there in weeks, I thought maybe I'd find him here. I know how much Caleb's business means to him. He works so hard to see that it prospers."

"I'm sorry, Virginia," James said, reaching out and patting her shoulder awkwardly. "But Daniel is not here, either."

"Do you have any idea where he might have gone?" she asked hopefully.

"No; maybe he caught a riverboat and is headed to New Orleans to visit his mother. Or maybe he's simply hiding out somewhere until he's had time to calm down. If I were you, I'd go on back to Valley Oaks and wait for him to come home. Try to get your mind off him as best you can. I'll bet he's back there before you know it."

"No, he's not coming back until I've left," she said, then told him about the letter. "What am I going to do? I love him so much! I can't bear the thought of living without him. I have to find him."

James turned and gazed sadly out a window that overlooked the wide, bustling Jefferson riverport. His hazel eyes scanned the activity along the docks. "Virginia: until Daniel wants to be found, he won't be. There really is no sense in making such an effort to look for him . . . you won't find him. All you can do is go back to Valley Oaks and hope that he comes to his senses."

Virginia had never felt such despair. "Eventually, I feel certain he will be in contact with you. I don't think he can allow himself to neglect Caleb's business for very long. When he does contact you, will you tell him that I was here looking for him? Will you tell him how important it is for me to talk with him? And tell him that I don't intend to leave Valley Oaks until I have had that chance to talk with him; but then, if he still wants me to go, I'll leave immediately."

James turned back to her and took her hands in his. "I'll tell him. I'll also tell him what a big mistake he's making."

"Thank you," she said. Her lower lip trembled enough to make her realize she was about to start crying again. After quickly telling James goodbye, she stopped by the hotel for her things, then returned to Valley Oaks, defeated. There was nothing else she could do but wait for him to return and hope that he was not still too angry to listen.

"I know you said you was not very hungry, but you have to keep up your strength for Mary's sake," Lizzie reminded Virginia when she set the breakfast tray on the narrow table beside the bed. "It was pretty late when you come back last night, so I was willin' to let you go without your supper, but there's no tellin' when you ate last. You have got to eat."

Virginia felt it was enough that she had agreed to return to Daniel's bedroom for Mary's sake, to make it appear everything was all right again, until after the child had left for her grandmother's. But the thought of forcing food into her mouth at that particular moment made her stomach coil into a

450

tight knot. Yet, to avoid an argument with the woman, who had nothing but her best interests at heart, Virginia watched while Lizzie pulled apart a steaming hot biscuit and placed a large dollop of strawberry jam inside.

"Here you go. One taste of that and your appetite's sure to return," Lizzie said as she handed the biscuit to Virginia. Then, while Virginia stared at the fluffy white mound of bread, with its tiny droplets of strawberry jam oozing out the sides, Lizzie turned her attention to finding her mistress something to wear. "You can't stay in that bed all day. It isn't good for you. I realize you are badly missin' Master Daniel, but you'll think less about him if you get yourself up from that bed and get to doin' something useful. Miss Mary could use some cheerin' up. She misses him too. Maybe the two of you could go for a walk, or somethin'. It's a pretty day."

Virginia had touched the large biscuit to her lips and tasted the sweetness, but could not bring herself to actually take a bite. Realizing Lizzie's attention was now on finding something appropriate for her to wear, she quickly tore off a piece of the biscuit and tossed it out the window Lizzie had conveniently just opened for her. She waited until Lizzie had glanced back to see that part of the biscuit was gone, then, as soon as she had looked away again, Virginia tossed the rest of it through the window, hoping there was no one outside to see the biscuit tumble to the ground. She hated deceiving the woman like that, but was not up to arguing further and really did not feel she could keep anything in her stomach at the moment.

Satisfied that Virginia was starting to eat and knowing her mistress's modest streak when it came to putting on her clothes, Lizzie left the room after she had everything laid out across the foot of the bed.

Though Virginia did not feel like getting out of bed at all, she realized Lizzie was right; Mary needed her, and she had only a few more days with the child. On wobbly legs Virginia eventually made it out of bed and got dressed.

The day passed slowly. Because Mary's appetite was also affected by Daniel's absence, Virginia forced herself to eat a hearty lunch, more as an example for the child than because she was finally hungry. The food made her feel a little better physically, but it in no way restored her spirits. By the time she had seen Mary safely tucked in bed that evening and had returned downstairs for a glassful of chilled milk, she was deep in a pit of gloom, willing to wallow there, no longer in search of a way out.

"I sure hate to see you sufferin' like you are," Lizzie said while she poured Virginia a tall glass of milk, happy to be providing her gaunt mistress with some form of nourishment. "I wish there was somethin' I could do to help."

"I know," Virginia said with a warm smile. "And I appreciate your concern."

"It's more than concern. I tell you one thing: when that man does decide to come on back here, I'm goin' to give him a big piece of my mind. Imagine him hittin' you the way he did, then runnin' off like that, and now sending Mary away." Lizzie's expression tightened. "You'd think he'd remember how bad bein' left all alone like that feels! You'd think he'd remember just how much he hurt when that first wife of his ran off and left him in much the same way! At least she left him Mary to help console him in those first, loneliest hours."

Virginia had been about to explain her bruise when the fact that Lizzie obviously knew something about Daniel's first wife caught her by surprise. "I wasn't aware you knew Daniel's wife."

"Didn't know her personally," Lizzie admitted. "Most of what I knowed about her I learned from Master Caleb. The rest Miss Mary told me."

"Mary did?"

"Yes, she told me all about the accident. And about how her mother had come back and taken her away from Master Daniel, then refused to let her go back home to see him until he had come up with a large sum of money." Lizzie's eyes narrowed. "That woman was a real witch. She only married Daniel as a way of gettin' back at another man who had refused to marry her."

Virginia's eyes widened with horror over what Lizzie had just told her. Though Virginia didn't ask any questions, Lizzie could sense her need to know more and continued.

"Master Daniel was stayin' most of the summer here with Master Caleb, like he always did, when he suddenly decided to start payin' calls on Miss Josie Kilburn. She had come to a few of the picnics Master Caleb was always havin', and she'd talked with Daniel some when she was here."

Lizzie tilted her head while she remembered. "But none of us ever realized Master Daniel was really interested in her until one evenin' he admitted he was seein' her. Master Caleb cautioned him against her, but Master Daniel was always the sort to have to find things out for himself, and Master Caleb did not try to stop him. He knew it would only turn the boy against him. But I tell you, it sure was a surprise to all of us when Master Daniel just up and married her the way he did — but it wasn't much of a surprise when he later admitted to his uncle how Miss Josie had told him she only married him to get back at that wealthy man she'd been seein' before. Seems when she'd started talking marriage, that other man had suddenly decided he preferred someone else's company."

Lizzie shook her head in disgust and began tapping her slippered foot in a subconscious show of anger. "Miss Mary was borned barely a year later. It wasn't long after that woman gave birth to the child that she decided she didn't like married life after all and up and left him. During an argument they had just before she walked out on him, he asked her if there was someone else. She just laughed at him and told him there were several men she'd been seein' on the sly. Seems Miss Josie preferred the company of lots of admirin' young men to that of one lovestruck husband and a demandin' baby.

"For years, that woman bled him for money until, because of advice Master Caleb had given him, he finally refused to do more than pay for her food and rent. It took him that long to quit lovin' her the way he did and pining over the loss. Even though he finally did get over her leavin' him, he refused to divorce her . . . he didn't believe in such as that. Then, after Master Caleb died and left most everythin' to Daniel and Daniel's mother, that wife somehow found out about it and demanded he give her part of the inheritance. He refused to give her anything more than she was already gettin' from him, which was generous enough, if you ask me. Barely a month later, she up and kidnapped Miss Mary and refused to return the child until he'd paid her a hefty ransom."

Lizzie looked away. "It was while she waited for Master Daniel's response and still held Miss Mary captive that the carriage accident happened, killing Miss Josie on the spot and severely injurin' Miss Mary."

Appalled by Lizzie's words, Virginia's hand went to cover her mouth, pressing hard against her lips. Suddenly it was easy to understand why Daniel mistrusted women so: the woman he had fallen in love with, who was supposed to have loved him too, enough to have agreed to marry him, had deceived him in the worst possible way and had had the gall to actually laugh about it.

Virginia's heart sank when she realized how Daniel must have felt to learn that like his first wife, she too had deceived him. She wondered what other parallels he had drawn between his two wives. Her stomach knotted when she realized exactly what he must have thought when he found her in Mark's arms: he must have believed she'd been seeing him on the sly all along. Desperately she wished she could talk with him, to explain that although she'd at first wanted to deceive him for her grandparents' sake and had married him for far less reason than she should have, she had indeed come to love him . . . only him. There could be no other man in her life. No other man could touch her heart in quite the same way he had.

But there was no way for her to tell him any of that. No one seemed to know where Daniel had gone—except maybe Amanda, who would not admit whether she'd heard from him or not. All she could do was refuse to leave Valley Oaks and hope that he'd give her the opportunity to explain everything when he eventually returned.

"I don't know what you two found to argue about that has caused you to be this angry, but it can't be all that serious if Virginia was willing to come here all alone to try and find you," James stated angrily while he leaned over the desk, his weight on his palms, facing Daniel. "You ought to at least have the courtesy of hearing her out."

"I've heard enough of her lies," Daniel said adamantly, then slammed his fist across the desk in emphasis. "I don't intend to give her the opportunity to tell me any more."

"She seemed sincere enough to me," James put in quickly.

"Oh, that was her, all right. She seemed pretty

456

damned sincere to me, too. But you'll just have to take my word for it, she's exactly like Josie in every way." His eyes narrowed as the image of his second wife locked in a passionate embrace with her not-so-secret lover came unbidden to mind.

"I can't believe that," James argued further. "Virginia can't be anything like Josie."

"She's *exactly* like Josie! In fact, it's ludicrous. She married me out of spite for something she thinks someone else did, even went so far as to tell me how very much she loved me, when all the time she was seeing someone else."

"I don't believe it," James said before he stood erect again and crossed his arms in front of him.

"Believe it. I saw them with my own eyes. And when I confronted her with the truth about her reasons for marrying me, she admitted everything. She married me just to get back at someone else." Daniel's fury grew when he realized that the person she had wanted to get back at was not even alive anymore. Still, she had done her evil deeds. "I never want to see her again."

James ran a hand through his thinning hair as if he considered arguing with his friend further, but in the end turned around and sank heavily into one of the handsomely upholstered leather chairs facing Daniel's desk. "So what do you plan to do? Avoid her forever?"

"Exactly. I'll provide her a place to live and food to eat, and even clothes to wear, but I never want to have to set eyes on her again." The muscles in Daniel's jaw worked furiously while he thought about it. How he could have ever believed she was a woman who'd be loyal was beyond him now. "As I told her in my letter, we've always been strangers and will remain strangers for the rest of our lives. I'll not put myself through any more hell for someone like her. I'm not going back to Valley Oaks until I have word from my lawyer, who is keeping an eye on things for me, that she has finally left."

"You won't even consider hearing what she has to say in her own defense?"

"All that needs to be said between us has already been said," Daniel stated with finality. "I won't give her the chance to do any more damage." Then a pain-filled smile lifted his lips. "And if it was a divorce she came looking for, she won't have it. She made her bed; now let her lie in it. Let them *both* lie in it."

Chapter Twenty-five

Virginia cried a lot over the next few days, sometimes over serious events, like Mary's leaving; but other times she cried over the most trivial of incidents. Everything seemed to bring tears to her eyes. Though she realized she missed Daniel and Mary dreadfully, she could not understand why it was so difficult for her to get her emotions under control. Nor could she understand why her stomach remained so obstinately rebellious in the mornings, yet extremely cooperative in the evenings, or why the cool October evenings should cause her such a chill through the night, so much so that she had to sleep with twice the covers she usually needed. It was not until Lizzie finally asked her straight out if she was "with child" that Virginia even considered she could be pregnant.

Suspecting it might be the case, for there had been ample opportunity for such to occur in the seven weeks before Daniel left, Virginia had Pete drive her into Pittsburg to see a doctor there. After a brief examination, he happily verified that she was indeed going to have a baby, and he suspected she was about to enter her third month.

Suddenly Virginia did not feel so all alone. Knowing there was a baby growing inside of her was like having a tiny part of Daniel returned to her. Though for now she still had Lizzie and the others at Valley Oaks to help her fill the long, lonely days without him, there had been no one to help her get through the nights. She felt certain the baby would change all that: just knowing there was a part of Daniel growing inside of her made her feel less alone. She could hardly wait to feel the baby actually moving about within her, which the doctor claimed could be as early as the following month.

Thrilled to learn her news, Lizzie decided a celebration was in order and immediately baked a four-layer chocolate cake, then decorated the dining room with flowers and brightly colored ribbons. All the workmen were told the good news and, once they had been made aware of her delicate condition, each took it upon himself to be her protector. From that moment on, Virginia could not step outside carrying as much as a pitcher of lemonade without having someone rush to her aid; but she had to admit, she enjoyed the attention. She knew it would help make the next two weeks that much more bearable. At that time, the month Daniel had given her would finally be up and she would finally be able to talk to Daniel. Sometimes Virginia even managed to pretend it was Daniel himself who doted upon her, demanding she take very special care of herself.

But, despite the fact she now had a small part

of Daniel living deep inside of her, it never fully made up for his absence; she missed him dreadfully. She missed his handsome smile, she missed the deep narrow dimples that formed along his lean cheeks whenever the devil had his thoughts, and she missed the special way he used to look at her from time to time—a look so deep, so very provocative that just thinking about it sent tiny shivers darting down her spine. But mostly she missed having him hold her at night. She missed the tender way he made love to her.

Virginia could not remember missing anyone so much, not even her grandparents. She loved him so very much that without him, she felt somehow incomplete. Even the baby inside her did not entirely fill the void that had been caused by his absence; nothing ever would. If only he would come home so they could talk, so she could somehow make him understand why she had done what she did, and how those feelings had changed—how everything had changed. All because she had allowed herself to fall in love with him!

How ironic it seemed to her now that Daniel had become more important to her than even Valley Oaks. And how it terrified her to realize she was on the verge of losing them both—and Mary too. All she could do was pray Daniel would set his stubborn pride aside long enough to give her the opportunity to explain everything to him when he finally did return.

Virginia was on pins and needles waiting for those final two weeks to pass. She realized she dreaded his return almost as much as she looked forward to it. She was well aware Daniel was going to be even angrier with her for having so blatantly defied his letter, but what other alternative did she have if she wanted to speak with him? He'd hidden himself away so well that her every attempt to locate him had failed.

When the full month finally passed and still Daniel did not return, Virginia began to wonder why. Day by day she watched for him, but he never came. Slowly she realized he had to have some way of knowing she was still there, but how? Who was reporting to him? Pete? Jack? Lizzie? Was one of them lying to her about not knowing where he had gone?

Unsure how long Daniel would remain stubborn about not returning while she was there, Virginia immediately resumed her search to try to locate him. While she wrote her letters to anyone he might eventually contact, she refused to give up hope that one day she would finally get the chance to explain how wrong she'd been and could at last beg him for his forgiveness.

Virginia had still made no effort to find another place to live, nor had she made any progress towards finding Daniel, when one day an older man in an olive-brown tailored suit came to leave a certain amount of money with her, along with specific instructions she get out of Valley Oaks within the week or chance being left penniless for the rest of her life. When she questioned who he was, the man staunchly refused to give even his name, but he had such a strongly professional air about him that Virginia guessed he was Daniel's lawyer.

Realizing the man must know where Daniel had

gone, or at least have a way of getting in contact with him, Virginia tried desperately to get him to reveal where or how she might find her husband. But no matter how she begged and pleaded, the man would not reveal Daniel's whereabouts, nor would he accept a message to be taken back with him.

"I have to get word to him," she tried to explain, her frustration evident in her quivering voice. "I've written letters to his mother and to his friend, James York, but they have been unable to help me locate him. It is almost as if he has vanished into thin air. But you know where he is. You can get a letter to him. That's all I ask, that you take a letter to him for me. Why can't you do that?"

"Because I have been instructed not to," he answered simply, unaffected by the tremor in her voice.

"He has instructed you not to bring him even a letter from me?" she asked, her frustration quickly giving way to anger. "He won't even allow me to write him? I understand why he is angry with me, but just how stubborn can one man be?"

"As he sees it, you are the stubborn one. You are the one who has refused to obey his decree that you get out of his home. My advice to you, Madam, is that you find somewhere else to go and be out of here within seven days. He told me that if you did not leave this time, he would no longer consider being so generous with your living expenses. Make him any angrier than he already is, and you will barely have enough money to get by. But if you leave within the week, he will still dutifully supply you with a decent place to live and enough spending money for ample food and clothing."

"I don't care about his money!" Virginia shouted, angered that anyone thought differently. "I can get by on my own as a teacher, thank you very much. But what I do care about is Daniel, and I'm not leaving here until I've had a chance to talk with him. And since I cannot send a letter to him, you will just have to *tell* him that for me!"

"Madam, you have one week to get out of this house," he stated again calmly, refusing to be affected by her sudden show of outrage.

"I'm *not* leaving until I've talked to Daniel," she repeated. Her eyes narrowed with determination. "If he is so eager to have me out of this place, then you tell him to come here and put me out himself. It's the only way he's ever going to get rid of me." She was so angry now that tears had started to well in her eyes. She didn't dare blink for fear of sending them down her cheeks.

"Mr. Pearson can have the sheriff come out here and force you to leave," the man pointed out, still calm, still unaffected by her emotional outburst.

Infuriated even more by the man's lack of emotion, Virginia clenched her hands into tight fists at her sides. "He can't have me evicted; I'm his wife. I have as much right to be here as he does."

"I'm afraid that's not so," the man responded quickly. "And because it is not so, and to avoid such embarassment, you really should start looking for someplace to go immediately. You have seven days."

And having said that, the man turned and

walked out of the house to the barn, where he then left another parcel of money with Pete, telling him he was to remain in charge of Valley Oaks until Daniel's return, much to the growing discontent of his brother, Jack.

More days passed, and still there was no direct word from Daniel. And though it was time for Mary to return from her grandmother's, she, too, failed to come back to Valley Oaks. Lizzie finally received a message that Mary's return was to be indefinitely delayed.

On the seventh day after Daniel's second ultimatum, while Virginia sat listlessly in the classroom, missing Mary and wondering if Daniel would really have the sheriff come out and force her to leave, a messenger came to the door with another letter for Virginia. Because the man had claimed it was important he deliver the letter personally into the hands of Virginia Pearson, Lizzie wasted no time in running to the back of the house to get her.

"He says it's important. He says he has to give the letter direct to you," Lizzie said breathlessly.

"Did he say who the letter was from?" Virginia asked, her heart frozen in her chest, her mind refusing to even guess.

Lizzie frowned. "No, I reckon I was too afraid to ask. Maybe it's from Master Daniel. Maybe it says when we can expect him back."

When they entered the area where the man waited patiently, Virginia was relieved to see that it was not the sheriff. Instead a man dressed in moleskin trousers and a flannel shirt stood patiently holding a sealed envelope. Virginia's stomach knotted for fear it held Daniel's final eviction notice, one that would clearly state the sheriff was on his way—which would explain why the man had to deliver the paper directly to her. But then she wondered why the lawyer-looking man had not been the one chosen to bring such a message to her.

With tears threatening her eyes, she reached out her hand and said, "I'm Virginia Pearson. I believe you have a letter for me."

"I sure do. I was told to personally see that you get this," he said as he quickly placed the letter in her outstretched hand. "And I am to wait for your reply."

Virginia glanced down at the letter and saw her name neatly scrawled across the front, but no indication of who might have sent it. She found herself too afraid to ask while she turned the envelope over and ran a trembling fingertip beneath the flap.

Virginia's blood seemed to turn to ice water when she slowly slipped the letter out of the envelope.

"It's from Lillian York," she said, having glanced at the signature first. She was unable to hide the odd mixture of relief and disappointment she felt to discover the letter was not from Daniel when she glanced up at Lizzie.

"What does she say?" Lizzie wanted to know.

"I don't know. I haven't read it yet," Virginia admitted and looked back down to read the short message. Her hand went immediately to her throat. The words struck her hard. "Oh no!"

"What?" Lizzie demanded while she stared down

at the paper too, dearly wishing she knew how to read. "What does it say?"

"Daniel's been in an accident of some sort. He's badly hurt. Lillian wants me to come to Jefferson right away."

"What happened to him?"

"It doesn't say," Virginia said, already feeling a strong surge of panic twisting wildly inside her heart. "But I have to go."

"Of course you do," Lizzie responded, turning to leave. "I'll go get your things packed. You go tell Mister Pete or Mister Jack to get your carriage ready."

"The letter says she'll explain more when I arrive at her house, but I don't even know where the Yorks live," Virginia said, tears starting to form in her eyes.

"Excuse me, Ma'am, but I was told to wait and ride back with you," the messenger interrupted, his face drawn with concern.

"I'll hurry," Virginia promised, already clutching her woolen shirts and running as fast as she could down the corridor.

Less than an hour later, Virginia and the messenger were on their way. He had volunteered to tie his horse onto the back of the carriage and drive for her, having realized how distraught the letter had made her.

The bright yet cold November day was just turning into night when the carriage pulled onto a wide graveled drive that circled in front of a lovely three-story home right outside Jefferson. The front door opened just as Virginia's blankets were removed and she was quickly helped down from the carriage. Lillian rushed to greet her.

"I'm so glad you decided to come. I was afraid you might not," Lillian said as she embraced Virginia warmly. Then, turning to an older man who had followed her outside, Lillian gestured to the large valise still in the carriage. "See that her things are taken up to Daniel's room."

"Daniel's room?" Virginia asked. Her heart jumped with anticipation. "He's here?"

"No, he's at Doctor Edison's. Come on in and I'll try to explain."

Lillian took Virginia's cloak, then directed her into an elegantly furnished parlor where a cozy fire awaited them before beginning her explanation. "Daniel has been staying here for several weeks. In fact, ever since he left Valley Oaks."

"But James said—" Virginia began, but was quickly interrupted.

"I know. James told me about your visit just days after Daniel came here. And I'm afraid he knew exactly where Daniel was the day you came by his office—which was right here in this house, locked away in one of our guest rooms."

"Why couldn't James have told me that?"

"Because Daniel had made James promise not to tell you where he was or that he had even seen him. It broke James's heart to have to lie to you the way he did, but he had promised he wouldn't tell you, mainly to keep Daniel from going somewhere else where he could not keep an eye on him. Even so, James tried to convince Daniel to change his mind and talk with you, but Daniel stubbornly refused to take his advice. I don't know what happened between the two of you, because both

468

Daniel and James have been very quiet about it; but whatever happened, it has been destroying Daniel, both physically and emotionally."

"It's a long story," Virginia admitted sadly. "I'm ashamed of my part in it, but I will tell you anything you wish to know."

"Well, you will have to tell me on the way to the doctor's. Daniel is badly hurt. Actually, we were afraid he was going to die before you got here."

"It's that serious?" Virginia asked. It felt as if someone had struck her hard just beneath her breast.

"It was; but according to last report, he is finally starting to show signs of improvement. Still, I think it would be best if we went right away. James is already there. In fact, he has rarely left Daniel's side in the three days since his injury. Even when the doctor demands he leave the room, James stays in the hall right outside his door. Daniel is his closest friend."

"Three days? What took you so long to notify me?" Virginia wanted to know as she followed Lillian back into the foyer to get their cloaks.

"James had to battle with his conscience first. After all, he had promised Daniel not to reveal his whereabouts to you. It took a while, but I was finally able to persuade him to do the right thing. We both thought you should be here."

On the drive over, Lillian explained that Daniel had not regained consciousness since the accident, but how James had sent word to her earlier that afternoon that his coloring was finally better and his breathing more stable. She admitted that all anyone really knew about the accident in itself was that Daniel had been out riding in the country, something that had become a habit with him, when his horse apparently stumbled or was frightened by something. Daniel was tossed through the railing of a bridge and fell quite a distance down the side of a deep ravine and might have fallen into the river had it not been for a tree at the river's edge.

When Virginia and Lillian finally arrived in front of a large, two-story house on Vale Street and had entered through a side door, the doctor came out to greet them. When he learned who she was, he led them back into the house to another room and let them in to see Daniel immediately. James sat in a straight-backed wooden chair, staring off into the corners of the room, his jaw unshaven and his expression sullen. Only one lamp burned low at Daniel's bedside, casting an eerie glow over both James and the bed in which Daniel lay.

"Virginia, you came!" James cried when he realized who had entered. With energy he did not look like he could possibly have, he rose from his chair and hurried to embrace her. "I'm so glad to see you. Daniel needs you. He wouldn't admit it for the world, but he desperately needs you — especially now."

"And I need him," she responded softly, then waited for James to move away from her so she could go to Daniel's bedside.

Tears sprang to Virginia's eyes when she stepped closer and could see how terribly thin and gaunt he looked as he lay unconscious on the stark white bedsheets. There were dark shadows beneath his eyes, and he looked as if he had lost at least twenty pounds. She quickly realized that could not have occurred in just three days.

Heartbroken, she pulled her gaze away from his unshaven face and glanced down at the rest of him. He was bandaged in more places than not and was covered from the waist down with a folded sheet, but still there were bruised flesh and several smaller cuts and scrapes exposed to her view. There was also a splint attached to his right wrist.

Reaching out a trembling hand, Virginia first touched his pale cheek, then quietly lifted his un-injured hand and held it gently. The doctor signaled for Lillian and James to leave the room with him so that she could have a moment alone with her husband.

The moment the door was closed and there was no longer a reason to be strong, Virginia bent over Daniel's bed, pressed her cheek to his bandaged chest, and began to weep uncontrollably, pleading with him to live.

"Daniel, even if you can never find it in your heart to forgive me, I want you to live. You have to live. Please, Daniel, don't die . . . please, don't die." Her voice was so strained with emotion that it sounded foreign, even to her. Closing her eyes, she continued to weep with violent, rasping sobs as she brought her arms around to gently hold him. When her furious weeping finally gave way to gentle sobs, she continued to hold him close, finding solace in the familiar rhythm of his heart-beat, in the warmth his body still held.

It was hours before the doctor returned and asked her to leave. He ordered the women home and told James he could only wait in the hall for an hour more, firmly stating that he did not need another patient to care for, and warned James that if he did not get some rest soon, he would be headed for a collapse; they all would.

Though Virginia and Lillian did not go on to bed when they first returned to the house and it was very late before they finally did go to sleep, Virginia awoke early the next morning, eager to return to Daniel's bedside. James had finally been banished from the doctor's home and had also returned during the night. He stayed long enough to have a quick breakfast with them before heading back over to the doctor's home to see about Daniel. Lillian and Virginia left together in a separate carriage only a few minutes after he did.

Arriving at almost the same time, the three entered the house together. As was the rule, they knocked at the doctor's office near the foot of the stairs before going on to Daniel's room. The doctor seemed eager to speak with them and asked them all to step inside the small, book-crowded room.

"Daniel has finally come to," the doctor told them with a pleased smile, "but he is very disoriented. I'm glad you knocked for me, because I want to warn you that, although he is indeed awake and seems to have very little pain considering the extent of his injuries, there are complications I had not realized."

The three of them exchanged worried glances. James was the one who finally asked the doctor to explain.

"It's his memory. It seems Daniel can't even remember his own name, nor can he recall anything at all about the accident, either before he mounted the horse or after he fell." Turning to Virginia, Dr. Edison's face grew solemn and he added, "Before you go in there, I want you to be fully prepared. It's possible he might not even know who you are when you first go in, but don't be too concerned; there's every possibility his memory loss is only temporary. That's usually the case. So don't try to force him to remember, because it will only frustrate him. Let his memory return at its own pace."

"Maybe we should wait to see him," James suggested, his gaze cutting to Virginia worriedly.

"No, don't do that," the doctor replied with a reassuring smile. "I've already told him he'd be having visitors today, and who you were. He's eager to see if he can remember you."

"Should we go in separately?" James then asked.

The doctor adjusted his eyeglasses as he thought about that. "Might be best. That way he has only to contend with one new piece of information at a time."

James turned to Virginia. "I need to go on to the office. I haven't been in since the accident, and problems have arisen that need my attention. Would you mind if I went in to see him first? I'll only stay a minute or two. Then you can stay as long as the doctor will allow."

Virginia was eager to go in, yet at the same time nervous about facing him again. "That will be fine. I'll wait out here with Lillian."

James was only in the room a few minutes, as promised, and when he came out, he shook his head worriedly. "He really doesn't remember me. He believes I am who I say I am, and he thanked me for my concern, but he didn't remember anything about me or about his business. The doctor is right. He doesn't even remember who he is."

James looked from Lillian to Virginia, then tried to smile. "But at least he doesn't seem to be in much pain. He says the worst of what pain he does have seems to be at the back of his head and in his wrist. He'll probably recover pretty quickly. He's eager to meet you two."

With her heart beating hard against her chest, Virginia was next to enter Daniel's room. She found him sitting in his bed, propped up with pillows. He smiled when she first entered and watched her expectantly while she crossed the room.

"And are you James York's wife or are you *my* wife?" he asked eagerly while his gaze swept down the length of her with obvious approval.

"I'm your wife," she answered hesitantly, wondering at what point in their conversation he would remember everything. And once he did remember just how angry he was with her and why, she wondered how long it would take him to have her sent from his room.

"Your name is Virginia," he added quickly. His handsome face twisted into a thoughtful frown.

Virginia's breath held. She feared he was starting to remember already. "Yes."

"That's what I thought the man said," he nodded, still studying her as if he was seeing her for the first time. "Pretty name for a pretty woman."

Unable to fully accept his memory loss, afraid he was playing some sort of evil game with her, she stepped closer and studied his expression while she carefully added, "My full name was Virginia Elaine Connors before we married. My grandparents were Joseph and Essie Elder."

"*Were?* Are they dead?"

She stared at his questioning face. "You really don't remember, do you?"

"No, and it frustrates me that I don't. But I'm trying. Did I know your grandparents?"

"No, not really. You knew *of* them," she answered honestly.

He frowned as if trying to figure out why she had mentioned them in the first place if he did not even know them. "Were they friends of my family?"

"Not exactly," she admitted, but was hesitant to go any further. Although eventually she planned to tell him everything she had found out from Mattie Williams, she wanted to do that only after he had his memory back. "They used to live near Valley Oaks."

"Valley Oaks?"

"Don't you even remember Valley Oaks? Your home?"

Daniel tried, but could not bring an image to mind. "Is it far from here?"

"It's about an eight-hour drive by carriage, but you've told me you can travel it in six hours on horseback.

"Who else lives with us in Valley Oaks? Do we have any children?"

Virginia thought about the baby growing inside of her, but decided not to tell him about that just yet. "You have a pretty little daughter who is worried sick about you. Her name is Mary."

"Mary," he said, trying the name out and finding it pleased him immensely. "How old is she?"

"She's eight. But she'll be nine next spring."

"Nine?" he asked, clearly surprised. "Any other children?"

"No. Just Mary." Though she was not really sure why, she still did not want to tell him about the son or daughter that would be born in almost six months. Briefly, she glanced down at her own stomach and was glad she had not yet begun to show any true evidence of her condition. "But believe me, she's a handful. Bright as they come."

He smiled and his long dimples curled deep into his cheeks, making her want to reach out and touch them as she had so many times in the past. He seemed oblivious to the effect he was having on her when he cocked his head at an angle and asked, "Smart, eh? I suppose she gets that from her father?"

Virginia smiled at his attempt at humor. It meant he was indeed feeling much better than they had expected. It also meant he did not have reason to hate her again. "She gets her quick temper from her father, too."

Daniel laughed. "I can't wait to meet her." Then, as if realizing how strange that must have sounded, he explained, "As long as my memory refuses to cooperate, *everyone* is a stranger to me. Even you." His hands clenched, further evidence of his frustration. "If only I could remember."

His mention of her being a stranger to him reminded her of the cruel remarks he had made in his parting letter, and she had to bite her lip to keep from letting the pain show. He had claimed she would always be a stranger to him; that was the way he wanted it. Odd, how fate had accommodated him on the matter.

How desperately she hoped that when he did remember her, he would be willing to change his mind about sending her away from Valley Oaks and putting her out of his life, and eventually forgive her.

"You will begin to remember soon enough. The doctor said it was best not to rush it. Just take it a little at a time."

Daniel's face relaxed. "I guess you're right; it's enough to know that I have such a beautiful wife and a little girl named Mary."

"And a very good friend named James," she reminded him, "whose wife is waiting outside to say hello. She is just as worried as the rest of us about you."

"Right, James told me she was out there. Ask her to come in," he said agreeably.

"I'll just wait outside," Virginia said before she reached for the door.

"No, you won't. You are my wife; I want you here by my side."

"But the doctor seemed to think it would be better for you if we came in one at a time."

"Doctors can be wrong about some things. I want you to stay." He was adamant.

Virginia was delighted to agree.

When Lillian entered the room moments later,

Daniel decided she seemed somehow familiar to him. Looking at her curiously, then back at Virginia, he wondered aloud, his brow drawn tight. "Why is it I can remember your face and can almost picture you sitting outside beneath a huge tree with an ivory fan in your hand, but I can't remember a thing about my own wife?"

Lillian did not want to even guess. Hoping to sound lighthearted, she hid her concern and answered cheerfully, "Maybe you fancy older women. Or maybe you have been secretly in love with me all these years."

"When I have such a beautiful wife of my own? I doubt that," he said with a grin.

"Well then, maybe you have a fancy for ivory fans," she suggested with an innocent lift of her brow that brought instant laughter from Daniel.

"That must be it," he agreed, then his face grew very serious. "I am lucky to have friends like you and James. The doctor told me how your husband has sat either by my side or out in the hall nearly the entire time I lay in here unconscious, and how you were always in and out demanding reports on my health. I want to thank you for your concern. And I want to thank you for thinking to send for my wife. I believe having you three around will help bring my memory back that much sooner."

Lillian chose not to comment on that remark and instead told him as much about the accident as she knew. She stayed for only a few minutes more, fearing two visitors might tire him twice as quickly as one, then went back out into the hall to wait for Virginia. Twenty minutes later, the doctor quietly stepped into the room and politely asked Virginia to leave, too, so that Daniel could get his much-needed rest.

James, Lillian, and Virginia agreed to restrict their visits during the following week, coming for no more than an hour in the mornings and not more than two hours in the evenings. Though Daniel protested such a decision, clearly eager for company, they knew it was for his own good that they must stay away the remainder of the time so he would be forced to rest.

Over the next two weeks, Daniel continued to get better, rapidly getting his strength back, and continued to ask everyone questions about his past, hoping something might eventually trigger his memory, but nothing seemed to work. By the end of the week, the doctor agreed he was well enough to leave his care, but cautioned him against doing anything stressful for at least a month, better yet, two.

He explained that although Daniel had been lucky enough to come away from the accident with only a few deep cuts, a broken wrist, and a sprained arm, his body had received quite a blow in general. He felt it would be best for him to rest as much as possible, quickly cautioning him that any injury which could cause him to be unconscious so long and then stunt his memory was serious in nature and should in no way be taken lightly. Though the doctor felt Daniel would want to be up and around within the next week or so, he said he was not to do anything strenuous.

Virginia vowed to see that he did not.

Daniel was released the next day into Virginia's care. Lillian and James invited them to stay at their house during the first few weeks of his recovery, but Daniel was adamant about wanting to go home. He was eager to meet his daughter and see if the familiar surroundings might help him regain his memory.

Having learned his daughter was away on a visit with his mother, he had immediately asked Virginia to have the child brought home so that she would be there when he returned. Virginia had reluctantly agreed; she knew how worried Mary had to be, having been kept away for so many weeks, and felt her return would be as much for the child's benefit as it would be for Daniel's. Though Virginia feared his returning to Valley Oaks and seeing his daughter again might indeed trigger his memory and as a result rekindle the anger he felt toward her, Virginia realized that eventually she would have to face his memory's return anyway.

But when they reached Valley Oaks and Daniel had to be reintroduced to Lizzie and the rest of his employees, Virginia realized it would take more than returning home to bring back his memories. It then occurred to her that maybe he did not want to remember; maybe his brain did not want any of the painful memories from his past ever to return.

The very day after his arrival back home, Mary returned, happy to see her father back with her stepmother, but making no mention of the fact he had ever left. Later that same afternoon, people who had been concerned to hear about the accident began to come by for short visits. Several of Daniel's business associates from the neighboring towns of Daingerfield and Mount Pleasant came by to make sure he was all right. Daniel could not remember any of them. Virginia feared that at any moment the man whom Daniel had sent with that last seven-day ultimatum might come by to see him and would wonder what she was still doing there.

Word spread quickly about the terrible accident and Daniel's return to Valley Oaks. Virginia felt certain the news would not only reach Daniel's lawyer, but also Amanda. Not at all ready to let Amanda have a go at him, knowing the woman would gladly supply Daniel with several vital pieces of information from his not-so-distant past, Virginia told Daniel that he should not be receiving so many visitors and convinced him it would be in his own best interest to leave Valley Oaks for a little while.

"Where would we go?" he wanted to know.

"To your house at River Ridge," she decided quickly, then explained to him where River Ridge was and how much privacy they could expect to have there. It also pleased her that the Edmonds did not know about her pregnancy and could not let her secret slip out at any moment — a situation entirely different from Valley Oaks, where every man who worked there knew and many had already inquired about her health, usually asking specifically about the baby. She knew it was only a matter of time before someone asked while Daniel was present.

"You mean there would only be you, me, Mary, and a few employees?" he asked, raising a brow. "And the employees don't even live in the house?

For the most part, we'd be all alone?"

"All alone," she agreed and felt a strong fluttering inside of her, for he was clearly fond of the idea of being alone with his family. "Visitors rarely come to River Ridge uninvited."

"When do we leave?"

Chapter Twenty-six

With Christmas only a week away, Daniel decided River Ridge deserved to look a little more festive and supervised the decorating he thought appropriate while Mary and Virginia happily did his bidding. Wherever he commanded they place a bow or a sprig of bright green holly, they were quick to do just that. Occasionally he would seem to forget he was still recovering from his accident, and they would find him up on a chair with a ribbon in his hand or kneeling on the stairs weaving branches of evergreen in and out of the banister columns.

Though still a few pounds thinner than he had been, Daniel looked almost as healthy as ever. A little of his memory had started to return while he was at River Ridge, meaningless bits of information like having climbed a particular tree in his youth, and the feeling that Louis Edmond was not just an employee but a long-time friend. Even so, most of his past remained a mystery to him.

Deep down, Virginia hoped that Daniel would never remember everything, even though she knew how much it frustrated him to have such a huge black void to overcome. It made her feel a little guilty, but she was too delighted with the amiable way he now behaved toward her to ever want his memory to return.

With his memory had gone that powerful demon which had been holding Daniel's heart just beyond her reach. The cold, hard barrier he had thrown up around himself in an obvious effort to protect himself from further heartaches and humiliation was gone. He had become a whole new Daniel, one who was frustrated by his inability to remember, but who tried to fit a life together with what he did know about himself. He was fun-loving and generous with his affection. He was all Virginia had ever hoped he could be. She had never known such happiness and tried not to think about how short-lived that happiness might prove to be.

Although nothing at Valley Oaks or River Ridge had caused Daniel to remember much about his past, he had come to the conclusion that he was a very lucky man to have such a beautiful, caring wife and such an adorable daughter. When he had first been reintroduced to Mary, he had wondered why she looked nothing like Virginia, because he had expected to see an smaller replica of his beautiful wife; but he quickly decided the girl did look a lot like himself, and that had pleased him. His life in general pleased him . . . so much so that his inability to remember the past had started to become less important that it once had been.

The night after the three of them had spent a joyous afternoon decorating the house at River Ridge both inside and out for the approaching holidays, Daniel was in such good spirits he decided the time had come to stop convalescing and get back into the mainstream of life. Though he had pretty much stayed in the house, as he had been ordered to, and climbed the stairs only once a day to go to bed, he was eager to do more. Despite Virginia's staunch protests — it had been only weeks since the doctor had told him to take it easy for the next two months — one night he decided the time had come to take a short walk to the river and back.

Stubborn about going, but willing to take the time to put on a heavy coat, since the temperatures had been near freezing the past few nights, Daniel allowed Virginia to pull his collar up to protect his ears from the cold and set off to get a closer look at the river, feeling there was a definite link to his past to be found there.

Afraid her husband might not be as strong as he thought he was, Virginia quickly put on her own woolen cloak and followed at a distance. Though his early recovery meant he would not need her help as much as he had over the past two weeks, she was glad to know he felt good enough to want to go against the doctor's orders.

When Daniel neared the riverbank, he slowed his pace and gazed appreciatively at his surroundings, feeling an inner sense of belonging. He was in immediate awe of the silvery beauty that encompassed the wide, slow moving river at night, and was almost certain the emotions which stirred within him were not new.

Taking deep breaths of the brisk night air, he stood near the pier, further admiring the scene which surrounded him. Virginia was not aware he knew she was there until he glanced back and held his arm out to her, motioning with a flick of his fingers for her to join him. She went to him eagerly, her heart singing aloud its strong messages of love while his arms came down around her.

"This place is special," he said softly, as if afraid he might break the magic spell the river had cast by speaking too loudly. "I have a feeling I've always been intrigued by this river."

"As I understand it, you spent many an hour playing in that river when you were young," Virginia supplied for him.

He turned to look at her then, her beautiful face bathed in the bright December moonlight. "You are special, too." Then for the first time since the accident, Daniel bent down to kiss her.

It was a long, lingering kiss, and Virginia savored the familiar warmth that quickly invaded her while his lips moved gently over hers. She was so pleased by the fact that he had wanted to kiss her, tears burned in her eyes, causing them to catch the moonlight and glimmer with joy.

"Let's go upstairs," he suggested in a husky voice when he pulled away from her and looked longingly into her eyes.

So very close to sobbing aloud her deep feeling of happiness and the strong desire she had for this man, Virginia was afraid to speak. She merely nodded her agreement, looking shyly away from him when they turned and walked back to the house.

Once in the privacy of their bedroom, with only a dimly glowing lamp to prevent them from drowning in total darkness, Daniel again took his wife into his arms, pressing her soft body close against him with the strength of his left hand.

Virginia heart was so filled with joy that it could no longer contain it. She decided to take a chance and reveal to her husband what she was feeling so strongly in her heart.

"Daniel, I love you." She tensed as she awaited his reaction.

Rather than go into a deep rage, as he might have if he were again in possession of his memory, Daniel brought his mouth down to covers hers with such tender passion that he did not have to speak aloud what he was feeling. It was evident in his kiss.

With the initial awkwardness of having to use his left hand when more accustomed to using his right, he quickly began to undo the many buttons along the back of her dress while she eagerly worked to remove his clothing. Soon, they were both gloriously naked and again locked in a passionate embrace.

United through their ardent kisses, his spicy male fragrance blended with her sweet, floral scent to create a heady, intoxicating aroma of sensuality. Closing her eyes, Virginia was immediately lost to the many sensations only Daniel could bring to life within her—lost in her love for him, in her undying love for her husband.

Eagerly, her lips moved from his mouth to seek other areas, exploring the taste of his cheeks, then his neck and collarbone, while he ravished similar kisses on her silken hair. Slowly his fingers moved to where two silvery combs anchored her thick tresses of dark hair at the back of her head and held the hair away from her face. Carefully, he eased the combs out of the thick mane and gently ran his fingertips through the soft tresses until the hair fell softly forward in a riotous mass and gently caressed her face.

"You are truly beautiful," he said huskily.

She smiled shyly before lifting her lips to his once again. Timidly at first, her hands roamed freely over the coarse texture of hair that covered his lower back and hips. As she pressed herself closer against him, she marveled once again in the feel of his firm, fit body against her soft, supple curves. The texture of his chest hair tickled the delicate peaks of her breasts when she moved against him. The sensual movements she made against his body aroused him to a point of madness.

Together, though their lips never parted, they moved toward the bed. As if of one mind, they lay down, still locked in passion's embrace. Eagerly each sought to bring the other pleasure, and hungrily they took that which was offered, until, when they could bear the sweet torture no longer, Daniel moved to fulfill her, bringing their passions to a peak of ecstasy so deeply shattering that they both cried out each other's names.

Sinking into a sensuous euphoria afterward, they continued to hold each other close. Daniel smiled and spoke the words Virginia thought she would never hear. "I love you, Virginia."

Then while he drifted off to sleep at her side, still holding her close, with his left arm beneath her back and his splinted right arm resting across her abdomen, Virginia's happiness gave way to a sudden burst of bitter despair. Aware this was all going to end the moment he remembered, she began to cry great silent tears. She was heartbroken to realize that when he did eventually remember, his demon would return. Again he would refuse to give her a chance to explain why she had been so willing to deceive him when she first came to Valley Oaks or why she had so blatantly defied his request for her to leave. He would be too angry to listen to her apologies. And when he realized she had purposely deceived him yet again, leading him to believe they were happily married when they were not, he would be angrier still.

Closing her eyes against the painful thoughts of having to lose Daniel a second time, Virginia prayed he would never regain his memory, then fought the guilt that came from making such a selfish wish.

After Christmas, Daniel continued to recover at a remarkable rate. Virginia stayed constantly by his side, helping him with the things that took two good hands to do, and seeing to it his bandages and injuries were kept clean. She continued to nag him when he tried to do something she thought too strenuous, and sometimes he listened to her, but usually he went ahead and did whatever it was he wanted to do. They fought goodnaturedly over who should be in charge and took turns letting each other win.

James had never found a real reason to tell Daniel any of what he knew about the earlier demand made of Virginia to leave Valley Oaks forever, and he had taken on far more responsibility with the shipping business. Pete had also already become so well accustomed to running Valley Oaks, it was as if he'd always been in charge. Neither found it necessary to call upon Daniel for his advice, knowing, too, that he might not remember enough to make a sound decision at this time. With none of the usual outside interferences to come between them, Daniel and Virginia managed to be together day and night. And during the day, they gladly shared their time with Mary. They were a family.

By mid-January, Virginia was living in constant dread he would at any moment start to remember everything about his past. She felt extremely guilty just knowing what a selfish pretense she lived, allowing Daniel to continue to believe they were happily married. But even so, she still could not bring herself to tell him the truth. Each day that passed was a day she could treasure, a day she could look back on in the long, lonely years ahead. Because as soon as he learned of her latest deceit, he would leave her again. But at least she would have something of him, and not just the memories of a few happy weeks spent together at River Ridge. She would also have his child, growing ever stronger inside of her—a child she had yet to tell him about.

Virginia had decided she did not want Daniel to stay with her out of a father's loyalty to his child after his memory did return — although she was not sure he would stay with her even for that. No, if he decided to forgive her and give their marriage a second chance, she wanted it to be for the right reasons, and she was glad that because of her height and frame she had yet to start to really reveal her condition, though she had to be well into her fifth month of pregnancy. So far, the only noticeable changes in her body had been an enlargement of her breasts and a gradually thickening middle. She had already started to let out the waistlines of several of her more closely fitted dresses. But luckily, Daniel did not remember her body as it had been and had not yet noticed the changes. She wanted to keep her secret for as long as she could, though she knew it was only a matter of time.

One afternoon, in the third week of January, while Virginia sat in the family parlor quietly altering one of her favorite dresses, Daniel and Mary decided to explore the house further, starting with a few boxes they had discovered earlier in the attic, then moving on to the lesser used rooms of the house. Virginia realized Daniel was still searching for clues to his past, and though it made her extremely apprehensive, she did not try to stop him.

After about an hour of noisy search in the rooms directly overhead, Daniel came back downstairs with a curious expression, holding a small, gold-plated box.

"Look what I found in one of the unused bedrooms," he said as he knelt beside her and opened the box so she could see the beautiful emerald and gold bracelet that was inside. "Is this yours?"

"No," she responded while she stared at it, feeling it looked vaguely familiar.

Daniel turned the box over in his hand and found an inscription: I will always love you, Caleb.

Suddenly, Virginia realized why the bracelet seemed so familiar. The design matched the necklace she had found among her grandmother's belongings. Baffled, she lifted the bracelet out of the narrow box and stared at it. Slowly she realized the real reason her grandmother had kept that necklace, when she could have sold it for greatly needed money at any time. There had been sentimental reasons all right — but those reasons had had nothing to do with her grandfather. Despite her grandmother's outward show of hatred, she must have actually loved Caleb — enough to have kept his necklace all those years.

She wondered then why Caleb had never given her grandmother the bracelet and realized her grandmother's announcement of her plans to marry Joseph must have come after Caleb had bought the bracelet, but before he had had the chance to give it to her. He too had kept the bracelet all those years, probably hoping to one day have the opportunity to give it to her.

Virginia leaned her head against the high upholstered back of her chair while she thought about it more. Her grandmother's deep bitterness must have stemmed from the fact that she had actually loved Caleb deeply, though for whatever reason she had chosen not to marry him. She had loved a man whom she thought had turned against her. If only her grandmother could have known the truth! If only she could have known just how deeply Caleb had loved her, right to the end.

Thinking further about her sudden discovery, Virginia closed her eyes against the sinking feeling that overtook her. It seemed ironic to realize that mere lack of truth could have caused such misery and heartache back then, yet it was a similar lack of truth that allowed her a moment's happiness now.

"What's wrong?" Daniel asked gently as he studied her solemn expression.

Realizing an open and honest answer would only create more questions in his mind, questions that might lead to his remembering, Virginia shrugged her shoulders and evaded the real truth. "Nothing, it is just that I've never seen a bracelet so beautiful."

"Then it is yours," he said without a moment's hesitation and quickly took the bracelet from her hand and put it around her wrist. "I'm sure my uncle wouldn't mind."

No, she thought morosely, he would probably have found great pleasure in knowing that at least Essie's granddaughter was able to wear it. Tears of sadness filled her eyes as she bent to kiss Daniel on his forehead. "Thank you."

"No, I should be the one thanking you," he answered with a gentle smile.

"What for?"

"For loving me the way you do," he said sincerely and returned her earlier show of affection by kissing her on the forehead. "And I should thank you for taking such good care of me while I still have this blasted splint on my wrist. I want to thank you—"—he shrugged for lack of words to explain exactly what he was feeling—"for being you."

"Oh, Daniel, I wish it could be like this forever," she said, able to feel her heart breaking into tiny pieces beneath her breast.

"As long as we have each other, it will be," he said in earnest, then bent forward to kiss her gently on the lips. A provocative smile played at the corners of his mouth. "And later, when Mary finally goes to bed, it will get better still."

"You promise?" she asked playfully, deciding to push her morose thoughts aside and enjoy each moment as it came.

"Are you sure you won't join us?" Daniel asked Virginia for the second time while he held Mary's linen cloak together so she could tie it closed. Though the day promised to be exceptionally warm for early February, the temperatures were still very cool beneath the trees, and Daniel did not want to chance the girl catching a chill.

"No, Daniel, I have too much to do around here," Virginia responded automatically. She did not want to intrude upon Mary's special time with her father. It had almost become custom for the two of them to take a brisk walk along the river early each morning, then return so Mary could start her lessons for the day. "And don't you forget that you and Louis are supposed to bring Ruby some more firewood when you get back."

"All the more reason to stay gone," Daniel said,

and winked at Mary, who broke into a fit of laughter.

Virginia gave them both an indulgent smile, then bent to kiss Mary on her cheek. "Just see that he doesn't run off. Now that his wrist is better, there is work for him to do."

Daniel waited with his cheek turned out for his kiss, and when no kiss immediately came, he pouted. "Why am I always the one who gets neglected around here?"

Rolling her eyes heavenward, Virginia sighed in exasperation, then bent over to give him a kiss as well. Smiling happily, she waited just outside the back door until the two of them were out of her sight before she turned to go back inside. As beautiful as the day promised to be, she was not especially fond of her decision to stay behind, but knew Daniel and Mary needed their special time together. It brought them all closer as a family and would help to bridge any gaps that might still lie between father and daughter once Daniel's memory had fully returned.

Virginia was grateful that Mary had agreed not to try to force her father to remember the past by supplying him with any information he did not come right out and ask for. And thus far, Daniel had not questioned his relationship with his wife, never once considering there could ever have been any real problems between them. But at the same time she hoped his memory would not return, she had to worry he would discover her pregnancy before it had—before they had their chance to talk out their earlier problems—before she could know without a doubt that any decision to stay with her would be for the right reasons. And she knew she could not keep her pregnancy a secret much longer, because her stomach was gradually growing rounder; and even though he did not remember her body the way it was before, he had to notice the changes in her soon.

Taking one last wistful look at the sunshine as it fell across the leafless trees near the river and brightened the dark greens of the tall pines that grew further up along the knoll, Virginia pushed her apprehension aside and went back inside to get Mary's vocabulary questions ready for their next lesson.

It was while she carefully wrote out the definitions on one side of the paper and the words those definitions could be matched with on the opposite side that she heard the distant jangling of a carriage. James and Lillian had been out once to visit, and Tony and Andy Edlan, brothers who lived just downriver, had come by a few times to see if Daniel needed any help; but other than that, there had been no visitors at River Ridge, so the sound of a carriage seemed a little strange.

Already frowning, Virginia went to the front of the house, to the wide double door which was so rarely used, and swung it open to see who their visitors might be. To her complete horror, it was Amanda Haught, alone and dressed in her finest.

Hurrying outside before Amanda could gather her silken skirts about her and climb down from the carriage, Virginia called out, "Amanda, what are you doing here?"

"I've come to see Daniel," she stated matter-of-factly, her head tossed back to reveal her cool determination.

"But he's been advised not to have visitors," Virginia quickly told her, hoping to convince the woman to leave before she could cause any great damage. "He is still recovering from his accident."

With determination in her overly large green eyes, Amanda climbed out of her carriage. "That was over two months ago. I'm sure he is well enough to have visitors by now."

"Amanda, he is not fully recovered," Virginia told her, which was the truth. He still wore the splint on his wrist, though he had already started to use his right hand again.

"Still, he will want to see me," Amanda said adamantly before she brushed passed Virginia on her way to the house.

"Amanda, please, Daniel is not up to having visitors," she tried again. But Amanda refused to listen and continued her march toward the house.

Never pausing in her quest, Amanda opened the front door and went inside, calling out Daniel's name as soon as she had stepped into the entrance hall. Virginia hurried after her, her heart hammering so violently that she could barely breathe.

"Amanda, this is my house and I must ask you to leave," she stated as soon as she had entered the house, trying to sound as authoritative as she knew how.

Amanda was already halfway up the stairs, but paused to look back at Virginia. "This is Daniel's house," she reminded her. "And you really have no right to be here."

"I have every right to be here," Virginia stated angrily.

"Do you really?" drawled Amanda and stared down at her with a deeply rooted look of disdain. Then she turned back to her quest of finding Daniel.

Virginia waited at the foot of the stairs, knowing Amanda would come back down when the realized Daniel was nowhere to be found on the second or third floor. Minutes later, just as she had predicted, Amanda reappeared at the top of the stairs, her face a fiery display of anger. "Where is he?"

"Amanda, please go home," Virginia tried again, though she knew her words would do no good. Her insides were a quivering mass of fear and apprehension, and by the time Amanda had rushed past her and began searching the other rooms, Virginia could hardly stand the pain that engulfed her. Finally Amanda realized her indoor search was futile and headed through the back door.

"Daniel!" she called out at the top of her voice. "Daniel, where are you? It's me . . . Amanda."

Virginia followed her outside on legs so weak they hurt. "As you can see, he's not even here."

No sooner had she spoken the words than Daniel and Mary appeared along the path, headed in their direction. "He's not here, is he?" Amanda asked triumphantly with a light shake of the shimmering black curls piled high atop her head. "What's that? His ghost?"

Virginia felt her insides tighten even more and began to feel a little nauseated, but realized she had to be strong. Holding a deep breath, she curled her arms around her stomach and watched

498

helplessly while Daniel and Mary came toward them arm in arm—Daniel's brow creased as if he was puzzled by something.

"Look what we found," Mary said when they came close enough to be heard without having to shout. Proudly, she held up her new treasure. "It's a ship's bell. Father says it probably came from a pirate ship."

Daniel's eyebrows rose as if innocent of having told such a tale. And though he continued to look curiously at Amanda, who stood impatiently waiting for a chance to speak, he nudged Mary near the small of her back. "Why don't you take it inside and see if you can clean it up a little. It looks as if it might be made of brass. Maybe you can bring back some of its shine."

Virginia realized he was trying to get Mary to go inside so she'd be out of earshot of whatever was about to be said. Suddenly she wondered if he remembered Amanda.

Mary cast Amanda a disapproving look before hurrying off to do as her father had requested.

Amanda waited just long enough for the child to get inside the house before rushing forward to fling her arms around Daniel's neck, pressing her body intimately close. "Oh, Daniel, I've been so worried. At first, I could not find out where you had gone after the accident—that housekeeper of yours can be quite stubborn when she wants to be—but eventually I heard that you'd been brought here. I don't know why I didn't think of it myself."

Daniel pulled shy of her and looked first at Virginia's paled expression, then back at Amanda.

"Who are you?"

"What do you mean? You know who I am," Amanda insisted, then the realization struck her. "You still haven't regained your memory. I'd heard you'd temporarily lost it, but I had hoped by now you would have gotten over that. But evidently you haven't. No wonder she's till here."

Daniel ran his tongue over his lower lip as he tried to make sense of what was being said.

Shrugging helplessly, Amanda finally stated, "I'm Amanda." When that brought no immediate response she spoke her name again, more slowly. "A-man-da." Looking at him with a sultry expression, she reached out and caressed his cheek with the curve of her hand. "Surely you remember me now. I'm an old and very *dear* friend of yours."

Daniel stared at her a moment, then glanced past her to where Virginia stood clutching her arms in front of her and chewing nervously at the corner of her lip, the way she always did whenever she was deeply worried about something. Quickly he stepped away from Amanda and went to Virginia's side. Putting a supportive arm around her shoulders, he bent to kiss his wife lightly on the temple as if hoping to reassure her somehow.

"How can you treat her like that?" Amanda cried out, infuriated by his actions. "Don't you remember how she deceived you? Don't you remember how you came to me for comfort the night you found out the horrible truth about her? I'm the one you should be holding, not her. Don't you remember telling me how very much you hated her and how you never wanted to lay eyes on her again?"

Daniel did not respond, but merely looked at her as if she had suddenly gone mad.

"Daniel! That is Virginia, the woman who tricked you into marrying her just so she could get Valley Oaks back. She tricked you just so she could get revenge against your family. She lied to you and cheated on you, just like that first wife of yours did."

"First wife?"

"Yes! Daniel! Don't you remember anything?"

Virginia could feel her world crumbling around her while she waited for his response. She fought valiantly not to show how deeply affected she was by what Amanda had just told him, but she could not seem to keep her shoulders and legs from trembling. Although she did not want Amanda to have the satisfaction of witnessing her distress, she knew it was only a matter of minutes before her traitorous tears flooded her cheeks. She wondered when Daniel was going to jerk his arm away, fearing that when he did, she would surely collapse, because her legs no longer felt strong enough to hold her weight.

"Amanda, are you sure you are an old and dear friend of mine?" Daniel asked, frowning, his brow pulled taut as he pieced what Amanda had said with Virginia's reaction.

"Very dear," Amanda responded quickly. "As a matter of fact, if this little harlot hadn't suddenly tricked you into marriage the way she did, *we* would have been married by now."

Daniel stared at her as he thought about that, then slowly turned to Virginia and looked at her for a moment. He could see the anguish on his wife's face, the tears that threatened to spill from her eyes at any moment. His next words were so softly spoken Virginia did not at first think she had heard them right. *"Thank you for saving me from someone like her."*

"You bastard!" Amanda screamed out in a rage. "How dare you treat me like this after all we have meant to each other. You've gone too far this time. This time I will not allow you to come crawling back to me. Daniel Pearson, I never want to speak to you again." Then spinning away from them, Amanda marched off in a fit of rage, muttering in a high voice something about how the two of them deserved each other. Only moments after her carriage drove off in a cloud of dust, Daniel pulled away from Virginia.

Virginia watched as he turned his back to her and stared out toward the river, his expression drawn. Her heart ached for him, knowing what a shock Amanda's remarks must have been for him. Taking a deep, steadying breath, she decided the time had come to tell him the truth.

"Daniel, it breaks my heart to have to tell you this, because I know it means I will lose you again, but you really should know that some of the things Amanda just said about me were true."

Daniel turned back to face her. Unwilling to hear what she had to say, he reached out and stilled her words by placing a finger against her lips. She sensed the extreme tension that had overtaken him. She could see it in his straining neck muscles and in the severe expression on his face. Bitter lines had formed along his hardened jaw, and his gaze had gone dark and distant. Suddenly, she realized the worst had finally happened. He remembered. Amanda had broken through the barrier and released his bitter memories. Daniel's demon was back.

Chapter Twenty-seven

Virginia tried to swallow back the pain gathered in her throat.

"Daniel? You remember?"

"Yes. Everything." Daniel admitted.

Virginia's heart filled with hopeless despair. "Everything?"

"While Mary and I were out walking, just before I heard Amanda call me back, we came across an old homesite out in the woods and noticed a danger sign sticking up out of the ground. When we went closer to investigate what possible danger could lie in the clearing, I discovered an old abandoned well. The boards across it had been broken as if someone or something had fallen in. It was then I knelt down to look into the dark hole to see if there might be an animal trapped inside and saw that someone had started to fill the hole with dirt. It was when I noticed how the well was almost completely full that things started to come back to me: I remembered having given Louis the order to have the well filled in. Next, visions of having found you there came to me. Then, one by one, other memories just started to unfold, and continued to unfold when I saw Amanda again."

His expression revealed his confusion. "Virginia, why did you let me believe we were happily married? Why didn't you tell me the truth?"

"I just couldn't. I tried, several times. I really did. I'm so sorry; I know I should have told you everything. It was very unfair of me not to."

Daniel stared at her in stunned amazement while he reached up to drag his hand through his thick hair. What she had said did not make sense to him. "Unfair of *you?* What about me? I was the one who was unfair. I treated you terribly."

"You what?"

"I well remember now the way I behaved toward you," he told her, slowly shaking his head at the realization. "I feel so guilty. Although I am very grateful to you for all you have done for me since the accident, I know now that I didn't deserve any of the kindnesses you have shown me. I punished you for all the hatred I still felt for my first wife. I never even gave you a chance to speak in your own defense. Even so, when you found out I had been injured in that accident, you stayed with me. Despite all I did to you, you stayed by my side when I needed you most." He stared at her as if he was seeing her for the first time. "You *are* something special."

"Don't be so quick to praise me. Don't you remember why I came to Valley Oaks in the first place? Amanda was right about one thing. I came here wanting nothing more than to get what I thought was rightfully mine, no matter what I had to do. I think I would have resorted to blackmail if I could have found something to use against you. I even stole into your library while you were away in the hopes of finding something just bad enough for me to use against you."

"Was Mark in it with you?" he wanted to know.

"No; Mark had no idea what I was up to," Virginia admitted. "He may be my best friend, but I was afraid to tell even him. I guess I was afraid he might try to talk me out of it, and at the time I thought I was in the right."

"Is that all he is? Just a friend?" Daniel asked doubtfully.

"That is *all* he is," she assured him. "I know what you must have thought, to have found me in his arms that day; but he was just trying to console me. I had just discovered the truth about Caleb and feared that because of my own foolishly misplaced family pride, I had lost you forever."

"What truth?" Daniel wanted to know.

"That Caleb had never cheated my grandmother out of Valley Oaks. My grandfather had come to him and asked him to buy it so that he could pay off some huge gambling debts. If anything, my grandfather cheated Caleb by making him promise never to reveal the truth about why he had bought Valley Oaks from him, because Grandfather then spread the story that Caleb had purposely given him bad advice on ways to invest his money until he ended up so broke he had to sell out. You were right about your uncle all along: he was a good and honorable man. And I hate myself for all that I so willingly believed about him."

Daniel stepped forward and took Virginia into

his arms. So many things were occurring to him that he had trouble grasping them all, but he was able to understand the importance of what Virginia had just told him. "That doesn't matter anymore. All that is in the past, anyway. What matters is now. Can you forgive me for all I've done to you? For the misery you must have gone through because of my childish behavior?"

"Forgive *you?* Can you forgive me?"

"I already have."

Tears of joy filled Virginia's eyes when Daniel tightened his embrace and brought his lips down to hers in a strongly possessive kiss. When he pulled away, his eyes had grown dark with the many passions that had flared back to life inside him. "Virginia, I don't ever want to have to live without you again. I want you to know that I love you. I have loved you from the very beginning, though at first I tried to convince myself otherwise."

"Is that really fair?" she wanted to know.

Daniel looked at her, confused. "Is what fair?"

"Is it fair for you to be allowed to tell me that you love me, yet you forbid me to express how very much I love you."

"I guess it is not very fair," he said with a smile. "You now have my permission to tell me you love me anytime you feel like saying it."

"I feel like saying it right now. I love you, Daniel Pearson. I also feel that I should tell you something else I have been keeping from you. I want to get everything out into the open. I want all secrets behind us."

"What is that?" His smile faded. Obviously he

feared the worst.

"That I am expecting," she said, feeling suddenly shy.

"Expecting what?" he wanted to know, not realizing that was the way some women announced they were with child.

"A baby, silly."

Daniel's blue eyes stretched wide. "A baby?"

Virginia could not speak. She merely smiled at him and nodded timidly.

"A baby!" he said again as the realization sank in. "I knew you were starting to put on a little weight, but I thought that was because you have had such a strong appetite here lately. We both have. But I had no idea it was because you were going to have a baby."

Quickly he scooped her into his arms and headed for the house, his eyes still wide and his mouth agape.

"What are you doing?"

"I'm carrying you inside," he stated matter-of-factly. "You have taken care of me long enough. Now it's time for me to start taking care of you for a while." He stared down at her stomach with amazed wonder, then grinned and corrected himself. "Both of you."

Though she worried a little about the strain her weight might cause Daniel's wrist, Virginia did not demand he put her down, knowing he wouldn't anyway. Instead she slipped her arms around her husband's neck and rested her cheek against his shoulder, smiling contentedly while he whisked her into the house.

Virginia's smile grew wider still at the gentle way

508

e placed her onto their bed, then lay down beside
her and quickly placed his ear over her abdomen.
Running a hand affectionately through Daniel's
hair, Virginia felt her love full force. She had a
feeling she was definitely going to enjoy being
pampered by Daniel. And when he then moved to
gently kiss her, his eyes brimming with love and
husbandly devotion, she realized that for the first
time since her grandparents' death, the future
looked bright and full of promise. With all the
demons from their past now buried, she and Daniel could look forward to a long and happy marriage.